BITTER SPIRITS

"You had me at booze, raw lust, and black magic! An inventive setting, delightfully sharp-tongued characters, white-hot chemistry, and wry, subtle humor make for a truly enjoyable read. I couldn't wait to meet each new character. It's *Boardwalk Empire* meets *Ghost Hunters*, but so much better."
—Molly Harper, national bestselling author of the Jane Jameson series

"I loved this book! Bennett delivers a sizzling-hot yet swoon-worthy love story with a mystery that keeps you guessing until the end, all set in the fresh and ultra cool world of Jazz Age San Francisco. Can't wait to read the next one!"
—Kristen Callihan, author of *Firelight*

"Complex and smart romantic leads . . . Expect historical romance authors and fans to eagerly hop on the Roaring Twenties bandwagon, following Bennett's very able lead."
—*Publishers Weekly* (starred review)

"Absolutely delightful . . . Stirs intrigue, paranormal activity, and romance into a wonderfully refreshing brew . . . Bennett's fast-paced dialogue, often witty and sharp, as well as her charming characters and detailed setting, will truly captivate romance readers." —*Booklist* (starred review)

"The combination of sizzling sex, gritty danger, and paranormal thrills adds up to one stupendous read!"
—*RT Book Reviews* (top pick)

PRAISE FOR
BITTER SPIRITS

Berkley Sensation titles by Jenn Bennett

BITTER SPIRITS
GRIM SHADOWS

GRIM
SHADOWS

JENN BENNETT

BERKLEY SENSATION, NEW YORK

THE BERKLEY PUBLISHING GROUP
Published by the Penguin Group
Penguin Group (USA) LLC
375 Hudson Street, New York, New York 10014

USA • Canada • UK • Ireland • Australia • New Zealand • India • South Africa • China

penguin.com

A Penguin Random House Company

GRIM SHADOWS

A Berkley Sensation Book / published by arrangement with the author

Copyright © 2014 by Jenn Bennett.
Excerpt from *Bitter Spirits* by Jenn Bennett copyright © 2013 by Jenn Bennett.
Penguin supports copyright. Copyright fuels creativity, encourages diverse voices,
promotes free speech, and creates a vibrant culture. Thank you for buying an authorized
edition of this book and for complying with copyright laws by not reproducing, scanning,
or distributing any part of it in any form without permission. You are supporting writers
and allowing Penguin to continue to publish books for every reader.

Berkley Sensation Books are published by The Berkley Publishing Group.
BERKLEY SENSATION® is a registered trademark of Penguin Group (USA) LLC.
The "B" design is a trademark of Penguin Group (USA) LLC.

For information, address: The Berkley Publishing Group,
a division of Penguin Group (USA) LLC,
375 Hudson Street, New York, New York 10014.

ISBN: 978-0-425-26958-9

PUBLISHING HISTORY
Berkley Sensation mass-market edition / June 2014

PRINTED IN THE UNITED STATES OF AMERICA

10 9 8 7 6 5 4 3 2 1

Cover art by Aleta Rafton.
Cover design by Lesley Worrell.
Interior text design by Kelly Lipovich.

This is a work of fiction. Names, characters, places, and incidents either are the product
of the author's imagination or are used fictitiously, and any resemblance to actual persons,
living or dead, business establishments, events, or locales is entirely coincidental.

The publisher does not have any control over and does not assume any responsibility for
author or third-party websites or their content.

If you purchased this book without a cover, you should be aware that this book is
stolen property. It was reported as "unsold and destroyed" to the publisher, and neither
the author nor the publisher has received any payment for this "stripped book."

This book is dedicated to ten-year-old Me, who decided that her early Nursing ambitions didn't jibe with her aversion to the sight of blood, and therefore being an Egyptologist was the next logical career dream; I think she'd be happy I finally settled on Writer.

ACKNOWLEDGMENTS

Much love and gratitude goes out to my wonderful agent, Laura Bradford, and to my lovely editor, Leis Pederson. Thanks also to my awesome publicist, Jessica Brock, and to Aleta Rafton for the beautiful cover—and the Berkley art department for the gorgeous layout.

A lot of research went into this humble tale, and I could not have written it without the help of the following people and institutions: *San Francisco Chronicle*, the M. H. de Young Memorial Museum, the Museum of Egyptian Antiquities in Cairo, the British Museum in London, the Bancroft Library at UC Berkley, Mark Bittner (who wrote the fascinating book, *The Wild Parrots of Telegraph Hill*), the San Francisco Cable Car Museum, the Jewish Home of San Francisco, Alioto's Italian Seafood at Fisherman's Wharf, the James Leary Flood Mansion, the CinemaTour project, the Shaping San Francisco community project, and the Western Neighborhoods Project of San Francisco.

Thanks to my brilliant husband for not only tolerating my Authorial Angst but also aiding and abetting it. Lastly, a big thanks to my readers for following me off the beaten path and into the secret garden of Unusual Historical Romances. This book was an absolute pleasure to write. If it gives you even half as much pleasure to read, consider me a happy writer!

ONE

JANUARY 1928

LOWE MAGNUSSON SCANNED THE DESOLATE UNION PACIFIC DEPOT lobby. A young couple he recognized from the train was spending the brief early evening stop flipping through magazines at the newsstand. A handful of other travelers loitered on benches. No sign of the two thugs, but it was only a matter of time. Easier to kill him in the dark corner of a rural station than in the middle of a crowded smoking car.

Satisfied he was at least temporarily safe, Lowe slid a bill through the ticket booth window. Not a large bill, but large enough to sway a hayseed Salt Lake City ticket agent. Surely.

"Look," he said in a much calmer voice. "You and I both know you have first-class tickets left on the second train bound for San Francisco. It departs at eight. If we wait for your manager to return from his dinner break, I'll have missed it. It's not like I'm asking for a new ticket. I just want to be moved from one train to another."

The young attendant exhaled heavily. "I'm sorry, sir. Like

I said, I don't have authorization to exchange tickets. Why can't you just wait for your current train to depart? An hour really isn't that much of a difference in the long run. It might even leave sooner if they get the supplies loaded quickly, and aside from a couple of extra stops, they're both going to the same place."

Yes, but the other train didn't have thugs with guns on it.

When he first noticed the men shadowing him, he thought sleep deprivation had gotten the best of him. After all, he hadn't had a decent night's sleep since Cairo. Food poisoning had made the usually tolerable Mediterranean crossing from Alexandria to Athens a waking nightmare. But just when he thought he was out of the woods, he spent the storm-cursed weeklong voyage from England to Baltimore hugging both the toilet and his pillow in turns, praying for death.

But God wasn't done punishing him, apparently. Now that he'd endured three nights of restless sleep on the worst train trip of his life and was less than a day's ride away from home, armed men were stalking him.

Where the hell had all his good luck gone?

Right now, all he wanted was to kiss solid ground in San Francisco, fall into his ridiculously luxurious feather bed—courtesy of his brother's ever-increasing bootlegging fortune—and sleep for a week. Some clam chowder would be nice. A two-hour hot bath. Maybe a small harem of nubile women to warm his sheets—dream big, he always said. But if he could manage to avoid getting shot and robbed during the last hours of this hellish trip home, he'd settle for ten hours of uninterrupted sleep and a home-cooked meal.

The attendant eyed Lowe's loosened necktie and three-day-old whiskers. "We wouldn't even have time to find your luggage and transfer it before departure, sir."

"Just forward it to my San Francisco address." Lowe begrudgingly placed another bill atop the first. Dammit. Only forty dollars left in his wallet. Ludicrous, really. A priceless artifact was in the satchel hanging across his chest, guarded with his damned life for the last two months, and all he had was forty dollars to his name.

Not to mention the massive debt hanging over his head after the botched deal with Monk.

The attendant shook his head. "I'm not supposed to accept tips, sir."

Lowe changed tactics, lowering his voice as he leaned on the counter. "Can I tell you something, just between you and me? I'm on a very important, very *secret* government assignment." He wasn't. "League of Nations business. Health committee," Lowe elaborated nonsensically.

"Health committee," the attendant repeated dryly. He couldn't have cared less.

"I wasn't aware the U.S. had joined the League," a voice called out.

Lowe looked up from the window to locate the voice's owner: a woman, standing a few yards away. She was long and thin, wearing a black dress with a black coat draped over one arm. Black gloves. Black shoes. Black hair bobbed below her chin. So much black. A walking funeral home, blocking his view of the platform entrance.

And she was staring at him with the intensity of a one-person firing squad.

"I did say it was a secret assignment," he called back. "In case you missed that part of my *private* conversation."

"Yes, I heard," she said in an upper-crust transatlantic accent, as if it were perfectly polite and normal for her to comment. No remorse whatsoever for butting into his business.

"Excuse me." *And please leave me alone,* he thought as he turned back to the ticket window. Concocting a believable story on no sleep wasn't the easiest task.

But she wasn't done. "Can I have a word, Mr. Magnusson?"

Had she heard him giving his name to the agent, too? Ears of an owl, apparently.

"Sir?"

Lowe's attention snapped back to the agent. "Look, just get me the ticket before the train leaves. Have a porter deliver my steamer trunk to my address. I'll be back in a minute."

He stepped away from the counter and strode toward the woman.

"Mr. Magnusson."

"Yes," he said irritably. "We've established you know who I am."

Her brow tightened. "You were to meet me." When he gave her a blank stare, she added, "My father cabled you when you arrived in Baltimore."

Shit.

In his haste to change trains, he'd forgotten about meeting up with Archibald Bacall's daughter, the oddball museum curator.

Not that she was unappealing, now that he was seeing her up close. Not plain, either. To complement her owl-sharp hearing, she had an angular face that reminded him of a bird of prey. Long face, long arms, and nice, long legs. Tall for a woman, too. The top of her narrow-brimmed hat might fit under his chin, so he guessed her height to be five foot ten. But her boyish, slender body made her seem smaller.

And the all-black widow's weeds buttoned up to her throat didn't do her any favors.

"Hadley Bacall." She stuck out a hand sheathed in a leather glove trimmed in black fur. More fur circled the collar of the coat draped on her arm. The Bacalls had money. Old San Francisco money, from the gold rush days—her deceased mother's fortune, if he wasn't mistaken. The Bacalls also had significant influence in the art museum at Golden Gate Park. Her father ran the Egyptian Antiquities wing and sat on the board of trustees; he'd been a field archaeologist when he was younger.

Not that Lowe had ever hobnobbed with the man. Without the amulet carefully tucked in Lowe's satchel, Dr. Archibald Bacall and his daughter would not be extending high-class handshakes in Lowe's direction. Hell, they wouldn't even give him the time of day.

"Yes, of course," he said. "Hadley, that's right."

Her grip was surprisingly evasive for someone whose arm was propping up a thousand dollars worth of fur and an aloof attitude to match. She tried to end the handshake as quickly as she'd offered it, but he held on. Just for a second. She glanced down at his hand, as if it were a misbehaving child. He reluctantly let go.

"You did get my father's telegram, did you not?" she asked.

"Sure." He'd received a lot of telegrams from the man after the photograph of Lowe and his uncle standing in front of the Philae excavation site circulated in newspapers on both sides of the Atlantic—a photograph that had been reprinted a month later in *National Geographic*.

"Why were you lying to the ticket agent?" she asked.

He coughed into his fist. "Ah, well. It's a long story, and one I'm afraid I don't have time to share. I'm switching trains, you see. So I won't be able to meet with you after all."

One slim brow arched. She was almost attractive when she was frustrated, very glacial and austere. The corners of her eyes tilted up in an appealing manner, and her gaze didn't waver. He liked that.

"You didn't come all the way out here just to meet me, I hope."

She shook her head. "I was giving a seminar on Middle Kingdom animal mummification at the University of Utah."

Fitting for a woman who specialized in funerary archaeology, he supposed. If he wasn't so goddamn tired, he might've been interested in hearing her theories, but his travel-weary gaze was wandering to her breasts. Nothing much to speak of, but that didn't stop him from looking.

"I'm on my way back to San Francisco," she said, diverting his attention back to her eyes. "But when my father found out you'd be coming in on this train, he thought it might be wise for me to book a ticket so I could speak at the university before you arrived. We aren't the only ones interested in your discovery. I'm not sure if you know what you're getting into by bringing the *djed* amulet here."

Oh, he knew, all right. He barely got the damned thing out of Egypt. While his uncle had battled the Egyptian Ministry of State, Lowe had defended their dig site from looters.

He'd been shot at, stoned, stabbed—twice—and had won a fair number of fistfights.

Once he'd made it back to the States, he thought he'd be done with all that, but now he worried his troubles were only getting started. He'd briefly considered the possibility that the hired thugs on the train tonight might be after him because of his debt to Monk Morales, but if Monk wanted to kill him, he'd wait until Lowe got home. No, these thugs were definitely after the *djed*.

"I've already received offers from a few collectors."

Her smile was tight. "My father is prepared to give you the best price. That's why I'm to speak with you now. I'd like to inspect the amulet. If it's truly the mythical Backbone of Osiris—"

"Christ, keep your voice down, would you?" Lowe quickly surveyed the lobby again. "I'm trying not to advertise, if you don't mind. Besides, all the artifacts from the excavation were shipped on another boat. They'll arrive next month. So I don't have it on me."

A hurried porter walked past them, wheeling a luggage cart. She kept quiet until the man was out of earshot. "You're lying."

"Excuse me?"

Her gaze dropped to his leather satchel. "From the way you're gripping that bag, I'd say it's inside. But whether it's there or in your jacket pocket, I can *feel* it."

The bizarre accusation hung between them for a long moment. If he hadn't "felt" the cursed object himself, he might've laughed in her face. But truth be told, the amulet emitted some sort of unexplainable current. His uncle hadn't felt it, but some of their hired Egyptian workers did. A fair number of them deserted their camp the night he'd brought it up from the half-flooded sinkhole. The artifact scared the hell out of him, frankly. And considering the way she was looking at him, all matter-of-factly and unblinking, well, that scared him a little, too.

"Mr. Magnusson," she said in a lower voice as her eyes

darted toward something behind his right shoulder. "Are you traveling with bodyguards?"

He stilled. "No."

"Don't turn around," she warned.

"Are there two of them? Black coats. Built like brick shithouses, pardon my French."

"No need to apologize. I prefer frank language. And if you are trying to ask if they are large men, then yes. They've been watching you for several minutes. One has slipped through a corridor behind the ticket windows and the other is approaching us."

A clammy panic slipped across Lowe's skin. His hand went to the Arabian curved dagger strapped to his belt and hidden under his coat over his left hip: a *janbiya*. In Egypt, he'd become accustomed to using it for protection. But after he'd left, he'd continued to wear it for peace of mind, more or less. Just in case.

Looked like he might be needing it now.

"Don't stare at the man approaching us," he instructed her. "Just pick up your luggage and follow me out to the platform. Quickly, but stay calm."

She didn't panic or question him. And thanks to those long legs of hers, their strides fell into a smart, matching rhythm. He caught the crisp scent of lilies drifting from her clothes as they strode past the newsstand, where neat rows of *Good Housekeeping* and *Collier's Weekly* blurred in his peripheral vision.

"Listen to me," he said as he placed an open palm at the small of her back. "Those men are armed with guns. They've been shadowing me on the train all day. I don't know for certain, but I've got a funny feeling they're after the amulet. It probably wasn't wise of you to talk to me, because now they'll think we're friendly, and that makes you a target, too."

"What do you plan to do about it?" she said calmly. Even in the panic of the moment, he had to admire her grit.

"You have a ticket for the 127?"

"Yes."

"Go ahead and board your train. Tell the porter suspicious men are following you."

"A porter's not going to shield me from gunfire."

"Lock yourself in your stateroom."

"I'll do no such thing."

Oh, she wouldn't, would she? He prodded her onto the shadowed train platform, where other travelers were waiting for their departure time to come, saying their good-byes to family members and loved ones. The chilly night air didn't stop a tickling bead of sweat from winding its way down his back.

"If they shoot you and take the amulet, I'll have failed my father," she said logically, as if she were making a decision about dinner plans. "So I'm sticking with you."

"Fine, see if I care if you get yourself killed. You're already dressed for an open-casket memorial service."

"And you're dressed like a Barbary Coast drunkard!"

"Is that so? Well, I'll have you know, I'm—"

Startled cries bounced around the platform. Right in front of them, exiting a door marked EMPLOYEES ONLY, was the second thug—the one who'd disappeared behind the ticket windows. He barreled onto the platform with a polished revolver leveled at Lowe's chest.

TWO

———❦———

LOWE SHOVED MISS BACALL TO THE SIDE. HER SUITCASE SKITTERED
across the platform as he reached inside his coat, drew the
curved *janbiya* dagger, and swung it through the air. Not
his best aim. But he felt fleshy resistance when it sliced
through the thug's shoulder.

At the exact moment the man pulled the trigger.

The rumble of two train engines absorbed the *crack!* of
the gun. Where the shot landed, Lowe didn't know—it just
missed his ear, he knew that much. And he damn well wasn't
about to find out where the next might land.

The thug growled, gritting his teeth as he cradled his
injured arm. The bright, coppery scent of blood wafted from
Lowe's blade. He readied himself to swing the dagger again,
but thought better of it when he glimpsed Miss Bacall rising
to her feet beside him. No, he decided, it really wasn't a
smart idea to engage in a knife fight in the middle of a train
station. Especially when the curator connected to his big
payout stood unprotected and the injured thug's much bigger
buddy was heading toward them with another gun.

Two guns, one knife . . . absolutely shit odds. No choice but to escape. So Lowe grabbed Miss Bacall around the waist and urged her into a run.

Screams from the lobby echoed off two idling locomotives. Fencing hemmed the station's platform. Nowhere to run but into the arms of the train he'd just been so desperate to leave.

She tripped on the metal steps leading into the first open car. Like a domino, he stumbled behind and nearly crushed her, but managed to save them both from landing on their faces at the last moment. Also managed not to stab her with his bloody dagger. Barely.

Brilliant, Magnusson.

"My luggage!" she shouted as he scooped her up and pushed her inside, wiping the blade on his pants.

"Forget it. Go!"

He sheathed the dagger as they raced through the deserted dining car, darting past compact tables draped in white linen. Heavy footfalls thundered behind them. The bigger thug had followed and was taking aim. Lowe covered Miss Bacall's body with his, bracing for the worst—

Goddammit, he really didn't want to get shot.

But instead of another revolver blast, he heard something different: a broader, *sharper* explosion, and then a surprised shout as the train carriage shuddered. A backward look revealed the thug sprawled in the floor, covered in broken glass. The train windows at the front of the dining car had . . . shattered?

Four windows, all blown out, as if a bomb had gone off. Cold night air whistled as it whipped past the jagged teeth of the smashed glass.

How in the living hell was that possible?

Did he care? No, he damn well didn't. Maybe his good luck was returning.

He thrust Miss Bacall farther down the aisle. Without a word, they dashed through the last quarter of the dining room and passed through the open door back onto the platform.

Just in time to see the injured thug warily inspecting the broken train windows as he clutched his wounded shoulder. He hadn't noticed them yet. Small miracle.

"Go, go, go," he said in Miss Bacall's ear. He grabbed her hand and raced down the platform, away from the lobby, away from the guns. And they followed the length of the idling train until they came to the last car.

The second train, the one he wanted to be on, sat alongside the 127. A whistle blew. Steam puffed from the engine. It was leaving the station. And the stairway that crossed the tracks to the opposite platform might as well have been in another city.

"Down!" he told Miss Bacall. She didn't seem to understand his plan, and he didn't have time to explain, so he jumped off the platform onto gravel-packed steel rails before helping her down into the darkness.

"Come on!" he yelled, pulling Miss Bacall alongside him to race behind the departing train as it chugged away from the station. They'd catch up easy as pie if they didn't hesitate. Thank God for her long legs; she'd make an excellent Olympic sprinter.

"Are you insane?" she shouted as they raced together.

A legitimate question, but he didn't answer. Nor did he consider leaving Miss Bacall behind. If the thugs were willing to shoot at him while she was standing at his side, God only knew what they'd do if he left her at the station, especially if they found out how rich her father was.

A small, railed platform cradled the back of the train, lit from above by a single light. A moving target, but a steady one. Like catching a cable car. Sort of.

Good sense be damned. He pumped his legs, grabbed the railing, and yelled, "Jump!"

Their combined landing wasn't as smooth as it could've been. His balance faltered. He heard a ripping sound, and for a moment he felt her falling. An image of her body being dragged behind the car flashed in his mind, but a quick shift in his weight brought her into his arms. And after some awkward flailing with her carried coat—how on earth had she managed to hang on to that thing?—they stood on the back platform, chests heaving with labored breaths.

They'd done it! He couldn't stop himself from hoo-ha-ing a little shout of triumph into the wind as they passed the engine of the idle 127. He caught a glimpse of a panicked crowd under the golden lights of the platform before their train chugged away into darkness.

He grinned down at Miss Bacall, thoroughly pleased with himself. Almost too pleased. The excited blood surging through his energized body was headed south, making him half-hard with the thrill of victory.

I am man! Hear me roar!

God, he almost wanted to kiss her. Probably all the surging blood between his legs was to blame, but still. A little kiss might make—

"What now?" she said, and not very happily.

His chaotic victory plans fizzled. He hadn't thought that far ahead.

Unaware of the inane thoughts running rampant in his head, Miss Bacall threw up a frustrated hand and turned away from him to tackle the door handle. With their luck it would be locked, and—

Dear God.

Unbeknownst to Miss Bacall, a ragged section of the back of her dress was missing—that would've been the ripping noise he'd heard when he pulled her onto the platform. The torn piece of cloth hung from a railing bolt, fluttering in the breeze like a flag. But his gaze narrowed on what that missing piece of dress exposed.

Miles and miles of leg covered in black stockings. A tease of pink skin above the garters. And lingerie the color of a ripe honeydew melon, trimmed with a border of embroidered peacock feathers.

His heart stopped.

Imagine that. All her dour, black clothes were a false front, like a Wild West building in a Hollywood film! And underneath was all this . . . *color.*

Color and more.

So much more.

Because filling out the melon-green step-in chemise was the roundest, most voluptuous ass he'd ever laid eyes on—hands down, no exaggeration. How could someone this skinny and long have a backside the size of a basketball?

It was the single greatest thing he'd ever seen in all his twenty-five years.

She grunted, completely oblivious to her situation. "The door's not locked, but the latch is stuck. Help me."

Should he tell her? He had to tell her, didn't he? How could she not feel cool air back there? Dammit, he had to tell her. And he would . . . but my *God*, that thing was round. If he was at half-mast before, she certainly had his full attention now.

"Mr. Magnusson?"

"What? Oh, yes. Let me . . . just shift over this way so I can reach. Never mind, I'll just do it this way. Stand still." Wind whipped across the back of his neck. He reached around her shoulders, and there was no getting around this part, because they really had no room on the platform, and the train was picking up speed. So he was forced—forced!—to flatten himself against her back to reach the latch. Gods above. It was like sinking into a warm pillow: not too soft, not too firm. Just right. And because she was tall, he didn't have to bend down too much for his victory-happy cock to nestle in the valley right between those plump, cushiony—

"Oh . . . God," she whispered.

Indeed. Guess he wouldn't have to break the bad news about the rip in her dress after all.

When the latch dropped, Hadley slid open the door and dashed inside the train car. Compartments stacked with baggage lined both sides of the otherwise deserted space.

Had that really just happened? Because "that" felt an

awful lot like an overexcited male. Cool air tickled the backs of her legs. She twisted to get a better look at her dress.

"You ripped it during the jump." He latched the outer door, halting the whistling wind and clack of the speeding train.

"You might've told me!"

"I didn't notice until you turned around. I was busy trying to save us from being shot."

"Save *us*?" She gathered the tattered edges of her dress together in an attempt to hide the tear. "You were the one being fired at, not me. And you were the one brandishing a—it looked like a ceremonial dagger."

"The ceremonial ones aren't sharp. Mine is." His deep voice carried a bit of an accent—not immediately percep-tible, but the cadence of his words had an almost songlike quality. A Scandinavian lilt. Oh, that's right—the Magnus-sons were Swedish immigrants. "And you should damn well be glad it is sharp," he continued. "Or that bullet might've re-killed the fox that gave up its short life for your coat collar."

"It's mink, and I don't remember asking to be saved."

"Oh, *w-e-ell*, pardon me for being a gentleman."

"Gentleman." She snorted a bitter laugh. What he'd thrust against her certainly wasn't gentlemanly. And despite her best efforts, her wanton mind now pounced upon the novelty of the feel of him, hanging it up in a gilded frame at the forefront of her thoughts.

"Fine. Shall I unlatch the door?" he said. "You can jump out and hobble back to the station on a broken leg. And after those thugs hold you hostage, you can sign over Daddy's check to pay the ransom and pat yourself on the back."

The edges of her vision darkened before she had a chance to dampen her mounting anger. Murky and foul, her specters emerged from the walls like shadows come to life. Though fully visible to her, they were—usually—imperceptible to anyone unlucky enough to be in their path when she couldn't send them back to whatever hellish place from which they came.

Or when she *wouldn't* send them back.

Caught in their grip, a row of leather suitcases slid from the rack above Mr. Magnusson and toppled. He lurched out of the way and nearly knocked her over in an attempt to save his own head.

Served him right.

She backed farther into the car as the next rack of baggage avalanched.

That was for lustily shoving himself against her undergarments and making her want something she couldn't have.

He shouted incoherently, ducking the falling bags. He moved with surprising grace for someone so tall. Still, better put a stop to this now before he was knocked unconscious or killed.

Or before he put two and two together and figured out it was her specters that had broken the windows in the first train.

One, two, three, four . . .

Anger blinded and stripped away her control. And when she was out of control, the specters would attack the object of her anger with deadly force, so she had to reel these dangerous emotions in. Must. Her father was relying on her to haggle with this man. The *djed* amulet meant something more to her father than an academic study or a bragging right, especially if he was willing to part with so much money to snag it before the museum or other collectors had a chance to bid. *Possessing this is the most important mission in my life,* he'd said.

Five, six, seven, eight . . . She counted until the specters faded back into the walls and Mr. Magnusson stopped shouting obscenities. She thought they were obscenities, anyway; he was speaking in Swedish now, so it was hard to be sure.

"What in the living hell?" he shouted, switching back to English. He stood at the ready, scanning the piles of baggage as he shoved disheveled locks of wavy blond hair out of his eyes. And what eyes they were, sharp and cunning—the bright, cool blue of the faience-ware lotus vase in case fourteen of the museum's Late New Kingdom exhibit. Those eyes were a distraction, as were the hollow cheeks and regal Scandinavian cheekbones, high and arching like the bow of a Viking longboat. And those lips . . . studded with dimpled corners and so full, they'd be the envy of any woman.

His only flaw was a broken nose that hadn't set correctly. It was just crooked enough below a bump in the middle to draw attention, but still not altogether unattractive. Ridiculously unfair that an opportunistic loot-hound could be so blindingly, roguishly handsome.

She'd seen his photograph—half the world had—but it didn't do him justice. Something about the way he carried his towering frame smacked of confidence and reprobation. And the unshaven jaw and scuffed shoes only made him look like a fairy-tale king dressed as a beggar. As if she could be fooled into thinking he needed her compassion. His brother was one of the richest bootleggers in town. She wouldn't be surprised if the Magnusson family's illegal gains exceeded what was left of her mother's fortune.

"Did you see that?" he said, holding his arms out as if he'd lost his balance.

"I saw it."

"Is the train rocking? What just happened?"

"It's over," she said, trying her best to play dumb. "So, what's your plan now, Mr. Magnusson? Do we hole up in here for the next, what, eighteen hours, until we make it to San Francisco? Or do we jump off at the next stop?"

"Christ. I don't know." He straightened the satchel strapped to his chest and cast one more bewildered look at the fallen luggage at his feet. "What's your thought on the matter?"

Oh, *now* he was asking her opinion?

She considered their situation. "No decent-sized stations until Reno, so chances of finding an open ticket office at this time of night are slim to none."

"Probably right about that. We'd have to sleep in the lobby and wait for the next train, maybe until this time tomorrow." He blew out a long breath. "And I haven't been home in nine months. Also haven't had a decent night's sleep in several weeks, so waiting's not my preference. What's in the next car? Can you peer through the window shade?"

She started for the inner door, but remembered what'd happened on the train's platform and hurriedly slipped into her coat.

"Too late. I've already seen everything." He turned sideways as he slipped past her. "Highlight of my entire trip home," he murmured with a merry lilt.

An unwanted thrill chased away any modicum of shame she might've felt. For the love of God, what was the matter with her, falling for empty flattery? And why was it so warm in here? She discreetly fanned her face while he peeked into the next car.

"Kitchen car. Looks to be empty." He motioned for her without looking. "If we get caught, leave the talking to me."

They hurried through. Fresh-brewed coffee and toasted bread made her stomach groan. The next car was a cigarette-smoke-filled observation room—only one passenger here, and he didn't even look up from his newspaper when they passed. The next car was a sleeper. A few private compartments lined the left side of a narrow passageway that spilled into the open public area.

"'Manager's Office,'" Mr. Magnusson read from gold-stenciled wood. They walked farther. "Ah, here are the compartments." Occupied, occupied, occupied. The last compartment door slid open, and out stepped a gangly young man in a railway uniform. He couldn't have been older than seventeen or eighteen.

"Pardon me, sir," he said, dropping his eyes as he stepped back into the stateroom to allow them room to pass.

"This one's not occupied?" Mr. Magnusson asked.

"Not at the moment, sir."

Mr. Magnusson flashed the porter a train ticket. "We were on the 127, my sister and I," he said, motioning to include her. "They switched us to this train in Salt Lake City. My sister's husband . . . well, there's no sense in mincing words. The man's a mean drunk, and he was threatening her, you see. And she's got a bun in the oven. A bad situation."

Hadley's mouth fell open.

The porter looked as confused as she felt. "Yes, sir."

"So they were kind enough to move us," Magnusson continued. "They told us to come aboard, and that the ticket office manager would bring us the new tickets while they called the police—you know, to detain her husband. For her protection."

"Oh, my," the porter said, leaning to get a better look at her.

"Only, the train left the station, and the manager never came. So now our luggage is on the 127, and we're stuck here without a stateroom assignment."

"No one informed me," the porter said.

"It happened so fast," Magnusson replied, shaking his head. "Her lousy husband had a revolver—can you imagine? Pointing a gun at a woman carrying his own child."

"Ma'am," the boy said with sympathy.

Hadley responded with a strangled noise.

"Now, now," Magnusson said, patting her shoulder. "Buck up, old gal. I know you say he only drinks when he's overworked, but this can't go on. Daddy will hire you a lawyer. It's just not safe. You have to think of your child, now."

"A crying shame," the porter mumbled.

"Amen," Magnusson agreed. "Do you think this is the stateroom they had in mind for us?"

"This one? It's been booked by a party scheduled to board in Nevada."

"Oh." Magnusson's face fell. He turned sad eyes on Hadley. "I know this is upsetting, and you're exhausted and terrified. I'm so sorry."

"I've already endured so much with you tonight . . . dear brother," she replied dryly.

The porter cleared his throat. "I suppose the couple who booked the compartment haven't been through your difficulties. I can put them in an open coach berth, if the two of you don't mind sharing this compartment."

Hadley didn't like the sound of that, not one bit, but her protest was buried under Mr. Magnusson's overdramatic sentiment.

"Oh, that would be wonderful. Just wonderful," he said, flashing the porter a grateful smile as he enthusiastically pumped the man's hand. "We're both grateful." He fumbled in his wallet and gave the boy a five-dollar bill. "Do you think you could do us one last favor and bring a pot of coffee and some sandwiches?"

"Yes, sir."

"Hot tea for me, please," she added. If they were doing this, she might as well have what she wanted.

"Yes, ma'am. Make yourselves comfortable. I'll be right back," the porter said, allowing them entry as he flicked the sign on the door to read OCCUPIED.

Hadley silenced her tongue and followed Mr. Magnusson inside the cramped stateroom. A small door led to a private toilet and shower on the right, and the parlor lay to the left: two cushioned seats faced each other in front of a wide picture window, capped by two pulldown sleeping berths above.

Mr. Magnusson pulled off his satchel and, along with his coat, hung his things on a hook. Then he ducked beneath the berth to plop down on one of the seats. His long body took up too much room. His shins brushed the edge of the facing seat.

"First class," he murmured on a sigh. "I think the public berths on the 127 were stuffed with hay."

Why on earth anyone with a bootlegging brother was riding coach was beyond her, but Hadley didn't care to find out. As she unwound the handbag chain looped over her wrist, she addressed her bigger gripe. "First you're on the health committee of the League, and now you're a heroic brother to a pregnant hussy—"

"Not a hussy. I said you were married."

"Is this what you do? Lie your way out of every situation you encounter?"

"I prefer to think of it as inventing a character. Acting."

"Acting," she repeated, hanging her handbag on the hook next to his satchel. She started to remove her coat, but remembered the rip in her dress. She wasn't the only one; a slow smile crept over Magnusson's face. She tightened the coat and perched on the facing seat. "Why wasn't the truth good enough?"

"You mean, I should've told him that I'm an archaeologist who found a piece of a mythical artifact purported to open a door to the land of the dead—and two hired thugs were shooting at us to get it, so we jumped the train like hobos?"

She crossed her legs. "You, sir, aren't an archaeologist. You're an entrepreneur."

"I have a degree."

"And I have two."

He casually kicked up his feet on the seat next to her, one ankle crossing its mate. "But no fieldwork."

"Not for lack of wanting, but kudos for making me feel small."

His face pinched as if she'd slapped him. But only for a moment before blankness settled over his features. He stretched his neck, loosening muscles. "You said you wanted honesty." With his head lolling on the seat back, he rested his hands on his chest and closed his eyes. "If you'd like me to tiptoe around your feminine feelings, I'm happy to do so."

"I want to be treated like a man."

He glanced at her from under squinting eyelids, one brow cocked.

"I mean to say, I want to be given the same directness you'd offer a trusted colleague. I am your equal. Speak frankly to me, or not at all." A quick anger flared inside her chest. She stared out the window, looking past her own tense reflection to the rolling black landscape.

One, two, three . . .

"All right, then," he said after a few moments. "If you were a man, and we were colleagues, the first thing I'd do is drop the formal address."

She hesitated. "Thank you . . . Lowe."

"You're welcome, Hadley." He smiled before closing his eyes.

They sat in silence. Perhaps she'd misjudged him. Now that she had time to think about the evening's events, she supposed some of his actions might have been well intentioned. He'd pushed her out of the first gunman's path and defended them with the knife. He'd also shielded her from the broken glass in the first train car, not knowing she'd been the cause of it. And now that they were settled, she could admit that she'd rather be here than taking her chances back at the station.

"You know, now that I'm thinking about it," he said with his eyes still closed, "if we were trusted male colleagues on a first-name basis with each other, I'd probably be bragging about how I just got a peek at a bea-*u*-tiful ass and nice pair of legs, and what a shame it was that the strange woman who curates mummified corpses in the antiquities wing of the de Young Museum dresses like an old maid."

The nerve.

"And I'd tell *you* that she dresses that way so that the men she works with treat her with respect, not as the privileged daughter of Archibald Bacall."

His voice softened. "Then I'd tell her that she shouldn't change herself to please anyone, and her coworkers are probably overeducated Stanford graduates with no real-world field experience, so who the hell cares what they think, anyway?"

"*I'm* a Stanford graduate."

A knock at the door halted whatever smart retort he was planning on releasing into the wild. The porter entered with a tray. Mr. Magnusson had the decency to remove his feet from her cushion so that a folding table could be erected between them. After piling the table with silver pots of steaming coffee and tea, a covered plate of sandwiches, and two table settings, the porter gave her a pity-filled look and left them alone.

"You're eating for two," Lowe said lightly, tugging a pair of thin, brown leather gloves off. When he laid them down, she noticed a strange alteration on the left glove. "So I'll leave you all the ones with . . . What is this? Olive spread? I think there might be chopped walnuts in here. *No-o-o*, thank you."

Left glove, left hand. By God, he was missing his pinky finger. Completely gone, all the way to the knuckle. His skin was discolored there. Stitches had left scars where the missing finger had been sewn up.

"Want a closer look?"

She glanced up, mildly embarrassed for staring. "Looks fairly recent. How did it happen?"

"Lost it in Alexandria." He made a chopping gesture. "Never steal a Muslim's woman."

A woman? Surprise faded into disbelief. Did he take her for an idiot? "Sharia law concerning amputation as punishment is for thieves. I believe what you are referring to would be considered adultery, punishable by stoning to death."

He lifted the top piece of bread from another sandwich. "Maybe he didn't like the woman all that much, so he gave me a warning."

"You know what? I don't even care why you lost it," she said, doing her best to curb the desire to call up her specters again. Maybe they'd unlatch the berth above him and re-break that crooked nose of his. "No more of your silly stories. Show me the amulet."

He stopped picking through the sandwiches. "Show me a check."

"Money. Of course. My father said that would be your first concern."

"It's everyone's first concern."

"You're wrong, and that's the difference between us."

"Oh, do enlighten me."

"You're a digger. I'm a scholar."

"If people like me didn't dig, what would you study? Mummified rats in the walls of your precious museum?"

They stared at each other through the whorls of steam rising from the coffeepot. She eventually gave in and dug out Father's check from her handbag, placing it on her side of the table.

He brushed breadcrumbs off his hands before reaching for his satchel. Ah-*ha!* She'd guessed correctly. No chance he'd pack the object in a shipping crate after all the hulla-baloo it had garnered in the press.

Moreover, she really did experience an inexplicable buzz-ing sensation when she'd walked into the train station. It wasn't the first time she'd sensed power coming from an object. The museum contained a door from Newgate Prison that made her head swim whenever she got within a few feet of it, and her father had occasionally acquired things over the years that made her hair stand on end. An object's power was like a perfume, recognized upon first scent, but fading into the background as one's nose became accustomed to it.

Lowe took out a small bundle of suede cloth and opened it on the table. Inside sat an elongated golden figure, about six inches tall, two inches wide. Osiris, funerary god of the Egyptian afterlife. The atef crown sat atop his head, and the iconic crook and flail crossed his chest. The figure was one component of the mythical Thoth *djed* amulet. Osiris's body was the base of a pillar. Missing were the four crossbars that stacked upon each other to create the top: a dark hole on the figure's crown hinted where the missing pieces would attach.

She fished out a folding magnifying glass from her handbag and examined the piece more closely. The style was right. Telltale metallurgy markings showed at the side seams, and the gold bore a distinct reddish coloration that gold from Ancient Egypt often possessed. According to the *National Geographic* article, Lowe claimed to have found the piece in a flooded secret room of the main temple at Philae.

Her throat went dry.

"Can I see the other side?" she said, her voice a raspy whisper.

He flipped it over. The back was flat, embossed by a series of hieroglyphs and unrecognizable symbols that abruptly cut off where the rest of the amulet's crossbars would attach. Was she really looking at magical symbols from the mythical Book of Thoth? God, it was thrilling to even allow herself a moment to believe it might be true.

If she was forced to validate the piece's authenticity and give a blind assessment on the spot, her education and experience told her that the object very well *could* be 3,000 years old—a priceless artifact, and a beautiful example of Amarna Period goldwork. Now, whether it actually opened a door to some mythical underworld was unknown, but something powerful crackled beneath the surface.

"If it's real, my father wants it," she finally said.

"I can't just hand it over to you right now," he said, reclaiming the amulet. "I'll need signatures, people present, that sort of thing. And you and your father will want the Egyptian documentation."

"You have it?"

"My uncle does."

Dear God. How thrilling.

Nothing mattered but this. All the insults he'd thrown her way were forgotten. Every strange feeling he'd dredged up inside her. Whatever she'd endured had been worth it to secure this arcane piece of history. The knowledge that it would also secure her the job promotion she so desperately wanted was, as they say, killing two birds.

She slid the check across the table. "Consider this a down payment. I want your word that you won't sell it to someone else. My father will give you the remainder when you meet."

"Gentlemen's agreement." He stuck out his hand— the one still flaunting all its digits—but shook his head when she offered hers in return. "No gloves. Like a man would."

Skin to skin? Not even the promise of the amulet could make her give him that. She avoided touching in general and skin contact at all costs. Beyond a few brief kisses at petting parties in high school and the loss of her virginity in college, she didn't remember the last time she'd touched someone with her bare hand on purpose.

Within the space of one afternoon, this walking vaude-ville act of a man had already touched her several times: his palm against her back when he was walking with her inside the station lobby; running hand-in-hand with her to catch the train; intimately pressing himself against her torn skirt. So much touching!

She supposed it was nothing to him—some people had no boundaries, after all—but it was something to *her*. "A gentleman would keep his gloves on," she insisted, thrusting her gloved hand forward.

"Fine. If you don't want it to be binding. There are special Man Rules, you know. Spitting, secret handshakes." Smiling a crooked smile, he took her hand.

His grip was firm and steady. Warm through the thin leather. Rational thought abandoned her until she realized they weren't shaking. Why weren't they shaking? A small noise vibrated from the back of his throat. Her gaze lifted to meet his.

Just like that, he'd captured her eyes above, and her hand below. His thumb swept over the tender skin of her wrist, grazing her pounding pulse. A whisper of a touch, barely there. Barely a touch at all, really—it might've even been accidental. But the tingles that rippled up her arm didn't care about distinctions.

She tore her hand away from his, back to safety.

"Mr. Magnusson," she said, hoping she sounded less frazzled than she felt. "It appears we have a deal."

THREE

———— ❦ ————

LOWE DIDN'T PLACE MUCH VALUE ON A GENTLEMEN'S AGREEMENT.
Any kind of agreement, really. Much like the rest of his
family, he saw words like "law" and "binding" as boundaries to be pushed—loose suggestions, if you will. It made no
difference if it was a handshake, committed to paper, or
filed in a government office.

His agreement with Hadley was no different than a hundred others he'd given without intent to follow through, so
he wasn't sure why it made him . . . uncomfortable. Maybe
it was her intense, too-serious personality that rattled him.
Or the way she looked at him with those discerning, hawk-like eyes of hers.

Or maybe it was because he actually felt guilty when
she'd trusted his lying handshake against her better instincts.
Why had she? Hadn't he given her every reason *not* to trust
him? He certainly didn't trust her. The woman was too
smart. Too rational. Too critical. He saw the wheels turning
inside her Stanford-educated mind.

Which was why, while she made use of the compartment's restroom, he tucked the amulet base beneath the pillow in his berth, as he'd done every night since he found the cursed thing. And like his previous nights spent on the train, he didn't expect to get much sleep. So when he woke up the next morning, he was surprised to realize he'd slept the entire night. And she'd slept, too.

Oddly pleasant to see her stretched out on the opposite berth, still wearing her coat. Her sharp, long features softened when she slept. She was rather pretty. Strikingly so.

Regardless, he damn sure wasn't selling the *djed* amulet to her father. If Bacall wanted it so badly, surely Lowe could find someone else to double the man's offer. Pointless to think about, because even that wouldn't be enough to cover his debt.

Big problems required creative solutions, and Lowe knew exactly what he was going to do to solve them. After he had a hot meal and a bath.

Talking shop with Hadley helped to pass time during the last leg of their journey. It was four in the afternoon when he finally stepped off the train onto the Twin Peaks station platform and breathed in San Francisco air. Home at last. Thank God.

"Lowe!"

His baby sister careened his way, her blond, bobbed hair swinging as she ran. She pounced on him like she used to when she was a child.

"Whoa, Astrid," he warned, but when her arms went around his neck, he found himself unable to stop from lifting her straight off the ground and hugging her back with the same enthusiasm. "All right, all right," he said, setting her back down. "Release me, she-demon."

She grinned up at him, running her gloved hand over his whiskers. "You look like a vagrant, *älskade broder*."

"I feel like one. And look at you! You've grown since the summer. Are you still just seventeen?"

"Last time I checked."

"You're wearing rouge now?"

"Maybe I am."

"Mamma and Pappa would roll over in their graves if they knew."

"I'm not a child, Lowe."

He laughed. "I didn't say it was unbecoming."

Her nose scrunched up as she smiled. He slung an arm around her shoulder and kissed her cheek as another familiar face came into view.

"Bo Yeung," he said, unhinging himself from Astrid to shake hands. The Chinese boy wasn't really a boy anymore— he was twenty-one, all lean muscle and handsome grace. Once an orphaned pickpocket, Bo had been the trusted assistant of Lowe's brother, Winter, for several years. When Bo wasn't helping Winter with the bootlegging, he did some driving for the family and played bodyguard to Astrid. A well-paid one, at that: he wore a plaid newsboy cap and matching dark green suit that looked as if it cost more than Lowe's entire steamer trunk of desert-friendly wear.

"She's right," Bo said, giving his hand a hearty shake. "You do look rough."

"I've been through hell the last few weeks. I can't tell you how good it is to see friendly faces."

"I'd say the house has been quiet without you, but that's a lie." Bo had lived at the Magnusson house in the servant's hall since their parents died in a car accident more than two years ago. Part of the family, really. But the way Bo was standing over Astrid—almost *too* protectively—and the way she was swaying nearer to Bo—almost *too* close—made Lowe think something had changed between them while he'd been in Egypt.

Interesting. Lowe loved a good scandal.

Astrid made a distressed noise. "What happened?"

"Oh, this? Didn't I write you about it?" he asked as she lifted his left hand. "I lost it in a game of Five-Finger Fillet."

"What?" Astrid and Bo said together before Astrid continued, "—in the world is that?"

"Knife game," Lowe said, holding out his hand, palm down. "You put your hand on the table, fingers spread, and

take the tip of your knife and stab between your fingers . . .
tap, tap tap!"

"You are a liar!" Astrid squealed, horrified, but laughing.
"Is it really gone? Is it a trick?"

"Wouldn't you like to know?" He wiggled his remaining
four fingers before lunging at her side to tickle her until she
squealed some more, begging him to stop. "All right," he said.
"Enough of that. Are the two of you my entire greeting party?
Where's my big brother and this fictional wife of his?"

A cheerful voice floated over his shoulder. "Fictional? I
thought you were the one with a thousand stories up your
sleeve."

He turned to find a small, heavily freckled woman in a
red silk dress with an oriental collar. She flashed him a pretty
smile and crossed her arms under a great pair of breasts.

"You must be the spirit medium."

"I'm also your brother's fictional wife."

"Hello, Aida." He started to shake her hand, then leaned
in and hugged her. "For the love of God, you're family now."
He held her at arm's length to look at her. "Are you really
having Winter's child?"

"The doctor says I am."

He hugged her again as she laughed. "God help you if
it's a boy."

"Christ alive, don't squeeze her to death," a deep, melodic
voice said at his side. His older brother, Winter Magnusson,
the mighty bootlegger. At twenty-nine, Winter was Lowe's
senior by four years and twice as burly. Lowe accepted his
embrace, clapping him on the shoulder.

"You look like death warmed over," Winter said. "Don't
they have a barber in first class?"

Yes, but he was too paranoid to allow anyone near him
with a straight razor. Not to mention the problem of his
dwindling funds. "I'm thinking of growing a beard."

"Not if you want to live in my house," Winter said.

Married or not, Winter was still his same old dictator
self.

Lowe was too tired to fight, so he turned his attention

back to Aida. How in the world his brother, with his gruff attitude and scarred eye, had been able to attract a pretty thing like her was beyond Lowe's comprehension. "Astrid described you perfectly in her letters." As for the breasts, Winter had mentioned those in the longest piece of correspondence he'd ever sent to Lowe. It said: *I'm in love. Got married to a tiny, freckled girl with nice breasts and good sense. You'll like her.* And then a telegram a month later: *You're going to be an uncle.*

She smiled back at him. "And everyone tells me you're the luckiest man alive."

Out of the corner of his eye, he spotted the porter helping Hadley onto the platform, like she was an invalid, or . . . Oh, that's right. She was still officially on the run from her fictional husband. Better put the kibosh on that, as his friend, Adam, would say, before the story spread to his family's ears. "Excuse me," he told Aida, before rushing back to the porter. "Thank you for everything. I've got her now," he told the young man, quickly taking her arm.

Just as quickly, she pulled away. "I can walk," she muttered.

After giving the porter another five-dollar bill—his last—Lowe turned to find his family staring. Expectantly.

He cleared his throat. "Hadley Bacall, meet the Magnusson clan." He hastily rattled off everyone's names. "Miss Bacall and I met on the train."

"That's one way of looking at it," Hadley muttered to herself.

"Her father works for the de Young Museum."

"As do I," she added.

"Right, of course," he said, mildly flustered. Why didn't he just say that to begin with? It's not like anything scandalous had happened between them. Well, minus the ripped the dress; his eyes instantly angled toward her coat while his brain remembered the stitched peacock feathers curving over her luscious backside for the umpteenth time.

For the love of God, wake up, man!

"She's a curator," he managed to spit out. "The museum is interested in what I uncovered in the desert."

There. That seemed to make sense to everyone. He struck his hands in his pockets and exhaled while Hadley politely elaborated on her undying love of mummies and the stories they told about the Egyptians' diet and way of life . . . talk, talk. And his family acted impressed . . . Yes, yes. Good. Everything was normal and fine.

Until Bo spoke up.

"Do you have a car picking you up, or would you like a ride home?"

"I'll just take a taxi, thank you," she answered.

Then Winter had to insert himself into the conversation. "Bo will take your luggage to the cab stand, then."

Luggage. Right. Time to invent another story. But Hadley was faster.

"Actually, your brother knocked my suitcase out of my hands in Salt Lake City during a knife fight, so God only knows if Union Pacific will find it."

Lowe cringed. "It wasn't exactly a 'knife fight,' per se."

"Correct me if I'm wrong," she said, her voice tarter than a Michigan cherry. "But during dinner on the train last night, when we were discussing you stabbing one of the thugs, I believe your exact quip was, 'That's what they get for bringing guns to a knife fight.'"

Oh, boy.

"A day in the life of a Magnusson," Aida murmured as Winter's face darkened.

Lowe wanted to drag Hadley aside. What happened to his partner in crime? She'd done so well in front of the porter this morning, and they'd spent the day chatting. He'd thought they were getting along. Now she was generating arctic winds strong enough to bury him under a snowy drift of resentment. What had changed?

He faked a smile in an attempt to charm his way back into her good graces. Or at least somewhere closer to her good graces than where he stood at the moment. "But, hey— I got us home in one piece. Mostly. Sorry about your luggage. And your dress."

She stared at him for a long moment, and then said, "You

have my father's check. He'll contact you about meeting up with him." She bid a polite good-bye to his family, nodded to him, then strolled away as if he were the last person she ever wanted to see again.

Even then, he was unable to tear his gaze from the hypnotic sway of her hips as she threaded her way through the boisterous travelers thronging the platform.

"Christ alive," Winter mumbled. "What on earth did you do to that lady?"

"Nothing," he protested.

Nothing he wanted to, that is.

A slow-walking group of elderly nuns split up their group and obscured his view of Hadley. As they shuffled by, Winter whispered in his ear, "Monk Morales has been sniffing around the pier, looking for you. Word is you sold him a forgery. Some kind of miniature golden statue. An animal."

Lowe scratched the back of his neck. "A crocodile."

"You been working with Adam Goldberg again?"

Lowe grunted.

"God*dammit*, Lowe."

"It wasn't Adam's fault—his reproduction was spotless. It was the fucking paperwork. Monk didn't even notice the error. It was the person he sold it to."

Winter's eyes briefly closed. "Which is who?"

"No idea. It was a silent sale."

"So what does Monk want from you now?"

"I think he wants his money back, but he might want my head, as well."

"Why don't you compromise and give him the real statue."

Impossible to give what he didn't have. The whole purpose of the forgery was to generate two sales. Lowe gave a polite nod to one of the nosier nuns as she passed. *Yes, Sister,* he thought, *you aren't wrong to suspect the Magnusson boys of vice and lies. We are the reason people need to purge themselves in your confessional booths. Nothing to see. Move along.*

Winter flexed his hand like he might be thinking about taking Monk's side. "How much do you owe him?"

"I've got a plan, don't worry."

"One that doesn't involve begging me for money?"

"Never begged you before. Don't plan to start now."

"Good, because my liquid assets this month are tied up in a new warehouse in Marin County, and I recently paid out Christmas bonuses to my people and—"

"*Ja, ja!* I said I wasn't asking." Not that he hadn't considered it, but still.

The last nun passed by. Winter gripped the back of Lowe's neck and whispered hotly into his ear, "Fix it with Morales. I've got a baby on the way. Don't bring that shit to our doorstep."

After leaving Lowe, Hadley spent several minutes calming her erratic feelings. Why she'd gotten so upset in front his family, she didn't really know. But once they were gone, she put Lowe out of her mind and waited nearly two hours in the Twin Peaks lobby, hoping her lost luggage was on the 127. It wasn't. So she filed a claim with the manager, listening to his secondhand account of the events at the Salt Lake City station. No one knew why the incident had happened and the police weren't able to apprehend the gunmen. Maybe they'd follow Lowe here to finish the job.

It was dark when the taxi took her through the Castro and the Mission District, and finally down the steep bend of California Street to her Nob Hill apartment building at Mason. The elegant nine-story high-rise was only a year old and very exclusive. Only the best, her father had encouraged when she'd decided to move out of the family home.

Tendrils of nighttime fog clung to French columns flanking the driveway. She paid the taxi driver and breezed through the small lobby, waving at an attendant who barely lifted his head—did he even know her name?—before stepping onto the elevator.

"Miss Bacall." Finally, a friendly face. The graying elevator operator greeted her with his usual broad smile. "How was your trip?"

"Hectic, Mr. Walter. Very hectic. I'm relieved to be home."

"No luggage?"

She wilted against the elevator wall. "No luggage. It's a long story, I'm afraid. Hopefully it will be delivered tomorrow."

He shut the scissor gate and engaged the elevator. "You're deliberately trying to intrigue me, I think. But I won't press. How about your class at the university? Did they like what you had to say about Egyptian cats?"

"They were attentive." The ones who didn't leave or fall asleep. She knew she wasn't the liveliest public speaker. One of her coworkers, George, said listening to her speak was akin to enduring an accountant's eulogy. She knew he wasn't wrong; giving seminars made her uncomfortable. But if she wanted to rise above her curation pay—and George—it was a necessary evil, and one that she'd gladly submit to. She wanted her father's position as department head more than just about anything.

But answering rote questions in front of bored college students at a podunk university was a one-way conversation. Not like the spirited discussion she'd had on the train that afternoon with Lowe. To her great surprise, he wasn't just a dumb treasure hunter who'd stumbled upon the *djed*. He knew things. He could read hieroglyphics, and he'd even learned some of the Nubi language from the local Aswan workers on his excavation. He told her stories about the historic book market in Alexandria, and asked for details about her seminar.

He listened. He asked questions.

He argued.

He might not agree with all her funerary tool theories, and he wasn't precise with dynasty dates, but he certainly wasn't stupid. And he had an easy, unpretentious way of talking that she didn't encounter much in her line of work.

He also lied about anything and everything under the sun. And beyond the seeming lightheartedness of it, she realized now that he was a master of deflection. All their chatting, all that time spent together, and he'd barely revealed a single personal detail about himself.

Floor numbers scrolled past the scissor gates as they ascended. Mr. Walter chatted about the winter rain they'd been getting and how it hadn't slowed a drunken hellfire party going on at the Pacific Union Club, the men's club across the street. On the ninth floor, he bid her good night.

In the entry to her apartment, she stepped on an envelope when she shrugged out of her coat. She weighted it in her hand. Not good, she feared.

"Mrs. Durer?" she called out.

Her maid did not answer.

A fitting end to her dreary day.

The click of her heels on polished marble bounced around the high walls of her spacious living room. The windows here looked out over the twinkling lights of the Fairmont Hotel—a beautiful building, always busy with people coming and going. And the steady rumble of cars and occasional clack of the cable cars braving the steep hill kept her company, night or day.

Like the rest of her apartment, the master bedroom contained a minimal amount of furniture. Everything was bolted down: bed, nightstand, chaise lounge. In the six months she'd lived there, her specters had blown out two windows and three light fixtures and had overturned a large armoire. Best not to give them any extra kindling, she found.

Her father called them Mori. Death specters. Her mother became cursed with them after a trip to Egypt, and when she died, they were passed on to Hadley. Strong, negative emotions called them up, fueled them. Shadowy tricksters, her father had explained when she was a child.

"Trickster" seemed too kind a word for spirits with the power to kill.

The only companion sturdy enough to survive her angry moods was a sleek black cat. Lounging on her silk coverlet, he stretched his long limbs in greeting when she dropped her handbag on the nightstand.

"Hello, Number Four," she said, running a hand along his soft belly. He answered with an enthusiastic purr.

Because of her unusual curse, she'd never been allowed

to have pets as a child. A necessary precaution, even now. God knew she wouldn't normally even consider subjecting an innocent life to her murderous moods. But she didn't seek out Number Four—she'd found him hiding in the pantry after she moved in. And though she'd tried to shoo him away, he just kept coming back, again and again, so she finally allowed the stubborn creature to stay.

A few months ago, he was Number Three, until he was caught in the cross fire of a fight between her and her father: the cat had hidden under a chair the specters reduced to matchsticks. But just as he'd done the first two times he'd gotten on the wrong side of the specters, the cat managed to pick himself back up and simply kept on ticking.

Nine lives, as the superstition goes. Seeing how he was on this fourth already, by her count, Hadley figured he had five more left. He was an odd sort of miracle, that cat of hers.

A lot like her, really.

She tried not to think about Lowe when she stripped off her clothes and tossed the ripped dress in a wastebasket. Unbelievable that she'd spent last night and most of today with him. The whole thing felt surreal to her now, like a dream. Or a gaudy nightmare.

Stretching out on the bed with Number Four, she held up the found envelope to her reading lamp above the headboard. The silhouette of a key and a letter appeared against the golden light. She ripped off the side of the envelope and tipped it into her open palm. Her apartment key fell out. The metal was cold against her fist as she skimmed the hand-written letter from her latest maid: *Miss Bacall . . . Grateful for my time in your service . . . however, I must take my leave . . . My nerves are frayed . . . Feel as if the devil dwells inside you . . . bad luck . . . Will pray for you and that demonic cat.*

"Another servant bites the dust," she said to Number Four. "Good riddance, you say? Why, Number Four, that's not very nice. Then again, neither was Mrs. Durer, and she did call you demonic. We'll contact the agency tomorrow and find someone less evangelical."

He purred in agreement.

She wasn't sad to see the woman go, exactly. But as she stared out the window past the city lights, she couldn't help but think of Lowe and his boisterous family. From the train's window, she'd watched the warm greeting they gave him, all hugs and smiles and laughter.

No one had bothered to welcome her home. Her father probably hadn't even remembered she'd left town. A shame that the only person who knew her comings and goings was the elevator operator.

No, she wasn't sad that another maid had quit. But she *was* sad that the old woman's quick departure left Hadley alone in the middle of a busy city. And she was sad that it made her feel so needy. Not for the first time, she wished that she could come home and count on someone being there. A warm body. Another voice.

Another soul.

She thought of last night, and how she'd spent much of it listening to the even rhythm of Lowe's breath as he slept peacefully on the berth across from her. How comforting it was to fall asleep to that sound.

She clung to the memory of that feeling while she curled up in an empty room, in an empty apartment, with nothing but herself and a cat for company.

FOUR

—◆—

AFTER SLEEPING IN TENTS AND DIRTY HOTELS FOR THE BETTER part of the year, Lowe found his beloved feather bed on the second floor of the Magnussons' sprawling Queen Anne to be everything he'd remembered: luxurious, comforting, and safe. Moreover, his en suite bathroom was blessedly clean, the polished floors of his room smelled like orange oil, and all of his things were just as he'd left them. But after catching up with his family and staff—and after their housekeeper, Greta, bemoaning the loss of his pinky finger, stuffed him with a homecoming feast of Swedish gravlax and dilled potatoes—he woke up the next morning feeling restless.

Maybe it was Winter's warnings about Monk Morales that did it. Or maybe it was the cursed *djed* amulet burning a proverbial hole in his soul. He needed to get that thing to a safe place, and fast. But before he could, he supposed he'd better let Archibald Bacall have a look. Maybe the man would like the damned thing so much, he'd triple his offer. Or quadruple it.

And perhaps while visiting Dr. Bacall, Lowe might see

Hadley again. After the way she'd left him at the train station, it might be in his best interest to avoid the woman. Why he was still thinking about her, he didn't understand.

The train company delivered his luggage early that morning. He looted it for gifts he'd brought back from Egypt before dressing in a freshly pressed suit and tie—possibly the cleanest clothes he'd worn in months. But old habits die hard, so he tucked his pants into knee-high brown leather boots and skipped the suspenders, opting for a belt. More comfortable, and it gave him something on which to anchor his curved dagger. He'd never admit it to Winter, but after the thugs with the guns in Salt Lake City, he wasn't exactly champing at the bit to march around the city unprotected. So he checked that his short coat covered the weapon and headed out.

"Oh, Lulu baby," he cooed to the poppy red Indian motorcycle gleaming in the late morning sunlight. God, he'd missed her. Conspicuous, yes, but also small and nimble; she could fit into places a big car couldn't.

He adjusted the fuel petcock and chock, and with one good kick-start, the engine rumbled to life. Beautiful. After tugging down the brim of his favorite brown herringbone flatcap, he maneuvered around Winter's limo and sped out of the gate. Sweet freedom! Everything disappeared but Lulu's weight beneath him and the road ahead.

The ride reacquainted him with the city's steep hills and the sweeping views of the sparkling Bay, an oasis after the prison sentence he'd served digging under Egypt's blistering sun. He was home, and he wasn't going to leave. Ever. He repeated this promise to familiar buildings as he passed until he'd crisscrossed his way through downtown.

No one seemed to be dogging his path, so he stopped at his favorite barbershop to rid himself of the itchy whiskers and have his mop of sun-bleached blond curls trimmed and pomaded back into manageable waves. Astrid would stop complaining now.

Feeling lighter, he zigzagged up through southwestern Pacific Heights past the old Laurel Hill Cemetery grounds to Golden Gate Park. The de Young Museum sat on green lawns and a palm-lined concourse. Throngs of people soaked up sunshine in front of the building's Spanish Plateresque facade. He zipped around the side road to the administrative offices.

Austere wood paneling and a pretty strawberry-haired receptionist greeted him.

"Why, hello," she said, flashing a dazzling smile as she chewed a piece of gum. "How may I help you, sir?"

"Mr. Magnusson to see Dr. Bacall." He handed her a business card and waited while she excused herself to announce his arrival. A few minutes later, she returned to lead him down a narrow hall past several closed doors to one of the bigger offices in the back.

Book-heavy shelves and numbered boxes lined the walls of the musty room, and paperwork collected on a corner conference table. Dust motes hung suspended in a slice of sunlight framing a thin, elderly man slumped behind a desk. More than elderly—on death's door. The man looked as if he were minutes away from drying up and blowing out the window.

"Dr. Bacall . . ." the redhead prompted.

"Lowe Magnusson?" the man answered. His head turned in Lowe's direction, but his eyes didn't see him. They were eerily blank. Albino white—no iris and barely a trace of pupil.

He was blind.

Good lord. What the hell had happened to Archibald Bacall? Lowe cleared his throat. "Ah, yes, sir. It's good to meet you."

"Come in, come in. I have trouble moving around these days, so you'll have to forgive me." He lifted his head and spoke to the receptionist. "Miss Tilly, can you show him a chair, then close the door, please? This is a private meeting. No interruptions."

As the door snicked shut behind him, Lowe removed his cap and studied the old man. Sagging, mottled skin. Frail bones. Balding. Liver spots. He'd seen fairly recent photographs of the man in archaeology publications—he'd had a head full of hair and didn't look a day over fifty.

"It's good to finally meet you after all our correspondence," Bacall said in a half-British, half-American transatlantic accent. The one Hadley shared. If Lowe remembered correctly, Bacall was from some titled English family or another—he'd married the gold rush heiress after moving here from across the pond.

"You, as well."

Could the man see him at all? Anything? Lowe waved his hand in the air. Bacall stared vacantly toward the back of the room.

"Quite a nest you stumbled upon outside the Philae temple," the old man said. "Hard to believe it's attracted so many scholars and tourists over the last couple of decades and no one noticed the sunken entrance."

Lowe peeled off his driving gloves and stuffed them in his coat pockets. "Just happened to decipher a code on the temple walls that led me to the secret room. Stroke of luck, really."

"I don't believe in luck. I think you're damn good at solving puzzles and finding things. Good scholars are a dime a dozen. In fact, we've got a dozen of them in these offices this afternoon. They can argue a theory and uncover new things sitting behind their desks, but they won't get their hands dirty. An educated treasure hunter like you with sharp field skills and the brains to decode riddles? You're a different breed altogether. An undervalued one."

"Thank you, sir."

Society snobs like Bacall didn't have respect for men like Lowe. Maybe the old man was trying to butter him up to get a better price, hard to tell. His daughter had been much easier to read.

The telephone rang.

"I thought I told her no interruptions," Bacall murmured. "Excuse me one moment."

Lowe sat back and waited for the man to finish his call. A few seconds into it, a brief knock sounded from an inner door in the corner of the room, and the door swung open.

A familiar willowy figure marched in lugging a stack of file folders up to her nose.

Dressed in a black pencil skirt and gray sweater, with a string of faceted black beads swinging down to her waist, Hadley looked more Casket Saleswoman than Wealthy Funeral Attendee today.

With a grunt, she lowered the files onto her father's conference table and attempted to straighten the teetering stack. She stilled and lifted her chin as if she were scenting the air. Then both her head and the string of black beads swung in his direction.

He grinned. Hard to tell if she was surprised or disgusted by his presence, but whatever it was, her hand slipped on the stack of folders. Half the files slid sideways and toppled onto the floor, paper scattering like autumn leaves.

He jumped to his feet to help her. "Funny seeing you here," he said in a low voice as he steadied the remaining folders threatening to fall. "Jumped any trains today?"

"Please don't mention that in front of Father," she whispered, looking over her shoulder to check that the man was still talking on the telephone.

"The jumping part, or the torn dress part, or the spending the night together part?"

"The part where we did anything other than meet briefly in the first-class dining car."

"Oh, ho-ho! Someone lied to dear old Daddy, did she?"

She glared at him like she was seconds away from scratching out his eyeballs.

"You have my word," he said, etching an invisible "X" over his heart.

"Which is worth less than a trapdoor on a lifeboat."

"Ooaf!" He bent with her to scoop up paperwork. "I get the distinct impression you aren't glad to see me again, Hadley."

"You aren't wrong, Lowe."

Despite her dour attitude, if he didn't know better, he'd think she was flirting with him. A strange little spark warmed his chest. "And to think, just yesterday morning I was waking up to the sight of your bed-mussed hair."

"Keep your voice down!" she said, glancing back at her father once more.

"If you lied to your old man, what did you tell your boy-friend?" No ring, and she hadn't mentioned anyone last night, but she wasn't exactly forthcoming about anything more than mummy dust. Maybe she kept time with some fancy-pants society doctor.

The barest of flushes colored her cheeks, but she didn't look up from her task. "Are you here to make my life miserable?"

"I'm here to empty your father's bank account. Making you miserable is a bonus."

"I do believe that's the first honest thing you've ever told me."

"Don't let it go to your head."

"The only thing in my head right now is that cock," she said, nodding toward the wall.

Lowe paused. "Pardon?"

"I'm in a hurry."

Another pause. Lowe looked where she'd gestured. "You mean . . . the *clock?*"

"That's what I said." But it wasn't, and her gaze flicked to his crotch—so fast he almost wasn't sure he saw it until a furious strawberry blush spilled over her cheeks and neck. "Th-that's what I meant," she stuttered, then whispered to herself, "Oh, God."

Well, well, *well*. When was the last time he'd heard *that* from a woman's mouth? Had he ever? Hadley Bacall, over-flowing with desire for . . . clock.

He didn't think she could redden any more, which made him feel a little pity for her. Best to let it go, as much as he hated to. So he gathered paperwork while she gathered her wits.

"Here, this one's intact." The fingers of his disfigured hand brushed hers as he passed a folder. She snatched her hand back like he was carrying the Black Death.

The sting of the rejection took him by surprise. He'd

become accustomed to people staring, but did his injury disgust her, too?

She cleared her throat and gestured to his hand. "Believe me, it's not that—not at all," she said in a low voice and looked into his eyes with startling sincerity. "Please . . ."

Her candid acknowledgment made him feel exposed, and for some bizarre reason, this also thrilled him. Why? It was as if the moment stretched between them and built a bridge. A rickety bridge, unsafe to cross, but he attempted anyway, irrational excitement urging him to lean closer. " 'Please' what?" he whispered, his breath fluttering a glossy strand of raven hair near her ear. "What do you want, Hadley?"

"What I want," she said in a controlled voice, "is for you to please shut up and sit down."

Well.

Can't cross a bridge when someone's shoving you off the side. He left her on the floor with the files and plopped back down in his chair, unsure why he even cared. Bacall was still on the telephone.

While one of his knees bounced out an anxious rhythm, Lowe attempted to divert his attention elsewhere. Lots of books on the shelves, but the titles were drier than the Sahara. He watched a bird alight on a branch outside the window . . . noted a frayed section of telephone cord. But a hushed whisper—*one, two, three*—brought his attention back to the conference table, where Hadley was counting under her breath while bending to pick up the folders.

He sucked in a sharp breath.

There it was, only a few feet away. How could he have forgotten? When she bent down, it tilted up to greet him. When she stood, it hiked up the hem of her pencil skirt by an inch or two.

If a salacious portrait of Hadley were painted on a carnival sideshow banner, it would read *Come See the Woman with the Roundest, Most Voluptuous Ass in the World!* Carnies would be able to charge whatever they wanted for a peek inside a dark tent, and Lowe would cash every penny he'd ever earned for five minutes alone with her in that tent.

Bend down. Pick up file. Stand up. Set file down.

All for his amusement, right there in front of him! Like watching a restaurant waiter flambé cherries jubilee at your table. Only, instead of making his mouth water, it was making his pants uncomfortable. He shifted in his seat and darted a glance at her father. Please God, let the man be totally and utterly blind.

Bend down. Stand up.

Oh, what he would give to angle her over that conference table, yank up that skirt, and find out if she was wearing more colorful lingerie today. Instead of peacock feathers, he imagined flaming cherries. And he imagined kneeling behind her and sinking his teeth into one of those oh-so-round cheeks.

Sweat beaded at his hairline. This was wrong, nursing an erection right in front of the woman's father. Wrong, wrong, wrong. He moved his cap further up his lap to cover himself and focused on book titles again. Dry, boring, academic titles about ancient pottery glazes and fourteenth-century crop rotation. Oh, look—her father's phone conversation was over.

Thank God.

"My apologies for the interruption," Dr. Bacall said as he groped the candlestick base of the telephone, seeking the hook for the earpiece by feel. "Is that you, Hadley?"

"Yes, Father."

"Everything okay?"

"I dropped some of the exhibit files, sorry."

"No reason to be upset." Her father said this in an odd manner, as if he were scolding her.

"It wasn't . . . it was—never mind. I'm fine."

"Good, good. That's my good girl," he said, speaking to her like she was a spooked horse.

Lowe glanced between the two Bacalls, feeling as if he were missing something.

"I have work to do," she said suddenly, and hurried out the way she came in.

"Nice seeing you again, Miss Bacall," Lowe called out.

"A pleasure to watch you work. Hope you don't find yourself watching the clock for the remainder of the day." Because, really, he should be awarded a medal for his earlier restraint.

A momentary look of horror crossed her face but she didn't blush or comment. Instead, she addressed her father. "He has the *djed* amulet base with him."

"Thank you, dear, I know. And no more interruptions, please."

Lowe tried to catch her gaze, but she exited with a dramatic slam of the door.

"You already know she can feel power coming from the amulet?" Bacall said when the brisk *click-click* of her heels faded. "Did she tell you that when you met her in Salt Lake City?"

"Yes," Lowe answered cautiously. "Would you like to . . ." *See* the amulet? That didn't sound right, considering the man's condition.

"No, no, no. If she's vouched for it, I trust her."

"And you still want to buy it?"

"Absolutely. Do you have the paperwork?"

"It's coming from Egypt," Lowe lied easily. "Should be ready in a month. I haven't cashed your check yet, but—"

"Cash it. I have had an agreement drawn up that you can sign. And if you can store the amulet safely for now, that's even better for me. But you must keep it somewhere safe and well guarded. There are people who will kill to get their hands on it. So I'd advise you not to keep it in your own home. You'll only invite a robbery. Safety-deposit box is no good, either. It needs to be well hidden."

"Don't worry about that."

"Yes, I suppose your family knows a thing or two about hiding goods, what with your brother's line of work."

"I suppose we do."

"You were happy with the deposit amount?"

"I've had better offers." Rather, he *would have* better ones, if he played his cards right.

"I thought as much. Money isn't a problem. Whatever you think is fair. But if you're interested, I have a proposition for you, related to the amulet, for which I'm willing to pay a much higher sum. It's right up your alley, I think."

"I'm listening."

"I used to excavate in Egypt every year when I was younger, you know." He leaned back in his chair. "Half the museum's Egyptian collection, I found personally."

"I'm aware," Lowe said.

"What if I were to tell you that I'd found the four missing crossbars of the *djed* years ago?"

Lowe stilled. Was the man serious? A piece of the amulet was one thing, but the entire thing, assembled? That would be worth—well . . . so much more.

"If that's true—" Lowe started.

"Why haven't I sold them? The first reason would be that the amulet has personal meaning. But the second reason, the pressing one, is why I'm interested in hiring your services. The four crossbars are here in the city. At least, I believe they are. I just don't know where, exactly."

"I'm not following."

The man felt around his desk for a gold cigarette case. He managed to extract a cigarette with some effort. Watching him was painful, so Lowe offered to strike a match. "Thank you," Bacall mumbled as he puffed the cigarette to life. "When I was younger, my excavation partner and I experienced what you might refer to as an occult phenomenon in Cairo. I won't bore you with the details—"

"I'm not easily bored."

"Suffice it to say, after that experience, we became enemies. Not the kind of enemies who squabble over petty things in the office, but the kind of enemies who spend much of their free time plotting to kill one another."

Well, well. "If you're going to do something, might as well do it right."

"This isn't a joking matter, Mr. Magnusson."

Grouchy old bastard, wasn't he? "My apologies," Lowe said. "Please continue."

Bacall took a long drag off his cigarette.

"Before we became enemies, we spent a lot of time

searching for mythical objects. The infamous Backbone of Osiris was one of them. Obsession does strange things to the mind, and I was obsessed to outdo my partner."

"So you hunted the amulet."

"For years. Such a disappointment to discover it had been split up in the Amarna Period. Imagine trying to find something whose pieces were scattered around an entire country almost three thousand years ago."

"But you did?"

"Spent a fortune scouring excavation sites, only to find them all in one place. Not in a tomb or temple or any sort of excavation site, but in the hands of a wealthy British earl, who'd bought them from grave robbers in 1879."

"Ah."

"Yes, not exactly the victory a young archaeologist craves, but I didn't care. So I gave the earl the better part of my wife's gold fortune to acquire them. That's when I ran into a problem."

"You didn't have the base of the amulet."

"That was one problem, yes. But at the time, I believed I could eventually find it. The problem was, my partner heard a rumor I'd found the crossbars. And I couldn't risk him stealing them from me before I found the last piece. Too dangerous to keep them, so I shipped them home to my wife."

Lowe crossed his legs. "Your deceased wife."

"She wasn't at the time," Bacall said. "The year was 1906. I had a lead on the last piece—a wrong lead, as you've proven—but I didn't know that at the time. So I chased the lead to Cairo and instructed my wife to hide the pieces in our house. She hid them, all right. Hid them around the city of San Francisco. I got a series of telegrams from her, in which she explained that she was ending my obsession with the amulet in some misguided attempt to mend the rift between me and my partner. She tried to destroy the pieces—said no fire would melt the gold."

Fascinating. "So she hid them around the city?"

"Indeed. Hid them, wrote a coded map of the hiding places, and hid the map as well. In her last telegram, he said no one would find the map or the pieces until I made peace with my partner. And before I could get back home to talk some sense into her, the earthquake hit. Vera didn't survive."

"I'm very sorry."

"More than twenty-one years have passed, but I still miss her." His mouth lifted in a soft smile. "Her hiding the amulet pieces didn't surprise me in hindsight. She was always fond of puzzles, you see. Very good at deciphering code. A bit like you, actually."

Lowe exhaled heavily. "You want me to decipher your wife's code?"

"I'd like you to decipher her code and find where she hid the pieces, yes. A sort of urban treasure hunt, if you will. If you find them all, and if you hand them over to me along with the amulet's base, which you've already found, I'll write you a check for a hundred grand."

A hundred thousand! Enough to cover his debt with Monk, with plenty left to burn. A familiar thrill—one of possibility and the promise of his luck changing—made his pulse pound.

"What's the catch?" Lowe asked. There was always a catch. Always, always, *always*.

The old man leaned back in his chair. "The catch is, you'll have to speak to my dead wife to find out where she hid the map."

FIVE

———◆———

LOWE STARED AT THE BLIND MAN. "YOU WANT ME TO . . . ?"

"Your sister-in-law is a spirit medium, I'm told. A real one."

According to Winter and Astrid, yes. Aida was channeling spirits on stage at one of the North Beach speakeasies, the Gris-Gris Club, when Winter first met her. She now worked out of a shop in Chinatown, holding private séances, performing exorcisms—that sort of thing.

Did Lowe believe in her ability? He didn't have any reason *not* to. If he saw it with his own eyes, he supposed he'd be swayed into a definite yes. He'd experienced some strange things in his life, the *djed* amulet's unexplainable power being one of them.

"Your sister-in-law can channel my wife's spirit," Bacall said. "You can talk with her, ask her about the map. Start there."

"Why don't you do that yourself?"

"She wouldn't tell me when she was alive. I seriously doubt she'd do so now."

"What about your daughter?"

"I don't want Hadley involved in this. Not at all. If you accept my proposition, I'll tell her you're hunting down old friends for me. She doesn't need to know about her mother's betrayal."

"Her mother hiding the pieces from you?"

A pause hung in the air. "Yes. All she needs to know is that I'm purchasing the amulet base from you. End of story. That's not negotiable."

Well, it certainly spoke to the man's trust of his own family. Then again, who was Lowe to judge another man's secrets? Especially not one who was willing to pay him.

"The payment I'm offering is generous," Bacall said. "Twice what the Alexandria stele sold for at auction last year. I'd wager you won't find a museum that will give you that price, nor a private collector. And I'm willing to offer something else to sweeten the pot."

"And what would that be?"

"Due to my declining health, I'm retiring my post here soon. The board of trustees will vote on my replacement in a month. If you find the hidden amulet pieces for me, I'd be more than happy to make sure your name is the only one considered for the job. It pays well, and puts you in a position to be sponsored if you want to continue digging. And if you don't? Well, it's a cushy desk job with a bit of status."

A lot of status. Enough that he'd never have to dig in that godforsaken desert again, which was tempting. Then again, he wasn't particularly excited by the prospect of being cooped up in an office, day in and day out.

"Think about my offer," Bacall said. "Our director is throwing our annual Friends of the Museum party this weekend. James Flood's widow is hosting it at her mansion on Broadway—just a few blocks down from your family home, I believe."

"Yes, I know the place." The Flood's marble palace. He drove past it all the time.

"Dinner, coats and tails, an orchestra," Bacall said. "Great chance to rub shoulders with donors and people who could help your career. I'll get you an invitation."

He glanced at the door Hadley had slammed, wondering if she'd be attending this soirée. Maybe he should stop fantasizing about erotic carnival sideshows and her interest in clocks, and concentrate on figuring out exactly why her father was offering him a small fortune served on a silver platter.

After all, there was always a catch.

Hadley stared out the window in her father's office, watching Lowe chat with one of the groundskeepers. Rather animatedly, at that. All smiles and laughter. Did he strike up friendly chats with every stranger he stumbled across during his day?

"Everything all right, my dear?" her father asked as he switched on a desktop radio.

Other than her complete and utter humiliation? Not really. Why in God's name had she said . . . *that*? "Just seeing what the weather looks like."

"It's going to rain. I can feel it in my knees."

"Mr. Magnusson took the amulet with him?" She didn't sense it anymore, so he must have.

"He's going to arrange storage for it until the paperwork arrives from the Egyptian Ministry." Her father fiddled with the radio dial, fine-tuning the signal until he was satisfied with the clarity of the music, some old-fashioned ragtime number.

"How did he get the thing out of the country without the paperwork?"

"Hmm? Oh, I don't know. His uncle is a fast talker. The whole family's filled with criminals and con artists."

"Why do you trust him, then?"

"Because I made him an offer he can't refuse, and people like him sell their loyalty to the highest bidder."

She moved the curtain to get a better view of Lowe. He was tipping the brim of his cap at grumpy old Mrs. Beckett, who looked up at his face when she strolled into the building and smiled like he was St. Peter and she was trying to cheat her way into heaven.

"What will you do with the amulet once you have it?" she asked her father. "Donate it to the museum?"

"Not sure."

A lie if she'd ever heard one. When Father had first insisted she meet Lowe at the train station, he told her he'd attempted to find it himself when he was younger, and that it was a lifelong dream to finally own it. He wouldn't go to so much trouble if he didn't have plans.

"By the way, I invited Mr. Magnusson to the party this weekend. Perhaps I'll ask Miss Tilly to play escort."

Her stomach tightened. "He's interested in Miss Tillly?"

"She's a lovely woman. Who wouldn't be?"

Who, indeed. Why this bothered her so much now, she didn't understand. Lowe had paid her a couple of rude comments and touched her hand, and now her brain was sending proprietary signals to her heart? Ridiculous. "I hardly think you'd want to offer up your favorite secretary like she's some kind of prostitute."

"Don't be vulgar, Hadley. Jealousy isn't becoming."

"I'm not jealous." But she was, stupidly. And before she could control her emotions, the Mori specters spied into her thoughts and rose up from the floorboards to childishly shove the radio off the desk. Static crackled through the speaker after it hit the floor.

Her father jumped. "What was that?"

"I bumped into it," she said, quickly snatching up the radio as she counted internally and turned the dial to find the station again. "It's nothing."

His shoulders relaxed. "I just want to keep him close until the sale of the amulet goes through, and Miss Tilly can introduce him to all the curators. I don't think she'll mind. She mentioned he was quite tall and uniquely handsome."

Oh, did she, now? Was that Miss Tilly's polite way of accommodating his broken nose in her assessment? Admittedly, Hadley had been surprised to see him clean-shaven and wearing a decent suit, though the dramatic brown boots that laced up to his knees were a little much. He looked like he was dressed for cavalry duty or hunting quail on horseback.

And why had Father asked a secretary her opinion about his looks instead of asking Hadley? Well, she supposed that was typical. Half the time, she swore he still thought she was a ten-year-old girl. If she told him Lowe had pressed his body against her underclothes, he'd expire from shock.

What do you want, Hadley?

She took one last look out the window. Lowe had finished his chat and was now straddling a bright red motorcycle. Why didn't this surprise her? Guess the riding boots *were* for a horse, after all—a mechanical one. The engine was so loud, it rattled the closed window.

He tugged his cap down and tapped the kickstand with his boot. My goodness, the man was nicely constructed. He took her breath away. Just a little.

Maybe a lot.

Because as he sped out of the parking lot, she felt unmoored.

And she wished she could've been on the back of that motorcycle, riding away with him.

Lowe took back roads from the museum to the Fillmore District and parked Lulu in an inconspicuous spot. Since the Great Fire, the neighborhood had become home to an eclectic mix of immigrants and working-class families. He'd spent the first ten years of his life in a row house here before his father's fishing business moved them closer to the Embarcadero.

The block he headed down was the center of the city's Jewish community; Russian Jews and Eastern Europeans owned most of the businesses here. He passed a Hebrew school, two kosher butchers, and several cigar shops before stepping into a movie theater alcove, where he stood in the shadow of the ticket booth for a minute—just to be safe.

No one was following.

The euphoric scent of freshly baked rye bread wafted

from Waxman's Bakery as he strode to the curb and waited to cross the busy street. Hopefully if any of Monk's men *were* trailing him, they'd seen him enter the museum earlier and assumed he left the amulet there. He tried to relax, but his mind drifted back to Hadley, which distracted him from what he should've been watching: the place he was headed.

Out of the corner of his eye, a flash of yellow darted from the delicatessen sitting catercornered and across the street from him. He turned his head in time to see Stella Goldberg bounding down the sidewalk in a buttercup dress.

For a moment, he was smiling at her plump face as the four-year-old girl silently ran down the sidewalk to greet him. Then he looked up and saw the obstacle in her path.

Two workers were hauling some sort of industrial fan up the side of the building with pulleys and ropes. The square fan was the size of a car hood, and from the way the men were straining, it was heavy. A foreman stood by, directing their efforts while shouting to another man on the roof.

The foreman saw Stella. He shouted for her to stop.

She couldn't hear him. Stella was deaf.

Unaware of their presence or the danger they posed, she plowed down the sidewalk beneath the rising fan, which dangled from the ropes a story above. And in her haste, she tripped over one of the worker's outstretched feet and fell facedown on the sidewalk.

Her ragged cry echoed off the building.

The man whose foot over which she tripped lost his balance. The rope slipped through his gloves. The fan plummeted several yards, its shadow growing larger over Stella's tiny body.

Lowe lunged off the curb and dashed across the road, his own hearing temporarily stunted by the blood pounding in his ears. His long legs carried him out of a Flivver's path on one side of the road—just barely. He reached the sidewalk in a leap. The foreman was grabbing the slack rope.

The pulleys squealed.

Someone was shouting.

Lowe didn't look up. Just leaned down and scooped her up as the fan dropped—

Inches above the sidewalk. That's where they stopped it. She was one extended second away from being crushed.

Lungs burning, he squeezed her against his chest, a ball of yellow flounce, dark curls, and fragile limbs. Her arms clung to his neck, her heartbeat like a hummingbird's.

"I've got you, I've got you," he assured her, speaking against her head so she could feel it.

As if a switch flipped somewhere inside her, she stopped sobbing.

A gaggle of women poured out from a nearby shop, shouting in distress. Stella peeled her tear-damp face from his shoulder and panicked when she saw the chaos surrounding them.

He held a hand up to the bystanders. "She's fine. Don't scare her." He ducked his head to catch her gaze and smiled. "Close one, old girl. You nearly had that last hurdle."

She gave him a toothy smile.

"There you go, right as rain." The workers lowered the fan to the sidewalk with a boom that shook the soles of his shoes. He adjusted Stella's weight onto his right hip and sidled around the downed fan. "You recognized your *Farbror* Lowe—and after six months away. Such a smart girl. Now then, let's find your papa before these men drop the damned thing again."

"That kid could've injured my man," the foreman shouted as his workers looked on in silence. "You're lucky we didn't drop this thing or you would've paid to repair it."

Lowe kept his face calm for Stella's sake and spoke through a tight smile. "You're lucky I don't beat your face into a pulp and break both your legs before I get my family's lawyer to sue your company for negligence."

"Now, you see here—"

Stella made an indistinct noise and looked toward Diller's Delicatessen, where her father burst from the door in a panic.

"Stella!"

"There's Papa," Lowe said as he gave one last malicious look to the foreman before striding off.

"Lowe, thank goodness." Adam Goldberg met them half-way. "I turned my back for a second. What happened?" He surveyed the scene on the sidewalk and frowned.

"Nothing a little hot water and salve won't cure." Lowe uncurled one of her skinned palms. "Stings, *ja*?" he said, tapping her fingers to show what he meant.

She flexed her hand and nodded.

Adam took her out of Lowe's arms, murmuring a quiet prayer beneath his breath. Once he'd inspected her knees, his shoulders fell. He chuckled the sort of terrified laugh that betrayed relief and fear—a laugh Lowe had heard a hundred times from his old friend.

"You look as if the desert sun tanned your hide," Adam said. "And I see you've lost a finger. Should I ask?"

"Probably not."

"Fair enough. Hungry?"

"Famished."

"So much for a discreet meeting. Come on."

The aroma of corned beef, chicken soup, and dill wafted toward them as they stepped into the delicatessen. Canned goods and bread were sold on one side of the shop, cold food behind a refrigerated counter on the other, and hot meals were cooked in a small kitchen in the back. A short menu of choices was scrawled in chalk on a standing board by the counter.

Adam set Stella down atop one of four tables near the windows and brushed dirt from her dress while Lowe dug around in his satchel, retrieving a windup toy for which he'd haggled in an open-air market in Cairo. He presented the black cat to Stella with a dramatic flourish. "What do you think? Hold on, you wind her like this." Lowe demonstrated and set the cat on the table. It rolled and wagged its tail up and down.

Stella grunted in joy, twisting around to touch it as it moved. A winner. Lowe never knew. She'd rejected half his presents. "She's grown a foot while I was gone," he remarked.

Adam smoothed back her bangs. "Twice as sassy lately, too."

An elderly woman came around the counter, smiling in their direction.

Adam nodded to her before speaking to Stella. "Take it to Mrs. Berkovich. You can play after washing up." He moved his hands to sign the word "wash" and pointed at the woman. Stella grabbed the toy and Mrs. Berkovich escorted her to the back.

"It's times like this when I think Miriam would've done a better job," Adam said wistfully as he watched his daughter disappear.

Adam's wife died of influenza a year after Stella was born—almost three years ago, now. The three of them had been friends since they were kids. Her death had devastated Adam. It had happened within a few months of Lowe's parents dying in the car crash, so Lowe and Adam grieved together. But though Lowe could say he'd come to terms with losing his parents—mostly—Adam never truly got over Miriam. And Lowe was worried he never would.

"I've told you a thousand times, it's not a defeat to hire a nanny."

"And I've told you a thousand more that I'm not taking a handout from the Magnusson family. I'm a watchmaker, not a bootlegger. I do the best I can."

"You're a goddamn genius with metal, is what you are. And if we can pull this off, we're going to make so much cash, *you* might be the one giving handouts."

"I've heard that a thousand times from you as well," his friend said, his mouth curling at the corners.

"We made a pretty penny off the crocodile statue forgery." Never mind that Lowe's uncle screwed up the paperwork, or that Monk wanted his head for it. None of that was Adam's problem.

"And I spent it paying off Stella's family debts."

"You're a better man than I, Goldberg."

Adam playfully slapped him on the arm. "Tell me something I don't know."

After Mrs. Berkovich brought steaming bowls of soup, fresh bread, and half-sour pickles pulled from fat wooden barrels near the counter, Lowe retrieved the amulet base. The strange, disconcerting vibration it emitted grew louder as he unwrapped it. "Take a look."

Adam whistled in appreciation. "This is it, eh?"

"What do you think? Can you do it?" Lowe glanced at Stella playing with the windup cat. She didn't seem to "hear" the amulet, which was probably a good thing. Adam didn't comment about it, either.

"May I?" Adam asked, pulling out a pair of jewelers' eyeglasses with extended magnifying lenses.

"Be my guest. I can't stand to touch the thing. Gives me the heebie-jeebies."

Adam turned it in his hand, leaning closer for inspection. "Same strange red tarnish to the gold as the crocodile statue, but completely different method of casting."

"A thousand years older, different place. Pay close attention to the hole at the top." Lowe pulled out a black pocket notebook from his suit and roughly sketched the finished shape of the amulet with the four crossbars stacked on the top—or how he theorized it would look, based on known descriptions and other *djed* pillars depicted in stoneware and jewelry from that time period.

"A curator at the de Young Museum looked at it—daughter of the antiquities department head."

"The one who offered to buy it?"

"The very one. I just came from seeing her." Lowe tapped his fingertips on the table and felt Adam's eyes boring into him. "Came from seeing her father, I mean. Her and her father."

Adam made a guttural noise that was both judgmental and amused. "Pretty?"

"The father?"

"Screw you."

"Hadley, then."

"Oh, *Hadley*," Adam drawled. "Ech. One day home and you're already on first-name basis? Damn you and your crazy Viking height and that lying smile of yours. What does she look like?"

"She's interesting." Well, she was. And he didn't really know how to describe her. Part of him wanted to tell Adam about the "cock" slip and the astounding shape of her ass, but some irrational part of his brain selfishly wanted to keep it all for himself.

"Fine, don't tell me. Is her father still buying this from you?"

"Even better. The man claims he found the crossbars that fit into the top. His dead wife hid them around the city years ago. He wants me to track them down and sell him this so he'll have the whole thing."

Adam looked at him above his magnifying spectacles. "How much?"

Lowe told him.

"No."

"Oh, yes," Lowe confirmed. "And God willing, if I find them, I want you to copy each piece exactly."

"It'll take me a couple of weeks to forge this one."

"That's fine. The crossbars will be smaller. Less detail." Lowe slipped his friend an envelope with a rather hefty wad of bills he'd pilfered from Winter's petty cash that morning; he'd have to replace it when Bacall's check cleared. "Money to purchase the gold. And keep that thing in the warded vault, Adam. Just in case anyone comes sniffing around."

"Why would anyone have reason to?"

"Well, for one, Monk is furious about the paperwork for the statue."

Adam raised his eyes to the ceiling. "Your uncle and his schemes. Are we in trouble?"

"Maybe, I don't know. I made sure I wasn't followed here, but watch yourself."

"Hold on a minute. Am I making the amulet copy for Monk? To repay him for the statue? Why would he trust you again if you've cheated him once and got caught?"

"He wouldn't. You're making the forgery for Dr. Bacall. I'll give Monk the real thing."

"Damn. Sure you're confident enough to pass off a forgery to an expert?"

Lowe leaned back in his chair and smiled. "Dr. Bacall is blind."

"Ah." Adam smiled. "That helps, I suppose."

"If those crossbars really do exist and you can forge the entire amulet, we'll be rich. Still, worse case scenario is no crossbars, Monk gets the real base for no charge, and we get fifty grand from Bacall for the forged base."

"Fifty grand. Even *that's* a fortune."

"Your cut's half."

"Lowe—"

"Half," he insisted, nodding to Stella. "For her, if not yourself. All I did was dig the thing up. Besides, Miriam would whip your ass from the Beyond if you didn't take it."

Adam sighed and removed his eyeglasses. "It's so much more than the statue. Maybe you should just clear your debt with Monk, sell Bacall the forged base, and be done with it."

"But if I can find the pieces, it's fifty a piece, Adam. *Fifty.*"

"If you find the pieces. *If.*"

"I found part of a mythical object buried in a flooded room halfway across the globe. Searching the city for a few more will be as easy as duck soup."

SIX

———◆———

LOWE WAS AN EXCELLENT SCHMOOZER, AS ADAM WOULD SAY. But several days later, when he climbed the white marble steps of the Beaux Arts–style Flood mansion and passed his things to the doorman—invitation, hat, white gloves, and overcoat—an old loathing resurfaced. Tailcoats and evening gowns thronged the Grand Hall and the adjoining rooms spilling into it. Old money. Prestige. San Francisco high society.

Everything Lowe was not.

Sure, his family home was in the same prestigious neighborhood, and his telephone number started with the same exchange name, but the Magnussons weren't exactly on the same level. To start, he doubted any of them had spent the week avoiding Monk Morales's telephone calls, completely paranoid that the man's goons were watching him. Nothing so far, but the shoe had to drop sometime, didn't it?

And even though no one here suspected Lowe owed a gangster fence a fortune for a forgery, everyone *did* know his family's money came from bootlegging. Hell, the entire police department knew: his brother dutifully paid them off every month.

So, yes. The champagne these partygoers were all tossing back might very well be Magnusson stock, but Lowe wasn't one of them. They knew it. He knew it. So he pasted on a smile as Dr. Bacall, walking with a gold-tipped cane, was steered in his direction by a much younger man.

"Mr. Magnusson?" The young man was built like a fire hydrant, low and squat. Seemed to be Bacall's guide dog for the night.

"Where is he?" The old man's white eyes stared at nothing as turned his head.

"Here, Dr. Bacall," Lowe answered, guiding the man's hand in a firm shake as the younger man assisted. "Thanks for inviting me."

"Think nothing of it, m'boy. They're pouring drinks down the hall, and I'm told dinner will be served soon. Miss Tilly couldn't make it tonight, I'm sorry. She had another commitment."

Lowe feigned disappointment. "Maybe some other time."

"Quite a few people here I'd like you to meet. Stan here helps me get around, but he doesn't know all the faces yet. So why don't you track down Hadley."

Hadley. Would she tell him to shut up again? He'd thought of little else the past few days. God only knew why. Maybe he was a glutton for punishment.

Bacall leaned closer, nearly butting Lowe's shoulder. "Have you considered my offer?"

Extensively. Lowe had also spent a little time getting to know Winter's spirit medium wife. But if Aida really *could* call up Bacall's dead wife, then she'd be privy to Lowe's business. And she was, unfortunately, married to his brother.

"I'm definitely interested in trying," Lowe told Bacall. "But if I do, I'm going to need something more tangible than a gentlemen's agreement before I bring my sister-in-law into this. I don't like family mixing with business, and keeping something like this under wraps will require tricky juggling."

Bacall nodded. "I know precisely what you mean, my man."

Good, because Lowe wanted to collect as much money as possible upfront, just in case Monk came calling and needed to be pacified with an installment payment.

"Dr. Bacall? Over here," someone called.

Lowe assured the old man he'd hunt down Hadley. "I'll catch up with you later."

Leaving Bacall and his assistant behind, Lowe meandered through the hall, grabbing a coupe of champagne on the way—definitely Winter's stock—and introduced himself to a widowed art critic he recognized from the newspaper. After his second glass of champagne, he bumped into a railroad tycoon who recognized *him* from the newspaper, but still no Hadley.

Until he glanced toward the end of the great hall.

Segregated from the main crowd on the far side of two immeasurably long tables set for formal dinner service, Hadley chatted with a man. Behind her, three bowed windows looked out over the night-blackened Bay. A single pendant light chased slow-moving shadows across her face as she talked.

Her pale arms and neck were bared by a layered sleeveless gown: silver bullion beneath a net of black beadwork. The beaded web gradually wove tighter and tighter to make ripples of sparkling obsidian strands that eddied around her hips and thighs, like a black whirlpool.

She wore curved silver heels on her feet, white gloves to her elbows, and diamonds on her wrists. And then, when she turned her head, something caught his attention. Something that softened every hard line on her face, every sharp note of her personality.

Every toughened wall of his lying heart.

Pinned behind her left ear, swaddled by a ruffle of raven hair, was a single star-shaped white Siberia lily.

Such an ordinary thing. But it unlocked an undiscovered door in his head. And when it creaked open, the music and clinking glasses and the snobby conversation in the hall faded to a muffled hum.

She wasn't skinny; she was elegant.

Her arms and legs weren't long; they were endless.

She wasn't pretty; she was knee-weakeningly, dazzlingly beautiful.

Lowe blinked several times and looked again. Not a dream. Still beautiful. She nodded her head in answer to her companion's question while stealing a glance at the crowd, and her gaze found his.

They stared at each other. Or rather, she looked at him while he stood rooted to the marble floor like a small child who'd been asked a question in class and was too embarrassed to admit he didn't know the answer. He became lost looking at her. For how long, he wasn't sure. But one moment he was drowning, and in the next, he felt the stem of his champagne coupe slipping through his fingers.

In a panic, he fumbled and juggled the glass until he gripped it with both hands.

Nice. Smooth. Oh so debonair. Probably looked drunker than Satan on vacation. Her squinting eyes only confirmed his fears. He set the empty coupe on a nearby table and did his best to regain his lost bravado as he headed her way.

Her companion was about Lowe's age, tall and lanky, dark hair. His formal tails were a little too long, his wing-tipped shirt a little too starched, and his face a lot too handsome. He was also alone with Hadley, so Lowe hated him on sight.

"Hello, Hadley."

"Hello, Mr. Magnusson."

No more first-name-basis, eh? Should've expected as much. "Hope I'm not interrupting an intimate conversation."

"Mr. Oliver Ginn, this is Mr. Lowe Magnusson." His own name fell off her tongue like a burden in that ridiculous posh accent.

"The treasure hunter," Mr. Ginn replied, sizing him up with a cool look.

"I prefer treasure *finder*."

"Mr. Ginn is a patron of the arts," Hadley said, as if she were defending his good character in front of a jury. "He has financed several excavations in Mexico through his contributions to university research grants."

"The Aztec program at Berkeley?" Lowe asked, trying to place the man's name.

Ginn shook his head. "I only moved here recently. My family is from Oregon."

Lowe honestly didn't give a damn.

"Mr. Ginn's the one who encouraged me to do more speaking engagements, so he's indirectly responsible for me accepting that seminar in Salt Lake City."

Oh, was he, now? "How kind," Lowe said. "I suppose I owe you thanks, Mr. Ginn, because if you hadn't encouraged her, then Hadley and I wouldn't have met and had our little adventure on the rails in that cozy little—"

"May I have a word in private, Mr. Magnusson?" Hadley said in a rush.

"Why, yes, you most certainly may."

Hadley excused herself from Moneypants and stormed off without a backward glance. Lowe guessed he was supposed to follow her like a dog, and he did—*oh*, he did. The spider web of black beads hugging her bountiful backside vibrated with every angry step she took. Mesmerizing. So much so, the great bronze door she opened nearly conked him in the head when it swung back.

Cool night air chilled his face as he trailed her into an Italian courtyard dotted with palm trees. A few stray partygoers mingled here. Servants smoked cigarettes in the shadows. Hadley strode to a marble gazing pool in the center of the cortile and stopped at the edge. Lowe heard her counting from several feet away.

Hadley focused on her watery reflection in the moonlit pool. Her specters gathered in the distance, hungry, waiting to be loosed. But somewhere between the count of eighteen and nineteen, another reflection floated over the water behind hers. It was enough of a distraction to send the specters scurrying away.

"I heard you doing that in your father's office." Lowe's

deep voice at the crown of her head sent chills down her neck. "Are you managing your anger?"

"That's none of your business." She crossed her arms over her breasts to ward off the chilly air. "Are you drunk?"

"I wondered that myself, actually. Because I can't seem to stop staring at you, and that doesn't make any sense."

The two statements dueled in her head. She'd seen him staring at her in the hall—how could she not? He stared so intensely, she'd *felt* it. And for a moment, she'd almost believed, stupidly, that he was seeing her for the first time. That they were explorers on Mount Sinai, trapped on opposite rocky cliffs, and he'd thrown her a rope, and she wasn't going to faint from starvation and lie there until vultures plucked her eyes out.

And then he'd acted like an ass in front of Mr. Ginn and her imaginary rope snapped.

"Staring at your backside, that's a given," he continued. "I'm a man, after all. If I were a religious man, I might believe the devil himself sculpted your ass to lure me into temptation. But your front side—"

"My front side?" She spun around to face him. "My front side is what, exactly? Harsh? Odd? Too skinny? Have I been studying mummies so long that I've started to look like one? Because I've heard all those things before, so do your worst."

He gaped at her for a moment, and then shut his mouth. Had she shocked him? Was he angry or embarrassed? Good.

"You want to know what I was going to say? Do you?"

"Say it," she challenged.

Agitation transformed him into something foreign. His eyes narrowed to dark slashes under a rocky brow; his jaw tightened. Nothing jovial or casual or charming about him now—all of that vanished and was replaced by brute intensity and darkness.

He loomed over her, leaning in far too close. Their noses nearly touched. "I was going to say that you look goddamn bewitching in that dress, and I hadn't realized how extraordinarily beautiful you are because all I've seen you wear are those ridiculous funerary outfits." He pulled back, putting some space between them. "There. Happy now?"

Happy? *Happy?* Hadley's heart nearly stopped beating.

The taut lines of his body softened. And in a low voice he added, "I was also going to say that your lily reminds me of a tomb painting I saw in the British Museum last spring, of Nebamun hunting in the marshes with a beautiful girl who wears a lotus in her hair. And that it's lovely on you. Extraordinarily lovely."

A strange sensation pinched her chest. No one had ever said anything like that to her. Why was *he* saying it, of all people? He wasn't teasing. He couldn't be teasing.

Please, let him mean it.

She blinked, pushing away unwanted emotion, waiting for a punch line that never came. He was so painfully attractive, towering over her in his black tuxedo jacket and white vest. His loose stance radiated confidence. Her body wanted to sway closer, as if it could drink up all his easy self-possession, all that golden light he seemed to emit.

Then she remembered what he was.

A liar. And a flatterer, too. He was good—very good. And she was a fool.

She snorted a bitter laugh. "After a man tells a woman the first untruth, the others come piling thick and fast," she quoted loosely.

"Fair enough. I've given you little reason to trust me. Tell me what I can do to gain it. Swear on a Bible? Get down on one knee? Name it, Hadley."

She shook her head, confused by feelings that tugged her good sense in different directions. In search of an anchor, her eyes followed the notch of his black tie to the broad ledge of his shoulder, limned with tawny light from the mansion. But when her gaze dropped to the crisp sliver of white cuff peeking from his dinner jacket, and his injured bare hand below, she decided to take him up on his offer.

"That," she said, nodding her chin at his hand. "Tell me what really happened to your finger." *Give me something real I can trust.*

Lowe lifted his bad hand and cradled it in his other, rubbing the scarred flesh with the pad of his thumb. "I haven't told anyone since I left Egypt."

"Not even your family?"

"Not even my closest friend."

Was that a lie, too? She couldn't tell. "Go on."

"It's not half as exciting as you're expecting," he said, stalling.

Was he waiting for her to revoke the request? Because she wouldn't. And after a long moment, he sighed.

"It was early September," he finally said. "My uncle had just moved us from Alexandria to Philae. It's an island, you know. Two islands. Nothing there but half-flooded ruins and ancient temples . . . a handful of archaeologists, locals making money ferrying tourists. We were working near a section of colonnade, and one day when my uncle was traveling in Aswan, I missed the last boat and got stuck on the island overnight with a few of the local workers."

Lowe turned and kicked at the edge of the reflecting pool. "I was supposed to be building scaffolding for the excavation. But the Nubi workers and I decided to have a few stiff drinks. By the time we got to the scaffolding, I was less alert than I should've been."

"Drunk, you mean."

"Fairly." He sniffed and rubbed his nose, looking so much more sober than she'd assumed he was earlier when he was juggling his wineglass.

"What happened?" she asked.

"I was sawing a board with my right hand," he said, pantomiming, "and holding the board with my left. And I couldn't get a good grip, so I switched angles and, well, to be perfectly frank, I sawed my own finger clean off."

The blood drained from Hadley's face.

"Granted, it was only to the first joint. I suppose the drink numbed my reaction and nerves. But we were stuck on the island with no doctor—no nothing. All I could do was bandage it up and drink until I passed out. By the time my uncle returned the next day and they got me to someone who could stitch it up, I was feverish. Infection set in. A few days later, I had to have the rest of it amputated or risk losing my whole hand."

"Good heavens," Hadley murmured.

"Took a couple of months to heal properly. I was almost useless to my uncle. Hard to work in the sand and dirt with one hand. Hard to do much at all when you're in constant pain. That's actually when I started deciphering pieces of the temple walls. Sheer boredom led me to the *djed*. Not a glamorous story, I'm afraid."

Hadley didn't intend to reach for his hand, but when her arm began moving, she didn't restrain herself as she normally would have when it came to her actively touching someone. The warmth of his skin penetrated her silk glove as she lifted it to inspect the scars in the light spilling into the courtyard. "It's not immediately noticeable that it's missing," she said. "Less conspicuous than a middle finger."

"That's one way to look at it." A gentle smile curved his mouth.

Well. Couldn't hold his hand forever. But as she withdrew, he held on to her, just as he had when they first met in the train station. This time she didn't fight it.

"I've often worried that I might never be able to touch a woman again without her having to swallow disgust in order to tolerate it."

"I suppose that would depend on the woman." A practical observation, or that was her intention, but the way his head tilted, just a bit—the slightest of movements—she knew he'd read more into it. Perhaps she didn't mind that he did. She certainly liked the sturdy feel of his hand holding hers. Some stranger living inside her head wistfully imagined that very hand running up her glove to her bare arm. Just a test, to see if she could "tolerate" it, as he'd said. Just the thought made her stomach flutter nervously.

"You don't think it's grotesque?" he asked.

"Haven't you heard? I'm an admirer of the grotesque and grim."

Lowe squinted one eye. "Are you flirting with me, Hadley Bacall?"

"I really wouldn't know where to start," she replied honestly.

A nearby couple shuffled past them to the other side of the pool. Lowe tugged her out of their earshot, into an awning's shadow. His head dipped lower, his face an inch away from hers again—only this time, she wasn't sure what intimidated her more: the angry Lowe, or the Lowe that looked as if he might ravish her right there in the dark of the courtyard. "What's the verdict? Do you trust me now?"

"Maybe."

"Only maybe?"

"Temporarily. Until the next lie."

"Maybe I won't tell another lie tonight. Maybe I'll be so virtuous, you'll nominate me for sainthood."

"Refraining from deception for one night is hardly virtue."

"Mm-hmm. Expert on virtue, are you?"

"Expert on several things, but virtue isn't one."

"Happy to hear it," he said with a conspiratorial grin. "You know, I always thought the wicked deserved their own sort of canonization. It's tough being immoral. Requires skill and perseverance."

"And a certain amount of natural talent, I'd think."

"Most definitely. I like to believe I was born bad. Shifts the burden of blame to my bloodline."

She chuckled softly.

"Fan," he murmured in Swedish. "You should do that more often."

The scent of laundry starch wafted when he lifted his good hand to her, slowly. The tips of his fingers traced the petals of the lily at her ear, sending a cascade of tremors through her hair, across her scalp, down her neck. It lit up her nerves and cells and spread like wildfire.

Pleasure.

She barely recognized the feeling. All her muscles tightened to hold back a shudder. Good God, it wasn't even a real touch and she was drowning in it. Perhaps it was halfway real, because she realized he was still holding her hand. Or she was holding his. Someone was gripping harder. It might've been her.

His head dipped lower. He inhaled the blossom and whispered, "Intoxicating."

He was so close. Close enough for her to catch a faint note of vanilla in his pomade. Close enough to shield her bare arms from the cool night air. Close enough that the lapel of his jacket brushed against her nipples.

Her breath caught as another wave of tremulous pleasure waterfalled over her skin, and she was drowning again. So very near. She wanted to lean her cheek against his. Wanted his mouth on—

A nearby booming voice tore into her thoughts.

"Dinner is served in ten minutes, ladies and gentlemen."

SEVEN

———— ❧ ————

WITH A START, HADLEY DROPPED LOWE'S HAND AND LOOKED around. Across the courtyard, a servant held a door open and beckoned the stragglers.

The loss of Lowe's warmth was acute and nearly painful to her confused body. Her mind slogged to catch up. "We should . . . dinner," Hadley said dumbly.

He cleared his throat. "Yes, of course."

"I was supposed to be helping Father with . . ." Helping with what? Why wasn't her brain working properly?

"Introductions," he offered helpfully.

"Right." Introductions. Yes. Something to focus on. Good.

They shuffled inside the hall, a short distance that seemed to take years to traverse. In a daze, she managed to introduce him to a few board members and one of the other curators before they were forced to hunt for their place cards and sit down for dinner. Oliver was seated to her left and Lowe was across from her, next to her father. She guiltily kept her eyes on the silver and china, as if nearby diners could guess what had recently transpired in the courtyard.

"Say, are you all right?" Oliver murmured, not once, but twice. Yes, yes. Fine. Was he still asking? The tone of his voice sounded like her father's nagging.

The soup arrived, but she was still in a trance. And when she dared look at Lowe, his waiting, heavy stare sent her heart racing again.

When the fish course was being cleared, her father patted along his place setting, and his beleaguered assistant emerged from the shadows to help. Father then dinged his spoon on his water glass until conversation sputtered to a halt. "Many thanks to the Widow Flood for opening up her lovely home for us this evening," he announced. Cheers and hurrahs circled the tables. "This night is always a special time for us each year, not just because many of you are graciously opening your pocketbooks for your annual tax break—I mean *donation* to our fine museum."

Laughter echoed off the marble walls.

"But it's also a time for us to see old friends. To reflect on what we've accomplished this year, and to share our hopes for the coming one. And as you all know, my health is not what it once was. Now, now. Don't pity me. I'm not at death's door yet. But I am old and tired, and I have given the antiquities department twenty-five good years. It's time to let someone younger and brighter have a crack at it."

Hadley's pulse doubled. The haze lifted from her brain. Was her father announcing his replacement tonight, right here, in front of the board of trustees and the director? She'd expected him to wait until next month's board meeting, but he was doing it now.

Oh, God. A speech would be expected. Nothing long, but she wasn't prepared to say anything in front of these people. It was a bittersweet surprise, but a thrilling one. All she had to do was say a few words and be gracious, and perhaps try not to gloat at George, who was whispering something to one of the patron's wives down the table.

Hadley glanced at Lowe and felt her cheeks heat. Why she wanted his respect, she couldn't say. Silly, really, but she was glad he was here to see this. All her hard work would finally be recognized.

Her father coughed before continuing. "As all of you know by now, Mr. Lowe Magnusson has just returned from a well-publicized excavation in Philae." Hold on. Why was he talking about Lowe? "He has graciously offered to give the museum an exclusive opportunity to bid on the Philae finds."

Hadley's pulse swished in her temples. She couldn't concentrate on her father's words. Degree. University of California, Berkeley. With honors. Rising star in his field. She stared at Lowe. He looked as confused as she felt. Her breath came too fast.

". . . and so it is with great enthusiasm that I nominate Mr. Magnusson as a candidate for primary consideration to continue my legacy."

A round of polite applause roared in her ears. Lowe was saying something in reply, how it was unexpected and an honor to even be considered, and something else she couldn't catch.

Considered for her job. *She* was her father's legacy. Heir apparent. She had studied for it. Worked for it. And she damn well deserved it. More than any man sitting at this table. A thousand times more than Lowe Magnusson.

He briefly shook his head at her, claiming innocence. Bravo. What a performance. Quietly charm the girl in the garden—an easy task, because she was so starved for company that any scrap of affection thrown her way would do then sit back and claim your crown.

What a fool she was.

Rage and hurt called the Mori, who rose up from the floor. Dark limbs, blinking eyes, grotesque features. Monsters, fueled by her pain. Dead things pulled from the Spirit World. Things she didn't understand and could barely control, but they coalesced into a writhing mass of gloom and shifting shadow, crawling up the marble walls and columns. Sniffing out opportunity as they tugged images from her mind.

Command us, they whispered inside her head. Dark avengers, ready and willing to do her bidding. To avenge her through abhorrent deeds. Through fright. Injury.

And death.

Her negative emotions were like carrion. Drawn to them, the specters scavenged her mind, always hungry. And they were hers to command.

Him, she thought, as angry tears flooded her eyes. No, both of them. Her father for his betrayal. And Lowe for carrying it out and lying to her face. Both of them.

The museum director was standing, raising a toast, while her specters slithered across the ceiling like a cloud of black exhaust toward their goal: a massive crystal chandelier dangling high above the table.

A rumble shook the ceiling.

The guests stilled, poised with glasses in hand.

Until his blindness, her father could see the specters. But now the great Dr. Bacall was as oblivious as the rest of the guests, who assigned an easy logical excuse to the unnatural act—

"Earthquake?"

Once the word flew out of someone's mouth, fear dominoed down the table.

At her elbow, Oliver lurched from his seat, looking up. Could he see them? How was that possible? It didn't matter. Too late to reel the specters back in now.

Hundreds of crystals clinked in unison. The ceiling cracked. Electricity sparked. And as the light dimmed in the chandelier, one of the cables suspending it snapped with a horrifying metallic *twang!* The chandelier swung on its side like a great glass pendulum.

Startled gasps bounced around the hall. Chairs skidded on marble. Guests scattered.

Everyone but Father, who couldn't see to move. And Lowe, who was struggling to pull a blind man out of his seat, just as Oliver was pulling her in the opposite direction.

"Hadley!" her father roared.

The sound of his voice penetrated the fog of her anger. Good sense flooded through.

Father knew it was her specters—he knew, he knew, he knew!

Oh, *God*. What had she done?

With monumental effort, she pushed the Mori away. They vanished into the ceiling as she despaired, shouting, "Run!"

Too late.

The second cable snapped. And like a car tumbling off a cliff, the glittering glass plummeted. Screams pierced the air.

Lowe's chair skidded backward. He threw an arm around her father and pulled him to the floor as the chandelier crashed onto the table in an explosion of glass and splintering wood.

Lowe crawled beneath the shuddering carcass that teetered precariously on the table above, dragging her father to safety. She flailed against Oliver's arms and shoved away from him, nearly falling on her face as she ran.

"Father!"

"I'm fine," he barked, using the wall for the leverage he needed to stand.

Lowe brushed glass from her father's shoulder, then glanced at his own clothes.

"Are you—" she started.

"In one piece? Think so." Slightly dazed, he shook out his jacket and glanced around at the destruction, mumbling, "What in the world just happened here?"

"You," her father said, his face red with emotion. "You and your petty anger. Your mother would be ashamed."

As shouts and animated conversation blew through the hall, Lowe narrowed his eyes and shifted a suspicious gaze between her and her father.

God only knew if her father's pronouncement of shame was on the mark—she didn't remember much about her mother. But he was right to be angry. She'd nearly killed him. And Lowe. And other guests. She glanced around at the chaos. No one seemed to be injured, but the poor staff was in a panic.

Tears threatened. Before her father could spit out another word, before Lowe could decipher her father's accusation, Hadley turned and marched out of the house.

EIGHT

———◆———

HEAVY FOG CLUNG TO THE ROOFTOPS LINING BROADWAY. HER
father's driver had taken her to the party, a small detail she
remembered once she made it outside. It was also nippy, and
not only had she forgotten her gloves, which she'd removed
for dinner—they'd likely fallen from her lap during the
fiasco—but she'd also failed to collect her coat. Now what?
Go back inside with her tail tucked between her legs?

"Hadley."

She turned to see Oliver striding down the sidewalk.

"Are you all right?" he asked in a calm, businesslike
voice as he slipped into his greatcoat, which looked warm
and tempting to Hadley's chilled body. Maybe he'd be a
gentleman and offer to return to the house and collect hers.
"I think we should talk about what just happened."

"I don't know what you're talking about."

"Nothing shocks me when it comes to matters beyond
this realm."

So he *had* seen the Mori. Rare that she encountered anyone who did. Very rare.

"I happen to have a lot of knowledge about the underworld," he said.

Funny way to put it, but, yes, she supposed that was as good a label as anything, though she really didn't know for certain where the Mori came from. She'd researched it over the years herself, but only found bits and pieces of information, nothing practical or definitive. It was like picking at a sweater: before long, the whole thing unraveled and one was left with a useless pile of yarn.

"A man of your wealth and stature?" she said. "I thought your obsession was Mexican ruins. When do you have time to research the underworld?"

"You'd be surprised what I've had time for over the years," he said. "Why don't we talk about it, yes? Maybe I can help you. Come back inside and let me—"

"I do appreciate your concern." He'd always been kind, since the moment he'd first introduced himself. Kind, handsome, interested in her work—supportive. And though she was quite sure by the way he stared at her that he wanted more from their relationship than the occasional shared luncheon or tea, she just wasn't sure if *she* did.

Silly, because she should. It wasn't as if men threw themselves at her every day. She hadn't even so much as kissed anyone since college. And, her personal touching issues aside, Oliver was probably the right sort of man for her, practically speaking. Yet the elusive spark that fueled a new romance seemed to be missing.

Maybe the fault was hers. Maybe she was broken and damaged. Wired incorrectly. Because instead of being interested in the right man, she was still thinking about the man who'd just conned the museum position away from her. The absolute wrong man.

The man she'd very nearly killed in a moment of poor impulse control.

"Let me help you, Miss Bacall," Oliver said. "Put your trust in me. You won't be sorry."

She let out a long breath and gathered her wits. "I don't

know what you think you saw. But right now, I prefer to be alone."

"Come now," he said in a sharper tone that took her aback. "You're hysterical. You've been agitated since before dinner. Let's go somewhere and talk about it."

Hysterical. No, that was one thing she *never* was. Angry, yes. Depressed. Cold. Aloof. Cursed. But not hysterical. And that single word soured her mood even further.

"You may call on me at the museum next week. Good night." She began to walk away, but he blocked her path.

"That's enough, now, Hadley. I'm—" He stopped mid-sentence when a shadow darkened his face.

"I believe she said good night." Lowe stepped from behind her and menacingly towered over Oliver. "And now I'm saying the same. Go on back to the party or go home. Just go."

"I will do no such thing."

"Did you escort the lady to the party?"

"Well, no, but—"

"Then you aren't leaving with her, either."

Oh my.

Oliver stuck his finger out, but seemed to have second thoughts about whatever he'd intended to argue. His forced smile seemed to mask whatever he was feeling. "It was enlightening to meet you, Mr. Magnusson. I look forward to crossing paths with you again. Good evening, Miss Bacall."

She watched Oliver march down the sidewalk until he got inside a parked car, unsure whether she was relieved or angry. She threw a mental die and decided on angry. "You didn't need to chase him off. He was only concerned about my well-being."

"Didn't sound that way to me. Here. It's cold as hell out here." Lowe held out her black mink. Why did he have to be the considerate one of the two men? Still, no sense in turning it away. She quickly slipped her arms inside the silk-lined sleeves.

"Is this your hat?" He held out an elaborate feathered thing. Garish red.

"Good God, no."

"Didn't think so, but wasn't going to waste time arguing with the doorman." He hung it on a nearby fence post bordering someone's yard and shrugged into his own coat. "If it makes you feel better, the staff lost my hat, too."

"No, what would make me feel better is if you just hadn't lied to my face with all your seductions in the courtyard before you colluded with my father to steal my damn job!"

Her shouted words bounced around the quiet street. He should be grateful her specters had already exhausted themselves for the time being, or she might have been tempted to give them a second shot.

Lowe held up an index finger. "First of all, I told you I wouldn't lie to you tonight, and I meant it. Second"—another finger joined the first—"I did not 'collude' with your father. He'd mentioned something about the department head position when I met with him at his office, but that was the last I'd heard of it."

"A likely story."

"Look, I was just as shocked as you. He didn't even ask if I wanted a desk job."

"You didn't stand up and protest."

"I didn't have a chance!" Lowe shook his head, as if to clear it, then held up a third finger. "Lastly, *you* were the one seducing me."

Her jaw dropped. "That's the most preposterous thing I've ever—"

"*You* touched me first. *You* gave me all those amorous looks."

"I did no such thing! You pulled me into a shadowed corner. And half an hour later you Judased me in front of my peers! You humiliated me."

"Your father humiliated you."

"You both did."

His head cocked. "And you . . . tried to kill us with that chandelier?"

Oh, God. She spun around and strode down the sidewalk. He followed.

"*Helvete*, you did!"

"That's ludicrous."

"Is it? Because I heard what your father said. And I caught some of Mr. Moneypants's conversation just now. I know a quake when I feel one, and this, Miss Bacall, was no earthquake. Hell, now that I'm thinking about it, I never could figure out what happened with those windows that broke on the train when that thug was chasing us. And then in the baggage car."

"You're mad."

"But not stupid."

"Please just leave me alone."

"I'm not abandoning a woman on a dark street in the middle of the night."

"It's eight o'clock and we're in a perfectly safe neighborhood. I told you when we met, I want to be treated like a man. Equal. Not like some frail doll with the brain of a pea. Not hysterical."

"Hey, that was Moneypants's word, not mine. But all right, I'm game. You're a man. Fine. Makes things a bit confusing for me when I consider all the lurid thoughts I've been entertaining about the two of us, but what the hell—I'm worldly. Suppose I'm open to new experiences."

Lurid thoughts. About her? A renewed thrill wove through her erratic thoughts. God, why did she even care? All she needed to focus on was the fact that her bastard of a father had betrayed her, after months of praising her work in front of the board. After *years* of telling her how smart she was, how capable.

Well. Not capable enough to dig in Egypt. He'd made that clear on numerous occasions. Women had no place in the desert. And when she'd argued that her mother had accompanied him, he said allowing her that liberty was the biggest mistake of his life. No amount of discussion changed his mind. So she gave up on that dream.

Now this one was crushed, too?

But Lowe swore he hadn't known. Did she believe him? And really, when she stopped to think about it with a clear head, wasn't the more important question *why?* Her father was getting what he wanted from Lowe already—the *djed*. And it's not as if Lowe had been on his radar before the amulet's discovery. She'd only heard the Magnusson name in passing.

Father had been so secretive about the *djed*, refusing to tell her why he wanted it so badly and what he was going to do with it. Did he really think the amulet had magical properties? It certainly gave off a strange energy, that much she knew for certain.

Osiris's Backbone supposedly opened up a door to the underworld. To the Egyptian Land of the Dead: *Duat*. But even if the *djed*'s powers *were* real, Lowe had only found a fragment of the amulet. Why would her father suddenly welcome Lowe into the museum with open arms—?

"Where are you going?"

Hadley halted and swung around to find Lowe standing on the opposite corner. She'd walked the entire block and crossed the street without realizing. "I'm looking for a taxicab."

Lowe surveyed the dark residential street. They'd long passed the line of parked limousines waiting on guests at the Flood house. A single car sped by. It was so quiet, she could practically hear the fog rolling in. "Might be hard to find a cabstand around here. If you'd like a ride home, our driver can take you. We're only two blocks from my home. I walked here."

She groaned.

He shoved his hands in his coat pockets and crossed the sloping side street. "My family's probably finishing dinner, so it's not like I'm hustling you into a secluded house to have my wicked way with you." He stopped in front of her, his gaze sliding down her coat. "Besides, you may or may not have just attempted to crush my body under two tons of glass. How, I really don't know. But I suspect I should be wary of you, not the other way around."

He suspected right.

"Truce?"

"Fine," she agreed. "On one condition."

His head lolled on a sigh. He stared at the foggy sky for a moment, muttering something in Swedish before answering, "Why the hell not. Go on. Name your condition."

"You tell me exactly why my father is bending over backward to let you have your wicked way with *him*."

NINE

―――――――◆―――――――

LOWE LAUGHED IN SURPRISE. A FLEETING PLAYFULNESS SOFTENED
the angry slant of her eyes, and this made him want to throw
her behind the bushes and roll around on the grass with her.

God. He really had no business chasing after this woman.
He promised her father he'd see her home when she left the
party, but he frankly couldn't give less of a damn about Dr.
Bacall at the moment. He did, however, care about Dr.
Bacall's money. So he needed to tread carefully here. Think
with his brain instead of his cock.

But *damn* if she wasn't twice as intriguing now that she'd
tried to kill him.

He suspected she had some intense kind of passion bubbling inside her. Now, what drove that passion to rip a fixture
off the ceiling with her mind? Well, God only knew how
she'd done it, but he'd seen it happen with his own two eyes.
It was as if invisible hands from the heavens had torn the
chandelier from the ceiling.

Maybe he was crazy.

But as best as he could tell, the world was filled with two

kinds of things: boring and interesting. And Hadley Bacall was not boring.

He fell in step with her as they strolled down the sidewalk. "I wouldn't say your father is bending over for me. He's offered to pay me for goods received, nothing more."

"I thought you were taking the night off from lying."

"That's not a lie."

"It's not the whole truth, either."

"Are you psychic? A mind reader?"

"If I were, I would've steered clear of you in Salt Lake City."

"Touché."

Their footsteps fell together, the *clop* of his shoe, the *click* of her heel. The darkness obscured her face and the shapeless fur of her coat hid the curves and planes of her body, but her presence beside him held his attention as sharply as a half-clothed burlesque dancer's would.

"Apparently, your father thinks I'm Howard Carter," Lowe said. "He's impressed by the amulet find. He wants to hire me to hunt other artifacts."

The scent of her Siberia lily wafted his way when she glanced up at him. "He wants to fund an excavation? In Egypt?"

"Not exactly."

"Just speak plainly."

"Look, he made me promise not to get you involved, all right? He's offering me a lot of money to find something for him, and he specifically warned me not to breathe a word to anyone in general, you in particular."

"Me? Why?"

"No idea. And you probably won't understand this, but I need the money your father's offering. Badly. I've got debts you can't imagine, and don't say it—I can see it on your lips already. I can't mooch off my family. And I'd just as soon saw off my other pinky finger than work for Winter. It's a matter of pride. I need to be my own man."

She didn't answer for several steps. "We aren't that different, Lowe. That's all I've ever wanted, to be judged fairly.

That job is everything to me. I've worked so hard to be worthy of it."

"I truly didn't ask your father for it."

After a few seconds she said, "I believe you."

Small miracle. The ironic thing about being a professional liar was that it was far more difficult to convince people to believe you when you were actually telling the truth.

"What does Father want you to find?"

"Hadley," he pleaded. He thought of Adam and Stella. Thought of his debt to Monk.

A cool wind ruffled her hair as she turned to face him, clutching her coat closed. "Tell me and you have my solemn oath that I won't run to my father and tattle. I can keep a secret."

"Give me your word, and I also want to know how you ripped out the chandelier."

"I can't do that." He almost said "no deal," but she added, "I barely know you."

Not an "I will never tell you" or "go to hell." No, not that. Perhaps his translation of her words was merely wishful thinking, but in his glass-half-full mind, she was saying, "I might tell you once I get to know you better."

Only a chance, yes, but one he wanted. Not more than her father's money, of course. But after the stunt the old man pulled at the dinner, Lowe felt more certain he'd get it. Because no way in hell did Dr. Bacall want Lowe to have that job. He only announced it after Lowe requested something "tangible" before dinner, and Bacall wasn't thick-headed. He damn well knew Lowe wanted money. But the job offer was a better move—for Dr. Bacall, that is. Without spending a dime, the offer kept Lowe tied to Bacall in a very public way. The old man might as well have pissed on his leg.

Bacall wanted the amulet crossbars very, very badly, and he was giving everything he had to Lowe in order to get them. Which put Lowe in the excellent position of being needed.

So, yes, Lowe felt more confident about Bacall paying out. He wasn't too worried that telling Hadley would mess that up for him. But something else was urging Lowe to tell her.

He remembered back to when Volstead passed, and his own father had thrown every chip on the table to trade fishing for bootlegging. From the beginning, Lowe had been disinterested in helping his father, while Winter enjoyed it—was good at it. And Pappa had groomed Winter to take over. If Pappa was still alive and retiring, and if he'd handed the reigns to someone else without telling Winter first . . . well, that wouldn't ever happen. Because Lowe's father would never have done that to one of his children.

Never.

Thinking of all this made Lowe a little angry on Hadley's behalf. Bacall truly had screwed her over. So because Lowe was softhearted—and maybe because he wanted to improve his chances of making his way up Hadley's skirt—he finally relented.

"All right," he said. "I'll tell you, but only on your word that you won't tell your father."

"I promise," she said as they walked together into the wind. "Let's hear it."

"The short story is that your father knows the approximate location of the remaining pieces of the *djed* amulet, and he wants me to find them and sell the base to him."

She made a low noise of surprise, but her stride didn't falter. "And the long story?"

"The long story is this . . ."

With her gaze trained to the sidewalk in front of them, she listened intently until he got to the part about calling up her mother's spirit. "Pardon?"

"My brother's new wife is a spirit medium—you met her at the train station. Apparently she can call up spirits of the dead and channel them long enough for their loved ones to find out where the family jewels are hidden. Or, in this case, a treasure map. And all that's needed to establish a connection is an object owned by the deceased."

Hadley lifted her coat sleeve to reveal her diamond bracelet. "Like this?"

"I suppose. Were you close to your mother? Would it bother you to speak with her again, as it were?"

"I was eight when she died and never really spent a lot of time with her." She shrugged. "I was closer to my nanny, if you want to know the truth."

A little sad. Lowe had beautiful memories of his mother. He still missed her.

He stopped in front of his house. Winter's red and black limousine wasn't in the driveway. He'd mentioned running out to oversee some big delivery at a hotel. Which meant he wasn't home, but with any luck, Aida was.

"What do you say? Are you curious?"

Hadley's head tilted to survey the Magnussons' gray green Queen Anne. Not the marble Flood mansion, not reputable, not society-approved, but easily the most expensive house on the block. And it must've been impressive enough to meet Hadley's standards, because she turned to him with a sly little smile and said, "Lead the way."

"Winter will bite my head off if he knows I'm channeling. He's worried the baby will be born with multiple souls," Aida joked as she closed the door. "So we'd better make it fast. He'll be back in an hour. A fisherman's day is never done." She winked and sat down on an antique Arabian chair across from Lowe and Hadley. An enormous brindled mastiff—Aida's dog, Sam, who was big as a small horse and blind in one eye—curled up around her feet.

The main floor parlor had been dubbed the Sheik Room by his baby sister. It was his mother's favorite space, and she'd had most of the furniture shipped from overseas. Lowe watched Hadley's gaze darting around the Arabian decor. She perched on the edge of the sofa with her back so straight, she might've been balancing an invisible book on her head. "You sure you want to do this?" he asked.

Hadley nodded. "I'm sure."

"All I need is the object owned by your mother," Aida said.

Hadley struggled to undo the bracelet's clasp with one hand.

"Here," Lowe offered, wanting an excuse to touch her. He bent over her wrist and used the edge of his fingernail to pry it open. As it fell in her lap, he ran a thumb over her pulse, greedy to feel the soft skin there. He swore she shivered, but she jerked her hand away and wouldn't look him in the eye, just handed the bracelet to Winter's wife.

"Very nice," Aida remarked as she turned it over in her freckled fingers. "What's your mother's name?"

"Vera Murray Bacall."

Aida shook her head. "All right. Give me a minute or so to sink into a light trance. I'll call out to your mother's spirit and try to pull her across the veil. Depending on her spirit's strength, she might occupy my body for a few seconds or a few minutes. Just depends. I normally advise my clients to question the spirit about something only the two of them would know—just to validate their identity."

"I can't think of anything like that," Hadley said.

"That's okay. It's more for your peace of mind. But if the information you need is as important as Lowe says it is, then you might want to ask your question straightaway. If you want to chitchat after, feel free. I'll try to hold her as long as possible. Any questions?"

"Will you hear the conversation?" Hadley asked.

"I will. But I hear a lot of conversations—hundreds this past year alone. That's a lot of secrets. What happens during a channeling is between you and the spirit. I don't yap about it to Winter in bed before we go to sleep." Her lips curled. "We have better things to do."

Lowe laughed. He liked Aida more and more. Hadley wasn't nearly as amused.

"All right. Try to remain quiet now," Aida said. "Let's begin."

The spirit medium closed her eyes as she gripped the bracelet in one hand. For a moment, he listened to distant voices deep within the house, dishes clanking in the kitchen, and creaking floorboards above. Then he slouched so he could watch Hadley without her knowledge.

Her lily was wilting, and the sparkling pin that kept it anchored to her black waves had slipped. How nice it would be to straighten it for her. Or remove it altogether. Work the pin down, then sink his fingers into her bobbed hair while he leaned in and put his mouth against her throat. The skin would be as soft as it was on her pale wrist. Would she like to be kissed there, right beneath her ear? He imagined her making little pleasured noises in response.

In the middle of his wandering fantasy, his mind fixed on something she'd said outside. She was eight years old when her mother died in '06. That meant she was twenty-nine. Four years older than him. An older woman. An educated society woman. And strong enough to rip a chandelier off the ceiling with—well, he didn't know how. But the muse in his head conjured an image of her using that strength to pin him to a bed while she climbed on top of him wearing nothing but that peacock-feathered chemise—

Hadley made a small noise and grabbed his arm.

Shit.

Was she a mind reader?

"Vera Murray Bacall."

Lowe sat up straight. Aida's breath was a white cloud, as if she'd stepped outside in winter and exhaled cold air. *Helvete*. It was just as Astrid said. And Hadley wasn't reading his salacious thoughts after all—she was just reacting to Aida, completely mesmerized.

And for good reason.

Aida's breath changed. Her eyes snapped open.

Chills trickled down the back of Lowe's neck and blanketed his arms.

"Who are you?" The voice was Aida's, but the tone damn sure wasn't.

"Is this it?" Hadley murmured to him. Her knee pressed firmly against his leg. She'd scooted closer? When had that happened?

"Do you see her breath?" he murmured to Hadley.

"Yes," Hadley whispered. "Good God."

Lowe cleared his throat. "Are we speaking to, uh, Mrs. Bacall?"

"Is Archie here? Or Noel?"

Archie must be her husband, Archibald Bacall, but who was Noel?

Hadley released his arm and straightened her shoulders. "No, but I am your daughter."

"You couldn't be . . . Hadley?"

"Yes."

"You were so small. I can hardly believe it."

If Hadley was emotional about this reunion, she didn't show it. She delivered her words with the passion one might give placing an order at a restaurant. "I have an important question for you and little time. You hid four pieces of the mythical Backbone of Osiris amulet. I need to know where they are."

"The amulet is dangerous."

"I understand its purpose," Hadley said. "Just tell me where you hid the pieces."

"I didn't hide them. I gave them away to keep them separated."

Was she speaking in riddles or being difficult? Regardless, they might be going about this the wrong way. Perhaps it was best to follow Dr. Bacall's original instructions. "Did you make a map of their locations?" he asked.

"A map?" The late Mrs. Bacall laughed with Aida's mouth. "Yes, I made a map, if that's what you choose to call it. A record of my great endeavor to keep Archie and Noel from killing each other, I suppose."

Ah, Noel was the partner, then.

"Listen closely, and I'll tell you where you can look for my map. You can find it in the Seine's cold quays, in the fields of gazing grain, on night's Plutonian Shore, and on a painted ship."

More riddles.

"You'd do well to leave it be," the spirit said before a short pause. "My darling. Your hair is blacker than pitch and impossibly thick. Just like mine."

"Please speak plainly and tell me where you've hidden the map," Hadley answered with a frustrated edge to her voice.

"Why, I have spoken plainly. Think about it a little, and you'll figure it out. You were always so bright. Seems fitting that you'd follow my trail of bread crumbs. A bit like Isis scouring the earth to find the scattered limbs of Osiris."

"This is a game to you?"

"Everything in life is a game. Listen, my dear, I can feel a dark presence attached to you. I hope that doesn't mean I passed the curse along. If I could go back and make different decisions, I would."

Hadley looked embarrassed.

Her mother's spirit then asked, "Was the base of the amulet located?"

No one answered.

"The object's purpose is no myth. That kind of magic is dangerous. The ancient priestesses stored the pieces in different temples for a reason, which is why I followed their example. Your father cannot be allowed near it. If you manage to find the crossbars and rejoin them to the base, under no circumstances whatsoever can you allow him to possess it."

Unless he was waving a hundred-grand check around. No disrespect to the dead, but Lowe was still alive, and he needed that cash.

"Noel either," she added. "I did my best to protect your father from him, but I fear what could happen if they were to compete again. Keep it away from the two of them. Please promise me."

"Why?" Hadley asked, but a strangled sound was the only answer given. Aida jerked and gulped air. And on her next exhalation, the eerie white breath had disappeared.

The late Mrs. Bacall had left the room.

"Whew, that one made me a little dizzy," Aida said, as if what she'd just done was no more miraculous than standing up too fast after a long nap. The mastiff never once lifted his big head. "Was anything she said helpful?"

"Not really," Lowe said at the exact moment Hadley answered, "Extremely."

Lowe squinted. "It was?"

"I'd say so." She stood and collected her coat from where it was draped on a tasseled silk cushion. "I do believe I know exactly where my mother hid that map."

TEN

———⊱⊰———

"I'LL TAKE A TAXI," HADLEY TOLD LOWE AFTER THEY STRODE INTO
the foyer. She glanced around to get her bearings and spotted
the spirit medium and her great beast of a dog entering a
birdcage elevator that flanked a grand staircase.

The Magnusson home was spacious and well kept.
Impressive, even. Much more welcoming than either her
apartment or her father's house. Livelier, too. She'd wondered what it would be like to live in a home like this, where
a radio played from the servants' hall and laugher seeped
through the ceiling from a room above.

"You want to take a taxi," Lowe repeated.

"If I can just borrow your telephone."

"Like hell you will. Where's the map?"

"Why should I tell you?"

"Why?" Lowe tilted his head to catch her gaze. "I'll tell
you why. Because we made a deal."

"Yes, a deal that I wouldn't tell my father. And I won't."

"No, no, no—this is my treasure hunt, not yours."

"All right. Go find the map yourself then."

"I will. As soon as you tell me where to look."

"Seems we're at a standstill."

A girl's voice called out a name from the second floor. The handsome young Chinese man she'd met at the train station, Bo, passed through the hallway behind Lowe and gave her a curious look before hiking up the staircase.

Lowe stepped closer. Her mind conjured an image of him stroking the flower in her hair, which temporarily disabled the more civilized parts of her brain. He spoke in a lowered voice. "Allow me to propose a compromise. On one hand, you know where the map is, and your mother seems to think you're smart enough to figure out her puzzle. On the other hand, you're not even supposed to know about the map or the pieces. I'm the one being paid to do the job, and I'm not so shabby with riddles myself. I *did* find the base."

Why did he have to smell so good? "Go on."

"Two heads might be better than one. So if you help me find the amulet pieces, I'll talk to your father and ensure that you get the department head position at the museum."

She snorted. "Like you have the power to do that."

"I can be persuasive when I want to be."

"Father's too smart to believe your silly stories."

"And too smart to disregard my request if I withhold the amulet in exchange for you getting the job?"

Hmm. He might actually have something there. Clearly after tonight's public betrayal—and her hotheaded reaction—Father wasn't interested in bargaining with her. It wasn't the first time she'd lashed out at him in anger with the Mori, but since he'd lost his sight, he was less trusting of her. Tonight might've been the final straw. She could appeal to the board for a chance at the position, but they'd never go against her father's wishes.

"We work as partners," she said after a long moment. "I help you, you help me. We keep everything honest between us. No lying to me about the hunt. No working behind each other's backs. You get the money, I get the job. And all of this is contingent on whether I'm right about the map's hiding place."

"Agreed."

"Do you want to start right now?" she asked.

"It just so happens that a falling chandelier has cleared my schedule."

She looked up. A copper and stained-glass Craftsman pendant hung from the ceiling. "The night's young," she said, giving Lowe a small smile.

He leaned in to murmur near her ear. "I really do like the way you flirt, Miss Bacall."

Before she could protest, he called out to the kitchen, informing them that he'd be home later. Then he shucked off his tuxedo jacket and exchanged it for a leather jacket snagged from a coat rack. "This way." He steered her into a hall that led to a covered side porch. On the other side of the railing stretched a driveway packed with cars. But Lowe was striding toward the red motorcycle. "Where are we headed?"

"What are you doing?"

"Dusting off the passenger seat," he said, brushing a small plank of wood that floated above the back tire. The rickety thing looked to be held in place by a few spindly scraps of metal and a couple of nuts and bolts.

"I'm not riding on that. Are you crazy?"

"Don't call her a 'that.' This is Lulu, and she's a custom-made Indian motorcycle. Goes ninety miles an hour on a straightaway. But no need to worry—I don't push her like that in the city. Astrid rides with me all the time on the second seat."

Lulu? How ridiculous. "My dress—"

"Will be protected by that million-dollar fur of yours. Just pull it tight around your legs so it doesn't get caught up in the wheel."

"There are several respectable cars here. Surely we can take one of them."

"Thought you wanted to be treated like a man, not a princess."

She stared at him for a long moment. Her emotions hovered between frustration and fear.

"Come on. It's perfectly safe."

She highly doubted that.

A dangerous smile tugged at his mouth. "I'll go slow." He held out his hand and nodded toward the motorcycle.

She reluctantly accepted. While he steadied the bike, she followed his instructions, stepping up on a small footrest jutting out from the wheel before throwing her leg over to straddle the seat. A metal handle shaped like a croquet wicket arched between her seat and his. She grabbed it for balance. "This won't work. My dress is too tight."

"Ruck it up under your coat. No one can see anything," he said as he mounted the driver's seat and fiddled with a couple of mechanical switches. "Not even me, unfortunately."

Using the heel of his shoe, Lowe roughly bore down on the starter lever near her right leg. The bike angrily rumbled to life like a bear awakened in the middle of a long winter nap, vibrating every bone in her body. No choice in the matter now. She quickly adjusted her dress and pulled her coat tight, tucking it around her thighs.

"Got everything out of harm's way?" he asked, glancing over his shoulder.

"This will never work," she repeated as she gripped the handle harder. "You'll kill me."

"Then we'll be even. Where to?"

She exhaled a long breath. "The museum."

He nodded, showing no surprise for their destination— just popped the kickstand and glided the bike down the driveway. Not so bad. Until he headed onto the street. The pavement seemed to peel away when the motorcycle sped into the night. Cool air rustled the hairs of the mink as they raced past the mansions on Broadway.

When he turned down a road that sloped toward the Bay, she lost faith in the handle and threw her arms around Lowe's torso, holding on for dear life. Her stomach dropped. Her heart drummed against her ribs. She pressed her cheek against his back and held on more tightly, wanting to scream for help or maybe even joy—*joy?* How was that possible?

But it was. An exhilarating sort of joy that bordered on madness. And even through the cantankerous roar of the engine, she could hear laughter rumbling inside his chest. He was deliciously warm and solid beneath her arms—so much so, she didn't care about the rickety wicket of a handle uncomfortably jabbing her stomach, or the sharp scent of gasoline and motor oil wafting past her face, or her no-touching rule. Nothing mattered but the shape of him—a living, breathing anchor. And while city lights blurred along the foggy roads they traveled, she did her best to memorize how it felt to hold on to something so reassuringly sturdy.

It didn't last long enough, because she soon recognized the familiar lawns of Golden Gate Park. And when he parked by the administrative offices, she nearly fell off the motorcycle trying to disentangle herself from him while quickly shifting her dress into place.

"Mind the engine," he said, helping to steady her while she stood on wobbly legs. "Burns like hell if you touch it. Believe me, I know from experience."

"I'm fine."

"You sure?"

If he said even a single word about her clinging to him, she would wither from humiliation. But when he didn't, she eventually answered, "It wasn't so bad."

"Better than 'awful,' I suppose. I'll take it."

Mildly self-conscious, she glanced around the back parking lot. Empty but for three cars belonging to security guards. "If the guards question us, let me do the talking this time," she said. "No more crazy stories of domestic abuse and pregnancy."

"If you insist. Now, what's the plan? Where do you think the map's hidden?"

She retrieved a set of keys from her coat pocket. "Right under my father's nose. Come on. Let's see if I'm right."

Shadows greeted them inside the office entrance. The guards concentrated their patrol on the museum proper, only occasionally making a pass through the administrative offices. Hadley would rather avoid them completely, so best to work quickly. She led Lowe directly to her father's office and closed the door behind them.

"You didn't recognize anything my mother said in regards to the location of the map?" she asked, switching on her father's desk lamp.

"Sounded like bad poetry."

"I suppose that depends on your tastes. Father used to give my mother books for every occasion—birthdays, anniversaries, Christmas. Expensive books. First editions. And they're right over here." She headed to one of the bookshelves on the far side of his office, near the door that connected to hers. "He said they were an investment, that he was giving her the pleasure of the words as well as something that would increase in value over time. But I remember hearing her tell my nanny that though Father may have given them to her, they were really more for him. Not that he's a lover of poetry, mind you. He's just a collector."

"These here?" Lowe's gaze darted over the shelves. "Must be a hundred or more. They survived the Great Fire?"

"My family home was just west of the fire line. We were lucky."

"We were in the Fillmore District at the time, so us, too." Lowe frowned. "You're certain your mother was referring to lines of published poetry?"

"My parents might've only been collectors of books, but I've probably read every volume in this room at least once."

"I read a lot in Egypt," he said. "Mostly *The Argosy* and *Weird Tales*."

"Pulp magazines don't count as reading."

"What a little snob you are," he said, slanting narrowed eyes her way. His smile told her he was teasing, but maybe he had a point.

"Regardless," she said. "If you'd read something with an actual spine, you might've figured this out. Because my mother said we could find the map in 'Seine's cold quays, in the fields of gazing grain, on night's Plutonian Shore, and on a painted ship.' I recognize at least two of those lines. 'Plutonian Shore' is from 'The Raven.'"

"Edgar Allan Poe."

"Very good. I suppose Berkeley didn't completely fail you," she murmured, scanning the shelves in front of them.

"There," Lowe said, pointing to the highest shelf. "Help me move this out of the way."

Together they dragged the wingback chair in which her father smoked cigars across the floor. Once it was out of the way, Lowe's impressive height gave him access to the top shelf. The tips of his fingers tugged out a volume. It was Poe, all right. He thumbed through it, once, twice. Tipped it sideways and fluttered it around to see if anything fell out of its pages. Nothing.

"Give it to me," she said. "Maybe there's a clue on the page with that line." She surveyed the index and found the poem. "I don't see anything."

He leaned over her shoulder to scan the pages with her, and she caught the scent of his leather coat—the scent she'd breathed in on the motorcycle when her cheek was against his back. Her pulse increased. "No marking," he noted. "No corner turned down." She felt his gaze shift to her face a moment before his fingers followed. "You're wilted."

"Pardon?"

"Your lily." Heat spread over her neck as he slid the flower out from its pin. "Bedraggled by the ride, I'm afraid. Shame. Still smells nice."

"Yes, well, nothing lasts forever." Her hand patted the space where the flower had been. "Unless it's been properly preserved, of course."

"A mummy joke?"

She smiled to herself. "Please focus on the task at hand. I'd prefer to avoid the guards."

"Well, the map's not here. Maybe we're looking in the wrong volume. Did your mother own two Poe books?"

She shook her head, fighting the disappointment unfurling in her chest. "Just this one."

"Let's try another verse, then. What was the other one you recognized?"

"On 'a painted ship upon a painted ocean.'"

"Sounds very familiar," Lowe mumbled.

"*The Rime of the Ancient Mariner* by Samuel Taylor Coleridge."

"Ah-ha! I saw Coleridge . . . there. Let me reshelve the Poe." He reached to slip the book back into place, then halted. "Hold on."

"What?"

"This feels odd."

ELEVEN

---※---

LOWE FLIPPED THE POE BOOK OVER TO STUDY THE LEATHER COVER. "I can't be sure. How attached to your mother's books are you?"

"Attached? If you mean sentimentally, not at all. Like I said—"

He reached inside his jacket before she could finish. Metal glinted. He could tell by her murmur that she was surprised he'd been wearing his dagger beneath his tuxedo. With the flick of a wrist, he slashed across the leather book cover with abandon and stuck a finger inside the gouge he'd made. Definitely something inside. A yellowed paper slid out.

"What is it?" Hadley pushed closer and grasped one edge while he held the other.

Textured artist's paper, about the size of his hand. And on it was a delicate watercolor painting of something he immediately recognized. Hadley, too.

"Canopic jar," they murmured in unison.

Pottery jars with lids shaped like heads of gods, used by ancient Egyptians to preserve their internal organs for the afterlife. Each tomb would contain four jars, holding four different organs. This painting's jar lid was rendered with Duamutef, the jackal-headed son of Horus and guardian of the stomach.

"Four poetry references," he said. "Four canopic jars. There's a date in the corner. February 5, 1906. And what's this?"

Running down the middle of the jar, carefully drawn over the watercolor with brown ink, were two columns of strange pictorial symbols. Hadley squinted. "This is where the hieroglyphic inscription would normally be—or the name of the god protecting the organs. But these aren't hieroglyphs."

"Not Egyptian ones," he corrected. "Appears to be an alphabet of pictograms. Look here—there's a flower and a knife."

"No, I think that's a blade of grass."

He darted a glance at her face, charmed by her scholarly seriousness. "Your father said your mother loved puzzles. Do you think she made up her own alphabet to mimic hieroglyphs?"

"Maybe," Hadley said. "But this isn't a map. What does it all mean?"

"Don't know, but ten dollars says paintings of the other three jars are inside other books." He relinquished the paper to her grasp and reached for Coleridge, gutting the book like he had the first. "Mother lode! This one's Hapy."

A baboon head was lovingly rendered on the lid of this jar. "Lungs. January 21, 1906. And there're the pictograms again."

"None match the first."

"Let me see." Her eyes flicked over both papers. "You're right—no matches. What a beautiful little alphabet, though, don't you think?"

"I'll reserve my judgment until we figure it out. What's next? The 'gazing grain' makes me think of Nebraska. Any Nebraskan poets who go crazy for wheat stalks?"

"I think Nebraska is better known for corn. Gazing grain, gazing grain . . ." She ran a finger along the spines lining the nearest shelf. "They're poems about death—the Poe and the Coleridge. 'Gazing grain' must be another death poem. Oh!"

"What?"

"'Because I could not stop for Death.'"

"'He kindly stopped for me,'" he finished. "Yes, I do know that one, Emily Dickinson. Though, I never managed to memorize anything past the first stanza in school. Nice memory you've got there, Bacall."

Hadley whooped a little laugh as a pretty pink color flushed her cheeks. He felt it, too, the thrill of discovery. What an unexpected pleasure to share it with her. Together they located the book and, sure enough, the third paper had been hidden inside the leather. A third canopic jar with a third set of pictograms, and a date of March 25, 1906.

"What about the last poem?" she asked.

"Well, the Seine's in France, so I'm betting on a French poet. Someone obsessed with death like Miss Dickinson, maybe?"

"Rimbaud, Hugo, Baudelaire . . ."

Lowe snagged all three volumes and ran his fingers along the back covers, stopping when he felt the telltale raised edge on the Baudelaire. And there it was: a fourth canopic jar painting, a fourth set of pictograms, and something new. Several things, actually.

"Dimensions," he said. "Fifteen inches tall, six inches wide at the base."

That wasn't all. Next to the watercolor of the jar, a cross section was drawn in ink. The jar was built with double walls and an empty section at the bottom, labeled with the description "sub compartment."

Lowe tapped the corner of the paper. "Notes for clay and glazes . . . prices. Looks like these are all commissioned sketches from a business called Cypress Pottery. 'Approved by client, VM. January 7, 1906.' It's the earliest of the four dates."

"VM," Hadley murmured. "Vera Murray. My mother's maiden name. She must've had these made. Look at the sub compartment. It's big enough to accommodate one of the amulet's crossbars, if they're in the same scale as the base you found."

He studied it. "By God, you're right. It's a hiding place. The jars are designed to be sealed after the pieces are inserted. Four jars to conceal four crossbars." He slid his finger across a smudged word near the cross section. "Arched? Ashes?" His gaze connected with hers. "Hadley, these are meant to be urns."

"Why, yes, they'd be about the right size."

"Look at the dates." He took the paintings from her and fanned them out on her father's conference table. "January, February, March—all four dates are in the months before the Great Earthquake."

"In the séance, my mother mentioned she gave the amulet crossbars away. She hid them in urns, and then hid the urns around the city. These are made for real ashes. Real people."

"I'll be damned."

They stared at each other for a long moment, both grinning.

She blew out a breath and surveyed the paintings. "That means these four pieces of paper really *are* a map. Because I'll bet *you* ten dollars, Mr. Magnusson, that the pictograms are the names of the deceased whose ashes are in these urns. If we want to find the pieces, we have to track down the families in possession of these urns."

She was right, of course. But finding them might prove difficult.

"A couple of ways we could approach this," he said. "Could try looking for this Cypress Pottery shop, but the chances that it's still around twenty-one years later, what with the earthquake and half the city burning to the ground . . . Better bet would be checking death records. How many people could've died in the city over those three months? A couple hundred?"

"So many records were destroyed in the Great Fire," she pointed out. "We could try the Columbarium north of Golden Gate Park."

"The what?"

"The domed building near the cemeteries. It houses funerary urns. A place for families to visit their loved one's ashes. An indoor graveyard, if you will."

"I wasn't aware any of that was still operational these days."

"The crematorium on premises hasn't been used since cremation was outlawed within city limits, but the Columbarium is still open for viewing. Survived the earthquake, so maybe there's a chance one or more of the canopic jars could be there."

Leave it to her to know something like that. Sort of endearing, in a macabre way.

She began gathering the paintings. "Tomorrow's Saturday, so I don't have to work. We can meet there in the morning and have a look around. In the meantime, I'll take these home and—"

He put a firm hand over hers. "Whoa. Who says you get to keep them?"

"They were my mother's."

"And it's my job. You're helping, not running the show."

A flash of anger bolted through her eyes. "She said I'd be able to solve her puzzle. This is what she meant. I'll look at them, then you can have them afterward."

Devious little thing, wasn't she? Had to admire her for trying, but no way in hell was he leaving without the paintings. And the heat of her knuckles under his made him greedy for something more. "I've found there are two ways to end an argument with a stubborn woman."

She snorted. "Please do enlighten me."

"The first way is to let her win." He allowed her fingers to slip away from his.

"Very wise. And what's the second way?"

His pulse pounded in his temples. "The second . . . is this."

Lifting her chin with one hand, he brought his mouth down on hers. Firmly. She stilled beneath him, not breathing. Probably just shocked. And maybe he was carried away with enthusiasm. He loosened up a bit, inhaled, and tried smaller kisses. Delicate and feather soft. Kisses even the purest of virgins wouldn't find offensive.

Nothing.

She was still as marble and twice as cold. Had he miscalculated? She wasn't pushing him away, but she wasn't exactly overcome with passion, either. A dead body would have more zeal.

This was definitely not what he'd conjured in his fantasies.

Christ. He'd never kissed a woman who didn't want to be kissed, but from the wooden indifference of her lips, he was fairly sure this was what it felt like. So different from the erotic pull he'd felt at the gazing pool back at the party. He could've sworn there was something between them. Had it all been in his mind?

Nothing to do but end it and let the fire of humiliation warm the arctic air between them. How could he have been so wrong?

He released her chin and pulled away. A look that was something close to horror harshened her features. Her hands were fisted at her sides.

"Guess that doesn't always work after all," he joked, trying to salvage his stinging pride.

A brisk knock sounded across the room. The office door creaked open to reveal a middle-aged man in a guard's uniform. "Dr. Bacall?"

"Ah, good evening, Mr. Hill."

"Miss Bacall. Sorry to bother you. I'd just punched out for the night and was headed home. Saw the light under the door and thought it was your father working late."

"No, it's just me. Oh, and Lo—umm, that is. I mean, this is—"

"Mr. Magnusson," Lowe said.

"Yes," she said, laughing nervously. "He's just back from Egypt. And we've both just come from the museum's party."

The guard's eyes narrowed. "I see . . ."

What had she said? Let *her* take care of the talking? She was terrible at lying. If she said much more, she'd end up turning herself in for a crime she hadn't committed.

Worse—she might tell the guard they'd been ripping up books to hunt down a map.

Oh, God.

The gouged books sat on the conference table with the paintings. Lowe quickly stepped in front of them, hoping to block the guard's view, and spoke over Hadley.

"We were planning a surprise for Dr. Bacall's retirement," Lowe said smoothly. "Collecting some old photographs of him in his younger days—so we could have an artist sketch him for a program highlighting his achievements."

The guard's posture relaxed. "I'm sure he'll be so pleased."

It was really too easy.

"You won't breathe a word, I trust," Lowe said. "We hoped to surprise the whole staff. That's why we rushed straight over here from the party. Don't want anyone spilling the secret until we could get the program to the printer."

"My lips are sealed," the guard assured him. "Well, then, I'll be on my way. You need a ride home or anything, Miss Bacall?"

"Yes, please," Hadley said. "That would be so kind, Mr. Hill. Will save me from catching a taxi."

A frustrated anger stole over Lowe. Had he not just invented an excuse to appease the guard? Was she so appalled by the kiss that she'd take any opening to remove herself from his presence?

She smiled at Mr. Hill. "If you could just wait for me at the entrance, I won't be a minute."

"Yes, ma'am. I'll wait." The guard tipped his hat to Lowe. As soon as he'd headed far enough down the hallway, Hadley surveyed the room with nervous eyes.

"I could've taken you home," he said.

She ignored that. "Put the books back exactly where you found them. Make sure your butchery job isn't noticeable. And I'll just—"

Oh, no. Lowe lunged for the table and managed to get his hand on two of the paintings. She'd already grabbed the others.

"A fair compromise," she said. "I'll keep these safe, you keep those safe. And I'll meet you at the Columbarium tomorrow morning at, shall we say ten?"

So she wanted to pretend the kiss had never happened? Fine. He didn't know why he was chasing after her in the first place.

During the ride back home, he reminded himself of all her irritating qualities. Bossy. Strange. Hot one minute, cold the next. Reserved. Bitter. Overeducated. Stubborn. Too old. Terrible sense of style—someone else must've picked out the evening gown, he decided.

And oh, that's right. She'd tried to *kill him*.

When he undressed for bed later, he found her wilted lily in his tuxedo jacket pocket. Nothing lasts forever, she'd said. How true. He dumped it in a wastebasket and turned off his bedside lamp, then lay there in the dark, still angry.

Gods above, he could still smell the damn thing.

He turned his lamp back on and dug the lily out of the trash. After a moment of thought, he flattened it between the pages of an old issue of *Weird Tales* and wedged it under the feather bed's mattress.

TWELVE

———◈———

GRAY FOG SALTED WITH DRIZZLE MET HADLEY WHEN SHE EXITED her taxi the next morning near the entrance to Odd Fellows Cemetery. The Columbarium's stately Greco-Roman columns and patina-green copper dome stood sentry above rolling grave-lined hills. She surveyed the grounds. Deserted. No cars. No visiting families.

No red motorcycle in sight.

Her rapid heartbeat relaxed its anxious pace.

As she approached the building's entrance, she straightened her cloche hat and brushed a few of Number Four's black hairs from her charcoal coat sleeve. The damned cat was going through another shedding season, and he'd offered little sympathy when she'd arrived home last night, fretting over Lowe.

And the worst kiss of her life.

What was the matter with her? Besides the obvious. But *really*. A devastatingly handsome, virile man had kissed her and she'd frozen up like a lake in winter. True, he'd caught her off guard, and she wasn't used to people touching her, much less kissing her. But she still should've been able to allow herself to enjoy the moment. Especially after he'd continued to try.

And try, and try . . .

Thinking about it made her teeth clench.

Loosen up. That's what George had told her in college. She wanted to—God, did she ever. Lowe's lips were warm, softer than she'd expected. She could only imagine what it would be like to surrender. She remembered how she felt with him at the gazing pool. If he'd kissed her then, in that moment? Well, things may have gone differently. But in the museum, her brain kept shouting at her, warning her not to let her guard down. Not to trust a man like Lowe, because he'd only kissed her to get his hands on the canopic jar paintings they'd found inside the books.

So why was she so embarrassed by her reaction? If that's the only reason he kissed her, she should hold her chin high and be proud of herself for not yielding. Instead, she was now wearing a dress with a low neck and—Dear God. She was unbuttoning her coat to ensure he saw it? What was the matter with her? She quickly buttoned it back up and glanced around guiltily, listening for the rumble of his ridiculous motorbike.

No sleep. That was her problem.

She'd meant to start translating her mother's pictograms, and she'd managed to copy them onto a larger piece of paper. Well, half of them, at least. She'd spent the rest of the night pacing the floors of her apartment in her stockings, imagining every detail of her evening with Lowe. And rearranging those details to include things she should've said and done.

She should've just kissed him back. *Wanted* to kiss him back.

Why didn't she kiss him back?

And why wasn't he here to meet her? If he was a different man, he might've thrown in the towel and decided he had better things to do. But he needed her father's money. He'd show.

Unless he'd solved her mother's alphabet and traced his two urns somewhere else already.

Best not to consider that possibility. Exhaling a long breath, she pushed the heavy door of the Columbarium's entrance and stepped into the rotunda. Four levels ringed in columns circled up toward a stained-glass ceiling capping the dome, and lining the walls were hundreds upon hundreds of niches that served as the final resting space for many of the city's residents. Most were no bigger than a post-office box. Some were covered by copper doors engraved with the name of the deceased, and others were fronted with glass windows, allowing visitors to see the urn or even a tableau of the deceased's favorite things: baseballs, books, curios, photographs.

Hadley's footfalls echoed around the rotunda. She stopped in front of a section of niches. She could spend all day browsing here. Maybe one day an archaeologist like her would uncover the Columbarium's ruins and try to divine details about San Francisco society.

"Found anything?"

She jumped and spun around. The brim of a tilted rust-colored fedora cast a shadow over Lowe's eyes, and his long brown coat covered the tops of his knee-high riding boots.

"I didn't hear your motorcycle."

"I didn't drive her," he said flatly, stuffing his hands into his pants pockets. "Took a cab. How's your father doing today?"

Her father? "I wouldn't know. We don't usually speak to each other much outside of work. When he's angry at me, we speak even less."

A grunt was his answer. "So, how are these niches arranged?" His usual good humor was missing. He wasn't angry—he just wasn't . . . anything. Guess they weren't discussing the kiss. Not that she wanted to rehash it.

"It would've been helpful if they were arranged by date, but no such luck," she said, craning her neck to look up into the dome. "We could look for a canopic jar in the niches with windows, but it might take a couple of hours, even if we split up."

"And it might be hidden behind a copper door without a window."

"True," she said. "Were you able to translate any of the pictograms?"

"Some of the characters are mirror images. Reversed."

"Oh?" She hadn't noticed that on the two paintings she'd taken home.

"There's got to be an office with files on the niches," he mumbled to himself.

She shook her head. "Wouldn't help. Why would they sort the files by date? Would most likely be by surname."

A throat cleared behind them. "Pardon, ma'am, but the crematory and offices were closed up when cremation was outlawed nearly twenty years ago." Standing in a prism of light spilling in from one of the angel windows, an elderly black man held a can of tarnish remover and a rag.

Lowe tipped his hat. "Good morning. You work here?"

"Caretaker," he said with a kind smile.

"My cousin and I have traveled from Salt Lake City to spend a weekend in town," Lowe started.

Good God, here we go again, Hadley thought.

"We were looking for our aunt Tessa's niche," he continued. "She died before the Great Fire. Pretty sure her ashes are here, but we don't know what surname was used. She'd been divorced a few times, you see. Anyway, we have fond memories of her from childhood. Thought we'd pay our respects."

At least this concocted fable didn't denigrate her character. Still, Lowe showed more cheer to the old man than he had toward her. Was he angry with her about the kiss? Upset? Or was she reading too much into his mood? Maybe he'd already forgotten it. She certainly wished *she* could.

"That is a problem," the caretaker said, nodding. "Even if you knew the surname, wouldn't help. The older files were relocated ten years back. A warehouse downtown. You'd have to contact the owners. If you're only here for the weekend, might not be able to catch them."

Lowe made a sound of disappointment and looked around the rotunda, where a dozen or more mismatched chairs sat empty. "Been the caretaker for long?"

"Thirteen years, now."

"Ever seen an Egyptian urn around here? It would have a sculpted lid about this high." Lowe measured with his hands. "Shaped like a head. A baboon or a jackal dog or—"

"Long ears?"

"Yes," Hadley said. "Long snout, too. Two rows of symbols on the front of the jar."

"Sounds like Mrs. Rosewood's urn."

A moment of silence hung in the rotunda as Lowe flashed her an expectant look. But Hadley didn't want to hope too much. Not about the urn. And definitely not about Lowe.

"Could you show us?" she asked.

He shook his head. "Sorry, it's not here. Back in my younger days, I used to work at Dolores Crematorium, between Telegraph Hill and North Beach. I remember an urn like that for Mrs. Rosewood's cremation."

"Who's this Mrs. Rosewood?" Lowe asked.

"A shipping heiress. Her death was quite the scandal. Folks said her sons killed her to get their hands on her mansion near the top of Telegraph Hill at the edge of the park. Rumor was, they wanted to turn it into a gambling den. That was right before the Quake in '06. The mansion survived, but once they took possession, they claimed her ghost haunted the place."

Hadley didn't care a thing about ghosts; she had her own to worry about. "Do you know where her urn was housed?" she asked. A few local churches had niches for funerary ashes, but she questioned whether churches would welcome a pagan urn shaped like a jackal-headed god.

"The family kept it, far as I know. Nice display piece like that? Probably on someone's mantelpiece."

Lowe relayed the caretaker's directions to the waiting taxi outside the Columbarium, and then rode in silence with Hadley as the car sped down rain-darkened streets. He'd done his damned best to leash his feelings and pretend as if nothing had happened between them the previous night. Well, nothing *had* happened on Hadley's end, so the charade was more a matter of his own self-preservation. Reclaiming his bruised male pride.

But it would've been a lot easier if the Cinderella spell he'd prayed she'd been under had magically faded overnight. After all, she wasn't wearing the fantasy whirlpool dress. No flower in her hair. In fact, she was back to her normal, funeral-colored, straightlaced curator self.

And even more damned beautiful than the night before. God help him.

She didn't smell like lilies today, so that was helpful. But when he'd held the taxi door for her, he'd noticed the backs of her stockings were decorated with a line of black bows. Different. A subtle sort of daring, especially for her. But the stockings weren't his primary distraction at the moment. No, that honor went to the thing that had caught his attention the moment he'd seen her in the Columbarium.

Her coat was mis-buttoned. Unusual for her to be sloppy. The top buttonhole was circling the second button instead of the first, which created a tunneled gap under the edge of the wool—a little shadowed hidey-hole. He imagined small woodland creatures burrowed inside it, right next to her breast, and had to refrain from teasing her about it.

But when the cab turned a corner and headed into North Beach, he spotted something more interesting than a wee mouse beneath her out-of-line buttons. A flash of skin. Was she wearing a low-cut dress beneath that drab gray coat? His thoughts strayed to her brightly colored underthings and it took the fortitude of a monk to stop himself from mentally flicking open the coat button.

Remember the terrible kiss, he thought. Should've been enough cold water to shift his concentration to their mission. But it only revived something that had been niggling his thoughts since he'd left Hadley the night before.

She caught him staring and offered a tight smile. "Dreary day."

"Hmm."

"Should've brought an umbrella."

"Are you and that fellow seeing each other?"

Sharp eyes widened. "Who?"

"That Oliver Ginn fellow."

"Oh." Did her shoulders fall? She definitely looked more relaxed, didn't she? "Mr. Ginn has been calling on me for a couple of months now, I suppose."

"I see." He didn't. "Serious, is it? Wedding bells in your future?"

One brow lifted. "None I'm aware of. I suspect someone would inform me first."

He tapped a random rhythm on one knee. She was teasing him. That was good, surely? Because it definitely didn't sound like the sort of response a girl who was madly in love would give. He thought perhaps the reason she'd been so unresponsive when he'd kissed her was because she had feelings for someone else.

"Oliver wasn't the reason," she said in a small voice, eyeing the taxi driver.

His hand stilled. "Pardon?"

"Firstly, I wasn't sure if you were only doing it to trick me."

Her voice was almost too low to hear, so he leaned closer. "I'm not following."

"Tricking me out of the canopic jar paintings."

Hold the line one second: she was talking about the kiss. "No, it wasn't a trick," he said quickly. "I mean, yes, I wanted the paintings. But I kissed you because I wanted to."

She blinked rapidly. "Well, regardless, my doubt about your motives wasn't the entire problem. It's just that I suppose I have trouble with touching." She watched the city rolling by her window, gloved hands clutched in her lap. "It's indirectly because of my . . . well, what happened with the chandelier."

"Death by crystal," he said.

She nodded, a nervous smile briefly lifting her mouth before she continued. "There was an incident when I was younger."

"What kind of incident?"

"I don't like to speak of it."

He paused. "Did someone hurt you?"

"No, not that," she said. "The details aren't important. It's in the past, but I haven't quite been able to overcome my negative feelings associated with it. It's usually not an issue, as people unconsciously tend to keep their distance from me. Which is fine. Things are easier at work, especially, when people stay out of my way. However, because of all this, I've become accustomed to having my private space."

"I see." Partly, anyway, but she didn't seem to be budging on the "incident."

"I'm sure it sounds pathetic. Maybe it is, I don't know. I'm just unused to being . . ." She struggled for words, gesturing with her hands in a way that didn't help to get her point across.

"Unused to being kissed?" he finally asked, fully intrigued.

Her cheeks flushed. "Don't flatter yourself. I'm not some chaste girl without worldly experience." Oh, really? Definitely intrigued. Lowe was rather fond of Unchaste Women with Worldly Experience. "I'm just unaccustomed to being touched so casually. I prefer a barrier."

"A barrier?"

"Gloves, or distance—I don't know." She shifted in her seat.

"No skin."

She nodded. "I suppose I've unintentionally nurtured a phobia."

"I scc."

"You do?"

He touched a gloved knuckle to her coat sleeve. "This is okay."

"Yes."

"But . . ."

"But," she agreed dramatically, as if that summed up everything she'd just explained. "I'm not saying I enjoy being this way. It's just something that seems to have happened." She shrugged and exhaled heavily.

He thought back to that first night on the train, and her

reluctance to shake his hand without gloves for their so-called gentlemen's agreement. And again the next day, her flinching away from him when they were picking up files, and her insistence that it wasn't caused by his disfigurement. And then the gazing pool. She'd gripped his hand tight enough then, but she'd been wearing opera gloves. And he'd never actually touched her face, had he? Only the flower in her hair. Even when she'd held on to him so tightly riding on the back of Lulu, there were clothes between them.

Sure, he'd grazed her bare wrist with his thumb a couple of times, but the first time he'd *really* touched her skin was when he'd clamped his bare hand on hers—when she was trying to take the paintings off the table. And seconds later he'd lunged and kissed her, thinking he'd grandly claim her and she'd just swoon in his arms. So much for that.

She smoothed the front of her coat. "Anyway, I suppose we're even now."

"How's that?"

"You'd never told anyone the real story behind your missing finger, and I've never told anyone about this."

"Not even Moneypants?"

The corners of her mouth quivered. She quickly shook her head.

Well, imagine that. She didn't shrivel up and die at the feel of his lips on hers—or, rather, she might, but it wasn't him in particular. And instead of just telling him never to try it again, she confessed her secret—partly, anyway.

It almost felt like a challenge. At least, that's how his ever-optimistic brain interpreted it, as if she were saying: *You want this? Good luck. You're going to have to work for it.*

Facing down a hurdle of this magnitude looked a bit like crossing the Rockies on a motorcycle during a snowstorm. But he'd always been fond of seemingly impossible and doomed tasks. So he spent the rest of the ride remembering what his uncle had told him about one of the Nubi workers who'd been deathly afraid of snakes. His uncle had said that the only way to rid the man of his fear was to feed him cake while he was forced to look at caged snakes from a distance, bringing the snakes closer and closer until the positive association of cake drowned the fear. Counterconditioning, he'd called it.

Simple as cake. Or was that pie? He wondered which Hadley preferred, because he suddenly had the most compelling urge to dabble in behavior therapy.

THIRTEEN

———◆———

HADLEY WAS GREATLY RELIEVED WHEN THEIR TAXI SLOWED NEAR
Pioneer Park. What on God's green earth had possessed her
to tell Lowe about her boundary issues? And now there was
nothing but heavy silence between them. God only knew
what he was thinking. She couldn't get out of the car fast
enough. Best to concentrate on the task at hand and pretend
that conversation had never happened.

  Rosewood Manor was one of a handful of buildings
clinging to the top of Telegraph Hill, and quite possibly the
wealthiest home in an otherwise working-class neighborhood. But it was far from impressive: the dull, gray paint
that covered the boxy Italianate Victorian was peeling; some
of the beveled glass twin-arched windows on the third floor
had been boarded up; and one of the overhanging eaves was
one storm away from being ripped off.

  "It's unoccupied," she said as she shut the taxi's door.
"What a terrible shame to let a home so grand slide into
such disrepair. Look at that stunning tower and those bracketed cornices."

"A shame?" Lowe's nose scrunched up. "It's spooky. 'Gloom Manor' is probably what the neighbors call it."

"I think it's handsome and rather pleasant up here. It's nice and quiet, away from all the traffic, and the views of the Bay are stunning. What a lovely old palm tree there in the side yard."

"To each their own. But the fact that it's clearly unoccupied doesn't help us today. Maybe we can track down—"

A bespectacled man with ginger hair emerged from the house. "Hello! Are you the Davidsons? I'm Mr. Farnsworth, the real estate agent."

Hadley's gaze flicked between Mr. Farnsworth and the FOR SALE sign hanging next to the front door. She immediately knew what Lowe was thinking: no sense kicking a gift horse in the mouth.

"Yes, we're the Davidsons," Lowe said with a smile. "Are we too late?"

"No, early, in fact. I just wanted to open up the house to air it out before our tour. You do want to see the inside, yes?"

"Absolutely."

"Some folks are only interested in the land, but the bones of the house are in excellent shape. Survived the Quake, so she's sturdy. Just needs some repair and paint. Electrical wiring and heating might need updating, and there's no telephone. But she's got a lot of character, don't you think?"

"I do," Hadley said, getting caught up in the charade. "A lovely old thing."

"Please, Mrs. Davidson, come inside and let me show you around. Then we can talk price."

The moment Hadley crossed the arched threshold, she felt it—just barely. The same unsettling twang she'd felt around the *djed*'s base. One of the crossbars was here!

She glanced over her shoulder at Lowe, who was craning his neck to survey the foyer. Oblivious. But he'd felt the energy in the amulet base—he'd admitted so on the train. Was she wrong? Because several other factors gave the old house a decidedly gloomy ambiance, as Lowe had put it. The thick layer of dust. The furniture draped in canvas cloth.

The pungent, musty scent. The crude drawings scrawled on the old wood walls and floor—occult symbols, cartoon depictions of sheet-covered ghosts having sex in multiple positions, and the words "Stay Away" painted in red on the stairwell wall.

"My apologies regarding the vulgar graffiti, Mrs. Davidson," the real estate agent said.

"I had no idea ghosts were so creative." Lowe turned his head sideways to examine the drawings. "It's hard to tell if this fellow here is more attracted to his ghost buddy or the girl ghost."

Farnsworth laughed nervously. "Seems the house was broken into several times before the bank took possession a few years ago. Probably just a roving group of youths."

"Oh, those roving youths," Lowe said with a slow shake of his head.

"I can assure you that once the house is occupied, that won't be an issue," Mr. Farnsworth said. "Now, if you'll notice all the natural light coming in from the living area at the back of the foyer . . ."

Hadley trailed the two men through several rooms, nearly tripping over an empty gin bottle in the kitchen doorway. "Not our stock," Lowe whispered as he steadied her with a firm hand on her arm. They both stared at the place where his hand rested. He cleared his throat and released her, reached inside his jacket, and pulled out a roll of peppermints. "Would you like one?" he said, peeling back a strip of the tinfoil wrapper.

She accepted and savored the minty white confection while he popped one in his mouth, too. As he repocketed the roll with one hand, he rested the other on her upper back. She eyed him suspiciously—had she not just opened her heart to him about her phobia?—then shuddered when his hand strayed down her spine. Down, slowly, then back up. A rub. Definitely a rub. Was he mocking her? Mild anger sifted with panic, but before she even had a chance to pull away, he withdrew his hand, loudly questioning Farnsworth on the total number of broken windows inside the home.

Seven was the man's answer. Seven was also the number of seconds it took her to grind the mint between her molars—something that did not escape Lowe's notice. She put some space between them and continued to keep a lookout for the urn while Lowe conducted a flawless performance of a wealthy husband looking for a quiet old home to renovate for his "mother-in-law."

The stairs were barely passable, and on the second story, a spacious landing ringed by four bedrooms greeted them. "Two full bathrooms on this floor," the real estate agent pointed out. "Not the prettiest things, but the plumbing seems to work. And there's a third one in the servant's hall behind the kitchen."

Hadley's sixth sense told her that they were getting closer to the piece of the amulet.

"What's that door, there?" Lowe asked.

"You know, I thought it was a closet, but there's a keyhole, isn't there?" the man answered, and proceeded to sort through a ring of keys, mumbling to himself as he shuffled toward the locked door. "Just a moment."

"I feel it," she whispered to Lowe as they hung back.

"Me, too." He rooted around in his pocket.

"Stronger up here. Maybe there's storage space in the attic? Because the"—she took another mint he offered—"only other logical place would be on a mantel or inside a glass case, I suppose. Maybe I'm just thinking of the urns on display at the Columbarium." She glanced down at Lowe's fingers, which were headed toward her chest. Bare fingers. When had he removed his gloves?

"You're buttoned up all wrong," he murmured, much closer to her face than she expected. So close, she could smell his minty breath, which distracted her from what his fingers were doing: unbuttoning her coat.

She wanted to protest, but he was right. How long had she been walking around with misaligned buttons? And why hadn't he said something sooner?

"One second, let me just . . ." Cool air drafted against the skin over her breastbone before warm fingertips brushed the same spot. Oh, God. The dress with the low neck. Terrible mistake. He made a low noise. Chills danced across her arms. She didn't dare glance up at his face as his fingers threaded the right button into the right hole. "There we go."

"Ah-ha! Success!" Farnsworth said at the same time from across the landing.

Hadley bit down on the mint and rapidly crunched it into dust as they made their way over to the real estate agent.

"Looks like a small storage room," the man said. "Electricity's out, so it's hard to see in the dark, but might be five by ten feet, I'd guess."

A distant knock turned their heads toward the stairs, from which floated up a tentative, "Hello?"

"Now, who could *that* be?" Mr. Farnsworth said. Clearly it was the real Davidsons, but Hadley wasn't going to offer this up. "I'll just be a moment," he said as he hurried toward the stairs. "Wait until you catch the view from the tower. Can see straight over to Angel Island and Alcatraz."

"Nothing quite like the pastoral elegance of a prison yard and an ill-managed immigration station," Lowe mumbled. "Help me. Hurry, before we're caught."

Hadley stumbled behind Lowe, practically running into him. "What?"

"Can't you feel it? The damned thing's practically screaming at me. Somewhere in here, I'd wager." He retrieved a small brass flashlight from his coat and flicked it on, shining it down the length of her coat. "Always prepared to explore small, dark places."

Dear God. Was he flirting with her? Now?

As Farnsworth's patent leather shoes tapped across the foyer, Lowe flicked the flashlight's beam into the closet and disappeared behind it. "Christ, this room is packed," he complained.

He wasn't wrong. Old crates, hatboxes, and stacked chairs lined one wall. They didn't have enough time to riffle through all this junk. But maybe they didn't have to.

"You feel it?" Lowe asked.

Maybe stronger than she had ever felt the base. "Right

here." It was emanating from one of three crates sitting in front of her. "They're nailed shut."

Lowe handed her the flashlight. "Hold this. Let me just . . ." A charming syncopation of Swedish and English curses filled the closet as he wiggled the corner of the middle crate. A second later, the shrill whine of wood pulling away from nails made Hadley wince.

"Come on, come on . . ." Lowe dug through excelsior wood wool packaging until he uncovered two things at once: an old Victrola and the sand-colored matte glaze of Duamutef, the jackal-headed son of Horus.

Her mother's canopic jar! It was lovely. Long, clean lines and perfectly painted details. Modern, yet ancient.

The front door squeaked closed on the floor below.

"Hurry!" Hadley said.

"Hurrying," he answered, hefting the urn out of the crate.

She flicked off his flashlight and pocketed it. "The real Davidsons sound confused. How are we getting this out of here? Back door?"

"Rule number one: never take the back door," he said, cradling the urn under one arm. "Better to talk your way out of a bind than run. Come on."

They bounded down the stairs. Mr. Farnsworth met them at the bottom, a stern look on his face. "Sir," he said sharply, as a middle-aged couple ghosted into the foyer behind him.

"Cousin!" Lowe announced, with a supremely joyous smile stretching his cheeks.

The cousin in question looked startled and confused.

"I see you've met the real estate agent. I wasn't sure if you were going to make it today and didn't want to miss a chance to make an offer."

"Richard," the man's wife mumbled. "What's going on?"

Lowe clapped Mr. Davidson on the shoulder and walked him toward the front door. "Now that you're here, old man, I'll let you handle it. I wouldn't take the missus through the main floor, though. Our dear agent here gave my wife quite a shock with all the lewd drawings scribbled on the walls."

"Now, you see here, sir—" Mr. Farnsworth started.

Lowe leaned closer to Mr. Davidson. "Looks like there's been some occult business going on here as well. Probably devil worship."

"Oh my goodness," Mrs. Davidson said as she rushed to keep up.

"True," Lowe said conspiratorially.

The real estate agent's face reddened. "It absolutely is *not* true."

Lowe stopped near the open door. "Occultists, perverts, drinking—God only knows what kind of wicked debauchery has been conducted in this house. And that's not to mention the ghost. Call me crazy, but I felt something cold upstairs in that closet." He nudged Hadley and held out his hand. "What do you think, darling?"

Hadley popped the proffered mint into her mouth. A funny sort of reserved panic made her head feel bright and empty. "I think that's why the neighbors call this place Gloom Manor."

A warm weight fell across her shoulders. Hadley looked up as Lowe tugged her against his hip. "Exactly right," he praised with the briefest of twinkling in his con artist eyes. "Gloom Manor, indeed. Now, we won't take up any more of your time. But it was good to see you. Please call your uncle. He's a lonely old man."

Lowe hurried Hadley around the murmuring couple and headed through the open door.

"Wait!" Mr. Farnsworth called. "What do you think you're doing with that?"

Lowe glanced at the urn under his arm. "This?"

"You can't just take whatever you please from this house. It belongs to the bank." In a startling show of nimbleness, the real estate agent lunged and grabbed the sculpted lid of the canopic jar. The scrawny man was outmatched by Lowe in every possible way: size, strength, age. But, unfortunately, he had the element of surprise.

The lid separated from the jar with a terrible grinding

sound. The men fell apart as a cloud of black ash billowed into the air between them. Hadley stumbled backward. Pottery crashed.

"Richard!" Mrs. Davidson shouted, as Mr. Farnsworth crashed into her husband.

"I'm all right," the man answered.

Lowe was, too, and he'd managed to avoid the bone dust. The downwind real estate agent, however, was doubled over coughing. Oh, and the poor canopic jar! Smashed to bits all over the front steps, nothing recognizable.

"What in the world is going on?" Mr. Davidson said to no one in particular. "Was that an urn?"

"Poor Mrs. Rosewood," Lowe mumbled.

Hadley spotted something sitting in the ashes accumulating on the walkway. Acting quickly, she snatched it up with gloved fingers: another beige nest of excelsior shavings. Cradled in the packing material was a slender rectangle of bright red-gold.

The crossbar!

"Got it," she mouthed to Lowe as a flash of bright spring-green zipped by her face. "What was that?"

"Feral parrot," Mrs. Davidson said. "There's a wild flock of them on Telegraph Hill. No one knows where they came from—oh, goodness!"

More green. A dozen or more parrots with red heads buzzed past, madly flapping their wings and squawking. "How odd. You'd almost think they were fleeing something," Mr. Davidson mumbled.

They were.

Something a lot bigger and stranger.

FOURTEEN

LOWE'S LEGS WEAKENED AS HE GAPED AT THE IMPOSSIBLE creature that had landed on the bracketed cornice above the house's entrance.

Like the Sphinx, it had a feline body, albeit more the size and shape of an alley cat than some majestic lioness. But its head was that of a hawk—curved beak, beady gold eyes. And it had enormous, feathered brown wings that were gilded at the tips.

A giant cat with wings. Or a giant bird with paws.

He must've inhaled some of the bone ash.

But the ragged screech that blasted from the open beak of the beast wasn't an illusion. And neither were the terrified shouts circling around him. Part of him wanted to join them.

Only one voice was calm. Firm. Steady. And it said, "A griffin."

He darted a glance at Hadley.

"Chimera," she elaborated. "Mythical beast."

"Egyptian?" he choked out.

"Maybe the canopic jar was warded with some sort of magic."

"Magic," he repeated. The Davidsons were running into Gloom Manor with Mr. Farnsworth. Perhaps Hadley and he should be doing the same.

Hadley wasn't paying attention. Her calm and collected scholar's gaze was fixated on the fantastical creature flapping its wings on the roof. "Or perhaps the crossbars are cursed, and that's why my mother—"

The griffin took flight, diving toward them like a fallen angel. The wings weren't just gilded; they were covered in golden symbols. Dozens. Hundreds. God, never mind all that—the thing was fast as lightning. Beak and claws, fur and feather, it all rushed through the air behind a disarming screech.

At the last moment, he shoved Hadley behind him. He hadn't realized he'd drawn his dagger until the beast was on him. He struck out blindly, shielding his face as it swooped past. A slash connected with flesh—real flesh that oozed blood. Real fur. *Horribly* real stink of something foul and putrid. Something dead and rotting and rancid.

Something from the grave.

He swung around to track it. The griffin made a massive, arcing turn in the air before coming at them again.

Jesus! Nowhere to go. And trying to stab it midflight was like fishing in the air with no line. "Get behind me!" he shouted at Hadley, but not soon enough. The thing was on them again, and this time Lowe spied golden claws extending from its paws.

He threw himself over Hadley's head and struck out at the incoming attacker. No hit with the dagger, but his hand knocked against a furry rib cage. Wings flapped. The beast struggled. And for a moment there was nothing but the stench of death and an ear-piercing squawk like a goddamn Harpy—so loud, he barely heard Hadley cry out when the bird swooped away.

"It took the crossbar!" She flailed against him and they stumbled to their feet. Her left glove was slashed.

In a panic, Lowe spun around to find the griffin flapping furiously against the palm tree. Either Lowe's blow had set him off balance, or whatever dark magic powered the creature was having trouble managing the weight of the crossbar. But sure enough, from the grip of his brown beak, a rod of gold flashed.

Gold worth about as much as his life, because without it, he had nothing.

Lowe raced for the griffin, not sure if it was out of his reach yet or what he'd do if it was. But something changed when he was still several strides away. The griffin was losing his battle with gravity. It was making horrific sounds, flapping and throwing itself against the palm tree's ringed bark, as if it were wrestling an invisible foe or swarmed by furious bees.

The crossbar dropped from its mouth.

Lowe swiped it off the lawn and backed away. The beast was still going down. Maybe the damn thing was going to explode like a magical bomb. Best not chance it.

"Run!" he told Hadley, grabbing her hand as he darted into the street. Where was the damned taxi? Did he not pay the man to wait, for the love of God?

Hadley pointed across the road. "There!"

He couldn't shove her into the backseat fast enough. He slammed the door behind him and looked out the back window, rubbing away condensation from the pane until he could see the dark shape of the griffin writhing at the base of the palm.

"You got it?" Hadley asked.

He opened his hand and showed her the crossbar before pocketing it.

"I thought you said the first rule was 'never run.'"

"I said never take the back door. You okay? Did it break skin?"

She tugged her glove off. "No. Just feels like there might be a bruise later."

He pulled her arm closer to inspect her hand. At the last moment, he remembered not to touch her and awkwardly withdrew, mumbling an apology. The look on her face was indeterminable. Hurt, wary, panicked? He had no idea.

"Go, please," he told the driver.

Dark eyes stared back at him in the rearview mirror. Now *that* was a panicked look. No telling how much the poor man had seen. "Where to?"

Where? Good question. Would the griffin revive itself and fly its rotting feline corpse around the city until it found them again? Regardless, he had to get the crossbar to a safe place.

On a sigh, Lowe collapsed against the seat. Dark blood tipped his blade. "Just get us off this damned hill as fast as you can. I'll decide once we're back in civilization."

LaZy SuZan's Automat was a café in North Beach that billed itself as San Francisco's only "European Electric Self-Serving Kitchen." Hand-lettered signs declared: NO WAITING. NO TIPPING. OPEN DAILY FROM SIX A.M. TIL MIDNIGHT.

While Lowe hunted a public telephone, Hadley found them an empty café table next to the expansive front window. She removed her coat and surveyed the far wall, where lunchtime crowds peered inside the glass doors of hundreds of tiny metal compartments, each fitted with a coin slot. Signs above indicated what was served: soups, hot meals, sandwiches, cakes, and pies. Coins went in, door popped open, food was taken. No servers, no hostess—a couple of uniformed employees cleaned tables as others bussed trays of dishes back and forth to the hidden kitchen.

"The temptation of unlimited food with the allure of slot machines," Hadley said when Lowe returned with a tray loaded down with slices of pie and two steaming cups. He'd actually remembered to get her tea and not coffee. "How charming."

He pulled a chair around the small round table until he had a better view of the window. A little too close for Hadley's comfort, especially when he paused in the middle of doling out silverware, eyes trained on the front of her dress. She wasn't sure if she was flattered that he'd noticed she'd removed her coat, or embarrassed. But she'd worn the damn dress, hadn't she?

He cleared his throat. "You've never eaten here?"

"I don't often find myself patronizing North Beach establishments," she said, eyeing the unmarked entrances across the street. Speakeasies. Gambling. Jazz.

"The Gris-Gris Club is right across the street—see that covered door on the side road? My brother met his wife there. Nice place. I'll take you sometime."

A nervous thrill surged inside her chest. He probably was just making conversation. "A nightclub," she scoffed, as if it was the silliest thing she'd ever heard. "Might be hard to dance when you're being attacked by flying cats."

"Been almost an hour," Lowe said, snapping his pocket watch shut. "Maybe we're in the clear. Try this." He slid a wedge of pale yellow pie in her direction. "Meyer lemon. Don't tell me you hate lemon or we can't be friends."

"I love any kind of pie. I have a terrible sweet tooth." After he dove into his, she took a bite. Tart, sweet, and cool. "It's delicious. Is this your usual lunch?"

"Lately, it's been whatever I'm in the mood for. I ate a lot of godawful food on the excavation. Every once in a while, we'd have something local that surprised me—the coffee was excellent—but mostly we ended up relying on tinned goods. But since I got back, I've been eating my way through all the things I've missed." He nodded at her plate and smiled. "Go on."

He'd already stuffed her full of mints, and now he was practically shoving the pie down her throat. She took another bite, then another, suddenly famished, before she noticed Lowe staring at her face. "What?"

A wolfish smile slowly lifted his cheeks. "Nothing. I just enjoy watching you eat."

"Well, I *do*, you know. Everyone always tells me I need to eat more, but I'm not some picky birdlike eater. My metabolism's high, or I'm just built this way, I don't know."

His gaze pored over her like sticky syrup. "I like the way you're built."

A vulnerable heat spread down her body. And to her great horror, her nipples tightened, bawdily prodding the thin fabric of her dress. She slowly set her fork down and crossed her arms over her breasts. When had he slung an arm around the back of her chair? She gave him a cross look, and he removed it.

"My guy is on his way. Before he gets here, maybe we need to take a good look at this." He glanced around and scooted his chair closer to hide what he laid on the table between them. "Too close?" he murmured near her ear. "I won't touch you again, I promise."

It sounded as though he meant it. Good. A relief. And at the same time muddily disappointing. Flustered, she took a sip of her tea, nearly scalding her lips—why in the world was it so damned hot?—and then promptly attempted to quiet her bouncing emotions.

"Are you counting again?" he whispered.

"I'm fine." She exhaled and slid a quick glance his way. "Really."

He lifted both brows but didn't push her. Whatever his faults, he had a knack for knowing when to stand down. Without another word, he unwrapped the handkerchief between their plates. Hadley stared down at it, grateful for the distraction.

The gold crossbar was startlingly bright in the gray light filtering in through the window. A conservative design bordered the front, and a small mechanism protruded from the bottom, presumably used to attach the bar to the base. Odd symbols were embossed into the back.

"Looks like a match to me," she said.

"Agreed." He rewrapped the crossbar.

But something else bothered her. "If the griffin was a magical construct, where was the spell?"

"The spell that released it, or brought it to life, you mean?"

"Yes. The crossbar wasn't housed inside any sort of wrapping when I found it, so the logical assumption would be that there was some sort of spell written on the inside of the urn."

"None of the canopic paintings showed additional symbols inside the jars, but maybe there was a spell scribbled on a piece of paper that was stashed with the crossbar. Could've fallen onto the lawn and we just didn't spot it."

"True, but regardless, why didn't my mother warn me about this?"

"She did mention the crossbars were dangerous," Lowe argued. "It wasn't attacking us—it wanted the crossbar."

"Protecting it. A final magical safety net, perhaps."

He propped his forearms against the edge of the table and leaned forward. "Seems odd that a griffin would guard the jackal-headed jar. Why not the falcon-headed one, Qebehsenuef?"

"I agree. If my mother was so meticulous about all the other details, why was she sloppy about that?"

"Especially when she could've buried the crossbars in a field and been done with it."

"Precisely. Details were important to her. The game was important. The magic doesn't seem to fit."

"And now we don't know what to expect if we find another one of the pieces. Another magical guardian? Maybe I need to listen to Winter and start carrying a gun."

Whatever made him feel better. At least she knew the Mori specters could take down the griffin. "I'm more concerned about where to look for another piece."

"I contacted someone this morning about death records. He's going to see what he can pull together. Hopefully he'll have it for me in a couple of days."

Oh.

"I wasn't trying to hide it," he argued. "We talked about this last night."

"But when were you going to tell me? And while we're on the subject, who is this man we're meeting? How do I know you aren't handing the crossbar off to someone who'll melt it down and sell it for gold?"

Lowe swigged his coffee. "Because the amulet pieces can't be destroyed, for one." He set his cup down and gave her a look weighted with a calm intensity. "And sometimes you just have to let go and trust people."

"Easier to do when the person you're trusting is principled."

"I've got more principles than you'd imagine." He leaned closer and spoke in a low voice. "Besides, you think keeping dark secrets isn't the same as lying? Maybe we've got more in common than you want to admit."

They stared at each other for a long moment. Too long. The heat she'd felt minutes before washed over her again.

"I want to be kept informed of your progress with the death records," she said, pulling the plate of pie closer. "Perhaps we should exchange telephone numbers."

And after they'd done so, he'd agreed—promised—to contact her the minute he got the list. And with that out of the way, they finished their sweet meal in silence until Lowe waved to someone through the window.

The front door opened and a halo of dark curls bounded into the automat. A toddler. Very pretty, with a plump face grinning above a coat buttoned to her chin. She flew into Lowe's arms, and he lifted her into his lap, smiling just as big.

"Stella," he said. "My favorite girl. All healed up from your fall?"

The girl didn't respond, but when he bit the tip of her nose, she opened her mouth and grinned some more.

Hadley glanced up at the man approaching the table. He had the same dark hair as the girl and was dressed in a plain suit and coat. A pleasant face. Kind.

"Got here quick," Lowe said to the man.

"Streetcar was almost empty, and we were already on our way out to the Japanese Tea Garden."

"To see the koi fish?" Lowe asked the girl, waving his hand like a fish tail swimming through water.

She nodded.

"If the weather holds, that is," the man said. "Might rain."

Lowe poked his head around Stella's curls. "Hadley Bacall, this is Adam Goldberg."

She stood. He was a few inches shorter than her, but many men were. She started to hold out her hand to shake, but realized her gloves were in her coat pocket, ruined by the griffin's beak. She canted her head instead. "A pleasure to meet you, Mr. Goldberg."

"Adam, please, and you, as well." Between two blinks, his gaze discreetly swept up and down her figure. "Lowe's mentioned you."

"Has he?"

"You're the curator."

"Yes." She gestured toward a seat. "Won't you join us?"

He hung his hat and sat next to Lowe as the girl looked up at Hadley. "This is Stella, my daughter."

"Hello," she said. "It's nice to meet you."

The girl didn't respond.

Hadley was terrible with children. She tried again. "What's that you have in your hand? A windup cat?"

No answer.

Her father spoke in her stead. "Lowe brought it back from Egypt." He turned to Lowe and said, "All week, it's been either the cat or Raggedy Ann."

"*Farbror* Lowe did a good job, *ja*?" He wiggled the cat before speaking to Hadley. "Adam and I are old friends. We grew up together."

"And you work together now?"

"On occasion," Adam said.

"What exactly do you do, if I may ask?"

Adam's eyes flicked toward Lowe's. "Whatever hare-brained thing he needs me to do."

Lowe turned Stella around in his lap to face the table. "In my family's business, it pays to have trustworthy people to make things disappear for short amounts of time. Think of Adam as the troll under the bridge."

"Troll?"

"Dragon!" Lowe said with a merry chuckle. "I meant a *dragon* guarding treasure."

"Better."

"Anyway, he keeps things safe. He's holding on to the base already. He's agreed to stash all of it." Lowe slid the handkerchief-wrapped crossbar across the table. "Just as we discussed."

A thousand doubts went through Hadley's mind. Where did this man live? Where was he "stashing" the amulet pieces? What was stopping him from selling them off to someone else?

Lowe's thigh knocked against hers. "Your father told me to keep them safe. Adam is very, very careful. And ten times more trustworthy than me."

She gave Lowe a sidelong look.

"Okay, a thousand times more trustworthy."

"That's better."

Adam laughed. "She already knows your con artist ways."

"Oh, I think there's another word for the kind of artist he is," she said, suppressing a smile. "And it starts with bull."

The men's hearty laughter surprised her. Stella, as well, who grinned along with them like she was in on the joke. Hadley glanced at the windup cat on the table.

"I have a cat, too," she told the girl. "He's black, just like yours."

The girl still didn't answer.

"She can't hear," Lowe said in quiet voice.

A prickling, warm embarrassment trickled through Hadley as she looked between Lowe and the girl's father. "I'm . . ." What? So sorry for the father? For the girl? Making a faux pas?

"She's an excellent lip-reader, though," Lowe said, smiling down at the girl. "And she's learning how to use sign language."

"Mostly she's learning to stomp her foot and shake her head," Adam said, giving Hadley a kind smile she didn't quite feel she deserved. Stella banged the cat on the table and made a gruff noise. "Like that," Adam said. "My wife passed a couple years back, so it's just the two of us. She could probably stand to learn some feminine manners."

"Absolutely not," Lowe said, winding up the black cat. "Feminine manners are overrated. You stomp your foot all you want, *sötnos*."

A rush of emotions welled in Hadley—tenderness for the father and his daughter. Pity, too. And something else: a nagging envy for the easy companionship and bond Lowe shared with these people, and a longing to have the same.

Watching Lowe hold the small girl tore something loose inside Hadley. This was real and good. He cared about them. Trusted them—and they trusted Lowe.

And for no real logical reason, she decided at that moment, she trusted him, too.

FIFTEEN

AFTER LEAVING LOWE AND ADAM THAT AFTERNOON, HADLEY SPENT
the rest of the weekend studying her mother's pictograms.
She didn't hear a peep out of her father regarding the fallen
chandelier at the museum party, which was fine. But he was
the last person she wanted to see when she walked into her
office on Monday. Having telephoned his house yesterday
to get word about his mood, she'd discovered from his staff
that he seemed to be in fine spirits. Father's cook said he
was singing to himself. Apparently he'd received a telephone
message from a Mr. Magnusson that brightened his day.

She wasn't sure why this bothered her. Lowe had told her
he'd need to inform her father about finding the crossbar.
Father was, after all, paying Lowe to hunt them down. And
she was not supposed to know about it, so there was nothing
to do but step aside, no matter how much this grated her
nerves.

But now that she had to sit in front of his desk and listen
to him rattle off all the reasons why Lowe was the best fit
for his replacement, she was feeling less bothered and more
insulted.

"I must say, you're taking all this well," he said after a long speech. "I'm glad your anger from this weekend has subsided."

"It was just the shock of it." In truth, her nails were biting into her thighs while she tightly controlled her feelings, for fear the Mori would attempt to murder the man again.

Unseeing eyes stared off over her shoulder. "Well, I'll admit my role in this. I should've told you before the dinner, but my mind was on other things. And no father wants to disappoint his daughter. I was a coward, and I'm sorry. Truly."

An apology? From the great Dr. Bacall? She was tempted to look around the room to see if he was talking to someone else. Instead, she took a deep breath and ate crow. "I'm sorry for losing control. I didn't mean for it to go that far."

"I feel certain you didn't. And I hope you won't hold a grudge against Mr. Magnusson. If he's appointed in my position, I'm certain he'd recognize what a tremendous talent you are. And perhaps something could be arranged for you to be interim head when he's out in the field."

Interim. Hadley rolled her eyes. Whatever feelings were stewing inside her over Lowe, she would hold him to his promise to turn down the position, and whether her father liked it or not, she would be sitting behind his desk come February.

"I hold no ill will toward Mr. Magnusson."

"Excellent to hear, darling. If you are to be working closely with him in the near future, it would be best for both of you to be professional. I know it's difficult sometimes. Maybe it would help to focus on your upcoming seminars to keep your emotions under control."

"Yes, that's probably wise advice." She'd be sure to relay it to her heart and brain, which were conspiring together behind her back to conjure up very unprofessional thoughts and feelings about Lowe.

Fifteen minutes after Hadley returned to her office, Miss Tilly's pretty face popped inside the doorway. "Oh, you're done meeting with your father. I wasn't sure how long it would take—he said no interruptions, so I told your visitor you weren't available."

Her heart leapt. "What visitor?"

"Mr. Ginn."

Oh. Oliver. After their parting at the Flood Mansion, she wasn't sure he'd call on her so soon. And it made her a little nervous that he did, because pieces of their conversation about her specters came back. "Did he say what he wanted?"

"No," she said, handing Hadley a small parcel. "But he was terribly disappointed that he couldn't see you. Wish I had someone pining over me like that. He asked me to give you this."

When the secretary left, Hadley opened a hastily scribbled folded note slipped under the parcel's string. *I hope you find chapter four enlightening. I have more information whenever you're ready to talk.*

Inside the brown wrapping was a small leather book. Not printed, but written in longhand. *Beliefs of the Arabian and Egyptian People.* A date—1895—but no author. A quick flip through the pages revealed the content of the chapter in question: Ifrit Spirits of the Djinn.

Thick pencil underlined several passages.

In Arabia, a rebellious class of infernal spirits said to be made of smoke and ash . . . some think they live underground, but others believe they are summoned from a netherworld.

Underworld. She turned the page.

They bear a striking resemblance to a kind of spirit feared by Egyptians, the Sheut, *or "shadow" . . . one of five parts of the human soul. Magical folklore explains the origins of the creatures as being created by Set, who separated Sheuts from 1,000 dead souls as they navigated the Egyptian underworld, Duat, realm of Osiris, and later loosed them in the Egyptian desert. Now considered an Egyptian version of the Grim Reaper myth, these spirits' purpose is to harvest intact living souls and drag them into the underworld.*

Grim Reapers. Where did Oliver get this? Who wrote it? Hadley had never heard of the shadow being separated from the other parts of the soul in Egyptian lore. Though, she had to admit that it sounded a bit like the Mori specters. But how did Oliver associate the two things after seeing her specters for a few seconds? Part of her wanted to ask him, and another part—a part reinforced by her father's admonitions over the years to keep the Mori secret—wanted to return the book and cut off all contact with the man.

Voices in the hall and a familiar booted gait dragged her out of her thoughts.

"If you don't mind, I'm just going to say a brief word to Miss Bacall while you let her father know I've arrived." Lowe's blond head appeared in the doorway, soon followed by his long body. He was back to his smart leather jacket and held a herringbone flatcap in his maimed hand.

Good lord, he was dashing. Just looking at him made her heart cartwheel madly. Was he this handsome on Saturday? Surely not.

"Miss Bacall," he said with a curling smile.

"Mr. Magnusson. What a nice surprise."

He glanced over his shoulder into the hall then strode to her desk as she stood. "Is it?" he said in a lower voice, eyes glinting with a half-hidden infectious kind of teasing cheerfulness.

"Is it what?"

"A nice surprise to see me."

She felt herself smiling and had to work to stop. "Perhaps it is."

His own smile widened into a stunning grin. Her stomach fluttered so violently, she pressed a palm to her middle, as if she could physically calm it.

"Why are you here?" she whispered.

"Your father left a message. I have some errands to run, so I thought I'd drop by and speak to him in person while I . . ." His gaze strayed over her top and skirt. "Well, while I saw you," he said with a wicked slant of one brow.

Desire leapt up inside her, hot and sudden. She shifted uncomfortably and struggled to keep her breath steady.

He glanced over his shoulder again and leaned closer. "My contact should have the list tomorrow. Would you like to meet somewhere for lunch and review it against our canopic jar paintings?"

"Yes," she said, far too eagerly. She cleared her throat and tried again, more softly. "Yes, that would be agreeable. Fine. Good. Sure. I probably can." Oh, God. She sounded like an idiot.

A loud *whap!* flew from the door, courtesy of her coworker, George. His irritating morning greeting consisted of smacking the doorframe with his briefcase—something that never failed to make her jump in her chair and tempted her to send the Mori down the hall to wallop him on the head with the damned briefcase.

"Who the hell was that?" Lowe asked.

"My biggest mistake," she answered as Miss Tilly's heels clicked toward her office.

During his brief visit with Dr. Bacall, Lowe gave him a pack-of-lies tale concerning the hunt for the crossbar pieces. Not only did he leave Hadley out of it, but he also concocted a completely different path for his search. No books of poetry, no canopic jars, no Columbarium, and no Gloom Manor. Lowe was simply deciphering a set of symbols and following where they led. Bacall was overjoyed just to have Lowe working on it. And Lowe would be overjoyed to take the man's money.

But at the moment, he was more interested in the younger man who'd passed by Hadley's office. A "mistake," she'd called him. Lowe intended to find out exactly what she meant by that. So after telling Dr. Bacall he'd show himself out, he strolled the maze of hallways until, in a quiet corner, he found a connecting corridor that led into the museum proper. A small office faced it, and the nameplate next to the open door said George Houston. Lowe ambled inside.

The man in question leaned against a file cabinet, looking into a small mirror as he ran a comb through dark hair. A cigarette dangled from his lips. He was tall—not as tall as Lowe, but probably a couple of inches over six feet—and his body looked as if it sat behind a desk all day doing nothing.

"You must be Mr. Houston," Lowe said.

"That's right." The man set his comb down and looked up. "Oh, yes. Dr. Bacall's golden boy," he said, giving "boy" extra emphasis before blowing out a cone of smoke. "Suppose it could be worse. At least I won't be working for a woman."

"Miss Bacall mentioned you."

Houston's eyes narrowed. "Did she? In what context?"

Lowe loosened his posture and gave a causal shrug, attempting to lure the man into dropping his guard. "Just mentioned you worked for her."

"*For* her?"

"With her," Lowe corrected with a causal shrug. "I can't remember. Didn't say much, but she's hard to read. Not exactly bubbly."

Houston chuckled. "No, B.L.B. isn't a charmer."

"Pardon?"

"Bad Luck Bacall. That's what we call her. You'll understand if you end up working here. She's a walking tornado of destruction. Wherever she goes, chairs break, books fall, light bulbs pop, and people end up in the hospital. You'd do well to stay out of her way, because if there's a chance for something unlucky happening, you can bet she'll be in the room."

He hadn't expected to hear all this, but if the idiot was leaking information like a busted tire, Lowe might as well help him along. "Is that right?"

"You were at the dinner party—could you believe that chandelier?"

"Yeah, that was something, all right." Would've been nice if Houston had been sitting under it instead of him.

Houston shook his head and ashed his cigarette on the floor, ignoring the ashtray sitting on top of the file cabinet. "I swear to God, as soon as it fell, I thought of her. We used to have one of those Safety First signs that said 'This

department has worked *blank* days without an accident'—
you know the ones with the black box where you chalk in
the number? We painted B.L.B. over the top of it and used
it every time something busted around here."

Lowe pretended to laugh. Goddamn arrogant little pis-
sant. No wonder Hadley kept to herself. If the office was
filled with pigs like this, he hoped she broke every chair in
the building.

"I went to college with her. She wasn't as bad back then,
but she was still a walking beacon for chaos."

"Stanford?" Lowe asked.

"Yep."

Lowe joined Hadley's comment to Houston's story, taking a guess. "She said someone in college was a 'mistake.'
That you?"

"Mistake?" Houston chuckled and opened the top drawer
of the file cabinet. "She liked it well enough." He made a
dismissive noise. "And if you want to know the truth, she
came to *me*. Offered to pay me to screw her."

Lowe's false front momentarily dropped.

"No kidding," Houston said, as if they were best buddies.
"She said a man could pay a prostitute for sex, so why
couldn't a woman pay a man? See, that's her fixation—she
always has to have control over a situation. Once she loses
that control? Forget it. She goes cuckoo. Terrible temper."

Lowe grunted vaguely as anger rolled over him in waves.

Houston thumbed through files with one hand as he
stubbed his cigarette out with the other. "Anyway, if she said
it was a mistake, that's her problem for lifting her skirt. I
enjoyed myself. I mean, come on. Have you gotten a look
at the ass on her? Now that's something to—"

Fury blotted out good sense, and Lowe finally snapped.
He shot forward on a growl and savagely slammed the file
cabinet drawer shut on the man's hand. Bone cracked. Houston cried out. Lowe released the drawer, and the curator fell
back, holding out his injured hand in horror.

"My fingers!"

Indeed. At least three were broken, judging from the

grotesque way they bent back at the knuckles. Bright red blood pooled in his palm. Tears of pain flowed as he grimaced and hollered again. "I'll have you arrested, you lunatic!" he bit out between sobs.

"What's my last name?" Lowe said. "Heard of my family? Go on, have me arrested. I dare you. In fact, I dare you to tell the entire museum that this wasn't a self-inflicted accident."

Realization flooded the man's face. He said nothing in response, just stumbled backward and shuddered violently while cradling his hand.

Lowe tugged on his cap and headed toward the door as people stampeded toward Houston's office. He reckoned he should be able to slip into the museum corridor before anyone saw him. "And if you say another crude word about Hadley—one fucking word—I'll break more than your fingers."

SIXTEEN

———◆———

THE FOLLOWING DAY, HADLEY BOARDED A STREETCAR A LITTLE
before noon. Because it was usually faster than calling a
cab, she often took public transportation during lunch, so
she knew her father wouldn't suspect anything amiss. Lowe
had called to suggest a meeting place; he had the list of
names.

After changing cars that climbed in and out of thickening
fog, she ended up at Fisherman's Wharf and immediately
spotted Lowe on the sidewalk, standing heads above hurried
pedestrians flanking Jefferson Street.

They strode toward each other and met near a newsstand.
She was breathing far too hard for ten paces—could she
look any more eager to see him? Good heavens.

"You managed to sneak out," he said, looking terribly
pleased and terribly handsome in his long blue gray coat
and matching fedora.

"I wouldn't call it sneaking, exactly. I told Miss Tilly I'd
be gone a couple of hours."

"The best lies are half truths," he quipped. "Hungry?"

"Famished."

"Me, too. I'm taking you to one of the best places to eat in the city."

She glanced around the wharf's warehouses, lumberyard, and boats. "I suppose I'll have to take your word for it. Do they serve lemon pie?"

He laughed. "No, but it's on my list of favorites. Trust me. Come on."

The scent of sharp ocean brine filled her nostrils as they made their way down the promenade. A row of Tin Lizzies and delivery trucks lined the curb to their left while fog-wreathed trawlers and seiners bobbed in the Bay on their right. "Did you take Lulu?"

He shook his head. "Bo dropped me off."

"You know, I did wonder what would happen if you'd driven the motorcycle and it rained."

"I'd get wet."

She squinted at him and smiled.

"How's the office?" he asked.

"It's calmed down since yesterday."

"Oh?" he said, the personification of innocence. "What happened yesterday?"

She lifted her mink coat collar to shield her neck from the nippy breeze. "Mr. Houston was rushed to the hospital. Word today is that he's resting at home with four broken fingers."

"You don't say."

"You wouldn't know anything about that, would you?"

"This is the first I'm hearing of it," he said cheerfully.

"So that wasn't you I saw racing through the back door into the museum."

"You know I never run out the back door, Hadley."

"Of course." She glanced at a trawler chugging closer to shore. "George didn't say anything about me, did he?"

"A jackass like that? Who would bother listening?" He straightened his hat brim. "But I'll tell you what, when you get your father's position? The first thing I'd do if I were you is fire dear old George Houston."

Hadley didn't respond, just lifted her collar higher to hide the smile she couldn't repress.

At the foot of Taylor Street, they strolled by wholesale fish stalls. Here, on the sidewalk over wood-burning stoves, peddlers stirred bubbling cauldrons of crab fresh off the boats and sold them to passersby for twenty cents each. But Lowe was headed to stall number eight, where an Italian couple was serving clam chowder. Dockworkers and a few middle-class businessmen sat at plain wooden tables with benches under a covered area. Lowe gave one of the diners a friendly wave and marched up to the counter.

"Lowe!" the pretty dark-haired woman said, coming around the counter to embrace him, kissing both his cheeks. "We saw your photograph in the newspaper. Struck it rich in Egypt, didya?"

"Not yet, but I'm trying," he said, shaking the man's hand across the counter.

"Famous archaeologist," the man said with a grin. "Be careful—you might give your family a good name."

"Where's the fun in that?"

The couple laughed, then Lowe introduced her to Rose and Nunzio Alioto. "They make the best chowder on the wharf," he praised. "And they catch the *second*-best crab. Magnusson may not run as many crabbers as we used to before Volstead, but we still catch the sweetest Dungeness." He winked at Mrs. Alioto.

"Glad to see your fame hasn't gone to your head," she said. "But as long as Winter keeps us wet, you can talk all the bull you want. You two want lunch?"

Lowe rubbed his hands together. "Chowder and beer. Extra sourdough on the side." He glanced at Hadley. "Sound okay?"

"Sounds terrific," she said to Lowe, then to Mrs. Alioto, "Thank you."

Under the curious gaze of the lunching dockworkers, Mrs. Alioto pointed them to a lone table at the back and soon followed with steaming bowls of clam chowder, two paper cups of beer—supplied by Lowe's brother, Hadley guessed—and a plate piled with sourdough rolls. "Monk's boys have been putting the word out that he's looking to talk to you," Mrs. Alioto said in a quiet voice. "Somebody's liable to tell him they saw you here today."

"Just a little misunderstanding," Lowe said as he set his fedora on the table and swept a hand over his hair. "If anyone asks, feel free to mention that you overhead me saying I was planning to call on him this week."

"I'll keep that in mind." She patted Lowe on the back. *"Buon appetito."*

"What was that about?" Hadley asked once the woman had left.

He gave her a sheepish smile and repeated her words from yesterday. "A mistake."

"Don't tell me he's planning to chop off your other pinky for stealing his wife."

He chuckled. "No women involved, cross my heart. Now dig in."

The creamy chowder was heavenly, the bread tangy and fresh. Lowe had been right to put the meal on his list of favorites—it might've been the most comforting food she'd had in years. And while they sat side by side on the weather-roughened bench and ate, Lowe pulled out a folded packet of paper, the top sheet of which was covered in typed columns.

"These are the names and addresses they could find. Over three hundred."

"Dear lord. How are we going to whittle it down?"

He reached in his coat to retrieve a small black notebook. Tucked inside were his two canopic jar paintings. He placed the jackal-headed one on top. "Because I've cracked your mother's code."

"You have?"

"Don't get too excited. Recognizing how she did it is only half the solution. Look here—each of her pictograms represents a letter. Since this was Mrs. Rosewood's jar, I worked backward from that: this hash mark is a railroad track. Railroad equals 'R.' This circle that looks like a golf ball? It's an orange—'O.' " He pointed to the other pictograms, naming words whose first letters spelled out Rosewood. "She used three different pictograms for 'O,' which makes it more difficult."

"But 'Rosewood' is only eight letters, and each jar has twenty symbols."

"Placeholders. Those are the reversed pictograms, and the only ones repeated. See this one that looks like a stick with a lump on the side? The mirror-image version is on the other painting I have. I'm guessing some of the other place-holders are on your paintings."

Hadley retrieved her share of the watercolors from her handbag and spread them out next to his. They studied the symbols together and identified all the reversed ones.

"Now we know the exact number of letters in each of the remaining three names. That helps. But it would help even more if we could compile a single list of the symbols along with any and all possible words associated with them. Because this symbol here looks like a moon, but is it 'moon' or 'crescent' or 'boomerang?' "

Now she understood the difficulty in translating the names. While he redrew all the pictograms in his notebook, she helped brainstorm. Working with him was pleasant and natural, and she found herself laughing at his jokes and stealing glimpses of him. The faint impression his fedora had pressed into his blond hair, and the bump in his crooked nose. The way his eyes squinted into long blue triangles when he was thinking. The masculine grace in his corded hands as he unconsciously seesawed his pencil between two fingers while he thought.

It wasn't until she marveled at the steely comfort of his shoulder butted against hers that she realized they were pressed against one another from shoulder to knee.

And to her surprise, she didn't mind. Not one bit.

In fact, she idly wished other parts of them were pressed together.

Lowe was having trouble concentrating on the pictograms. Every instinct he had was shouting at him to pull Hadley into his lap and kiss the bejesus out of her. He doodled spirals on the page's border and analyzed the logistics of having sex with her, right there on the bench. Would require balance, but he'd already run through three different positions and a couple of variations. As he was debating the possibility of bringing the table into it, she made a small noise.

"Trotter."

"What?"

She stared at his list of dead people. "Henrietta Trotter. That's one of Hugo Trotter's sisters. The funeral director who was rumored to have killed his siblings."

Lowe vaguely remembered the legend of Hugo Trotter. Police never could find evidence that he'd done anything wrong, but the man had made several jokes at dinner parties that he was planning to kill and cremate two sisters and one brother, and all three siblings died suspiciously, one by one, over a yearlong period.

"People said he talked to their urns as if they could hear him," Hadley said. "This must've been the last sister, because he moved out of town after the earthquake. Which canopic jar has seven unique pictograms? Ah—the baboon. See if the symbols could possibly spell Trotter."

"That's . . ." Crazy, he was going to say, but after sorting through their word list, he picked out the letters with ease. "T-r-o-t-t-e-r. *Helvete*, Hadley—you think it's possible?"

"He was known for having a strange sense of humor. Maybe he didn't really kill them, but I definitely remember stories in college about him talking to the urns. Just to be sure, we should try to match up other seven-letter names, see if anything else fits."

And they did, for nearly an hour. One name was off by only one letter, but nothing else matched exactly. They finally gave up and decided to investigate Trotter. "I'll make a few calls and come up with a plan," he said as he stacked the papers into a neat pile.

"Do I get half of the list?" she asked, narrowing her eyes at his busy hands.

Part of him didn't want to let it go. The sensible part. The part that was slightly worried about Monk asking around for him at the wharf.

But another part of his brain—the part that had filled her up with bread and chowder just so he could lull her into letting him feel her thigh against his—remembered George goddamn Houston saying Hadley needed to be in control. And really, what was she going to do? Run off and track down the amulet crossbars without him and disappear to Mexico? She had as much of a right to be on this godforsaken quest as he did—it was her mother's doing, after all. And if she was correct about this Trotter fellow, then that would make her instincts two for two. She definitely knew the macabre underbelly of the city better than he did.

He tore out his scribbled key to the pictograms and slid it in front of her, along with the list and the paintings. "All yours," he said, grabbing his leather gloves off the table and tugging them on. "Just make sure you keep it all safe and locked up. No desk drawers, no obvious places your maid might find while cleaning. We can switch up every few days. Two pairs of eyes are better than one."

She didn't reply, just stared at the packet of papers like they might self-combust. Brown eyes widened as they flicked up to meet his. A faint thrill warmed his chest. God, he was a sucker, because there was nothing better than her features softening. He liked her unguarded. He liked her guarded, too. Hell, he just liked her.

It was past time for her to head back to work, so they bid the Aliotos good-bye and left Taylor Street, heading back up to where the streetcar had dropped her off. Half a block before they got there, the bottom fell out of the sky.

"Oh, no—my mink collar!" she cried as rain began beading on their coats.

Lowe hurried her toward the dry stoop of a nearby warehouse and squeezed into the alcove with her. The smell of wet pavement and Hadley surrounded him. A man could get used to that. He even thought he caught the grassy scent of lily—perfume, perhaps. Or maybe his memory of the night by the gazing pool was shifting things around in his head.

Just relax and enjoy being close to her, he told himself. Don't get carried away and do anything stupid. Deep breath. Keep your coat buttoned and your hands to yourself. Do not think about sex gymnastics on a bench.

"Thank God you put the papers inside your coat," he said, shaking rain off his hat.

She didn't answer. Something gripped his arm. He glanced down to find her gloved hand there. When he looked back up, she was a moving blur—one that erased the small space between them. He staggered back against the alcove wall in surprise as her mouth clamped on his. Suddenly there was nothing but her wet lips on his and warm softness pressing against his chest.

Dear God, she was kissing him.

Wake up, idiot! Kiss her back!

He grabbed fistfuls of fur and wool and crushed her body to his, returning the kiss with equal ferocity. This wasn't a repeat of the kiss in her father's office; she actually wanted him. The difference was staggering.

A joyful pleasure rushed toward the base of his spine as slender arms wrapped around his neck. Closer? Gladly, yes. He pushed her against the alcove wall. She moaned, and he swore his heart shuddered. And as he sank against her, the kiss deepened from tight and frantic to open and slow and ardent.

Nothing existed but their warm bodies and the sound of the rain outside their shadowed alcove.

His tongue slipped between her lips, just once. Testing. Then he kissed the corner of her mouth. Slid his tongue in again. Kissed the other corner. Licked the salt from her bottom lip. And, Gods above, her tongue finally joined in, rolling with his. Dancing, exploring. Tasting.

And he wanted more.

He kissed her chin, her jaw, nuzzling his way into the soft ebony hair beneath the edge of her cloche, smelling both the citrusy brightness of her shampoo and the scent of her skin.

Another moan. Fingers grasped the back of his neck. One hand ghosted down the front of his coat, planting on his chest. She was touching him! Glorious, absolutely glorious. He wanted that hand inside his coat, under his shirt.

And look how well they fit together. He didn't have to hunch over to kiss her.

"Hadley," he murmured, kissing her cheek, one eyelid, then the next—like he was some sort of erotic priest administering a blessing with his mouth. "Hadley, Hadley, Hadley."

Christ, he was punch-drunk with arousal, his cock hard and heavy. He rocked his hips against hers, pinning her against the wall, and had begun taking his erotic blessing south of her neck when a foghorn's bellow made her jump. She immediately shoved him away.

They stood a foot apart, breathing heavily, mouths open.

Her knees buckled. He reached out to help her as she slid down the wall.

She flinched away from his touch.

He lifted both hands in surrender.

"I'm fine, I'm fine," she insisted in a hoarse voice, pushing herself back up. She wouldn't meet his eyes.

"Hadley—"

"Oh, there's a taxi. I really must . . ."

"Are you sure?"

"I—"

"Christ, Hadley. That was—" Amazing. Sexy. Far better than he'd imagined.

"I should go. Please call when you're ready to . . . Trotter, you know." Then she darted into the rain and disappeared into the taxicab at the curb. The last thing he saw was her touching the backs of her gloved fingers to her lips as the car drove away.

Instead of heading straight back to work, Hadley took a detour downtown and darted down the sidewalk into a shop upon whose window was painted in fine script:

Madame Dubois
Lingerie Couture

A bell tinkled to announce her entrance. She strode between a wooden table displaying a fanned-out selection of silky tap pants and a canvas-covered mannequin to which a half-finished nightgown was pinned. As she approached a glass display counter, a plump middle-aged woman with a perfectly coiffed silver bob looked up and smiled. "Good afternoon, Mademoiselle Bacall."

"Madame Dubois," she said with a nod.

The back of the tiny shop was a riot of silk, lace, and colorful spools of glossy embroidery thread. Neatly folded negligées and stockings lined the shelves behind the counter. And on the glass counter, cream boxes were stacked near a roll of apricot tissue paper. Madame Dubois's creations were the finest in the city. They were also Hadley's most extravagant weakness.

The scent of rose powder wafted in the air as the Parisian expat seamstress leaned over the counter, a long tape measure hanging around her neck. "And what may I do for you? Special order?"

"Yes."

"Wonderful! Your designs are some of my favorites. What shall it be today?"

Hadley's heart fluttered faster than hummingbird wings as she unfolded a color page ripped from a recent museum exhibit program. Briefly wondering if this was how her mother had felt years ago when she'd approached the ceramic artist to commission the canopic jar designs, she smiled at Madame Dubois and said, "I'd like you to copy this . . ."

SEVENTEEN

———◆———

LOWE TELEPHONED HADLEY AT WORK THE FOLLOWING DAY TO cheerfully inform her he'd found Hugo Trotter. Apparently, the alleged killer had done what many other funeral directors did when San Francisco decided land was too scarce and valuable for the funerary arts: moved his business to the nearby necropolis of Lawndale.

Hadley wasn't all that jazzed to call on a murderer. But Lowe assured her it would be fine: Mr. Trotter had died ten years ago, so they'd be calling on his son. Hugo Junior had apparently followed in his father's footsteps. Hopefully not the murderous ones.

Lawndale—"the City of the Silent"—was half an hour from San Francisco. And this is where the younger Mr. Trotter now ran his father's business, the Gilded Rest Funeral Home and Crematorium. Lowe had reserved the last appointment of the following day, so that he and his "sister" could make funeral arrangements.

He provided all this information without a word about the subject that hadn't left her thoughts since she'd left him at the wharf.

The kiss.

She'd crashed into him like she was outrunning a storm. And it was indescribably wonderful. Until she panicked. Now she teetered between the fear that it would happen again and the fear that it wouldn't.

"I'd like to leave at four in the afternoon tomorrow, just to make sure we make it in plenty of time," his voice said over the crackling line in her office. "We'll be playing the role of well-to-do siblings, so you'll need to look as if you have money."

"I *do* have money," she reminded him.

"And you have plenty of mourning clothes, which finally works in your favor. But wear the most expensive ones—not something you'd wear to work."

"Yes, yes," she said irritably, even though she could hear the teasing in his voice over the line. "It'll look suspicious if I come to work dressed to the nines, so I suppose I'll have to invent an excuse to leave."

"Headache or a cold coming on," he suggested. "I'm sure even you can dream up a lie that small."

"I'll manage."

"Then I'll pick you up outside your apartment building around four."

"Not on Lulu," she insisted.

"No, an actual car. Must play the part. Are you game?"

Was she?

Come the next day, she spent all afternoon trying on clothes and worrying herself into a frazzled knot. What was she supposed to do when she saw him? Pretend the kiss never happened? Angry with both herself and him, she finally picked a dress that covered up as much skin as possible. She further armored herself with gloves and fur and a brimmed hat that cast half her face in shadow. Then she took the elevator down to the lobby.

He was already waiting for her.

With the exception of a white shirt, every stitch of clothing was black, from the silk band of his fedora, to the well-cut lines of his bespoke suit, to the perfect polish of his shoes. A silver pocket watch chain looped from one button to a pocket on his vest, and his overcoat flowed to his calves.

Gone was the treasure hunter with a lawbreaking family, and in his place stood a well-to-do society man—an unbearably handsome one. Her heart hammered as if it didn't give a damn about her fears and worries, as if it were saying: *Look! There's the beautiful man who kissed you like you were the most desirable woman on earth. Go throw yourself at him again!*

She ignored these instincts and halted several feet away. He ducked his head to catch her gaze beneath the brim of her hat, and he smiled slowly as he said, "Hello."

Her reply sounded like the gurgle of an old drain. Dear God. He was making her stupid. Before the night was over, she'd have forgotten how to spell and count.

Dusk fell as he led her to a silver Packard out front. "Very nice," she remarked, regaining her grasp of the English language.

"It was my mother's," he said, holding the passenger door open for her. "Aida's been driving it. I switched out the license plate, just in case."

"You did what?"

"My brother's got a stack of them for bootlegging," he said, as if that made it better.

The car was as beautiful inside as she was on the outside—all leather and wood and polished chrome. The two-seater's top was up and the interior was warm. A little too warm when Lowe's long legs stretched into the driver's seat. He smelled clean. Like lemon and rosemary.

"What's the story you've concocted?" she asked as he started the rumbling engine and pulled out of her apartment building's entrance.

"Our older sister died. We want her cremated."

"That's it?"

"I don't like to plan too far in advance," he said. "Comes off as rehearsed. So just follow my lead and we'll be fine."

Easier said than done. As dusk deepened and lights began twinkling, they drove south through the city until the buildings grew shorter and farther apart, the road patchy and dotted with ruts. And all the while, a heavy silence sat between them. Until Lowe broke it.

"You look lovely."

Her response leapt out of her mouth before she could stop it. "Yesterday was a mistake."

"I disagree."

"Well, it will never happen again."

A long pause. "All right."

She forced her twined fingers to relax and gazed out the window. Was he going to say nothing more about it? She tried again. "I'm not sure what came over me."

"If you're not interested, you're not interested."

"It's not—"

"No need to explain yourself. Consider the matter in the past."

She couldn't make out his expression in the shadowed car. This was not going how she wanted it to. She struggled to put words to her thoughts, but he beat her to it.

"Glad I didn't make a fool of myself asking you out this weekend," he said.

"Pardon?"

"Some friends of mine from the history department at Berkeley are meeting up for drinks and dancing in North Beach. I knew it wasn't your thing, but everyone's bringing dates."

"Oh."

"Anyway, an old college sweetheart recently broke off her engagement and left me a couple of messages, wanting to reconnect."

She stilled. "Oh?"

"Good old Ruby. A little wild. God knows she cheated on me left and right. But she's fun at a party. I'll see if she wants to go."

Ruby. What a wretched name.

She rolled down the window to get some air as images of supper clubs and jazz bands collided in her head. Jazz bands and dancing and a wild woman who wanted to reconnect with him. A woman he'd taken to bed? Did the time they'd spent together mean so little to him that he could just shrug it off and start up with another girl?

But if she cared that much, she shouldn't have told him their kiss was a mistake. Why did she say that, anyway? She was terrible at relationships. Part of her had given up on men entirely, and was convinced she'd never fall in love or have a family. But another part of her still hoped. The same part that lay awake at night wanting Lowe. Fantasizing he did the same for her.

Her chest ached. Raw, hurt feelings tightened her throat. Tears threatened.

"Hey," he said in a softer voice. "You okay?"

"Just a little warm in here," she said, calming her emotions. This was not the time to fall apart like a small child who hadn't gotten her way. They had work to do.

"Mint?" he asked, offering her the open roll of candy in his hand.

She took three.

After the San Mateo County sign, they drove through the rural town of Lawndale, or Colma, as it used to be known. The necropolis. In the distance, rolling hills were lined with cemetery after cemetery, each privately owned and operated. Graves aside, there wasn't much more in town but an athletic club, a train depot, and a downtown area filled with funeral homes.

Trotter's place was a fat two-story home. The scent of cleaning fluid greeted them at the door, along with a cheerless elderly secretary, who led them into Trotter's empty office.

"I'll tell him you're here," she said, as they perched on two visitors chairs in front of an old desk. Business licenses and funerary certifications hung in dusty frames along the wall. No urns in sight, but Hadley thought she possibly detected a strange energy; another crossbar might be here.

"You need anything?" the secretary asked. "Coffee? Water? I'm just about to lock up and leave for the day."

"Nothing, thank you," Lowe said, sounding weary and empty. Was he already in character? Now she wished she would've spent the ride over pressing him for more information on his plan instead of pining over him like a lovesick girl. As soon as the secretary closed the door, Lowe leaned closer and whispered, "You don't feel anything?"

"I don't want to talk about that here," she whispered back. "Later."

"What?"

She glanced at him. "What *what*?"

"I meant the amulet crossbar. Do you feel its presence?"

Her cheeks heated. "Yes, I believe so. But it's hard to tell. This place makes me anxious." She took off her hat and fanned herself.

The door to the office opened, and a portly blond man wearing an ill-fitting suit entered. He looked Hadley's age. Maybe younger. "Good evening, Mr. Smith," he said to Lowe, extending his hand. "I'm Bill Trotter."

Lowe shook and said, "This is my sister, Ruby."

Ruby? His nightclub floozy? What in the world was he playing at?

"Miss Smith," the young funeral director said, bowing his head. "I'm very sorry for your loss." He didn't sound all that sorry. If she didn't know any better, she might think he was looking her over. That didn't happen often. Maybe he recognized a kindred spirit whose life work also centered on death. "Won't you please sit down? I'll try to make this as easy for you as possible."

The man's chair creaked as he lowered himself into it. "Mr. Smith, I believe you told my secretary that your sister passed two days ago?"

"Poor Esmerelda," Lowe said. "We came home to find her bludgeoned on the parlor floor."

"Robbery?"

"Nothing was taken, so we don't really know why it happened. Only that she wasn't a well-liked person, to be honest. Always shooting her mouth off. There was no love between the three of us." He grasped Hadley's hand on the armrest; she had to fight every instinct not to jerk it back. "Ruby and I are close. We felt an obligation to take care of

Esmerelda, even though she's only our half sister. But I won't lie—it'll be more pleasant around the house now that we can keep her contained, so to speak."

Good heavens. Lowe was telling the man a version of his own father's myth—Hugo Trotter's siblings were bludgeoned and stabbed.

"I hope you don't find my honesty off-putting," Lowe added.

"Not at all, Mr. Smith. Not everyone who walks in this door is wracked with grief." He gave Hadley another glance. Or her legs, at least. She crossed them in the opposite direction and rearranged her dress over her knee.

Lowe cleared his throat. "Since I don't want to waste your time, I'll get right to the point. Esmerelda's body isn't viewable, which is why we'd like her cremated. But she did leave us a great deal of her father's fortune, so we'd like to"—he gave Hadley a secret smile—"shall I tell him, dear?"

"Please do." She had no idea where he was going with this ruse.

"Well, we'd like something extravagant to hold Esmerelda's ashes. A showpiece—not your usual fare. Something we can put on a shelf and raise a glass to now and then. Money is no object, God rest her soul."

Trotter brightened. "I'm sure we can find something to meet your needs. I have several unique pieces in stock. Would you like to see them?" He gave Hadley a hopeful smile. And another glance at her legs. Maybe he really was smitten with her.

They followed Mr. Trotter into a small showroom that featured a variety of urn options lined on shelves. Small paper placards provided pricing. A few of the urns were gaudy, but no strange energy, and no canopic jars.

"These are nice," Lowe said, running his hand along the marble of the most expensive urn on the wall. "But what we had in mind was something exotic. Maybe something Roman or Greek. Something classic."

"Something sculpted," Hadley added.

Trotter's brow lifted. "You know, my aunt Hilda's urn sounds a little like that. Only, it's sculpted in an Egyptian fashion. I—"

"O-oh, Egyptian," Lowe said, as if it were the most intriguing thing in the world. "That's very exotic. What do you think, Ruby?"

What she thought was that she wanted to brain him over the head with the marble urn he was stroking. "Egyptian would be perfect."

Trotter chuckled. "Well, I can't exactly dump out her ashes and sell it to you."

"Of course not," Lowe said with a smile. "But would it be too much trouble for us to take a look at it? Might give us a better idea of what we want. As I said, money is no object."

Trotter jingled change in his pocket as he rocked back on his heels. "Well . . ."

Lowe elbowed Hadley discreetly. She looked up at him and elbowed him back. He made an urgent face, dramatically flicking his eyes toward the funeral director when the man wasn't looking. She took a guess as to what he wanted her to do.

"Oh, please, Mr. Trotter," she said, trying her best to sound like a fetching young girl with nothing inside her head. "It would mean so much to us. So much to me."

Two pink circles blossomed on the man's cheeks. "The urn is downstairs in the basement, though. It might be upsetting to see my work area. Maybe I should bring it up."

"I have a strong stomach," she told him. "Nothing shocks me."

He smiled at her as if she'd just unlocked the key to his funeral-director heart. "This way, then."

EIGHTEEN

———— ⌣ ————

THE BASEMENT WAS ONE LARGE ROOM, LIT BY TWO ROWS OF hanging bulbs that weren't bright enough to chase away shadows in the corners. The cremation area took up one side, where a large iron door protruded from the brick wall lined with steel gurneys, rubber tubing, and ash shovels. Across the room near a desk, a wooden display cabinet held three objects on a single shelf. And even though age and smoke had discolored the glass front, obscuring the view, Hadley knew the Hapy canopic jar was one of the contained objects; she'd felt its eerie energy the moment Trotter opened the creaking basement door.

"Here's the urn," he said, unlocking the cabinet. "My father kept all the family urns here, and I just haven't bothered to move them somewhere else." He opened the doors and stepped aside to let them have a look.

The sand-colored canopic jar sat right in the middle, a baboon's head crowning the top.

"It's exquisite," Lowe praised.

"Perfect," Hadley agreed. "Exactly what we were looking for."

"Are you sure you won't sell it to us?" Lowe asked. "I feel just plain rotten for asking, but if you don't have any attachment to it, can't the ashes be transferred to another container?"

Mr. Trotter scratched his ear. "I really hate to tell a customer no—"

"I've got three hundred in cash in my pocket," Lowe added.

Trotter coughed, his face reddening. A strong temptation, to be sure—the amount was likely a solid three months' salary for a man of his class, and the most expensive urn upstairs was priced at twenty-nine dollars.

"It's very generous, but I'm sorry, Mr. Smith," he finally said. "I really can't, not for any amount. If my father were alive, he'd never forgive me. It was even mentioned in his will—he requested that I be a steward to these urns in exchange for inheriting the business."

Lowe sighed. "Can't blame a man for trying." He turned toward the case and slung an arm around Hadley's shoulders. "Maybe we can have one sculpted," he said, hugging her closer. "You're not crying are you, dear?"

Before she could think of a response, he kissed her cheek and whispered in her ear, "Distract him. Flirt."

Hadley's stomach knotted. Firstly, he was clearly planning on stealing the jar. She didn't see this going as well as it had at the house on Telegraph Hill—and that had gone *terribly*. Secondly, she was an awful flirt. George once told her that she wouldn't even be able to lure a child into a carnival if she held an oversized lollipop in one hand and cotton candy in the other.

She gave Mr. Trotter a forced smile over her shoulder and nervously turned around.

"I'm certain I can have another one made," Trotter assured her, studying her face as if checking for tears.

"If you could, that would be marvelous," she said. How in the world was she supposed to do this? She glanced at the oven in the far corner and fixed on the only topic of conversation she was comfortable pursuing. "Ah, so that's where it's done," she said, crossing the cement floor to inspect it. "Rather a solid-looking workhorse."

He followed her. "Yes. She's thirty years old, but still works wonderfully."

"Why, that's exactly my own motto."

Trotter's mouth opened. He sucked in a breath and chuckled. "An excellent one to have," he said, sweeping a glance over her body. "And no doubt it's true."

Perhaps this was easier than she'd feared. She gave him a coy smile and nodded to the oven. "I hope you don't think I'm macabre, but I'm quite interested in how it works."

"What a fascinating woman you are. I'd be happy to show you." Trotter enthusiastically pointed out where the bodies were placed, and when she begged to see the inner workings of the oven, he gladly turned on the pilot and struck a match. Orange fire roared inside the dark tunnel.

"Oh, my," she said. "How very—"

A crash behind them made her jump.

They both swung around to find Lowe crouching inside a cloud of dust in front of the cabinet. His coat was pulled up over his face.

"What in God's name?" Trotter shouted.

Hadley's pulse hammered inside her temples. She spied Lowe snatching up something from the broken shards on the floor and stuffing it inside his coat. He'd gotten the crossbar.

"I don't know what happened," Lowe said, waving away ash as he stood. "It slipped off the shelf."

"Oh my lord, my lord," Trotter said, reaching for a shard. "My father would never forgive me—this is terrible. Just terrible."

"I'm so sorry." Lowe glanced around the room, searching. "I'll compensate you."

"How?" Trotter stood, a look of fury tightening his face. "Just how in heavens do you plan on doing that? This can't be repaired. And you are stepping on my aunt's remains!"

Lowe gingerly stepped out of the ash pile, shaking out his pant legs and kicking his heels against the floor. "Let me give you the three hundred I'd offered previously."

"Your money won't fix this." The man was verging on hysterics.

Lowe reached for his wallet. "But it's a start, yes?"

A floorboard creaked above Hadley's head. Was someone upstairs? She glanced at the ceiling and spotted something dripping onto the floor. Something dark and viscous. It pooled on the cement in the middle of the room as a burning stench filled her nostrils. A strange heat warmed her back. She swiveled around to see a ball of flames shoot from the oven and arrow across the brick wall until it leapt on the pool of black liquid.

Uh-oh.

She watched in horror as flames roared, climbing several feet high in a flash. But this wasn't a simple fire. The strange inferno coalesced into a distinctly *human* shape—a shape which took a step forward, detaching itself from the floor, a fiery shadow come to life.

Like something out of an infernal hellscape, a behemoth of a figure solidified before them. A female. One that was a good two feet taller than Lowe, with tree-trunk legs and shoulders as big as a barge. The giantess stood in the center of the room, a monstrosity of blackened naked flesh with fire licking around its shoulders, hands, and feet.

In place of a human head was the head of a lion.

Hadley's academic mind put two and two together and vaguely recollected seeing photographs of ancient statues bearing lion heads. They all belonged to the Egyptian goddess of fire, Sekhmet.

The creature's back arched as she took a step toward Lowe, shaking the crematorium trolley with her heavy footfall. And that's when Hadley saw what fueled it. Hairline cracks in the creature's skin glowed with orange light, like lava flowing beneath furrowed dry earth. They spelled out some sort of hieroglyphic message—a spell, she reckoned, just like the one on the flesh of the griffin.

Not a goddess, but a magical replica of one.

Mr. Trotter screamed like a child. Lowe merely groaned and reached inside his jacket. But instead of pulling out his curved dagger, he retrieved a pistol.

The gun's report cracked through the air. The bullet went right through the fire giant and exploded the bricks a few inches from Hadley's arm. She shouted and stumbled against the cremation trolley, life flashing before her eyes.

"Shit!" Lowe shouted.

Mr. Trotter ducked behind the trolley, using it as a shield. Useless, cowardly man. So much for their passionate funerary bond.

"Shoot it in the heart! In the heart!" she shouted at Lowe, then added, "But don't kill me in the process!"

Lowe shifted his stance, backing up and rotating his aim. *Bam! Bam! Bam!*

He unloaded three bullets into the creature's torso, and all of them embedded into the wall near Hadley, showering Mr. Trotter's head with brick dust.

Whatever the creature was, it was different than the griffin. Not only did it make no sound, but at the bullet wounds, where there should be blood, a black substance oozed down its muscles.

The silent creature lunged for Lowe with a fiery hand and grabbed his shoulder. Lowe cried out. Flames erupted over the front of his coat as he growled and tore away from the monster's hold. The giantess faltered, losing her footing while Lowe stumbled backward and fell against Trotter's desk—

On fire! Lowe was on fire!

He flung off his hat and wildly slapped at the flames rippling over his arm.

Hadley sprinted for the cremation sink and twisted the rusty handle. Pipes creaked. Liquid spiraled through the rubber hose attached to the tap. She grabbed the end and aimed it toward Lowe. A spray of water arced through the air and doused Lowe in the eyes.

He jerked his head away and shouted obscenities in Swedish. Quickly redirecting her aim, she soaked his clothes and doused the flames.

"Not me!" he shouted as he hurdled himself over the desk. "Her!"

The creature made a grab across the desk, setting a stack

of files on fire. Hadley increased the water pressure with a thumb covering half the hose's opening and pointed the spray at the giant's face. Flames sizzled and popped. Steam rose.

It was working!

"Brilliant!" Lowe shouted. "Keep it up!"

The creature shuddered, twisting her neck back unnaturally as the water extinguished flames on one side of her head. A foul stench swept through the room, like wet cat and burned grease. Hadley's mind conjured the image of a rotting animal corpse being roasted on a spit, fur and all. And some chemical note lay beneath it, like a car overheating.

With his half-burned coat steaming and water dripping from his hair, Lowe skittered around the desk and stuck his gun in the waistband of his pants. He circled the giantess and dashed toward Hadley. "Let me have it," he said, reaching out his hand for the hose.

Lava-red eyes turned in their direction. Blackened flesh and fur shimmered under the hanging lights. Shimmered like oil. That was the chemical scent: motor oil! Was this also what had dripped from the ceiling before the creature formed?

Motor oil wasn't exactly something she associated with ancient Egypt or magical creatures. But she didn't have time to puzzle it out. The fire around the beast's shoulders roared up, spreading flames across its furry lioness crown. It was reigniting itself.

They were fighting a losing battle. The meager flow of water from the tap would never be enough to douse oil-fueled flames. Lowe ripped the hose out of her hands and sprayed the creature's face with a sharper stream of water. "Get Trotter out of here!"

Trotter could rot in his hiding space behind the trolley for all she cared, the whimpering coward. "I'm not leaving you here," she told Lowe.

"Believe me, I'm right behind you. Go!"

Begrudgingly, she tugged the funeral director's arm, shouting at him to stand. Once he was on his feet, he took off running for the basement stairs without a single look back. Good riddance. Hadley raced to Lowe's side and prepared to help him fight the best way she knew how.

She called for the Mori.

They stirred from the darkened corners, pushing their way out of the wall. As they were forming, dark faces turned toward the fire goddess. *Yes,* she thought. Take the damned creature down. She expected to feel their excitement, a sort of buzzing energy they gave off whenever she gave in and unleashed them, but it didn't come. Worse, she felt them cower, turning away from the creature as if it physically hurt them to look at the fire. Then they did something she'd never seen. They rejected her command and disappeared back into the walls.

If the Mori were afraid of the creature, what the hell were Lowe and Hadley doing standing there?

Lowe seemed to be thinking the same thing. With a grunt, he ripped the hose off the tap and flung the snaking rubber at the giantess. "Go, go, go!"

They raced up the stairs, Lowe urging her forward with a firm hand on her back, and surfaced on the main floor to find Trotter holding a kitchen knife in one hand and a telephone's earpiece in the other as he recited his address into the mouthpiece on the wall. "Sorry for the urn, Mr. Trotter," Lowe said, throwing a shower of bills at the man as they ran by. "We won't be needing your services after all."

Wood exploded.

Hadley turned to see the fire goddess at the top of the stairs. The basement door dangled on one hinge; flames leapt across the splintered wood. The creature stepped through it and swung her lioness head around, looking toward Trotter. He dropped the telephone earpiece and fled down the hallway and out of sight. The creature immediately fixed her eyes on them.

"She's after the crossbar!" Hadley shouted at Lowe as she backed away.

"And she's damn well not getting it—come on!"

NINETEEN

———— ❧ ————

LOWE GRABBED HADLEY'S HAND. THEY RAN THROUGH THE HALL
past Trotter's office, bursting through the front door into
cool night air. The hellish lion-headed giantess was dogging
them—no mistaking the boom of her feet pounding through
Trotter's house.

Want the amulet piece, don't you, old girl? he thought.
You'll have to catch me first, you sack of flaming shit.

He dug car keys out of his pocket as they raced toward
the silver Packard. The giantess smashed through Trotter's
front door. Christ. The sleepy town of Lawndale was going
to love seeing this. He unlocked the driver's door and shoved
Hadley inside, practically sitting in her lap before she had
time to scoot across the front seat. A moment later, the
engine roared to life. Tires squealed as he flicked on the
headlights and sped away.

"Good lord," she said, twisting around to peek out the
back window. "She's still coming."

Haloed in flames, the creature bounded after the Packard,
her bare feet scattering sparks over the asphalt. The Packard's engine protested when Lowe switched gears and

pushed it faster, but she didn't fail him. And as he put some distance between them and the creature, he kept his eye on the rearview mirror, watching the monster's frantic pace slow to a lope. Then a hobble. Then one of its legs seemed to give out, and the creature collapsed in the middle of the road and its body disintegrated into a roaring pyre.

"*Hurra!*" Lowe shouted excitedly, pounding the steering wheel with his fist. He grinned at Hadley. "Packard beats magic."

She flipped back around and melted into the seat. "That was a disaster. Poor Mr. Trotter."

"I gave him money—money that I couldn't really afford to throw away, at that. You're only upset because he was drooling over your legs."

"He was most certainly not."

"He was ready to drop to his knees and suck your toes."

"Don't be crude."

"Oh, pardon me. I thought you wanted to be treated like a man. Are you now wanting me to sanitize everything for your delicate feminine ears?"

She rolled her eyes and crossed her arms over her coat. Something was bothering her, and it wasn't him this time.

"You okay?" Lowe asked after a few seconds of silence.

Her eyes remained fixed on the road ahead as they headed back to the city. "You know that was Sekhmet's form."

"The breath that gave birth to the desert," Lowe said. "Yes, I recognized the likeness."

"And did you see the oil dripping from the ceiling before the creature formed?"

"What are you talking about?"

"I thought I heard someone upstairs right before, then a black liquid leaked from the rafters. The creature formed where it pooled on the floor. It seemed to be the substance on its skin. It was as if she were conjured or created out of that liquid."

Lowe thought about that for several moments. "At Gloom Manor, when I dropped the jar, the griffin didn't rise out of the ashes, so to speak. Remember how the parrots were fleeing it? It came from a distance."

"Yes."

"And if someone was upstairs in Trotter's office pouring some sort of hellish oil into the basement, then the jars aren't loaded with protective magic. Someone is following us and sending magical creatures—"

"To get the crossbar pieces," she finished. "Both times, the creatures were after the pieces. Can I please see it?"

Lowe fished the crossbar out of his pocket and handed it to her. She inspected it, reporting that it looked much the same as the first one, and that the magical symbols continued on the back. "It's real," she said, handing it back.

"I'll take it to Adam as soon as possible."

Oncoming headlights beamed a triangle of slow-moving light across the front seat as a car drove past. Lowe thought of all the trouble he'd had in Egypt when news of his discovery spread. But all of those attacks had been dumb and brute. No finesse. No magic.

Monk was still looking for him. And Lowe was counting on the fact that Monk had heard about the amulet—he needed Monk to trust that Lowe would be offering him the real deal and not a forgery to pay his debt. But Monk would stick a gun in his face or pressure Winter to drag Lowe into his office for a meeting. He wouldn't bother fooling around with stealth and magic. Especially not Egyptian magic. That significantly narrowed the possibilities.

He supposed it was possible a wealthy Egyptian had sent someone after him to steal the amulet. But how would any of these people know about their search for the crossbars? The only person who knew was Bacall, and it didn't make sense that he would he pay Lowe to find the pieces, only to go to all this trouble to steal them.

Something else troubled Lowe. Dr. Bacall had never told him why he wanted the complete amulet so badly. Yes, he'd claimed it was an obsession, and that it was something in the middle of a longtime quarrel between him and his old partner.

But he never would say what started the quarrel.

And then there was the warning Bacall's wife's spirit had given during Aida's channeling. She said to keep the amulet away from both Dr. Bacall and "Noel." Why? Maybe this was a question best put to Dr. Bacall. He made a mental note to do so before pain in his left arm suddenly became unbearable.

"What's the matter?" Hadley asked.

"Nothing."

"What?"

"I think I may have a small burn."

"Where?"

Lowe shifted his hand on the steering wheel and winced. Now that his victory buzz was wearing off, his body decided to tell him something was wrong. "My shoulder." He ducked his chin to get a better look at it. "Damned bitch burned a couple of holes right through my coat."

Hadley leaned surprisingly close and tried to inspect it, nearly blocking his view of the road. "When she grabbed you?"

"Apparently. Hurt like hell. Hurts worse now, to be perfectly honest."

"I've got first aid supplies at my apartment. I'll bandage you up."

He nearly ran off the road. Well. If he wanted a distraction from the pain, he certainly got one. Her apartment. Him. Her. Touching. Yes, please.

"No sense in paying for medical care if you aren't badly injured," she said in a defensive voice that made him want to grin deliriously. Oh, yes, please do argue your point, Miss That-Kiss-Can-Never-Happen-Again. Because a man and a woman didn't kiss each other like there was no tomorrow and then walk away. That was the kind of kiss that inspired poetry. Just the memory of it was inspiring something beneath the fly of his pants even now.

But another thought sobered his good mood. "If someone's following us, I don't want to lead them to your apartment."

"If someone's following us, they already know where I live," she said in a quiet voice.

That certainly didn't calm his fears.

Half an hour later, with his shoulder throbbing in pain, Lowe pulled into her building's entrance and parked the Packard in the shadow of a wall covered in climbing bougainvillea. It was nearly eight, and traffic up and down California Street was still brisk. He followed her into a swank lobby, where they entered an elevator.

"Mr. Walter must be on break," she surmised, looking at the crank mechanism as if it were an unsolvable math problem.

Lowe shut the scissor gate. "I think we can manage on our own. What floor?"

"Nine."

He flipped a switch and slowly moved the lever until they began ascending. Neither of them said a word, not even when they got to her floor and she unlocked her apartment.

"Mrs. Wentworth?" Hadley called out. No reply came. "My maid must have stayed with her daughter tonight. She only started last week, and we haven't got her schedule worked out."

She flipped a switch and a pair of etched sconces came to life on the nearby walls, casting light into the room. It was spacious and elegant, just as he suspected, all polished marble and clean, modern lines. It was also very formal. Not exactly a welcoming place to cozy up.

"I'll just get my supplies," she said, hanging up her coat and hat.

He glanced out the window while she rummaged in one of the back rooms. No new cars at the entrance. Nothing suspicious. Carefully peeling his wet coat off his injured arm, he surveyed the apartment. Very little furniture. No decor but a mirror and two paintings, which were fixed to the wall with corner brackets, as if she were afraid someone would try to steal them. Odd.

A radiator beneath the windows felt hot enough to dry his clothes. He shrugged off his vest and long sleeves and hung them over the radiator's fancy silver fins. His undershirt was mostly dry, but it wasn't every day that he found himself with a believable excuse to rid himself of clothes inside a woman's apartment. So he stripped to the waist and admired himself in the mirror for a moment—not bad at all, if he did say so himself—before turning to the side to wince at the burn on his arm. Then he plopped down onto a gray velvet slipper chair and stilled when he felt something brush up against his leg.

Hadley strode into the living room with her hands full and nearly dropped it all when her gaze landed on Lowe. Dear lord. He was half naked.

Yellow lamp light spilled over his bare torso. His body was strong and tightly muscled—a body that knew labor. Her gaze crept over burnished arms to an impossibly well-constructed broad chest and broader shoulders. Muscles everywhere. Muscles on his stomach—his *stomach*! And the middle of it was covered in golden hair that darkened as it arrowed beneath his belt buckle.

George certainly didn't look like that. In fact, she was quite sure every unclothed male torso she'd ever seen—and there weren't many, including her own father and the occasional movie star in the theater—were all lumps of dough and loose skin held up by a few bones.

They weren't *this*.

If her mind was impressed, her body was ecstatic. A tremor started in her chest and ran through her center, until she was hot all over. She licked dry lips and swallowed nothing. Tried to remember what she'd been doing before her knees had gone weak.

Deep breath.

She calmed down enough to notice Number Four. The damn cat was on his back, stretched out lengthwise on the seam between Lowe's closed thighs, all four paws in the air. Lowe slowly scratched the beast's belly.

"I guess that means you're welcome." She marched toward them, as if it were the most normal thing in the world that a beautiful man with the body of a god sat in her living room wearing nothing but his pants and shoes. "Though I should warn you that he's got a nasty biting habit. The building superintendent thinks he's a demon in disguise."

"Animals love me."

"Of course they do," she mumbled irritably. Animals, secretaries, her father. Lowe had everyone wrapped around his finger. She supposed she could add her name to the list.

"I wouldn't have taken you for a cat lover. What's his name?"

She set her armload down on the nearby end table. "Number Four."

He squinted for a moment before chuckling. "A curious cat, is he? Did he go through those first three lives before or after he came into your possession?"

"I didn't choose him. He chose me. Now I can't seem to get rid of him." She reached to scoop him up, but hesitated when she realized where her hands were headed. "How's the pain?"

"Fine."

"Liar."

"I thought we'd established that as an invariable fact." He groaned and plucked Number Four out of his lap, setting the cat down on the floor. "All right, if you want to know the truth, the pain's pretty goddamn awful."

Easy to believe when she tilted her head to get a look at the burn. Nasty. His left biceps were splotched with an angry red patch of blistered skin. "My God," she murmured. No telling how much he was hurting. "Would you like aspirin or whiskey?"

"Both."

She screwed off the cap and poured him a couple of fingers of scotch. "Would be funny if this was your brother's booze," she said, handing him several aspirin and the liquor. He downed it in one gulp.

"Didn't envision you as a big drinker." He handed her the empty glass.

"I'm not." But liquid courage might be needed if she was going to be near so much bare skin. Skin she'd have to touch if she was going to do this. So she poured herself a drink and tipped it back, shaking off the burn. Malted warmth spread through her stomach. "Every once in a while I can't sleep, and this does the trick. Though, I do try to avoid drinking while sawing."

His laugh sounded pained. "Wish I'd taken that advice. Don't be stingy."

She poured him another and opened a tin of ointment while he tipped the glass back a second time. "Better?"

"Much. But I have a feeling you're about to change that," he said, eyeing the scoop of salve in her fingers. "Be gentle, Nurse Hadley. I wouldn't want to faint on you."

"You aren't the only one." She knelt next to the chair. Her eyes darted to his nipples and the dusting of honey hair ringing them. Best to get this over with, and fast. "Take a deep breath."

As he followed her instruction, she swabbed the ointment over the top of his burn. He jumped, then stilled himself and spoke through gritted teeth. "Your furniture is bolted to the floor."

She flinched and reached for more ointment. "Yes."

"Mirror's bracketed to the wall."

"Yes."

"No chandeliers."

"Mmm." She gouged out another measure of ointment. Felt the scotch's pleasant warmth in her belly. Then she sighed and let the words come.

TWENTY

———⚜———

"MY FATHER CALLS THEM MORI SPECTERS," SHE SAID. "SHADES of death. I suppose they look a bit like ghosts made of smoke and shadow. I don't know if they are actual ghosts or demons or something else entirely." The ointment was cool on her fingers. She gently spread it over the rest of Lowe's burn. "I inherited them from my mother."

"That was the curse she spoke of when Aida channeled her spirit?"

Hadley nodded. "Once she died, they started showing up. Whenever I'd have temper tantrums, they'd float up from floorboards and attack the cause of my anger. They like to use nearby objects to inflict damage. Glass, wood, metal— whatever they can manipulate. When I called them up to attack the griffin, that was the first time I'd seen them attack something directly."

"I *knew* it," he whispered.

She kept her eyes down and cut a square of gauze with a pair of scissors. "My father says my mother never knew anything about their origins. They just started appearing to her one day after a trip my parents made to Egypt, apparently.

He said it must've been some bizarre mummy's curse. I never saw them until they started appearing to me. They're fueled by negative emotions. When I'm very angry, they are difficult to control. It's hard to explain. They . . ."

She sat back on her heels, reaching for the right words.

"They don't speak or communicate with me in any way," she finally said. "But it's as though they can pick out my thoughts and act on that information. And I can feel their energy. They're hungry, I guess you'd say. To be blunt, they want to hurt people. And if I loosened their leash and let them go wild, they wouldn't stop until they'd killed."

He didn't ask her how she'd tested this theory, and she was grateful for that. "So you have some control over them? Oww." He flinched and hissed as she covered the ointment with gauze.

"Sorry," she murmured. "And yes, a little. I didn't send them out specifically to pull that chandelier down, if that's what you're thinking. They are, well, I like to think of them as bounty hunters. My mind gives them the target name, and they do whatever they must to bring down the target."

"Are they here now?"

She shook her head. "Remember how Aida told us she had to summon my mother across the veil? I don't know for certain, but I feel like they live in another place, and they only come here when they catch scent of my emotional state."

"And these specters are the reason for your touching phobia."

Her hand stilled. "When I was thirteen, a family named Price lived next door to my father. Mrs. Price's cousin moved in with them. The man wasn't right in the head. He'd been arrested for crimes related to the molestation of children, but beat the charges on a technicality."

Lowe watched her without comment, so she continued.

"My father was having our downstairs floors polished. The doors were open for ventilation. Mr. Price's cousin walked into the house without anyone noticing, right as I was getting out of the bathtub upstairs." She took a deep breath and plunged through the rest of the story before she lost her nerve. "He pinned me to the floor. I was terrified. The Mori came so fast. He was horrible and crazy and I was frightened. Before I knew what was happening, the Mori caused his footing to slip on the wet tile as he was struggling to hold me down. His head smashed against the porcelain tub. He died almost instantly."

"Oh, Hadley," he whispered, his face twisting up in sympathy.

"To be clear, he never managed to do anything but hold me down. Had I been a normal girl, I suppose it would've played out differently. But it didn't, and the death was ruled accidental. My father wasn't angry, nor the Prices."

"And they damn well shouldn't have been," he snapped. The strength of his anger took her aback. "If a man like that lived next door to us, while Astrid was living in the house?" He shook his head. "I guarantee you it wouldn't be for long. And neither Winter nor I would be feeling any sort of remorse. Neither should you."

She tried to explain. "I'm not sorry I did it. It's just that my brain mixed up the fear I felt at the time with the guilt that came later. And I logically understand why, I suppose. But understanding something and changing it are two different things."

"Asking for help isn't weakness."

"It's more a matter of trust. Not just trust in someone else, but in myself."

"Maybe fixing one also repairs the other," he said with a soft smile.

"Perhaps." Neither one of them said anything for a long moment. She snipped off a longer strip of gauze and wound it around his arm to hold everything in place.

"And you're the only person who sees them?" he asked.

"Pardon?"

"The Mori."

"Every once in a while, I run across someone else who can. One of my maids could. She quit after she saw them— was terrified out of her mind. My father used to see them, before the blindness. Oh, and Oliver Ginn saw them at the dinner party."

He growled. "Moneypants?"

"He seems to believe they're a kind of trickster spirit created by Set."

"The Egyptian god?"

She nodded. "Apparently there's a myth that Set harvested a group of soul shadows to wreak havoc in the underworld."

"*Sheuts.*"

"You've heard about this myth?"

"Not just a pretty face, you know," he said, and her eyes involuntarily flicked over his muscled chest. She looked away and busied herself with taping up her bandaging while he continued. "The Nubi workers at the site used to tell stories of spirits that would change into black dogs to trick wandering strangers into losing their way in the desert. Some said they were made out of shadow. Called them *Sheuts.*"

"So Oliver might be on to something?"

"Oliver," he said, as if it were a bad word. "You're talking to him about this? What is he to you, Hadley?"

"And I might ask what *Ruby* is to you." Now finished with the bandage, she pushed herself up to stand.

"I already told you."

She threw the roll of tape down in frustration. "You told me you were going to take her dancing, and then you used her name for my disguise in front of Mr. Trotter. Probably half of what you tell me is a lie—how am I supposed to separate fact from fiction when it comes to you?"

His hand grabbed hers. She jumped and tried to pull away, but his grip was like steel. "Let go! You're hurting me." He wasn't, really, but panic had a way of scrambling things in her head.

"Goddammit! Stop struggling and listen to me for one second."

The exasperation in his voice startled her. She stilled, her breath coming fast and hard.

"You're right," he said, lessening the intensity of his grip.

"I'm a liar, and we both know it. But even if I weren't, I'd never be an upstanding man. My family are immigrants. I grew up poor. I'm not part of your circle of society and never will be, no matter how much money and power we have."

"Money and power don't make a man trustworthy."

"And not everything I say is a lie. Let's make a deal, you and me, *ja*?" His voice softened. "Remember when we stood in the courtyard by the gazing pool? I told you the truth about my injury. No one else—only you. And I said I was worried that women would find this hand repellent, and you told me the right woman wouldn't care. Do you remember?"

"Yes."

He pulled her closer. "See, I've got this funny idea in my head that you might be that right woman. Someone who won't reject me when I touch her."

Raw emotion tightened her throat.

"See this hand?" He gently squeezed her fingers, drawing her attention to the scarred skin where his missing finger once was. "Just like I told you the truth that night about my injury, from now on, whenever I hold your hand with this one, you can trust what I'm telling you is the truth. I promise to give you that. Do you believe me?"

Hadley's heart drummed inside her breast. She lifted her gaze to his. "I can try. I want to."

"That's all I'm asking." He lifted her hand to his lips and kissed her knuckles, sending a chill up her arm. Blue eyes squinted up at her with disarming intensity. "Now, let me prove it. I'm holding your hand, so tell me what truths you need from me right now. You need to know that I won't tell anyone about your secrets? I won't tell a soul. But you already knew that, or you wouldn't have confessed."

"You aren't afraid of me, now that you know?"

"Afraid of whatever it is you call up? Abso-goddamn-*lute*-ly. Every man's afraid of the unknown. But I'm not afraid of *you*, and that's the difference. What else, Hadley?" He pulled her closer, until her legs brushed against his. "You brought up Ruby. You want to know about her? Because there's nothing to tell. I'm not interested in renewing anything with

Ruby, which is partly why I haven't answered her calls. But mostly, I haven't had time. Seems lately I've spent most of my days with you, and I've spent most of my nights thinking about the days."

"Lowe." She tried to say something more, but nothing came out.

A second later, he let go of her hand, only to wrangle her around the waist, pulling her down to sit sideways on his lap. His chest was a warm brick wall against her shoulder. So much bare skin. A little shiver of panic raced through her as one hand slid around her back and settled on her hip. The other tilted her chin toward his face.

His voice was low and firm. "I understand why you're uncomfortable with other people touching you, but you can't be that way with me, and that's all there is to it. Because when I told you in the car that it didn't matter if you weren't interested in me, I lied. It *does* matter. It matters a lot." He slowly released her chin. "Did you lie to me when you said you never wanted to kiss me again?"

Her gaze dropped to his chest as she whispered, "Yes. I lied."

The muffled noise from the yawning city outside her windows sounded far away as she listened to his breath. Movement stirred against her thigh. But with her nerves stretched tight, it took her several moments to comprehend what was happening—plenty of time for him to gentlemanly move away or shift positions. He clearly had no intention of doing so.

Good God.

Her face heated in embarrassment, but that quickly changed into something else when her nipples stiffened into hard points. Her hands lay in her lap. She clenched them, fingernails biting into her palms, as she pressed her thighs together, praying he wouldn't touch her.

Praying he would.

He brushed a slow touch along the curve of her shoulder and spoke in a deep, rough voice. "You've made yourself a fine little island, not getting close to people, haven't you? But you can't survive like that forever. I think I'm going to have to send out a rescue boat and haul you back onto the mainland."

"Lowe."

He nuzzled his nose into her hair and inhaled. "This is what's going to happen. You're going to kiss me. And I'm going to touch you."

"I—"

"Nuh-uh-uh," he warned. "I'm in charge now, Miss Bacall. Here, hold my hand again so you can be sure I'm not lying . . ." He forced open one of her fists and threaded three long fingers between hers. "This hand only, that's all I'll use. We won't move from this chair, and I promise not to touch any skin. I'll only touch you over your clothes. That's all. Nothing more. Agreed?"

"Over my clothes?"

"Yes."

"Where?" she whispered, and immediately regretted the question.

He whispered back, lips brushing her ear. "Wherever I choose. Yes?"

Her heart galloped inside her chest. "Yes."

"Good." His lips grazed hers. "Now, kiss me like you did on the wharf."

She hesitated, but only for a moment.

A carnival of current jolted through her center when their mouths met. Lips pressed against lips. Closed. Firm. A tentative investigation that soon opened to something deeper. Not rough and breathless like their last kiss. A slow-moving, rolling one that tasted of scotch—but sent a hotter flame through her belly than the liquor had. She was lightheaded and stupid within seconds, melting against him.

His fingers untwined from hers. She pulled out of the kiss.

"Now, now," he chastised. "If you stop kissing me, my promise goes out the window."

How absurd. She was not playing these games with—

He clamped a hand around her bare arm and slid it upward, into her sleeve. "Will you kiss me, or shall I touch your bare skin like this?"

No-no-no-no! She anxiously pressed wet lips to his to stop him.

"Good girl," he whispered into her mouth before swiping his tongue over hers. His hand abandoned the skin of her arm and moved to the safety of her waist. But it didn't linger there long. She felt its warmth tracing a slow line down over her hip, and up again. Up further, brailling over her side.

Old, critical words from George resurfaced, and for a moment she worried he'd feel her ribs and think her too skinny. But there was no hesitation in his touch. No recoil or pause in his kiss. He touched her like he enjoyed what he found, and when his fingers curved over a breast, all her old worries dropped away.

"Mmm," he said against her lips. "A nice palmful. Just enough." His thumb found the hard peak of her nipple. Pleasure shot through her. She gasped. He groaned, pushing his erection into her hip. A joyful sort of carnal amusement weighted his voice. "Feels good, does it? Let's try the other. Put your arm around my neck." As she did, he pinched a nipple, worrying it back and forth through the fabric of her dress. Her legs wantonly parted like the Red Sea in front of Moses. She nearly fell off his lap.

"C'mere," he whispered, shuffling her around to face him.

"Your burn," she protested.

"Hush, Nurse Bacall." He pulled one leg across his lap until she straddled him like she was riding his motorcycle, dress rucked up around her thighs. Only, instead of a cold metal bar threatening the vee between her legs, the tented bulge of his erection loomed between them. A very significant bulge. The academic part of her wanted to reach between them and run her hand over it for analysis.

Shocked at the thought, she looked away and circled his neck with her arms to keep herself in check. Dear lord, his body was hot. "Lowe—"

"Rule still stands. No skin. I just need to feel this." He helped himself to two handfuls of her backside, kneading her flesh with abandon. "Lush." He wiggled her cheeks in his hands. "Best ass I've ever seen in my life. God*damn*, you feel incredible."

It felt incredible to her, too. All her muscles had turned to jelly.

"What've you got back here? More peacock feathers?" He craned his neck over her shoulder and lifted her dress before she could protest. "Purple. Are those grape vines?"

She reached back to pull her dress down. "Don't make fun."

"Believe me, I'm not. I've fantasized about your fancy lingerie since the first night I met you." He swept his hands up and down her back while he nipped at her neck, just under her ear. She groaned in surprise, and that was distraction enough to overlook his straying hand until it was now already under the front of her dress, sliding over her stocking.

"Oh, God," she murmured.

"No skin," he assured her, sounding almost gleeful with victory as he came to the rubber garter clamp holding up the top of her stocking. He slowed there and walked his fingers up the narrow garter, chuckling low when she meeped in distress. Then he found what he'd been hunting. Over her tap pants, he cupped her and slid a finger over the silk between her legs.

She lifted off his lap and cried out, her back bowing as she shuddered in pleasure. He kept a steady arm around her waist, holding her in place.

"Soaking wet. My, my," he whispered, slowing rubbing the damp fabric back and forth over her clitoris. "Right here?"

Her head fell against his shoulder. "Yes."

"Mmm. I feel it through the silk. Think you're almost as hard as I am."

Good God. No one had ever talked to her so candidly. A shaky inhalation was her answer.

"Want to know a secret?" he whispered, changing the direction of his fingers, side to side. "I stroke myself to sleep every night thinking of you."

His words sent an electric bolt of pleasure through her center. She rested her brow against his. "God . . . *Lowe.*"

"You feel marvelous. So damn marvelous." Fingertips slid farther back, and even with the barrier of her tap pants limiting his explorations, he did his best to dip into the wetness pooling at her center. Nice, but not as nice as what he'd been doing.

"Please don't stop."

"Yes, ma'am, so sorry," he said, not sounding sorry at all, but returning to his previous ministrations and rubbing her sensitive bud. "I couldn't help myself. Better?"

He knew it was. She bowed her head, cheek against cheek, and moaned.

It had been so long since she'd been touched this way. So very long.

And it felt so spectacular and new that she wondered if she'd ever been touched at all—everything in the past was a dream and this was her new reality. The standard by which any other touch should be measured.

"Tell me how it feels," he demanded.

"So good" was all she could manage, but he made a pleased noise in the back of his throat, as if it were exactly what he wanted to hear. So she repeated it like a mantra between hard breaths until—

What was that noise?

The door. *The door!*

"No, no, no!" She jumped off his lap to pull her dress down before moving in front of the chair, as if she could block the view of a six-and-a-half-foot-tall Scandinavian with no shirt and an enormous erection.

Keys jingled as an elderly woman with white hair stepped into the apartment. She looked up and stopped dead in her tracks, eyes big as dinner plates.

Hadley straightened her posture and pasted on a smile. "Good evening, Mrs. Wentworth."

TWENTY-ONE

LOWE PRETENDED TO LEAVE. HE PARKED THE PACKARD ACROSS the street and sat in the driver's seat half the night, watching Hadley's apartment building to make sure they hadn't been followed. No flaming lioness goddesses, no suspicious cars. The lights in Hadley's windows flicked off. Maybe she was in bed now. After conjuring the memory of her moaning on his lap, he unbuttoned his fly and pleasured himself in the darkened car until he came on his hand, hoping she was doing the same, nine stories above him. When the milkmen began making their rounds in the wee hours of the morning, he finally went home and slept.

The next afternoon, he headed into the Fillmore District and stashed Lulu in a new hiding place. Then he walked a meandering path to ensure he wasn't being tailed. Along the way, he smelled something achingly familiar and stopped in front of a florist. Wooden buckets of greenhouse tulips and daisies lined the sidewalk, but he looked past them and spotted the star-shaped Siberia lilies. A middle-aged blond woman brushed off her hands. Norwegian, he guessed, from the flag in the window. "Like a bouquet for your sweetheart?" she asked.

"Not a bouquet, but I do have something in mind."

"Anything you want, we can do," she said, waving him inside.

Fifteen minutes later, he emerged from the shop and headed down a side street to Adam's. Stella looked up from her doll party and spied him at the back door before running to greet him.

"Hello, Miss Goldberg," he said, hauling her into his arms as Adam appeared.

"Found another piece to that amulet, did you?" Adam said with a grin. "Let's see it."

After returning Stella to her dolls, Lowe gave his friend the second crossbar and inspected the finished copy he'd made of the base. An exact match. Even Hadley might be fooled, though this particular thought made him feel a little guilty. More than a little, truth be told.

"What's the matter with you?" Adam asked after the pieces were stashed in the vault.

"Had a long night, that's all."

"Are you sure? Because the way you're smiling and frowning at the same time, it looks like you're either ill or doped up. Maybe both."

Lowe slouched in his chair. "How did you know Miriam was the one?"

Adam stared at him for a long moment. "Oh, no."

"Look, I'm not saying I have feelings for anyone."

"For Hadley," Adam corrected.

Lowe groaned. "I'm just saying I *think* there might be the chance that what I once thought was just lust could be something more. Maybe. Possibly."

"You think? Listen, you either have feelings or you don't."

He ran a hand over his face and rubbed the heel of his palm over a brow. "I just advanced a florist one hundred dollars."

"Are you mad? That was—"

"Stupid."

"Most definitely stupid."

Lowe's shoulders slumped. "It really was." Then again, he had a long history of making stupid mistakes. Maybe this was nothing out of the ordinary.

Hadley rarely made stupid mistakes, so she had to assume that her inability to add simple numbers and use the telephone without accidentally hanging up on the caller were indirectly related to the time spent on Lowe's lap. And her newfound stupidity continued to hobble her throughout her workday. The other curators squinted at her like there was dirt smeared on her face. George asked why she was smiling to herself. Her father—blind, at that—suspected illness and suggested she go home and rest.

Rest was the last thing she needed. She was wound tighter than a cheap watch, bursting at the seams with an antsy sort of elation.

But as the hours passed, all that elation shifted into a nervous anticipation that created a dull fog over her brain. When five o'clock finally came, and she was on her way out of the office, she found herself standing at the front desk while Miss Tilly slowly repeated what she'd already said twice, looking at Hadley as if she'd lost her mind. Maybe she had.

She stared at the secretary's hand in disbelief, her insides jumping with glee. "For me?" she said dumbly, finally catching on to what the woman was telling her.

"I know. I thought the same thing," Miss Tilly said before glancing up at Hadley's irritated reaction. "Oh, no—I didn't mean that no one would ever send you flowers, it's just that no one has."

"Yes, I'm quite aware, but thank you for the reminder," Hadley said dryly. "Who brought it into the building?"

"A delivery boy. He was sort of handsome," the secretary said, flouncing her too-perfect strawberry hair. "Anyway, he said I could expect to see him a lot, because the gentleman who ordered it paid for daily delivery." *Daily?* "Every kind of lily they can get their hands on, a different one each day." She handed Hadley the single oriental lily, snowy white and smelling both sweet and spicy. On its long stem, a brilliant purple ribbon was tied in a bow. "Terribly romantic, don't you think?"

Hadley had no experience with which to judge such a thing, but her heart was beating so fast, she feared she might break down and do something embarrassing, like laugh inappropriately or twirl in circles. It was all she could do to squeeze out a disinterested, "Mmm."

"Is it from Mr. Ginn?" Miss Tilly whispered, wide eyes blinking with interest.

"Probably," Hadley lied. She knew exactly whom it was from, and why no card was provided. After all, her father couldn't find out they were working together.

She bid the secretary good night and stepped out into the parking lot. Should she call Lowe? They didn't make plans after Mrs. Wentworth walked in on their erotic tête-à-tête last night. And though Hadley expected to find the woman's resignation when she got home, she was more concerned about what to expect from Lowe. He said a lot of things that pointed to something of substance between them, but her mind still tugged her back to his casual "I'll just call Ruby" speech from their trip to Lawndale. And though he'd flat-out told her he wasn't interested in Ruby or any other girl, doubt lingered.

Because if she let herself believe in the possibility that he meant everything he said in her apartment, a dark fear whispered that she'd be setting herself up for disappointment.

Normal women probably didn't have these obsessive reservations. And if Hadley wanted a shot at being normal, she reckoned she'd better shake off the fear and figure out what she wanted from Lowe. She sniffed the lily and pictured his muscled chest and arms.

I stroke myself to sleep every night thinking of you.

She glanced around guiltily, as if passersby could hear her thoughts.

All the tumbling joy and the nervous anticipation and the heavy fog swirled around her head like a mad game of musical chairs. If she wasn't careful, she might trip over her own feet. So she pushed his words from her thoughts and focused on heading to the spot her usual taxicab sat every day at five. Standing on the sidewalk between her and the waiting yellow car was Oliver Ginn.

"Pretty flower," he said, hands shoved in his pockets.

"Hello, Oliver."

"Who gave it to you? That Magnusson fellow? He seemed awfully territorial that night at the Flood Mansion party. I would've thought you preferred brains over brawn."

She brushed off the insult. "If you wanted to send me flowers, nothing was stopping you. Instead, you send me strange books."

A wounded look flashed over his face. "I thought you liked books."

"I do," she said, wishing he wouldn't make her feel so guilty. "Where did you find it? No author was listed."

"It's something from my family's library. Did the passage strike a chord?"

"How did you see what you claimed to see at the Flood Mansion party and associate it with that particular myth?"

He exhaled heavily. "If you want to know the truth, I've seen them before."

The muscles in Hadley's neck tightened. "Where?"

"Someone I used to know," he said, removing his hat. "Someone I used to care about. I didn't understand what was happening at the time, but I've since learned things. And I can help you, I promise. If you give me a chance, there are so many things I could teach you. So much I could show you."

He sounded so sincere, and if it were any other matter but this, she might give him the benefit of the doubt. "I've never even heard of another person plagued by such a thing. And yet, you've somehow met two of us?"

"When I first came into town, I heard rumors from other curators about strange things happening in the de Young Museum. All of those rumors seemed to lead me to you."

Anger swelled. The edges of her vision darkened. "You courted me under false pretenses?"

"No! I was curious, of course, but when I saw you, everything changed. My entire world opened up. Look at you—brilliant and strong. A scholar who's not afraid to make her mark in a man's world. Just like your mother."

"My mother?"

"I know you say you don't remember her, but surely you've read about her achievements. That photograph of her standing in front of the temple at Karnak with your father was printed in a dozen publications—you look just like her. It's uncanny."

Yes, her father had often said the same thing when he was feeling sentimental. But when Hadley looked at her mother's image, all she saw was the woman who had paid her nanny.

"Everyone said your father stood upon her genius, and you have that same spark," Oliver insisted, his hand reaching out for her face. "And so much more."

She drew back sharply. "I'm sorry to disappoint you, but I am *not* my mother's daughter. Nor am I some curiosity to be studied."

His dark brows knitted. "Of course you aren't. And I can't apologize enough for not telling you sooner that I knew about your gift. It's just that I wanted to make sure the rumors were true, and I wanted you to trust me. I'm not interested in you as a curiosity or a whim. I truly believe fate brought you into my life. Fate brought us together," he insisted, reaching out unexpectedly to trace her jaw with the tips of his gloved fingers. "You're not cursed, Hadley. You're blessed. Let me into your life, and I'll prove it."

His hand curled around the back of her neck. He leaned in before she could pull away. Cool lips pressed against hers, unyielding and insistent. Tobacco and the strong scent of bay rum smothered her senses as a keening anxiety turned her muscles to stone.

Everything inside her screamed *no!* And that was enough

to tear her out of her panic. She shoved at his chest and stumbled backward, wiping her mouth on her coat sleeve. Good God. If she ever had any doubt about the lack of spark between them, she certainly didn't now.

Wrong man. Absolutely the wrong man.

Jaw slack, he blinked as if dazed for several moments. His chest heaved with labored breath. Then his mouth warred with a manic smile. "Oh, Hadley. My darling—"

"I'm late for an appointment." She brushed by him and headed toward the waiting cab.

"If you give me a chance, I will give you the world," he called out behind her. "And instead of suppressing your gift, you can be what you were born to be."

What exactly he thought that was, she didn't bother to ask.

Lowe followed Dr. Bacall's butler through a drafty Russian Hill mansion. The old man sat in a wheelchair on a closed-in porch that overlooked a sizable backyard for this part of the city, and, in the distance, San Francisco Bay, shrouded in dusk. A fine view, no doubt, but the blind man couldn't see it. And yet he faced a large window as if he could still picture it all, a plaid blanket over his lap and a cup of steaming tea in his hands.

The servant announced Lowe.

"How are you, m'boy?" Bacall said, seemingly glad for the company.

"I'm sorry to bother you right when you've just gotten home from your workday, but I was hoping you might have a minute to answer some questions."

"Sit," the man said. "I'll be glad to help however I can. Tell me about the search while you're at it. Do you have good news?"

Lowe pulled a wicker chair closer to Bacall and tossed a glance toward the door to ensure servants weren't lingering. "I've found the second crossbar."

"Indeed?" Bacall grinned. "That's marvelous!"

"Yes, but I'm a little worried about looking for a third piece." Lowe set his hat on his lap. "Someone nearly killed me. I'm being tracked, and not in the usual manner. Someone's using a very specific kind of magic to try to steal the crossbars."

The man stilled. "What do you mean?"

"Someone who has the power to manifest mythical Egyptian chimera."

The surface of the tea inside Dr. Bacall's cup wobbled, but he didn't answer.

"When my sister-in-law channeled your wife, her spirit warned me to keep the amulet away from Noel. I'm going to take a wild guess and assume this is your old excavation partner."

Bacall nodded. "Noel Irving."

"Perhaps it's time for me to know exactly why you want the amulet so badly and what it has to do with this man."

"You won't believe me."

"Won't I? I was nearly burned alive by an Egyptian fire goddess. And before that, a griffin tried to peck my eyes out. So maybe you'd better tell me who I'm dealing with so I have a better idea about what kind of magic I'm up against."

After using one hand to find a side table by touch, Bacall set his tea down with shaky fingers. "Tell me, Mr. Magnusson. Do you believe a woman can be in love with two men at the same time?"

Lowe's jaw tightened. "No, I don't."

"I once shared that sentiment." Bacall sighed deeply and leaned back in the wheelchair. "But I suppose I should start from the beginning. Back when Noel and I were still friends, in the late eighteen hundreds, he was terribly interested in the occult, and dabbled in magic to mixed success. Little spells to increase our luck in finding treasure, or to create light in a dark tunnel—nothing extraordinary. Though, looking back years later, I often wondered if he used a love spell to coerce my wife into sleeping with him. Or maybe that's just my pride talking."

Lowe shifted in his seat, feeling extremely uncomfortable. "I'm sorry."

"You and me both. But they were lovers for several years. I suspected, but didn't know for sure until 1898. I left Noel to watch over Vera in Cairo while I traveled for a month. When I came back, I found them both seriously ill with a local infectious disease. They needed Western medicine but were too weak to get out of bed, much less travel. The local doctor said they had days to live, if not hours. Noel begged me to fetch a witch he'd met on our previous trip."

"And you did?" Lowe asked in a quiet voice.

"I felt I had no choice. Vera was several months pregnant with Hadley. If she died, I'd lose them both."

"Christ."

Bacall shifted in his wheelchair. "So I tracked the witch down. She said she could save them from death, but there would be consequences. You don't upset the natural order of things without paying a price."

"There's always a catch," Lowe murmured.

"Indeed. And this one was eight years," Dr. Bacall said. "Eight extra years of life, then they'd die. That was the curse. What could I do? Watch them die in front of me? Lose my unborn daughter? I was out of my mind with grief—over their betrayal, over the loss of my innocence and trust in the two people I cared most about in the world."

Bacall shook his head, remembering, then sighed deeply and continued.

"The witch pulled them both back from death's grip and saved Hadley in the process. I was elated for a time. It wasn't until much later that I learned the true nature of that magic and what had gone wrong. Because the spell, you see, was intended to make the recipient deathless."

"Deathless?"

"Indestructible. For eight years, anyway. And I saw it with my own eyes. Death wouldn't touch Noel. He would not bleed out from a stabbing, nor die from a bullet. Disease and poison had no effect. I pushed him off a cliff in 1901.

He fell several hundred feet, brushed himself off, and walked away."

Dear God.

"Terribly inconvenient for me, as the more I learned about the length of their affair, and how much my wife still cared for him, I was rather sorry I saved him. The only thing I wanted in those ensuing years was to bury the bastard—and it was the one thing I couldn't do."

"And your wife had this same advantage? This death-lessness?"

"No." The blind man felt around the table for his tea and took a sip. "My wife seemed perfectly normal. Human. And Hadley was born healthy. Nothing was amiss. I began to hope perhaps she got lucky, and that since Noel got the curse's blessing, he'd also be the one to pay its price after eight years—that Vera would live a normal life."

The old man shook his head and continued.

"But eight years is a long time when you're young. And spell or no spell, Vera just would not give Noel up. She insisted she loved us both equally, but would leave both Hadley and me if I forced her to end the affair. I couldn't risk that. If she wouldn't leave him, I figured I'd just take him off the playing field. So, two years into the curse, I began searching for a way to kill a man who can't die."

"The amulet," Lowe whispered.

Bacall nodded. "If it were assembled, I could call up a door and Noel would be claimed. Maybe it would be enough to pay the ferryman, so to speak. Or, if nothing else, Vera might borrow Noel's extra years once he was out of the picture."

"So you searched for the amulet and found the crossbars, but you couldn't find the base."

"Exactly. I sent them home, hoping to keep them hidden from Vera. But she was smart. And she couldn't bear to lose Noel, which is why she hid the crossbars when she realized what I was planning on using them to do. She couldn't let me kill him."

Lowe remembered Vera's words during the channeling,

warning Hadley to keep the amulet out of both men's hands. "But after she hid the crossbars, the earthquake hit."

"Exactly eight years to the day that the witch had cast the curse on them," Bacall said. "I arrived home from England an hour before the earthquake struck." Unseeing eyes blinked away tears. He shook his head and composed himself. "As you can see, this house survived both the quake and the Great Fire. But Vera was not so lucky."

He leaned toward Lowe, as if he could see him. "You see, the spell was meant for one person—not two. And because it was cast on both Vera and Noel at the same time, the magic split. My partner got the advantageous part of the spell—the immunity from death. And my wife's soul was dragged into the underworld, harvested by dark reapers."

Hadley's Mori.

"And as if that weren't enough," Bacall continued, "not only did these reapers take my wife's life, they somehow got passed along to my daughter. I suppose it's because Vera was pregnant with Hadley when the original spell was cast, because after my wife died, the spirits started appearing to my daughter."

Christ. Mummy's curse, he'd told Hadley all these years.

Anger tinted Bacall's voice. "You can't fathom how shocked I was to see them again after they'd taken Vera's life. I thought they'd come to take Hadley, too. But no. They were just attached to her, appearing for short times, then disappearing. It was as if she was being haunted by ghosts—ghosts that never seemed to scare her, even when she was a child."

"Did she see her mother taken by them?"

"No, and I never told her. You can't imagine how terrifying it was to watch them following my daughter around like hellhounds. They are a plague. Nasty, evil creatures. They'd taken my wife, and for eight years after Vera's death, I was terrified they'd take Hadley, too. I prepared for the worst, waiting for them to turn on her."

"But they didn't," Lowe said quietly.

Bacall shook his head. "They seem to be merely bound

to her without purpose. I've come to believe they are still hanging around because of Noel. He tricked death. That spell should've taken his life, too—not just Vera's. But as long as he's alive, Hadley bears the burden of the specters."

They may not want Hadley's life, but they were still hungry to reap souls. Lowe nearly said this out loud, but caught himself. In Dr. Bacall's mind, Lowe barely knew Hadley at all. And if the man got an inkling of what Lowe had been doing to his daughter? Well, he damn sure could take away the dangling check, couldn't he?

"We haven't spoken for years, Noel and I," Bacall said. "But I knew he'd heard about your discovery of the amulet base, because a week after it appeared in the papers, I received an anonymous note telling me I'd never see the amulet rejoined with my own eyes. Later that day I lost my sight."

"The blindness is magically induced?"

"Quite. I believe the spell was embedded into his note. And it's degenerative. I seem to be aging at an inhuman rate. He's slowly killing me."

Lowe exhaled a long breath. "And there's nothing you can do to stop the aging?"

"All my hope rides on the amulet. If he dies, I live—if he lives, I die. It's not just revenge anymore. It's both self-preservation and concern for Hadley's well-being. If I die, I'm not sure what he might do to her."

As long as Lowe was still breathing, not a damn thing.

Christ. He now understood why Bacall was willing to part with a small fortune to obtain the amulet. And consequently, why Noel Irving would go to any lengths to stop him. Lowe would have to give Bacall the real amulet—not Monk. That's all there was to it. He'd figure out some way to make it work. He always did.

"Where can I find your partner?"

Bacall shook his head. "He officially dropped off the map after Vera died. I can tell you where he might be hiding, but if he's trailing you, you're going to need to seek out some stronger protection."

Lowe began to assure the man that he would, but Bacall seemed to struggle with several breaths. Sweat broke over the man's brow. "Are you all right?" Lowe asked.

"My neck seems to be—" The blind man slammed a fist to his own chest and clutched at his shirt before his body began slipping out of the wheelchair.

TWENTY-TWO

———❧———

HADLEY GLANCED UP AT THE OVERSIZED CLOCK IN THE HOSPITAL waiting room after the doctor strode away. It was nearly midnight, and she and Lowe were the last people sitting on a cold bench in a long, sterile hallway. She could hardly believe mere hours had passed since she'd gotten Lowe's phone call. It seemed like days. But now that she could finally take a moment to exhale and relax her alert posture, her mind decided to crackle into action.

"Only a mild heart attack," Lowe said at her side. "You heard the doctor. It happens all the time. Some people never even seek medical help."

"Yes, but those people aren't having the life sucked out of their bones by a madman wielding dark magic."

"It was likely just the natural progression of the original aging spell, not a new attack."

"Not much of a consolation."

"And he'll be able to come home in a day or two," Lowe said. "He's going to be fine."

"For how long?"

"Long enough for us to either find his old partner and

send him to the bottom of the Bay in a bag filled with rocks, or to find the last two crossbars." He ducked to catch her gaze. "Listen to me, Hadley. We won't fail him."

She slumped against the stiff bench and sighed. "All of this is simply overwhelming. The heart attack and everything he told you before it happened. I'm torn between feeling sorry for my father and selfishly angry with him for not telling me sooner. And the worst part is that I have to pretend I don't know."

"Perhaps you can sort it out with him when this is over."

She nodded, but her mind was elsewhere. In the stress of the last few hours, she'd completely forgotten about something. Now it hit her like a punch to the gut. "Lowe? You're going to think I'm mad, but . . ."

"Madness is in the eye of the beholder. Try me."

"You said my father called his former partner 'deathless,' and that nothing could kill him."

"Yes."

"Are we to assume that means the man doesn't age?"

Blue eyes slanted her way. "I didn't ask, but anything's possible."

"Oliver confronted me at the museum this afternoon." She told him everything he'd said. Told him about the kiss. Lowe made a low, growling noise in the back of his throat. "I pushed him away," she argued. "It wasn't reciprocated, and he's never been that brash before. It's just you've told me all this about my mother and Noel Irving, and Oliver said . . ." She looked up at Lowe, too shocked to finish.

"Impossible," Lowe mumbled. He swiped a hand over his hair and jostled his foot nervously. "I mean, you've seen photographs of your father's partner, haven't you?"

"Yes, but the man had a beard and mustache. Besides, all those photographs are from the turn of the century—all blurry or from a distance. Taken on antiquated equipment."

Lowe exhaled through his nostrils and frowned. "When exactly did you first meet Oliver?"

"Exactly? I don't know."

"Three months ago?"

She started to pick at her coat and stopped. "Yes."

"When I uncovered the amulet base in Egypt. When your father got the note from Noel Irving and started aging."

"But . . ." Her brain grasped for anything at all that would disprove this madness. "If Noel Irving was interested in finding the amulet—"

"Not interested in *finding* it. Interested in stopping your father from assembling it. If he believed that the amulet would be the end to his ill-gained immortality, he'd damn sure want to ensure that door never opened."

"Easiest way would be to take one of the pieces," she said.

"And your mother hid the crossbars, but the newspaper reports of my find might as well have put a gigantic red arrow pointing to me."

"Yes, yes," she said impatiently. "But if Noel Irving is Oliver Ginn, why in the world would he try to get to know me? Why not just befriend you if that would better serve his purpose?"

A string of Swedish curses spilled from his lips. "Oliver's got family in Oregon?"

"That's what he told me."

"What about your father's partner? Any idea where he's originally from?"

She shook her head, suddenly sickened. "I don't know anything about Oliver. He always called on me at work—he never picked me up from home. Never even asked for my home telephone number." Panic sunk its claws into her belly. "Lowe, I don't even know where the man lives. And my God, if Oliver is Noel, he's been flaunting himself under my father's nose, courting me at the museum in the room right next to his own enemy?"

Lowe whistled sharply and put a firm hand on her shoulder. "Let's not get ahead of ourselves, okay? One thing at a time."

"Yes," she said, forcing her frantic breathing to slow on a long exhalation. "Yes, of course. You're right. Panic will get us nowhere. Must stay clearheaded. For Father's sake."

He squeezed her shoulder. "I'll see what I can dig up on Oliver, and I'll ask my brother if he can send someone here to keep an eye on you and your father. Until we know for sure, I don't want Ginn within a hundred feet of either one of you."

"I have the Mori," she argued, more to calm her own nerves. Because of course she had them, and cursed though they may be, they would protect her.

"That's well and good, but I'm still calling someone out here to watch the two of you. Not taking any chances. If that jackass is Noel Irving, he's a dangerous maniac. And if he's not, he's got ulterior motives. Not to mention, he put his hands on you. And no one gets to do that but me, *ja*?"

She nodded as warmth bloomed over her cheeks.

A thousand thoughts swirled in her head. Noel. Oliver. All the secrets her father had kept from her. "What if I'd gotten married and had a child? Would the curse pass on when I died? Was my father ever going to tell me?"

"I don't know."

"And how could he still worship that woman?"

"What woman?"

"My mother. She was having an affair with his best friend while pregnant with me? That's ghastly. Scandalous. And goddamn selfish."

"She paid for it in spades," Lowe said.

She slanted him a sharp look beneath her lashes. "You just don't want me to get angry and smash you with an operating table."

"I'd prefer not, given the choice," he said, smiling softly.

She attempted to smile back, but ended up merely wilting against his shoulder. He slung a strong arm around her and tucked her tighter into the diminishing space between them. She didn't resist. He was warm and reassuringly solid. Even his clothes smelled comforting. And if one of the nurses told her father of seeing them like this, she didn't really give a damn at the moment.

All of this was madness. Pure, unbridled insanity. Thank God Lowe had been there. If not, would she be picking out caskets for her father? Heading out to Lawndale again to make funeral arrangements? No matter what problems stood between them, she couldn't bear to lose Father right now. Not like this.

Feeling uncharacteristically fragile, she reached across Lowe's lap for his maimed hand. A small noise vibrated in his chest before he curled his fingers around hers. How quickly things had changed between them. When they'd met on the train, she'd avoided shaking his bare hand, but now his touch was a balm to her shattered nerves. She shoved aside her worries for the moment as exhaustion settled. "I haven't had a chance to thank you for the lily."

"You liked it?" He said this with a boyish tilt to his lips, as if he wanted to be proud of himself for thinking of it but needed her confirmation to be sure.

"It was terribly romantic," she said, repeating Miss Tilly's pronouncement.

"Oh, good." His squinting eyes twinkled with muted joy. "My pleasure."

"I'm not sure what the proper thing to do now is—after last night I mean."

"None of what we did was proper," he said in a hushed, teasing voice that sent a little shiver through her. "Just please don't tell me you regret it."

"No." She smiled softly, feeling unusually shy. "Definitely not."

"Thank God," he said, squeezing her hand. "That's all that matters for now."

Noel Irving's home was destroyed in the earthquake of 1906. Lowe made a couple of phone calls the next day and discovered the man's name popping up again in 1910 as the owner of a small bungalow in Noe Valley. But when Lowe went there to investigate, he found it occupied by a family of Greek immigrants who didn't speak much English—barely enough to tell him they'd purchased the house a decade ago.

He changed tactics and began searching for Oliver Ginn. The man had told Hadley he was looking for a house to purchase in Pacific Heights, but Lowe couldn't find an address there, nor in any other neighborhood—not at the telephone company, the electric company, or the property tax office. And a quick flirtation with a young operator got him a tally of all the telephone numbers assigned to any people with the surname Ginn in the state of Oregon: zero.

Lowe took a different approach and began telephoning all his archaeological contacts from Berkeley, asking if they'd ever heard of Ginn and his financed digs in Mexico. A couple of them had, but only vaguely.

He finally thought they had something when Hadley had Miss Tilly dig through her files and they found the business card Ginn had presented when he first showed up at the museum's offices. No telephone, and the address printed on the card belonged to a bakery in Russian Hill.

The family who owned the bakery had, indeed, heard of Mr. Ginn: he'd rented an apartment above their shop for several months. He'd also packed up and left two weeks ago. No forwarding address.

"Why would he give me one?" the shop owner asked with a shrug. "The apartment is a weekly rental. We had almost a dozen boarders come and go last year alone. As long as they paid rent, we didn't ask questions."

Might as well be chasing down ghosts.

If he couldn't find either man, then he'd have to make it difficult for either man to find him and Hadley. The one person Lowe knew who could help with that was the owner of the Gris-Gris Club.

Two days after Dr. Bacall's heart attack, Lowe called Velma Toussaint and gave her a general idea of his problem. Anyone else would laugh at his crazy request. She merely said, "You can come by on Friday. I'll have something ready for you then."

And so, he waited.

The hospital released Dr. Bacall. He looked weak, but

was well enough to complain constantly, so Hadley thought that was a good sign. Even though she was staying with him at his house, she wisely hired two full-time nurses to oversee his care.

For his part, Lowe talked to Winter's assistant, Bo, who wrangled two intimidating men to stand guard over the Bacall house, watching out for anyone fitting either Noel Irving or Oliver Ginn's descriptions. Though Lowe desperately wanted to get a better idea about what Noel Irving might look like these days, questioning Hadley's father didn't prove helpful; Bacall hadn't seen his partner in twenty years, and had no idea if the deathless magic would also preserve his age.

When Friday night finally arrived, Lowe ate dinner with his family before heading to Gris-Gris. Only a few blocks from Chinatown, the North Beach speakeasy's entrance sat behind a locked door. A long line of patrons already waited to show their membership cards, but like the rest of the Magnusson family, who supplied the club's booze, Lowe only needed to flash his smile to the doorman to receive a cheery welcome. He was waved in immediately and run through a gauntlet of handshakes—half the staff having heard about his return from Egypt—before being shown to a table on the main floor to wait for Velma.

A round of applause ended a jazz trio's set, and after the club's master of ceremonies announced a short piano interlude between acts, Lowe watched couples leave the dance floor to converge upon the bar for drinks. He spotted a black-haired woman in the crowd and thought of Hadley. Five days had passed since she'd patched him up in her apartment. Five days since he'd kissed her. Held her. Made her moan with pleasure.

A goddamn eternity.

He'd seen her briefly the previous afternoon at the museum. Too briefly. With her father recovering at home, she was handling both their workloads and juggling telephone inquiries about his health. No Oliver Ginn sightings, thank God.

She'd given him the canopic jar paintings and their list of names, since he had more time to decipher the last two jars. He'd narrowed one of them down to four possible names on the list, and once he had Velma's magical protection in his hands, Lowe was eager to start looking for the crossbars. He'd do it alone if he had to, but he secretly hoped Hadley might be ready to continue the hunt with him. And because he was a selfish dog, he also hoped she'd soon be ready to continue putting their hands on each other.

Mostly, though—and this was the most pathetic part—he just missed her. God, was he actually moping over a woman? A cursed one, at that. With an entourage of dark spirits and a fear of being touched. Why was nothing in his life ever easy or normal?

Maybe he needed a drink.

A flickering candle cast shadows on the white linen table-cloth near his elbow. He measured his desire for a glass of gin against the effort it would take to brave the crowd at the bar. And while he considered it, his gaze fell on a woman who had stopped in the aisle a few tables down. She was accompanied by the club's floor manager, and the two of them were scanning the room, searching for someone. Her back faced him, so he couldn't see her face. Didn't have to. The hem of her black dress was hiked up unevenly in the middle.

Only one ass he knew would cause a dress to defy gravity like that. And for one moment, he felt like one of those housewives who got chosen to participate in those radio game shows that are always giving away new electric washing machines for answering trivia questions.

He never knew he wanted a washing machine so badly.

Hadley turned around and her eyes locked with his. Her unrestrained smile made him want knock over tables to get to her. She gave him a little wave and ducked around club patrons to make her way toward him. Her boxy dress had short sleeves, and he suddenly realized he hadn't seen her elbows since that night at the Flood Mansion. The ash gray bohemian silk scarf banded around her forehead and tied around the back of her jet black bob made him think of a dour fortune-teller who always gave depressing news.

God, how he loved her fatalistic sense of style. Curse or no curse, he didn't give a damn. Every fiber of his being screamed, *Her—she's the one you want.*

And damn, did he ever.

He stood as she approached the table.

"Mr. Magnusson," the club manager said at her side. "She insisted—"

"Yes," Lowe replied. "It's fine, Daniels. Thank you for letting her in."

The man nodded, a palpable relief winding through his posture as he took his leave.

"What are you doing here?" Lowe asked in a rush, suddenly worried her father's condition might've taken a turn for the worse.

But she appeared to be in good spirits and relaxed. She squinted up at him and gestured toward the arch leading to the lobby, a beaded handbag dangling from her wrist. "If you'd like me leave . . ."

"Oh, no—I'll chase you down if you do." He tugged the handbag until she stepped closer, grinning. "What I *meant* to say was hello, and have a seat, won't you? You look stunning. And please tell me how you ended up in the same speakeasy."

"Astrid."

"Say again?"

"I called your house. Your sister told me I'd just missed you and where you were headed."

God bless Astrid and her big mouth.

He pulled a seat out for her, then quickly shifted it closer to his. She laughed and sat down, holding a long strand of faceted black beads against her breasts to stop it from clinking. She looked a little breathless. About as breathless as he felt when he smelled her citrusy shampoo as he scooted her chair under the table. "I haven't been inside a speakeasy since college," she said. "I had no idea this one was so big. Elegant, even. Are your friends here?"

"What friends? Oh, them. No, they're meeting at Coffee Dan's. I decided not to go. I'm here to pick up something from the club owner. Magical charms."

"Oh?"

"The woman who owns this club practices hoodoo." He leaned closer and spoke in a lower voice. Mostly to catch the scent of her skin, but he also didn't want to shout all his secrets to a crowded room. "She created the warding spell on Adam's vault—which is where he's keeping, you know, *important things* for us."

"How intriguing." She removed her gloves and tucked them inside her handbag.

"I should ask about your father and your day, but I really want to kiss you, so I'm feeling conflicted right now. I'm so glad you're here. Why are you here, by the way?"

"Let's see." She ticked off a list of answers with her fingers. "My father is grouchy, so I couldn't have been happier to move back into my apartment last night. I came here to make sure you weren't meeting up with Ruby. And I really wish you'd kiss me, too."

No need to tell him twice. He pressed his eager mouth to hers, smiling as he kissed her several times in quick succession. Then he slid his hand around the side of her neck to hold her captive and lingered a little longer. He was just about to deepen the kiss when another female voice addressed him.

"If you wanted a private balcony room, you should've told Daniels."

Hadley jerked away. Standing in front of the table was a tall woman in her mid-thirties with pale nutmeg skin of indeterminable ancestry. Her hair was cut short in an Eton crop, styled into shiny brown finger waves molded close to her head, and she was dressed in a soft blue gown that glittered with beads.

He jumped to his feet to greet her. "Did you miss me?"

"The poker games upstairs sure did," she said, a smile curling her lips. She set a pocket-sized cigarillo tin on the table before hugging him. Then she held him at arm's length to look him over. "Your hair's blonder on top. And you're missing something." She glanced down at his maimed hand.

"Gardening accident."

Never one to believe his stories, she rolled her eyes to the ceiling before glancing at Hadley.

He placed a hand on Hadley's chairback. "Velma Toussaint, this is Hadley Bacall, a curator at the de Young Museum. Hadley, this is Velma. She owns Gris-Gris."

The women nodded at each other politely.

"Curious energy you've got there, dear," Velma remarked.

Hadley's eyes widened. She shifted in her seat as Velma looked askance at Lowe, as if asking for an explanation.

Not his place to tell Hadley's secrets, so he just gave Velma a smile that was probably cockier than he intended. "Hadley knows why I'm here to see you. We're working together, so she'll be using the charm with me."

"Well, then. Isn't *this* interesting," she said, keeping her eyes on Hadley as she flicked open the cigarillo tin's lid. An herbal scent wafted out. Inside the slim box sat a glass vial and several small pouches made of red flannel, each about the size of a quarter. The tops were tied with white string. "Five mojo bags. They will keep your enemies away and give you protection from magical tracking spells, but only for a brief time. To activate a bag, you must feed it by anointing it with oil. A drop will do, right on the outside of the bag. Keep it in your pocket and don't let anyone else touch it."

"How long will the effects last?"

"Fifteen minutes, an hour. It's hard to say. It'll be strongest right when you feed it. Gradually wears off. One-time use only. When you're done with it, you'll need to throw it away at a crossroads. Any crossroads will do. Just toss it out of your car window if you're in a hurry."

"What's inside them?" Hadley asked, sniffing the contents of the tin.

Velma shut the lid. "Herbs, charms. Innocuous ingredients. It's the way they're combined and prayed over that gives them power. And it's the intent behind their deployment that makes them work. So while you feed a bag, if you have a specific enemy in mind to avoid, best to think hard about them. Understand?"

Hadley nodded.

"You're a peach, Velma. How much do I owe you?"

"Just tell your sister-in-law to come see me. I've got a client who needs to have a word with their dead grandmother." Velma slid the box toward Lowe and smiled as she took her leave from the table. "Don't be a stranger."

Lowe watched her depart as he stashed the tin in his inner suit pocket.

"Fascinating," Hadley said.

"She is," he agreed. "And now that we have some protection, we can begin searching for the third crossbar."

Her reply was lost under a booming voice from the stage. The tuxedoed house band was taking its place to play their first set of the night. And as the drummer teased out a snappy rhythm, the clubgoers who'd been taking a breather at the bar now returned to the dance floor like ants infiltrating a picnic. Then the chords of "Bye, Bye, Blackbird" started up, and conversation became an impossibility.

He glanced at Hadley.

"Care to dance?" he said near her ear, raising his voice to be heard over the music.

She quickly shook her head and stiffened her posture. But curious eyes slid toward the dancers and a soft smile tilted her lips. She gave him a look that said "maybe."

He pulled her to her feet and led her past tables to the crowded dance floor. And before she could change her mind, he gathered her close, one arm around her back, hands clasped, and swayed her into the crowd. A look of exhilaration swept over her features as they fell into step with ease. She was a good dancer, only looking at their feet long enough to catch the beat. He wasn't sure why this surprised him. But he soon took advantage of it, swinging her around and laughing as she mouthed the song's chorus along with the crooning singer on stage.

What an unexpected pleasure it was to watch her cheeks flush with excitement. He liked seeing her happy. It was infectious. They danced through another up-tempo song, and then he drew her closer for a Gershwin ballad. Closer still, holding her with both arms as she flattened her palms against his chest. He bowed his head to catch the scent of her hair and felt her breath tickling the skin between his ear and shirt collar. It made him dizzy with arousal and an aching, over-warm contentment.

"Take me home."

He barely heard the words against his ear. Barely believed them. His breath came faster. Maybe he was giving them unintended meaning. Maybe she only wanted a repeat of the chair. Which, to be honest, he wouldn't turn down in a hundred years, especially if they weren't interrupted by her maid.

But if there was a chance she meant something more . . .

"I want to forget about everything," she said. "Please."

"Not sure I can do what we did again and survive—a man has his limits," he said. "Let's just dance."

Tension tightened her shoulders for a moment. Then she relaxed and spoke into his ear again as if she were bartering for goods at one of the street markets in Cairo. "No clothes."

"You or me?"

She hesitated for a moment, and then said, "Both of us."

TWENTY-THREE

———◆———

HE DIDN'T HAVE TO TALK HER INTO RIDING ON THE BACK OF LULU
again. It felt good to have her arms around him, but he
would've given anything to be in the darkened backseat of
a taxicab instead. And the torturous wait didn't end once
they got to her apartment building, where tenants were coming and going and chatting in the lobby. They hurried into
the elevator, only to be forced to make small talk with the
elevator man. By the time they made it inside her apartment,
Lowe had adopted her counting technique.

He couldn't lock the door behind them fast enough.

"Please tell me there's no maid getting ready for bed in
another room," he said, shrugging out of his outer garments
while she did the same.

She smiled nervously. "No maid."

"No maid coming later?"

She shook her head, backing farther into the darkened
apartment.

Thank God. "Where are you going?"

"It's warmer back here."

He paused mid-step, his eyes nearly fluttering shut with

anticipation. He followed the sway of her hips through a hall-way into a room that *was* warmer in both temperature and color. Dusky rose covered the windows and floors. Her black cat lounged on a pile of crumpled clothes in the corner, his tail lazily switching as he yawned at his owner in greeting.

"Sorry," Hadley mumbled as she turned on a stained-glass dragonfly lamp. "No maid."

Well, well. He rather liked seeing her messy. His gaze fell to the unmade bed, and alongside it, a wide vase of lilies sat on her nightstand, all different sizes and shapes and colors. *His* lilies: the ribbons were still tied to the stems.

It was all he could do not to grin like an idiot.

She untied the scarf around her head and dropped it on the bed. They stared at each other for several beats. Gone was the smiling confidence he'd held in his arms on the speakeasy dance floor. She looked wary now. A hand flattened over her stomach, as if she were trying to tame her nerves.

She was distressed.

Not exactly what a man wanted to realize while he stood in a woman's bedroom. But what did he expect—that a few minutes in his lap a week ago would wipe away years of aversion? Sad thing was, he stupidly *hoped* it had. And something base inside him saw her unguarded and fragile, and it wanted nothing more than to rip off her clothes, throw her across the bed, and sink inside her.

What little blood was left in his brain whispered that this might not be the best approach.

Hadley was a prickly cactus. He could take his time to slowly, delicately find his way between her defensive spines. Or he could craftily trick her into shedding the spines on her own.

He crooked a finger. "Come here."

She hesitated, then closed the distance between them, stopping a foot away.

"This is what we're going to do," he said, removing his suit jacket. "I'm going to take off every stitch of clothing." He hung the jacket on the metal footboard of her bed and watched her eyes following its path. "And you get to keep your clothes on"—he slid a glance over her breasts—"for now. But only if you help me undress."

She made a small noise, looking him over as if his clothes were an unsolvable puzzle.

He unfastened a cuff link and dropped it in his pants pocket. "You'll be touching me while I keep my hands to myself. You're still in control." She absolutely wasn't, and he hoped like hell she wouldn't notice. Like a cardsharp using sleight of hand to trick his mark, he added a little misdirection. "Now, I'm going to remove everything above my waist while you take off my boots. Whoever finishes last has to take care of my pants."

Her wide eyes fell to his bulging fly.

Suppressing a smile, he dropped the other cuff link in his pocket. "You'd better hurry," he warned, tapping heel against toe. "These things are a bitch to unlace."

Without a word, she crouched at his feet, dark head bent just south of where he wanted it, and untied the long bow at the top of his right boot. Then her fingers raced to loosen the crossed laces, from knee to ankle. Each pluck reverberated through his bones and sent muted thumps of pleasure through his tightening balls.

He nearly forgot they were racing. Vest, tie tack, necktie . . . he practically ripped them all off before yanking his shirt out of his pants.

Glancing up, she whined and frantically wiggled the boot's heel. He curled his toes to impede her progress. "No fair!" she said, breathless, before tugging the leather off with a grunt and nearly falling backward.

"Told you they wouldn't be easy," he said with a chuckle.

Undeterred, she quickly loosened the second set of laces. My, she was motivated. But so was he. A shortcut made quick work of his shirt—once the first four buttons were unfastened, he easily slid the linen over his head while she wiggled the second heel.

"Socks, too."

"That's cheating!" she said, yanking the boot free and tossing it to the side with a *thunk*.

"Socks, Hadley," he insisted.

She cursed under her breath but began stripping his socks off. He reached over his shoulder and waited until she believed she still had a chance to win before pulling off his undershirt in one smooth movement. "So sorry, *min käraste*. You lose."

"You're not sorry at all," she said, throwing down the second sock as she pushed herself to her feet.

He clucked his tongue and pushed disheveled hair out of his eyes. "Don't be a sore loser."

Her blinking gaze flicked over his chest. She blew out a long breath and stepped closer. He inhaled the scent of her hair while they both stared down at the space between them. Slender fingers unbuckled and pulled his belt free from the belt loops, one by one. His curved dagger and its leather sheath slid free into his waiting palm.

Determined, she unbuttoned his fly, each tug of her fingers exquisite torture. Christ, he was harder than a brickbat. When she let his pants fall to the floor and hesitated, he took pity on her, tucking his thumbs into the waist of his shorts to spring his proud erection. Her little gasp and the accompanying scarlet blush that bloomed over her face made him want to throw his hands up in victory.

"Good God," she murmured.

"It's one of my better features," he teased. Bet George didn't have half of this. He wanted to ask, but didn't want the bastard's name floating around her bedroom. She already had enough baggage, and he wanted to deal with that first. "C'mere."

"Lowe . . ."

Ignoring her weak protests, he gathered her in his arms and pulled her down to the rose-covered rug until she straddled him while he lay on his back. "Pin me down," he said, throwing his hands over his head in surrender.

"What—*oh* . . ." She slanted him an irritated look. "I know what you're trying to do."

"Then humor me. Pin me down. Go on."

Hesitantly, she stretched out and bowed over him. The

black beads of her long necklace cascaded against his chest as her hands pinned his to the rug. Sweet Jesus, her body felt good on his. Her face hovered over his, strands of her bobbed hair tickling his cheeks with every hard inhalation of breath. Stockinged knees pressed against his outer thighs. It took every ounce of control he had not to pull her against him and roll her onto her back.

"Most interesting," he murmured in a voice that sounded shakier than he intended. "What does it feel like to hold down a man twice your size?"

"You're letting me."

"Pretend I'm not. What would you do next?"

"This is silly."

"Is it?" He slowly thrust his hips toward the thighs arching above him.

She groaned. He closed his eyes and waited, listening to her quickening breath. After a long moment, he felt warmth on his forehead. Her lips, kissing him. Once, then twice, on his eyebrow. And as she kissed a slow path from his temple to his jaw, chills raced over his skin. She picked up speed and confidence, opening her mouth against the frantic pulse on his neck, swiping a hesitant tongue over his Adam's apple as he swallowed.

Keeping a grip on his arms, she slid lower and pressed kisses on his chest. Did she know what she was doing? Because, for a moment, he couldn't figure out who was the manipulator. Her lips grazed his nipple, almost seemingly accidentally. Pleasure rocketed straight to his balls. Now he was the one groaning. And when her kiss gained suction—God!—his tenuous restraint eroded. Again, he thrust his hips upward, and this time his cock rubbed against the silk between her legs—this time she squirmed and pushed back.

Out of nowhere, a familiar pressure gathered at the base of his spine.

Shit.

It was all too much. Far too long since he'd had a woman. He might've been able to hold out if it was anyone else but Hadley. But he'd never wanted anything so badly and his body was going haywire. Somewhere God was laughing as he cruelly took away all of Lowe's willpower and turned him back into a fifteen-year-old boy who was on the verge of coming in his pants when the wind gusted.

"You're killing me," he whispered. "I'm not going to last. You've got to give me relief." His hips thrust on their own accord now. It was nearly painful. "Please."

Just as he was about to break free of her grip and take care of himself, she released one arm and slid her hand between them. He pushed himself into her palm and her slender fingers circled. Absolute bliss. One uneven pump of her hand and his hips lifted off the rug. A second, and he was struggling for breath. Two more and the floor fell away. He came, quickly, violently, as he spilled onto his stomach and the front of her dress.

His head lolled against the floor as he closed his eyes, reeling with relief and regret. If he was attempting to cure her touching phobia, he was fairly certain this wasn't the way to go about it. "Sorry," he mumbled as she released him. "I'm normally not this eager."

A rustling movement tore him out of his thoughts. Soft fabric brushed his stomach. Was she cleaning him up? Before he could analyze this too closely, her warm touch disappeared.

He cracked open an eye to see Hadley straddling above him on her knees as the inner lining of her black dress glided over her shoulders. She tossed the dress aside and shook her hair out, breathing hard. Bare arms. Bare thighs, banded by ribbon-adorned black garters. And in the middle, a golden silk step-in chemise—so fine, he could see right through to her nipples and the dark triangle of hair between her thighs.

The chemise's loose legs were embroidered with a field of alternating lotus flowers and fanning papyrus stalks. And over the tops of her breasts stretched the green and blue winged figure of Maat, Egyptian goddess of balance and truth.

Hadley shyly smiled down at him and he wasn't entirely

convinced he hadn't died and ascended to some sort of heaven.

Hadley held her breath as Lowe's gaze raked over the chemise. It was Madame Dubois's finest embroidery work, and Hadley had sighed blissfully when she'd picked it up that afternoon. Silly, but she couldn't curb the careening hope that he'd like it just as much.

"O-oh," Lowe moaned, rising up on his elbows. Half of her wanted to cover herself up. The other half wanted him to put his hands everywhere his heavy gaze roamed. He pushed himself up until she was forced to sit back on his thighs. "*Vacker.* So beautiful—my God, Hadley." His knuckles grazed her clavicle and stroked over the embroidered neck of the chemise, sending goose bumps down her arms. Thick blond eyelashes fanned over blue eyes as he blinked. His voice was low and gravelly. "Can I please touch you now? I need to touch you. I *have to touch you.*"

"Yes," she said, gaining confidence. "Definitely yes."

A heavy arm slung around her waist, and with a grunt, he pushed himself off the floor, hauling her with him as he stood. He set her on wobbly feet. "Steady, now." Two big hands swiveled her around to face her bed.

"What—" She twisted around to see him ogling the embroidered papyrus fans that curved over her backside.

"Jesus Christ," he mumbled. His willpower seemed to snap. One moment he was in a daze, and the next, his hands were all over her, sliding beneath the loose legs of her step-in chemise to palm her ass, igniting a thousand sparks across her skin. He kneeled behind her, talking more to himself than her. "These have to go."

He lifted her foot and unbuckled the T-bar strap of one Mary Jane pump, forcing her to grasp a rail of the metal footboard for balance. The other quickly followed. Warm fingers pushed down her garters before circling her thigh to roll a stocking down. Shocking wet heat followed the stocking's path down her leg—his mouth on the back of her thigh. Down, down, until he licked the sensitive hollow behind her knee.

The second stocking went twice as fast. He seemed to be racing her quickening pulse. She felt him stand behind her before he tugged golden straps down her arms. Silk whispered across her skin as the chemise fell, puddling at her feet.

She was naked. Utterly, completely naked. Her bare skin on display to his hungry gaze. Never had anyone seen her this exposed—not since the incident. Not even George; their brief encounters had been in the dark, beneath the cover of her skirt.

A powerful shudder went through her.

"Shh," he whispered. Heavy heat prodded her lower back. Good God! Already? Her mind flashed back to the night they met and the shock of his erection pressing against her on the back of the moving train . . . and the ensuing panic she'd felt at the shocking intimacy.

"It's only me," he whispered against her ear. "Just me."

She stilled, bracing for the inevitable cringe as his arms wound around her. Tonight she was ready to fight that feeling. To count it away, or drown it in liquor again if she had to. But—

But it didn't come. Not even when he pulled her tight against the solid muscle of his chest, bare skin against skin. Or when his wet mouth opened against the side of her throat.

This time, she didn't feel the panic that blackened her senses and stole her free will.

This time, she felt . . .

Safe.

Her body sagged in relief.

She spun in his arms as unshed tears stung her eyes. His mouth crushed against hers, and he kissed her like he was bound for the gallows and she was his last hope for salvation. His hands were suddenly everywhere, all at once, a whirlwind of heat and sensation, sending pleasurable chills over her skin. He pushed her back on the mattress a second before he bent his head to her breast. No soft kisses. No teasing. He just sucked her nipple into his mouth and pulled. Lightning shot down her center, electrifying her with an intense bolt of lust.

He released her flesh with a wet pop and moved his attention to her other breast. She cried out and scissored her legs together in an attempt to get relief from the building ache between her thighs. She was embarrassingly wet, wantonly rubbing herself against his erection . . . drowning in want and a startling neediness. She tried to calm herself down, but some animalistic part of her wasn't willing. Her legs fell apart around his. His long middle finger parted her damp curls. She jerked and writhed against him.

"You're so wet. *Jesus*, Hadley." Wonder coated his words as he whispered, "You want me."

More than anything. She moaned, half-ashamed as his hand ran through the slickness that coated her inner thighs. Half-amazed, too. She'd never been so aroused. When his thumb circled her clitoris, she felt a tickling warmth as pooling liquid trickled down her flesh.

Lowe groaned, a rich baritone rumble she felt through her bones. She couldn't stop her plea from jumping overboard. "Please, Lowe. God, now. *Please*."

He immediately pulled away. Where was he going?

She lifted her head to see him reaching for his suit jacket that hung on her bedpost. He fumbled for a small tin and flung the quickly discarded lid on her coverlet—where Hadley caught a glimpse of its printed front, a chariot drawn by a pair of racing lions.

Oh.

Interesting. She'd never seen any in person. She wanted to tell him that she'd followed a new method of counting the days in her cycle. That they should be in the clear. Instead, she found herself caught in a fascinated daze as she watched him retrieve a ring of latex and unroll it down his length. Good grief. He could sell tickets to this show—every hot-blooded girl in town would pay to see such a spectacle. If he'd felt impossibly thick and heavy in her hand minutes ago, he looked even more intimidating now. She didn't know whether to be worried or impressed.

Impressed, her body decided, as another wave of need warmed her aching sex.

His shadow fell as his body covered hers again, warm and strong and big. A welcome weight. His maimed hand pushed one arm above her head, like she'd pinned him moments before. "It's only me," he said again, kissing her bottom lip. Their fingers threaded together as he prodded her legs apart, making room between her thighs for his hips. He pressed his forehead to hers. "I've never wanted anyone so badly. Never. My God, Hadley. Tell me you want me inside you."

"Yes." She could barely speak.

"Tell me." He guided her free hand to hook around his neck and shifted his weight to his forearms. Back bowed, he pushed himself against her entrance, a teasing pressure that made her want to writhe beneath him. "Say it."

"I want you—"

He plunged inside her before she could finish. One punishing stroke, no quarter. She cried out, digging her nails into his neck, shocked by the near-painful intrusion.

"Don't move," he said sharply as his muscles strained.

She didn't. Couldn't. All she could do was hold her breath. *One, two, three* . . . Her body relaxed. He groaned and pulled back—no!—before pushing into her again, more slowly. Terribly slow. Perfectly slow. Slow enough to make her squeeze her eyes shut as desire rolled through her.

"Yes?" he murmured.

"Lowe," she answered.

He kissed her and she let go, giving in to the feel of his hips driving against hers and the beautiful friction that whorled between them where their bodies were joined. Her free hand roamed over his warm skin, exploring, delighting in the hard lines of his shoulders and back. The way he shivered beneath her touch when her nails swept down his side.

She stretched out below him, lifting her knees to invite him deeper. They both groaned as her muscles tightened around him. She gasped and shifted her hips, testing the angle until she felt the brush of his wiry curls teasing the sensitive bundle of nerves pulsing in her clitoris.

So much pleasure. Enough to erase years of martyrdom. Every fear, every worry, every night she'd spent alone, wondering if there was nothing more—it was all gone. Swept away. She felt warm tears streaming down her temples as joy caught in her throat.

"Hadley."

"It's so good," she said dumbly.

"This is how it's supposed to be," he murmured, kissing her eyes. "This is what I've wanted." His lips pressed against hers and she tasted salt.

Me, too, she thought. And so badly.

Never expect anything and you'll never be disappointed. She told herself if this was all there was—this closeness, this dismantling of her phobia, this fuzzy pleasure—that it would be enough.

But it wasn't.

Never mind that she'd had sex with George a handful of times and never once had an orgasm. Or that she hadn't so much as kissed another man in years. None of that mattered. She suddenly wanted it all, and she wanted it with Lowe. Right now. How easily he'd come apart earlier beneath her inexperienced hand. No shame, no struggle. Just total abandon and trust. She wanted that, too. And when her body greedily fisted around him again, that *want* intensified into something more than determination.

"Goddamn," Lowe murmured. "Yes, *min älskling, ja.*"

O-oh. *Oh!*

This is really happening.

Urgently needing an anchor, her free hand clung to his straining biceps as her toes curled, bobbing above the increasing pace of his pumping hips.

Sweat beaded on his brow. His fingers tightened around the hand he held captive above her head while he pinned her to the mattress below. She was so close. And so very desperate for it. And within the span of two heartbeats, there was no stopping. A horde of people could burst in the door and she wouldn't be able to muster enough shame to halt it. She was gone. Lost. Racing toward oblivion and uncertainty and a gathering darkness that threatened to swallow her whole, if she was willing to dive into it.

And she was. God, she was!

The climax ripped through her like a summer storm, jerking a long, carnal cry from her lungs. She came endlessly, pleasure tumbling and shaking and squeezing her until she couldn't breathe. Until she thought she might die from it. Until she felt Lowe's body seize and heard his answering roar as he came inside her. He sounded just as lost and bewildered as she felt. And as he collapsed against her, she threw her arms around his neck, curled her legs around his hips, and pulled him down with her.

TWENTY-FOUR

―――――◆―――――

HADLEY DOUBLE-CHECKED HER BEDSIDE ALARM CLOCK. THREE. She didn't remember falling asleep, but must have. The bed was achingly empty. But the panic she'd felt when she first realized this a few moments ago was fading, now that she knew for certain he was still here. She'd never been so happy to hear noise in her apartment. Clinks and bumps, water running in the pipes, cheerful whistling. The pleasant sounds of someone else in her home. And not a maid that would abandon her tomorrow, but Lowe.

Lowe.

She grinned at the ceiling, squeezing her eyes shut as a silent joy washed over her, and pushed out of bed.

After a hurried trip to the bathroom, she slipped into a plover gray Habutai silk peignoir dotted with bright begonias, quickly tying the sash as she hunted the location of the noise. Kitchen. She rounded the doorway, wincing at the harsh pendant lighting reflecting off white subway tile. When her eyes adjusted, she found herself staring at a very interesting view of Lowe's thoroughly naked backside.

Arm draped over her icebox door, he was bent over,

peering inside. Long legs dusted with blond hair supported well-shaped buttocks with muscled hollows. But it was the shadowed glimpse of what hung between those legs that made her chest warm.

My God, the things he'd done to her over the last few hours . . . the things she'd done to him. She could scarcely believe any of it had happened. And now, here he still was. No dream—solid flesh. Very solid flesh. She liked the way his back rippled as he poked through jars and containers. Not much to see. Butter. Fig preserves. Blood oranges. Some cooked chicken for Number Four, who was spooling around Lowe's feet like they were best of friends.

"What is this, do you think?" he asked the cat. "The green fuzz isn't giving me hope. Looks vaguely meat-based."

"Week-old deviled ham," she warned, voice cracking with sleep. "What are you doing?"

He glanced over his shoulder and stood. A shame. She'd been enjoying that. But the slow grin he gave her made up for the loss. The long top of his sandy hair was a messy mop of loose curls limned in pale light. He pushed away a thick lock that hung over one eye and shut the icebox door.

"I'm making breakfast," he answered, corded arms crossing his broad chest as he leaned a shoulder against the icebox.

"Naked?"

One shoulder lazily lifted and fell. "Why not?"

Indeed. Walking pornography, right in her kitchen. She drifted closer, feeling a bit like a wealthy tourist on a safari trying to get a better view of a grazing gazelle. "At three in the morning?"

"I'm famished."

"Me, too," she admitted.

His eyes sparkled with good humor. "All that touching and moaning exhausts a body's resources."

"You aren't kidding," she murmured, all too aware of the dull soreness between her thighs.

He swayed closer and dropped a peck on her forehead. So casual and affectionate, as if they'd been doing this for years. She caught the unique scent of his skin and breathed

in deeply. Better than the lilies by her bed. Better than anything she could think of at the moment.

His appreciative gaze roamed over her dressing gown.
He made a satisfied noise before scratching the back of his
neck. "I washed up the dishes in your sink, by the way."

"You didn't have to do that," she said, feeling mildly
embarrassed.

"Someone did. Why do I get the distinct feeling that
you're unfamiliar with manual labor?"

"Because I am," she said, prodding his toes with hers.
He had the loveliest arch to his feet. "I'm not going to apologize for my family's money. It's not as if I sit around doing
nothing. I work, after all. And I'll have you know that I
dirtied those dishes, so I'm not completely useless around
the kitchen. I can make toast. And tea."

His big toe wiggled in answer as it drifted over her foot.
"And peel oranges."

"And peel oranges," she agreed with a smile.

"Well, together we might get somewhere, because if you
can brew us up some tea and make toast, I'll fry us up some
eggs." He glanced down at the purring ball of fur nosing his
way into their toe conversation. "Eggs for three, I suppose.
Or maybe we should feed him the deviled ham and see if
it'll turn him into Number Five."

"Big talk. At the rate you two are going, you'll be kicking
me out of the covers and cuddling up with him instead."

"Not on your life." He grazed a barely-there finger down
her hip as she passed, sending a tiny shiver racing below the
silk of her robe. "I like your claws better."

While she set a kettle on to boil and pulled down the
smallest metal canister from a set of FLOUR-SUGAR-COFFEE-
TEA—the one marked "coffee" was only filled with loose
coins and nails—Lowe found a cast-iron skillet and struck
a match to light the stove.

"I meant to say this earlier, but your burn looks much
better," she said, nodding toward his arm.

"Lucky for me, I had a skilled nurse to bandage it up
properly."

She chuckled and set two empty teacups on saucers. "It's rather strange to spend my Friday night making breakfast with a naked man in my kitchen," she said, spooning tea leaves into two cups as she stole a glance at his body. "Strange, but good."

"If I wasn't here, what would you be doing?"

"Sleeping. Or, if you take into account the events of the last week, I'd be *trying* to sleep at my father's house and failing. If I had to spend one more night in that depressing old place, I might've gone crazy."

"He probably doesn't want you doting over him anyway."

"I'm sure you're right." She set the tea canister back in its place on the shelf and fitted bread into both sides of an electric toaster. Then she bent to pick up Number Four, who lazily draped his front legs over her shoulder. "Have you had a chance to look at the pictograms?"

"I think I've narrowed the third canopic jar down to a handful of names." He cut off a nub of butter into the pan. "You ready to get back to our task?"

"We can start tomorrow, if you'd like. My weekend is free." What she really meant to say was that she wanted him to stay here with her. That all of this was so wonderfully new, and now that she'd broken her touching phobia, she felt like a child who'd tasted sugar for the first time—buzzing with joy and delight and a glorious sort of satiated warmth.

And it wasn't enough.

She wanted more. Both more of what she'd already had and the promise of new experiences. She wanted to know what it felt like to wake up in his arms. To bathe with him. To walk to the market and buy bags of food to fill up her empty icebox and cupboards.

Silly things.

Lowe cracked eggs into the hot butter and rattled off the names he'd matched to the pictograms. They debated the meanings behind one of the symbols. And when their humble late-night dinner came together, she pried Number Four from her shoulder, happy to have a plan for tomorrow.

They set steaming cups and plates down on a small round table sitting beneath a window that framed a view of the sleeping city. Lowe glanced at the pair of polished café chairs sitting beneath the table and tested their mobility, shifting one chair closer to the other. "Well, what do you know. Looks like you've got a few things around here that aren't nailed down."

"Don't laugh," she said. "You'd be surprised what the Mori can do with two chairs and a glass window."

"I'm more concerned about the frying pan and the knives in the drawer."

"You'd be wise to confine any arguments with me to the bedroom."

"More than happy to test that later," he teased, directing her into a chair.

As they dined on their impromptu meal, she fed scraps to Number Four under the table while asking Lowe about his family. He told her how his parents emigrated from Sweden and founded a small fishing company that grew into something successful. How his father decided to risk everything when he traded half his fishing fleet for rumrunners after Volstead. But when she asked him about his childhood, and then about Adam Goldberg and his daughter, something in his posture changed.

"I don't mean to pry," she said, sopping up orange egg yolk with a corner of toast.

He didn't reply for several seconds. "I think I need to tell you something. Well, I don't *need* to, but I want to."

When he didn't continue, she prompted, "Something about Adam?"

"More about Stella, actually." He tapped the tines of his fork against the plate. "There's a small chance she might be mine."

Shock halted her next breath as his words sunk in. "Your . . . child?"

He sighed heavily. "Adam and I were in the same class in elementary school. Miriam was a grade younger. We were all friends, but as we hit our teens, things changed. My father was making more money, so we moved into a nicer house, different neighborhood. I made new friends. And Miriam and Adam began dating. After graduation, I went to college. They stayed and got married."

He pushed his plate away. "Within a year or so, everything was different. Bootlegging made my family wealthy almost overnight. Adam resented that, I think. He threw himself into his work and he and Miriam went through a bad patch. The two of us exchanged letters while I was studying at Berkeley, and during a holiday weekend at home . . ."

Hadley blinked at her plate, unable to look at him.

"It was only the one time—never happened again," he said. "But it was absolutely the stupidest thing I'd ever done."

"Did you love her?"

"Not in a romantic way. I don't know if I was trying to hold on to a life I didn't have anymore, or if I was jealous of them. They were adults. Working, married. Paying rent. I was still a boy, getting drunk at college and playing stupid pranks, not knowing who I was or what I wanted to do with my life. And then Miriam began reaching out to me."

"And you didn't push her away."

"Adam was my best friend, and I . . ." He shook his head. "The guilt ate me up. I nearly quit school. And then Miriam announced she was pregnant. And, well, give or take a couple of weeks, either one of us could've been the father. She begged me not to say anything, and I tried to keep my mouth shut. Usually I'm pretty good at lying." He forced a stilted laugh.

"But you told him."

"I'd want to know if it were me. And he wasn't happy, of course. Half my size, but the man's got a wicked hook," he said, pointing to his nose. "He told me plainly that no matter if the child was blue-eyed and blond, it was his, not mine. They worked out their problems, and eventually he forgave me, too. I didn't deserve it, but there you go."

"And Stella . . ."

"Looks like Miriam, through and through. Even the curls could be Miriam's." He gave her a brief, tight smile. "And

Stella's only four. They say you can better see resemblances when they're a little older."

"There's the new test—it matches blood types."

"And that test is what? Not even fifty percent accurate?" He shrugged. "Adam wouldn't want to know, so I have to respect that. And I'm not sure knowing would change anything. I've tried to offer financial help over the years—for doctors and special schools, you know? But he won't take handouts."

She lifted her head to study his face. "That's why he looks after things for you, isn't it?"

"It's the only way I can get him to accept any money. He's stubborn. And that's his prerogative." He gave her a sad smile. "In the end, it doesn't matter. They are still my family, whether she's got my blood or Adam's. I feel lucky to be in both their lives, and that's enough."

Hadley didn't know what to say. Her feelings ran the gamut from jealousy and distress to pity and respect. And something more, she realized. Not only had he torn down the barrier she'd constructed around herself, he was dismantling bricks from his own wall—an invisible bulwark she hadn't even known existed. He was right when he said he didn't need to tell her any of this. If he hadn't, she may never have been the wiser.

But now she did know. And what he'd revealed didn't matter. She only cared that he'd wanted to share it with her. And her heart swelled with this new awareness.

"Do you think less of me now?" he asked softly. "Do you want me to go?"

She swirled tea leaves in the last bit of golden liquid at the bottom of her cup. "Awfully inconsiderate for you to leave now. Who would wash the dishes?"

Out of the corner of her eye, she saw his shoulders relax as he blew out a long breath. A few moments later, his hand slid across the table to coax her fingers into his. "What would you say to a nice hot bath?" he asked in a hopeful voice. "I saw your tub earlier. Looks big enough for both of us."

"I seriously doubt that."

"But it will be fun to try, *ja*?"

"Ja," she repeated as a quiet joy warmed her chest. "I think it really might."

TWENTY-FIVE

———◆———

LOWE WOULD'VE BEEN HAPPY TO NEVER LEAVE HADLEY'S BED, but his need for a change of clothes finally spurred him out of her apartment the next day. They'd made plans to regroup in the afternoon to hunt the third crossbar. But at this point, Lowe almost didn't care if they were hunting rabbits, as long as he got to see her.

He rode Lulu down Mason like a madman, buzzing with bright satisfaction; when he came to a stop sign, he had to force himself not to stupidly grin at the passengers in the nearby car. A single night with Hadley and he was euphoric. Drunk on sex and the deep contentment of holding her in his arms. Nothing was better than feeling all her hard angles and sharp edges soften beneath his fingertips. Or collapsing on her breast after they'd come together and listening to her crazed heartbeat slow to a fierce, strong pulse that matched his. As if they were both sinking underwater, slowly drowning in pleasure.

But it wasn't just that. It was everything. Her company. Her sharp wit. The way those dark eyes squinted when she smiled, with their upturned corners creating a shadowed line that seemed to go on forever. The way one slim brow lifted critically as she upbraided his wild ideas in that acerbic, posh accent of hers.

He had prepared himself for rebuke when he told her about Stella. He certainly wouldn't have blamed her if it were too much for her to deal with. He'd never forget how his mother had wept uncontrollably when he told her. Disappointed in him, devastated by the impossible nature of the situation—no joy of grandchildren running around her home or even watching Stella from afar. Adam refused; he didn't want to confuse the girl. And rightly so.

But Hadley accepted it. He'd watched her carefully later, sure that once she'd had time to think about it, she'd start pulling away from his touch again. But no. A small miracle. He'd never been so thankful.

As he urged Lulu toward Pacific Heights, the city became a blur, a little like the lazy thoughts streaming through his head. His world felt as if it had been tipped over, then righted. Like he hadn't known how unbalanced he'd been until he experienced how much better it felt to be standing straight.

Every worry he'd had since he'd returned home seemed a little less hopeless. Every problem, fixable. His mind raced the motorcycle, churning out images of a shiny future with Hadley. A big house. A family. Her running the antiquities department. Him . . . well, he hadn't figured that out yet. Traveling with his uncle wasn't looking as exciting as it once did. Bad food, sweaty clothes, hard labor, illness, and no sleep. All of that was tolerable when you were running away from something. But not when you had something to run to. Or someone.

Maybe going back to dig in the wretched sun wouldn't be so bad if she was at his side. He pictured her walking around the desert in a traditional Egyptian *galabiya* dress and smiled. Maybe she'd have an easier time than he did. Maybe it would be worth it to see the look on her face when she strolled around the temple ruins.

He was considering all this as he galloped up the side

steps of his family home. And after swinging open the screen door, he nearly slammed into Winter, who stood unmoving and icier than a side of beef in a cooler.

"Where the hell have you been?"

"And a fine fucking day to you," Lowe said, shouldering around him.

Winter held out a hand. "Out all night and you come in looking like this? What were you out doing? Whoring?"

Lowe angled his face inches away from his brother's. "Say that again. I dare you."

"Defensive about that curator, aren't you?" Mismatched eyes narrowed over a dark, stilted smile. "Oh, yes. I know. Greta told me you brought the woman here."

Damn the staff and their wagging tongues.

"Not the first time you've been keeping graveyard hours," Winter said. "A week ago Jonte told me you rolled home inside the Packard in the dregs of the night. You with the curator then, too?"

"She's none of your goddamn business."

"She's a gold heiress—a society girl. Dammit, Lowe. You want to see a woman like that, you do it properly. If everyone here is talking, don't you think her people are talking, too?"

Lowe started to protest that she didn't have a maid, but thought better of it. And Winter wasn't wrong, exactly. Hadley seemed friendly with the elevator man, who gave Lowe a frigid look today during the trip downstairs. Not to mention all the other apartment tenants—they would definitely talk if they saw him skulking around at odd hours. He wasn't exactly inconspicuous.

"Antiquities business isn't all that big in San Francisco. Word gets out you're seeing her, everyone in that museum's going to talk. Patrons, donors . . . You need to be careful you don't hurt that lady's reputation."

"I'm careful."

"And you've also got a habit of making promises you don't keep and leaving by the bedroom window. Don't salt the ground under her feet."

"Always good to know the strength of your faith in me," Lowe said sourly.

"Why were you bothering Velma?"

Was there anyone he could trust to keep their damn mouth shut? "Not that it's any of your concern, but Hadley and I are working together on something for the museum. At the request of her father."

Winter's scarred brow lifted. "Please tell me it doesn't involve Goldberg."

"Of course not." Well, not in Hadley's eyes. Not in the way she believed, at least. But he didn't want to think about that right now. Or ever. Jesus, it was hot in the house. Lowe loosened his necktie as sweat bloomed on his brow.

A tense pause stretched between them before Winter seemed to give up the fight, sighing heavily. "Lowe," he pleaded, using the Old World pronunciation, *Low-va*. He continued in Swedish. "You can't go on like this. I know you want to make your own way, but you can't spend your life running around the globe with Uncle, or you'll end up like him: alone."

"I hate Egypt," Lowe admitted angrily in Swedish. "I hate digging."

"Then *don't*! Come work for me. You can run the new warehouse. Wine and dine clients."

"Nej." Lowe shook his head. "I can't do that. I'm so close to a big break, if I can just . . ." He trailed off. "I don't want to do it forever, but I have to see this last thing through."

Winter stared at him for a long moment, as if he wanted to say more, but thought better of it. He switched back to English when he finally said, "The shipping company called. The crates you sent from Egypt will be delivered next week. Greta has the details."

Lowe mumbled his thanks and sidled around his brother.

"You square things with Monk yet?"

For the love of God. Winter was worse than a mother. Lowe had to get out of this house before he went crazy. Maybe get an apartment downtown. It wasn't part of his bigger plan, which was to buy a comfortable house and make sure Adam and Stella were taken care of. But that wasn't going to happen tomorrow, and there were other things at the top of his to-do list. The most pressing of which was to secure enough cash to pay off Monk—sooner rather than later.

And the closest funding within his reach was tied up in the crossbars hunt, something that was turning out to be much more complicated than he'd originally hoped, what with Dr. Bacall's health, Noel Irving, Oliver, magic . . . Hadley.

Hadley.

Lowe could get by without the flock of servants and all the luxuries. Better to live free and poor. But what he'd told Winter was true—the crossbars *had* to be his last forgery, and that's all there was to it. Hadley would never tolerate it, not in a million years. And he wanted her more than the money. As long as Adam and Stella had what they needed, Lowe could take his share and retire, so to speak.

All he had to do was find the rest of the crossbars, sell the real amulet to Dr. Bacall, and hand off the forgery to Monk to pay for the crocodile statue forgery—he'd just talk Bacall into giving him the original bill of sale for the crossbars. Give Monk that along with his official documentation for the amulet base. Bacall didn't care about reselling the damned thing. He wanted it to get rid of Noel Irving.

Simple, really. No one gets hurt; everyone's happy. And Hadley would never have to know that he'd intended to cheat her father in the first place. But in order for everything to work, he needed to find the last two crossbars.

And in order to do that, he first needed a shave and another bath.

The hunt awaited him, along with his raven-haired hunting partner.

The joy of seeing Hadley again didn't disappoint. In the space of one night, everything had changed between them. Her boundaries were felled. She now greeted him with open arms. He scooped her up with a racing heart and no intention of ever letting her go. He'd never been so happy.

And yet, so anxious at the same time . . .

Because the easy luck they'd experienced tracking the first two crossbars seemed to have dissipated. They plowed through two addresses over the weekend, then two more at the beginning of the following week, sneaking out during Hadley's lunch break and after she got off work. Each time they used Velma's charmed bags to hide their trail. They posed as charity workers, door-to-door sales representatives, long-lost relatives, and their finest bit of acting: country preacher and demure wife.

A waste of choice vaudeville, as all names led to dead ends.

Utterly vexing.

Still, the week wasn't without merit. Her father's health improved, and even though he couldn't confirm the existence of Noel/Oliver, they saw not hide nor hair of Oliver and no magical chimeras pecked at their heads.

But, best of all, they buried their failures in consolatory rounds of increasingly daring sexual athletics: in the passenger seat of the silver Packard, darkened hallways, a public restroom, and—during a particularly blasphemous afternoon—on the back steps of an empty church when they were investigating a crumbling graveyard.

Every time he saw her was a gift. Even so, a mounting frustration dogged him that had nothing to do with the crossbars. Winter's words echoed in his head. *You want to see a woman like that, you do it properly.* Why did his brother have to be right? Because damned if Lowe didn't spend half his time trying to keep their affair quiet: tiptoeing around her father and her coworkers; sneaking around her apartment building at odd hours, while he trudged up a million flights of stairs to avoid the elevator man; parking Lulu across the street at the Fairmont Hotel.

It was demeaning to both of them.

And almost a week after their first night together, here he was at ten in the evening, lurking around the cypress trees at the base of the museum's front tower while he waited for Mr. Hill to take his break—the same guard who'd caught them in Dr. Bacall's office when this whole thing started. When the man's car sped around the side of the building, the museum door cracked open and Hadley's face popped out.

"All clear!" she whispered cheerfully before ushering him inside the door and bolting it.

His eyes darted around the museum's shadowed front lobby. Eerie to be in here alone. "Another guard is definitely not going to waltz in here, right?" he asked.

"The other two are stationed outside."

"And Mr. Hill—"

"Won't be back until after midnight."

"If the wrong person knew this, you could be robbed blind."

"We've only had two break-in attempts in ten years. And it's not as if someone could pull up a truck to the front door and bust it down without someone hearing. Where's your sense of adventure, Mr. Treasure Hunter?"

"Hmph. I think it got trampled beneath the wheels of our failure this week." He bumped into a stanchion and gritted his teeth as the sound of grating metal bounced off the walls. "Jesus, Hadley. I feel like a misbehaving boy, sneaking into a building on a dare."

"Well, hopefully the elevator in my apartment building will be repaired tomorrow. Then you can use your misbehaving ways to sneak up the stairwell without bumping into every tenant on the way up."

"Oh, joy."

She placed flattened palms on his chest and tilted her face up to his. "Grumpy."

"Frustrated." But now that he caught the scent of her hair, a part of him relaxed. He dipped his head to press his forehead against hers for a moment, and then kissed the tip of her nose.

"I'm so happy you're here," she whispered. "I had trouble sleeping without you last night."

"I hate being away from you. It makes me physically ill,"

he whispered back. "I want this hunt to be over, so we can stop hiding and lying."

"I thought you lived for lying," she teased.

"You're ruining me, Miss Bacall," he said against her lips.

"I don't believe I've ever ruined anyone before."

"Best make it good, because I don't want you ruining anyone else ever again."

She arched into him, smiling a delightfully silly smile that he promptly kissed away. And just when he was warming up, she broke the kiss and wound her fingers through his. "We can hear Mr. Hill's car in the antiquities wing. And there's something there I want you to see."

Feeling a little less anxious and a lot more motivated, he followed her past the ticketing windows and an army of silent statues lining the walls. The high ceilings and tiled marble floor seemed to simultaneously magnify and swallow their footfalls as they strolled by framed paintings worth more than any one of the Magnusson's luxury cars.

Past the Pacific Art collection, an arched entrance was marked with a hand-painted sign that read: TREASURES OF ANCIENT EGYPT—MUMMIFICATION, MAGIC, AND RITUAL. He'd seen this exhibit many times over the years, even when most of it was housed in the old Midwinter building. As a boy, it held enormous fascination for him and was one of the main catalysts that spurred him into pursing an archaeology degree. Strange to think that the objects his ten-year-old self gazed upon with delight would later be placed under Hadley's stewardship.

He stopped in front of a case that held a female mummy. Sprigs of hair were still attached to her preserved skin. Most of her teeth were still intact, but she was missing a leg; half the museum's mummies were damaged or crushed to shards in the earthquake. But the thing that made her such a crowd-pleaser sat in the adjoining case: a tightly wrapped mummified cat, which was found in the same tomb.

"The best feline specimen on the West Coast," Hadley

bragged. "Excellent example of geometric patterned wrapping from the Ptolemaic Period."

"Is this what you'll do for Number Four when the time comes?"

She clasped her hands behind her back and gazed at the case with a satisfied smile, head tilted. "I think he'd like that. A tiny sarcophagus might be nice, too. Who knows—perhaps one day we'll both end up on display. People will study our preserved corpses and call *me* the Cat Lady."

"You're a morbid woman, *min kära*."

A mischievous smile hoisted her cheeks. "I do love the way you flirt, Mr. Magnusson." Gaze locked with his, hands still clasped behind her back, she took a couple of backward steps. Lowe might as well have been mummified himself, for it felt like she could tug on his wrappings and wind him toward her with a single look.

If she wanted her preserved body to be on display, he wanted to be the one lying beside her.

"Over here," she said, beckoning him with excited eyes. "This is what I wanted you to see."

TWENTY-SIX

———— ❧ ————

LOWE WATCHED HADLEY AS SHE TURNED ON A HEEL AND LED HIM to a waist-high glass case that sat against a square pillar in the middle of the hall. Inside was a small collection of personal items found in the Cat Lady's tomb: perfume jars, a comb, jewelry. And in the middle of the case sat three canopic jars; the fourth one had been lost in the earthquake.

She leaned over the case to peer down into it. "My parents found this tomb at the necropolis near Thebes in 1895. Only three years before I was born. I wondered if my mother used these as inspiration when she decided to hide the crossbars."

"Different era design than the ones she had made," he noted.

"Yes. Still, I imagine her walking in here, angry with my father for wanting to kill Noel. Desperate to keep the peace between the two of them so that she could selfishly hang on to both husband and lover. And she sees these." Hadley tapped on the glass with one nail.

"The solution to her problem," Lowe agreed, stepping behind her to peer over her shoulder as he gingerly wrapped one arm around her waist, testing. "Hide them in something that people would keep safe and treasure."

"Exactly." She snaked a hand around the arm that held her, quietly voicing her approval. "And I thought if we looked at them in the right way, maybe we'd see something that would help us decipher the last two pictograms."

How he hated those unsolvable pictograms. Both them and her mother be damned. He inhaled the clean scent of her skin, smelling soap and the bright note of her shampoo and beneath it all, *Hadley*. Intoxicating. He felt powerless to stop himself from nuzzling below the sharp line of her bob to kiss the fine hairs that veed at the nape of her neck.

She shuddered ever so slightly, but continued with her train of thought, albeit in a breathier voice. "You know, I think Father's decision to gift the Cat Lady to the museum was tied to the caveat that he be appointed director of this department."

"Mmm." Lowe trailed two more kisses down her spine, stopping where the top button of her oh-so-serious black dress prevented him from going further. "Maybe that's why he thought I'd be champing at the bit for a chance to be his successor."

Two slim fingers slid beneath the cuff of his shirtsleeve, stroking the skin over his wrist. The barest of touches, but the shiver it coaxed jumped straight to his cock.

"You haven't changed your mind, have you?" she murmured. "Because you should be warned, if you break our agreement, I will bury you under ten chandeliers."

"I love it when you're romantic," he said, holding her tighter as he nudged himself into the cleft of her ass.

She jumped and made a little noise. "Oh, dear."

"Oh, yes." He opened his mouth to nip the skin below her ear.

"What a big clock you have, Mr. Magnusson."

He laughed against her hair. "I nearly fell on my face when that slipped out of your mouth in your father's office that morning. For a Stanford-educated mind, you're a terrible speller."

Her snorted chuckle was quickly broken by a hissed intake of air. "My office . . ."

"I thought you wanted me to look at the canopic jars." He released her waist and urged her forward. "Bend over the case with your hands there," he instructed.

"Right here? We might be seen."

"I damn well hope we are," he said—partly agitated, partly thrilled. "Then maybe we can stop sneaking around like we're doing something wrong. Nuh-uh, no you don't," he scolded, pushing her down on the glass. "Hands right there and don't move unless I say so."

"Or what?"

"Or I'll yell for the guards and tell them you've gone mad and are trying to steal the Cat Lady's eternal companion. Stay still." He held her down with one hand on the small of her back while his free hand pulled up the hem of her dress to expose her beautiful backside. "What do we have here?" Bright cobalt blue tap pants strewn with golden stars, and in the center, back to back, two intertwined crescent moons. "Your adventurous taste in lingerie never ceases to amaze me. You look like an erotic Van Gogh painting."

She chuckled once, twisting to look back at him, then sucked in a breath and wilted atop the display glass when he slid a hand beneath the loose embroidered fabric. Christ, she had the softest skin. He reverently kneaded one plump cheek, then the other, tugging the silk until it wedged between both cheeks and bared the lower half of her pale ass. A beautiful sight. He especially liked the way she was squirming beneath his hand. Like waving a red flag at a bull. His cock was definitely paying attention.

He pulled down the starry-starry tap pants. Slowly, slowly. From this angle, her ass looked like an upside-down heart. But it was space between that drew his attention. "Foot up," he said in a hoarse voice, kicking the tap pants aside after she stepped out of them. Then he nudged her legs apart. "Wider."

"Lowe . . ."

"Hush." He sank to his knees behind her and kissed the tops of her stockings. Licked along the shadowed crevice beneath each ample buttock. She made small, breathy noises. And when she fidgeted, shifting her weight from one leg to the other, he spread her open with both hands. "My *God*," he murmured. So slick and swollen, her flushed pink flesh was framed by damp, dark curls.

Drugged by the scent of her sex, he leaned in and took a long, lazy taste from front to back, until she whimpered and her knees bent. Then he did it again, dipping into the warm liquid that pooled at her center. So wet. All for him.

"Please," she murmured.

Oh, how he loved it when she begged. If he could hear her repeat that *one* word every day for the rest of his life, he'd die happy. And he tried to hold out, to coax it from her again, but at the moment, he was just as greedy for her pleasure as she was.

He pressed his face closer and found the small bud with the tip of his tongue, flicking it from side to side several times to gauge her reaction. And when she cried out and tilted her ass up to give him better access, he gave in completely and gave her what she wanted: Steady licks with the flat of his tongue. Up and down, down and up, sucking and flicking. Circling this way, and then the other. As long as he gave her a steady rhythm, she gave him the most glorious noises in return.

And for a time, he almost thought he could go on like this, giving and not taking, but the insistent ache in his balls was too much to bear. Christ, she turned him into a ravenous animal, unable to control himself. No one else had ever had this unrelenting pull on him. Her scent, taste, shape. Her laugh. Her icy stare. Her posh accent. The way she squinted one eye when solving a problem. Every bit of it made him hard. Thank God he hadn't met her when he was seventeen and barely able to make it through a few hours at school without a release—he might never have graduated.

Holding her open to him with one hand, he struggled to unbutton his fly, fingers shaking. His cock sprang into his palm, heavy and hard as steel. A shuddering relief passed through him as he stroked himself. Goddammit, he just couldn't wait.

Ignoring her vocal protest, he stood, spread her wide, and, guiding himself with one hand, sank into her wet heat with a unsteady groan. She tensed, shouting as her body arched off the glass.

"Whoa," he cautioned, and put a firm hand on her back to force her down as he began moving. Fast. Hard. No inhibition or restraint. Just a manic rush toward oblivion and an unyielding drive to push her further than he ever had. To conquer and claim her.

And if some quiet voice inside him was warning him to be careful and consider the ghosts from her past as he held her down, thrusting into her wildly, then a much louder voice extinguished his doubts.

"Yes, yes, yes," she cried. "Thank you, God, yes, thank you . . ." Holding on to the edge of the case, she turned her head to the side, one cheek against the glass and an open-mouthed look of rapture on her face.

Not fragile. Not broken. Not haunted.

Her cries echoed around the shadowed room, bouncing off the display cases and pillars. They truly might be caught after all. But damned if he was going to reel her in. He just shifted his grip, grabbing hold of her fleshy hips in both hands, and rode her until sweat trickled down his neck. Until they were nothing but two parts of a machine, each fueling the other's pleasure. Until her punctuated moans and prayers grew desperate and she clenched around him.

"That's it," he murmured. "Come for me."

He slipped his hand around her hip, to plunder her damp curls. His middle finger grazed the tight bud once, twice . . . She gasped for a breath. Jerked. Clutched around his cock until he groaned and thrust harder. And then . . .

Yes.

There it was: the bewildered, broken wail. He pushed her through the orgasm, hips pumping, finger rubbing her clitoris until her cries calmed and she pulsed around him. Thrust her hand over his to signal that she couldn't take any more.

A possessive joy rang inside his chest as warmth gathered at the base of his spine. Christ, his balls were ready to explode. Picking up speed, he drove into her with hellbent purpose, ready to join her. And, oh, God—no.

No wonder it felt so good. He'd forgotten the goddamn condom.

How didn't matter. He just had to pull out. Now.

Acting on some crazed, feral impulse, he groaned and jerked himself out of her wet heat—a fucking saint, he was—and grabbed her arm. He vaguely heard a surprised moan as he urged her onto her knees, one hand on the back of her head. Christ, she had every right to hate him for this, but he just couldn't stop as he took himself in hand and prodded the tip of his cock against her mouth.

"Hadley," he begged. He was a dog, and he knew it, but please just . . .

Her lips parted. Wide brown eyes locked with his as she closed her mouth around him and sucked.

His mind emptied. Head tipped back. Ecstasy rushed forward. He thrust into her mouth and came.

And came.

Gods above, it felt like he was spilling his very soul into her. He shuddered, nearly losing his footing as he swayed over her, hand fisted in her hair. Christ! He could barely breathe. But as heady gratification pulsed in his veins, the outer edges of his world bled back into view. And with that, a slow, heavy shame moved into his chest.

Any second she'd push him away and tell him to go to hell. Any second. He was sure of it. So when she extracted him from her lips, he didn't expect the loose, tender strokes from her hand. Or the light kiss on the tip of his cock that sent frantic tremors through his legs, intense enough to make him rock forward on his toes.

And when she finally released him, and pushed herself to her feet, he definitely did not expect the playful smile. Gods above, that smile! Wicked and shy, all at once. It bowled him over. He wrapped his arms around her and kissed her head, repeating her name like a sacrament as they swayed together on unsteady legs.

"I don't know what I was thinking. I forgot the condom,"

he mumbled against the citrusy perfume of her hair. "I'm sorry."

"I'm not."

He lifted her face to his and said, in wonder, "You really aren't."

She shook her head.

He exhaled heavily, a stupid grin spreading across his face as he tucked himself into his pants and buttoned back up.

She tucked his shirt a little tighter. "And what's more, it jostled a thought out of my brain."

"Eh?" It jostled a lot of things in him, but thoughts weren't one of them.

She explained. "When I was, well, bent over the glass, I kept thinking that there was something wrong with the third name."

"And here I was, thinking I was transporting you to euphoric bliss."

"Oh, you did. Believe me," she said dreamily, a lusty satisfaction weighing down her eyelids. "But after, when you pulled me off the glass like some kind of violent marauder—"

He groaned.

"No need to be sorry. I rather enjoyed it. Quite a lot, actually," she said with one brow cocked and a brief, sheepish smile. "But—"

"But?"

"I guess I had 'clock' on the brain, and your teasing me about my poor spelling skills, and I realized the problem with the name. Our interpretation of the pictograms wasn't wrong. My mother misspelled the name."

"She did?"

Hadley gripped the lapels of his jacket and spoke in an excited voice. "Lowe, I know exactly where the third canopic jar is, and it's not anywhere near a grave."

TWENTY-SEVEN

⌦

"IT'S NOT L-E-V-I-N-E. IT'S L-E-V-I-N. FIVE LETTERS, NOT SIX."

"Levin?" He studied her face, still a little dazed and stupid from the massive orgasm. "I don't remember a Levin on the list."

"That's because there wasn't one. But I was just reading an article in the *Chronicle* yesterday about all the movie theaters being built around San Francisco. Quite a few of them have been financed by the Levin brothers. Including the one in the Richmond District. The Alexandria. Pet project for Sammy Levin."

"Why does that name ring a bell?"

"Because he shares an obsession." She straightened the knot on his necktie. "We have one mojo bag left?"

"Yes."

"We'll need it. The newspaper mentioned a gala being held Sunday night. The owner's trying to court Hollywood to film more pictures in San Francisco, and he's putting his personal collection on display. Bet you anything we'll find the Qebehsenuef jar there."

Definitely worth a try.

And try, they did . . .

Early Sunday evening, Lowe held open the silver Packard's passenger door and helped Hadley onto the curb, where other well-heeled gala attendees were gathered in front of the Alexandria Theater. Walking through lotus-topped columns, they stepped beneath the Egyptian-revival entrance and got in line near a ticket booth that was closed for the night—a tuxedoed man collected private invitations at the door. Nearby, reporters snapped photographs of a handsome couple—motion-picture stars, according to the buzzing chatter. But even the minor Hollywood dazzle couldn't distract Lowe from the strange, prickling sensation that they were being watched. He'd used Velma's last mojo bag, so they should be safely hidden. But he just couldn't shake the feeling that something was wrong.

"Everyone has invitations," Hadley whispered.

"I'll think of something."

"Please do, because I think I see someone I know in a car that just pulled up."

Lowe groaned. All they needed was someone to blow their cover. Big, public con jobs were so much more trouble than the intimate ones. He watched the line for a break, and when no one was paying attention, quickly prodded Hadley forward to skip several couples.

The doorman looked up and smiled. "Good evening."

"It will be once we're inside," Lowe said, matching the man's enthusiasm. "Damn cold night. Say, I hate to be trouble, but my assistant here accidentally left our invitation at the hotel. It's my fault, really. We drove up from Los Angeles this afternoon, and I guess it was a longer trip than I thought, because I fell asleep in the room when I should've been changing clothes."

"Well, it's just that—"

"Then when she rang me to say that the car was ready, I had to scramble to get ready and we barely made it here on time. Anyway, if you really need the invitation, I'm sure we can telephone the Palace Hotel inside the lobby and ask one of the managers to open the room and verify it's there."

The attendant glanced at the impatient people in line behind them and scratched his ear.

"We're booked under Columbia Pictures, if you want to call the hotel yourself," Lowe added.

"Columbia?" He glanced at Hadley's fur and extended an arm into the lobby. "I don't think that'll be necessary. Please, do come in."

Well. That wasn't so bad, after all.

Lowe led Hadley inside. Green patterned carpet spanned the spacious lobby. Lots of columns. Bronze Egyptian bas-relief on the walls. A train of attendees headed up and down an attractive staircase to a curved landing where drinks and finger food were being served. But it was what was on display at the back of the lobby that captured Lowe's attention.

Sammy Levin's private collection.

Hadley was right. They all shared a common obsession, all right. Mr. Levin's, however, leaned toward the surreal. The centerpiece of his collection was a massive Egyptian throne with thick, carved arms lined with lotus blossoms. The sign above identified it as a prop from the movie *Cleopatra*, which meant that Theda Bara's barely covered ass once sat upon that wood. How Mr. Levin managed to obtain it wasn't much of a mystery, because lining the shelves around the throne was an expensive, if not eclectic, mix of Egyptian objects, from painted Hollywood paste to some statuary that looked very ancient, and *very* real.

Mr. Levin was loaded.

And with pockets deep enough to not only build a handful of neighborhood theaters like this but also acquire treasures that rightly belonged in Hadley's antiquities wing. "Did you know he had all this?" Lowe whispered in Hadley's ear.

"He's outbid the museum on a few occasions," she said. "Nothing big. A few pieces of jewelry and a broken funerary mask. I'd heard he has little academic knowledge of what he collects. He's like a small boy in a toy store. He just desires and takes what he wants. The glitzier, the better."

Hadley hadn't met the man in person—Lowe knew that

much. She'd said she caught a glimpse of him at a charity function last year, and had heard rumors he might be missing a few marbles upstairs. People said he had secret living quarters on the second floor of the theater and could sometimes be spotted in the balcony drinking whiskey in his bathrobe between shows.

Lowe could clearly imagine one of the canopic jars sitting pretty among all of this strange mix of old and new. But his curiosity warred with a renewed itch that they were being trailed. Would Dr. Bacall's old partner dare attack them with magical creatures in a public place like this?

Best find the damned thing and get out. Fast.

After scanning the crowd for suspicious eyes, Lowe protectively drew Hadley closer and joined the line of people filing past the uniformed police guarding the display shelves. Half of them didn't have any idea of the worth that sat inches away from their fingers. Hell, most folks just wanted their photograph taken as they perched on the throne. Hollywood trumped dusty relics.

Fine by him. It left half the exhibition wide open for their perusal. His gaze skipped over the objects, looking for the distinctive urn. But as they rounded a bay of shelves, Lowe's eyes fixed on something else. Something horribly, horribly familiar.

The golden crocodile statue.

Levin was Monk's silent customer.

No. It couldn't be. Absolutely impossible. He squeezed his eyes shut, as if he could will it away, then looked again. Oh, yes. It was the crocodile. And since he knew for a fact that the other statue—the real crocodile—was resting in a display case in New York, this had to be Adam's forgery.

Lowe's entire body seemed to catch fire from within. He loosened his tie, momentarily numb as panic jumbled his thoughts. He wiped his brow and glanced behind him. Okay, all wasn't lost. All they had to do was find the damn urn and run for the door. And maybe it wasn't even here. Maybe Hadley had guessed wrong. He swung back around to suggest it, only to find her leaning inches away from the shelf, staring at the crocodile.

"Lowe," she whispered. "This looks exactly like the Late Period statue that was stolen from the tomb at Faiyum. How in the world did it end up here?"

He stood mute, feeling dangerously unsteady, as if the floor had liquefied beneath his feet. His body flashed from hot to cool. Sweat coated his skin.

He'd have to tell her now. And when he did, she'd suspect forgery with the amulet. She'd know he'd been planning to cheat her father, and she'd hate him for it. For the past week, he'd been thinking he was uncomfortable about all the sneaking around he'd been doing to keep their affair hidden, but that was only half the problem, wasn't it? That was him lying to himself about lying to *her*, thinking that he could somehow juggle all the deceptions and sweep the forgeries under the proverbial rug. That he could cancel his debt to Monk and help Hadley's father, all without her knowing. Which would've been a fine plan if it were only a simple affair.

But somewhere between the time he first saw her in the train station and the last night he'd slept in her bed, it became so much more, and now he was well and truly fucked.

He was going to lose her over this. He should've just told her. She'd understood about Adam and Stella—maybe she would've understood this, too. But not now. It was too late.

He was an idiot. A goddamn idiot.

A tall, thin man in full tails approached. At his temples, two gray streaks ran through dark hair, swooping up like wings. "Good evening," he said. "Are you enjoying my collection?"

"Mr. Levin," Hadley answered, one octave too high. *Helvete.*

Levin squinted at Hadley. "Have we met? You look terribly familiar, my dear."

"No, I'm afraid not."

"We've just arrived from Los Angeles today," Lowe

quickly said, somehow gathering the wherewithal to pull himself together.

"Yes, from Columbia Studios—is that right? The doorman told one of my men, and I had to come meet you myself. What exactly do you do?"

Terrific. The man would know they'd lied about leaving the invitation at the hotel, wouldn't he? Lowe stuck out his hand and quickly concocted a second story. "James Anderson, producer. And this my assistant, Miss Black. We're here to scout locations for a mystery picture. Heard about your gala and decided to drop by. Hope you don't mind that we showed up uninvited."

"Of course not. I'm pleasantly surprised."

Might've been Lowe's imagination, but Levin seemed to squeeze his hand a little too hard. He reminded himself that Monk often conducted silent deals, and surely hadn't given out Lowe's name. So there was no reason to panic.

Levin's eyes narrowed. "What's your picture about, exactly?"

Lowe summarized a Dashiell Hammett serial from *Black Mask* magazine about a hard-boiled private detective solving a missing gem case on the streets of San Francisco. Levin appeared to be listening. Hadley, however, did not. Throughout Lowe's story, she stole several curious glances at the crocodile statue, and upon hearing Levin's enthusiastic response to Lowe's fake script, stepped forward and pointed to the statue.

"Pardon, Mr. Levin," she said. "But I'm quite taken with this. Where in the world did you acquire such a thing?"

"My dear, it's funny you should ask. I purchased it from a man who deals in, shall we say, under-the-table sales of antiquities."

"Oh, my."

Levin crossed his arms and leaned closer to Hadley.

"Have I shocked you?" Levin asked her. "Because it quite shocked me when my lawyer discovered the paperwork was not in order. And it shocked me even more when I heard there was another statue just like it rumored to be in the private collection of a Scottish laird now living in Manhattan."

"A forgery?" Hadley squinted at the statue. "How intriguing. It looks quite original."

Levin smiled. "Doesn't it? Your partner here does excellent work."

A silence hung between the three of them, one that ballooned inside the stuffy theater lobby until it muted everything. It wasn't the first time Lowe had been in situations like this—in which he needed to make a split-second decision to either bullshit his way around the problem or flee. But damned if he wasn't rooted to the floor right now without a single word on his tongue.

All at once, everything suddenly slipped out of his reach. His money. His future. His pride. And from the look on her face, Hadley herself.

And, as if God hadn't smote him well and good enough already, a dark-headed man in a long brown coat stepped out from Levin's shadow.

"Good to see you again, Magnusson. Was worried you might be avoiding me."

Monk Morales.

Not Bacall's ex-partner following them, after all. If Lowe's world hadn't just fallen apart, he might've laughed at the irony; he'd used Velma's last mojo bag on the wrong person.

Levin nodded to a couple of policemen guarding his collection and spoke to Lowe. "Why don't the four of us have a little talk in my office upstairs. These officers will make sure we aren't interrupted."

TWENTY-EIGHT

―――⚜―――

HADLEY DIDN'T SAY A WORD AS LEVIN LED THEM INTO A LOCKED
hallway on the second floor of the theater. Surely this was
all wrong. There was an explanation of some sort. A good
reason. She remembered back to that afternoon they'd eaten
clam chowder at the wharf, and Mrs. Alioto had mentioned
Monk Morales was looking for him. Lowe had trivialized
it. Made it sound like it was nothing.

Running a forgery ring was not her idea of *nothing*.

In her mind, Lowe's face splintered into two images: the
Lowe she knew—the one she'd given her body and heart
to—and the Lowe she'd pictured before they ever met. The
digger. Treasure hunter. Part of a family of criminals.

Forger.

Levin unlocked a door. The policemen waited outside
while she trailed Lowe and Mr. Morales into a grand office
that had dark wood, expensive rugs, a fireplace, and a ridiculously dramatic desk that took up half the room. The walls
were lined with shelves. Mostly books, but a few stray Egyptian pieces. No canopic jars. And at the moment, she couldn't
even make herself care.

Levin paused in front of the fireplace. He warmed his hands for a moment, and then settled behind his enormous desk, looking more like a king than a theater owner in his high-backed leather chair. "I must say, Miss Bacall, I wouldn't have guessed you'd have friends in such low places."

Her shoulders went rigid. "You know who I am?"

"Spitting image of your mother. My late wife was friendly with her. They used to rub elbows at museum parties."

Maybe it was his late wife who acquired the canopic jar from her mother.

Levin reached in a desk drawer and pulled out a cigar. "And everyone knows your father, of course. We run into each other in New York now and then. Or we used to, when he'd make the trip out East to bid on pieces for the museum."

"He's never spoken of you," she said tartly.

Levin snipped off the tip of his cigar. "It's been a few years since I've seen him. But when Monk's men reported hearing about the two of you"—he nodded at Lowe—"gallivanting around town together, I was surprised. Does Dr. Bacall know you're making time with a con artist? Because I would think the museum would frown upon such affiliations. Could tarnish their reputation—especially if word got out that Mr. Magnusson is playing the forgery game."

"Leave her out of this," Lowe said. "She has no knowledge of any of it. And frankly, Mr. Levin, I didn't make the deal with you—this matter is between Monk and me."

"It damn sure is," Monk said, pushing the brim of his hat high on his brow until it looked as if it might fall off his head. "And what are you gonna do to square it?"

"The only thing I can do. Return your money." Lowe narrowed his eyes and raised his hand as if to calm the air between them. "I can stop by your place and give you half in cash tomorrow—"

"I don't want my money back," Levin said, throwing the cigar on his desk like an overgrown child. "I want the real statue."

"Not mine to give," Lowe said.

"Is that right?" Levin snagged the base of his candlestick telephone and angrily set it down in front of him with a thud. "Then shall I call the Scottish collector myself and let him know there's a possibility his crocodile is a forgery, as well?"

Lowe closed his eyes briefly and exhaled heavily through his nostrils. "Listen—"

"How long have you been doing this?" Hadley said, interrupting the conversation. She really didn't care if the other men were gangsters or kings. "How long?"

Lowe's face turned toward hers. "Hadley—"

"Is that what you're doing with all the finds you bring back from Egypt?"

"No. *No*," he repeated. "I'll tell you everything." His voice was low. Eyes, pleading. "Please. Just let me talk to Monk."

All at once, the heat left her body as her mind drew a line from the crocodile statue to the reason they were at the theater. "The amulet," she whispered, covering her mouth with her fingers. "That too?"

"Hadley—"

She jerked away from his reach. "Tell me, right now. Look me in the eye and tell me you weren't going to cheat my father. That you weren't going to let him hand you a check while . . ." God, she couldn't breathe. Could barely talk. "Please tell me that you weren't going to let him die to make a dollar."

Lowe rushed for her as she tried to back up. He managed to grabbed her hand and pull it against his chest. She could feel his heart racing. "I swear to all things holy, I wasn't. I mean, I *was*—at the beginning. I needed the money, and fast. I didn't know you, or your father. I didn't know this would happen between us."

Her eyes blurred. "But it did."

"And I changed my plans to go through with it," Lowe insisted, his bright blue eyes rapidly darting back and forth, as he intently tried to trap her gaze. "I couldn't—wouldn't. God, Hadley, please believe me. I promised you I wouldn't lie when this hand is holding yours."

"You should've told me!" Hadley jerked away from his grip and swiped at her eyes. Hurt and anger shredded her good sense into tiny pieces that blew away like confetti. Her chest hurt. She couldn't breathe. Couldn't see. And like a siren's call, her swell of grief called to the specters, clanging a silent alarm. She felt them come: shadows slithering in the corners of the room . . . dark shapes shifting in the background of her bleary vision. The temperature in the cozy office dropped several degrees.

"Your personal problems are riveting," Levin said dryly. "And I'm sure your father will be thrilled to hear that you're consorting with men like Magnusson. But unless you want the entire city to know, I suggest you convince your beau here to do what I've asked. I want the real statue. Immediately."

Lowe ignored the man and held his hands out as she backed away. "Hadley, don't. Take a deep breath. You can kill me later if you want, but don't hurt them. You'll regret it."

"You should've told me," she repeated. A black sea of Mori specters covered the room, climbing the bookshelves. Scurrying across the ceiling. Rising up from the floor. Their half-human shapes circled Lowe.

They were so hungry.

Hadley's control was slipping. She heard an anguished growl and was distantly aware it came from her.

"What the hell is going on?" Levin mumbled.

"Magnusson," Monk barked. "If you ever want to work again, you'd better pay attention. I want my money back, and Levin wants the real statue. Get your ass over here and start making calls."

"Hadley, please. Count if you need to," Lowe said.

She was beyond counting. Or caring.

"I'm not screwing around." Monk's arm lifted. Metal clicked.

Hadley swiveled in time to see a gun pointed in Lowe's direction. And that's when she snapped.

The Mori swarmed to a shelf near Monk and pushed a vase over the edge. It tumbled through the air and shattered on his shoulder, sending out a shower of ceramic shards.

"Arghhhh!" Monk stumbled as the gun flew from his hand.

Lowe lunged after it, while Levin leapt up from his chair with a confused shout.

And in the scuffle, Hadley gave the Mori their freedom. *They're yours,* she thought.

Their collective dark shiver reverberated through her bones.

Books shot off the shelves, pages flapping—leather-bound bullets sailing from every direction, pummeling the three men. Monk's knees buckled. He fell to the floor under a pile of books. Glass shattered. Light bulbs popped, shrouding the room in shadow, but for the orange glow flickering in the fireplace.

"Hadley!"

The office door flung open. White light poured in from the hallway as the two policemen rushed into the room. "What the—"

Chaos. Shouting. Banging. File cabinet doors crashed open, one by one—their contents gusting into the air, fluttering around Levin. A horrible scraping whine rocketed through the room as the specters shoved the enormous desk backward. Levin jumped in time. Barely. He was inches away from being crushed against the wall along with his chair.

A silhouette dove toward her. She was knocked sideways and fell. Her back hit the floor. Air whooshed out of her lungs.

Pain. Sharp pain. A terrible brightness swelled and faded. She forced her muscles to cooperate and finally sucked in air. Opened her eyes. She was crushed beneath something. Not a specter—warm, not cold. "Hadley!" Her name, repeated several times. Then numbers.

She blinked away confusion, struggling against an impossible weight.

"Ten, eleven, twelve . . ."

Above her, Lowe's face materialized in the shadows. She saw his lips moving. Heard the counting. And when those two things merged, a horrible sob wracked her chest.

"It's okay," he said. "I've got you. It's okay."

Anger leaked away with her tears. She felt the Mori weakening. Felt their anguished protest as the chaotic frenzy in the room began quieting. And one by one, the specters faded away.

She distantly heard angry shouting. Confusion. Acrid smoke—someone was swatting out a fire. But all of that muffled sound snapped to the foreground when Lowe cried out near her ear. His weight and warmth suddenly disappeared.

She raised her head to see the policemen hauling Lowe to his feet.

"Arrest him," Levin was shouting angrily as he wiped his hands on the front of his disheveled tuxedo. Nearby, smoke curled from a pile of books beside the fireplace.

"What charge?" one of the cops asked, his skittish gaze jumping around the room, sweeping the shadows, taking in the mounds of book carcasses and scattered broken pottery. Lines creased his tight brow. He was clearly worried the invisible tornado might start whirling again.

"What the hell do I care?" Levin said. "Destruction of property? Theft?"

The second cop kicked away a book and picked up Monk's gun from where it had landed on the floor. "How about brandishing an unregistered gun?"

Levin bent to help Monk. "Just take him in and make sure his bail is sky high."

"What about her?"

"Touch her and I'll strangle you," Lowe said through gritted teeth, struggling against the policemen's hold.

"He threatened me," Levin said. "You all heard it."

As Hadley rose up on one knee, Levin jerked back, eyeing her with fear and disbelief. She'd seen the same crazed uncertainty in other faces, a dozen times over. He knew she was responsible for all this, and yet, it made no rational sense. But he was too much of a coward to ask questions. Better to blame it on something ordinary, no matter how improbable.

"Let her go," Levin said. "I'll contact her father later."

Anger pricked her cheeks, but before she could respond, footsteps thundered in the hallway outside the office. More people on their way. More questions. The press was already here for the gala; the last thing she needed was to be publicly identified in the middle of all this.

She stood on trembling legs and faced Lowe. In the shifting firelight, she could see cuts on his face. A splatter of blood, dark against the white of his shirt collar. A fresh wave of hurt threatened to take her under again. The pain of betrayal and loss crisscrossed over her heart like wild brambles.

She couldn't be in the same room with him. Not now. If she lost control again, her Mori might burn the whole damn theater down.

TWENTY-NINE

***

WITHOUT ANOTHER WORD, SHE STRODE FOR THE DOOR AND slipped past a small group of concerned employees clamoring to get inside the office. Down the staircase, she shouldered her way through chattering onlookers. Speculation volleyed past her ears as she descended: *What's going on? A fight? The police are arresting someone.* When she stumbled her way out of the crowd, she ran into more theater employees. Police. And the front door was still being manned by the ass who'd reported them to Levin.

Where to go? She pulled her fur coat closed and ducked her head as she made her way to the opposite side of the lobby. Panic sharpened her senses. And though her mind urged her to flee, a queer feeling gave her pause, one that lifted the hairs on the arms. She took a few experimental steps down one of the side corridors and the feeling strengthened. Where?

She spotted a sign—LADIES' OASIS—and quickly darted through the swinging door into an elegant lounge. Potted palms, sofas, and stuffed chairs. Beyond the small room, bright lights lit up the washroom. All was quiet and calm. Deceptively normal.

But across the powder room, a long gilded mirror hung on the wall, embossed with papyrus. And below, sitting innocently on a narrow marble makeup table, was the falcon-headed canopic jar.

She quelled her frazzled nerves as a toilet flushed in the next room, and then she waited, listening as heels clicked and water ran. A middle-aged woman finally walked through the powder room, smiling stiffly at Hadley as she passed. As soon as the door swung shut, Hadley rushed for the urn, hoisted it in the air over her head, and brought it down violently over the marble table.

Gold glinted. The crossbar bounced across the table. Hadley grabbed it, ignoring the foul energy it radiated, and slipped it into her coat pocket.

"My goodness!" a woman said behind her. "Are you all right, dear?"

Hadley pushed through the swinging door without an answer. Her head was clearer than it had been in weeks. If love was a thick fog, then heartbreak was the cold winter rain that washed it all away. For all the deceptions she'd stumbled upon over the last few weeks—her father's secrets about her mother's affair, Oliver Ginn's hidden agenda—this was the last thing she expected to face. But she would, no matter how much it hurt.

And she knew there was one person who could give her the whole truth.

A blond head bobbed above the crowd on the balcony's landing. Gala attendees swarmed around the staircase, watching the police forcibly haul Lowe down the stairs. He could rot in a jail cell for all she cared. Hadley moved quickly, slipping past the roped-off area housing Levin's ramshackle collection, and snagged the last thing she needed.

She didn't sleep that night, having spent half of it crying and the other half pushing back the Mori so that Number Four wasn't caught in the cross fire. At one point, the emotional pain had been so intense that she'd tried to rationalize a path to forgiving him.

But would this be the last time?

She couldn't help but picture a bumpy future with Lowe, filled with lies and deceit that never ended. Imagined herself sitting at home pining for him while he was halfway across the globe, betraying her in other ways . . . maybe even with other women.

Perhaps her original assessment of him had been right. He was too handsome, too quick with false words and easy deceptions. He had a way of making all of that seem charming, but it was a false front. Nothing charming about building your life around lies. And when did it stop? She wouldn't be surprised to discover other deceptions—ones she just hadn't caught yet.

How big a fool was she, anyway?

Focusing on her self-appointed task gave her the motivation she needed to seek an answer to that question. And the following morning, she brushed aside tears and set out alone.

It wasn't hard to find Adam Goldberg. Lowe might've claimed his friend was merely a dragon guarding his treasure, but she was quite certain he was something much more. A friendly chat with an eager young telephone operator got her a list of Fillmore District businesses with Goldberg in the name, and when the word "watchmaker" crackled over the line, she knew it had to be him.

Heading out into gray drizzle, she wore a hat with a broad brim that was several years out of fashion to hide her face and took two taxis—to shake anyone who might be trailing her. Convinced she hadn't been followed, she paid the driver to wait at the curb and stepped inside a small shop.

A bell rang above the door to announce her entrance. She tugged at her gloves and glanced around at the small, warm room as the scents of solder flux and coppery metal filled her nostrils. A wooden counter stood between a narrow area and the back workspace, where saws and ball-peen hammers lined the wall near a forge and buffing machines. Across the room, a bright swing-arm lamp shone over a desk lined with neat trays of wire, cogs, and screws. And tucked in the corner near the desk was a smaller table, where Stella bent over a colorful drawing. Lowe's windup black cat sat near her elbow.

Hadley's chest tightened as she watched the girl, who was oblivious to her entry. Was she really Lowe's child? And how many times had he gazed at the girl's curling hair and wondered the same thing? She could only imagine how painful it must be for Lowe to stand aside and watch her grow up with the burden of guilt and a yawning unknown hanging over his head.

He'd betrayed Adam—his best friend. Why was it such a shock that he'd do the same to her?

Footsteps marched down a narrow set of stairs, ones that looked as though they might lead to an apartment above the shop, and Adam stepped into view. Wiping his hands on a work towel, he glanced toward the door. His face brightened momentarily as he recognized her, but quickly tightened with anxiety and wariness.

"Good morning, Mr. Goldberg," she said crisply.

"Hadley—"

Stella glanced up from her drawing and blinked. A grin spread over her plump face. She dropped her crayon and started toward Hadley, but stopped halfway, unsure, and backtracked to the safety of her father's legs.

Adam glanced over her shoulder. "Is Lowe here, too?"

"When we parted last night, Lowe was on his way to jail," Hadley said

"Good grief, what's happened?"

Hadley reached inside her coat pocket and placed the golden crocodile on the glass top of the counter, beneath which laid rows of gold and silver pocket watches on a burgundy strip of velvet. "This has happened. We ran into Monk Morales last night. I'm assuming you're intimately familiar with this statue."

Adam swore softly in Yiddish.

She turned the crocodile to face her. "Extraordinary work, I must say. It fooled me, and that's saying a lot. But it appears that the buyer, Mr. Samuel Levin, is quite angry that Lowe deceived him, so he had him arrested."

Adam put a protective hand on Stella's head and drew her closer. "Does he know I made the forgery?"

"No, I figured that out myself." She pulled out the small golden crossbar. "I should've known it was strange that you were merely hiding the pieces for Lowe, especially after he told me that Velma Toussaint had warded the safe where you kept valuables. If the safe was protected by magic, why didn't Lowe just keep it himself at his own house?"

Adam's shoulders dropped. "Why, indeed." After settling Stella back down at her tiny table, he locked the shop door, pulled down the window shade, and disappeared through a door. A minute later, he returned with a box shaped like a miniature trunk, whose painted black surface was covered in red symbols. "Can you lay that down over the glass, please?" he asked, arms straining.

Hadley unfolded a scrap of soft brown leather and spread it upon the glass countertop. She soon understood why: the box was rough enough to scratch the glass. "Cast iron," he explained. "Keeps things hidden, according to Velma. Seems to work, so no reason to doubt her, I suppose."

The moment he unlocked the box and swung open the lid, Hadley grimaced and turned her head away. Dark energy rose from the box, so strong, it was nearly palpable.

Adam made a low noise in the back of his throat. "You can feel it, too? Lowe says he does. Stella and I can't, thank goodness." He lifted two items from the box and laid them down side by side on the leather. "This is the original, and this one's mine."

Bracing herself against the bad energy, Hadley leaned over the counter. Her mouth dropped open. Two identical amulets, each assembled with the Osiris base and two crossbars. "Good lord," she murmured. "You've been copying it as we've found the pieces?"

He nodded. "Lowe wanted to replicate it so he could . . ." Brown eyes shifted and lowered as he cleared his throat.

"Yes, he told me," she said. "He'd planned to cheat my

father out of a hundred thousand dollars and sell the original to someone else."

"Not sell—it was to pay off Monk for the crocodile forgery. Monk's got no qualms about putting a bullet in your head."

"Yes, he nearly did just that last night." She picked up the copy of the amulet and tested its weight in her palm against the real thing. Aside from the intense energy emanating from the artifact, she could detect no difference between the two. Even the reddish hue to the gold was right. And Lowe intended to use the real amulet to pay off his debt to Monk? A fair chunk of cash, she had no doubt, but surely Lowe could've asked his bootlegger brother for it. Hell, if he would've just been honest and asked *her*, she would've gladly given it.

"Oh, boy." Adam sighed and scratched the back of his neck. "I wonder if he's called his brother to bail him out?"

"As of an hour ago, no," she said. "I called the precinct and they said he hasn't made a telephone call."

"Probably because Winter will skin him alive if he finds out. And Lowe's pride is bigger than the Golden Gate, in case you haven't noticed."

How a liar and a fraud had any pride at all, Hadley couldn't comprehend. She wished she had brawn enough to punch him repeatedly and knock some sense into his stupid male brain. To make him see how ridiculous all of this was. How boneheaded he was to lose what they had over something as meaningless as money and as useless as pride.

"This is beautiful," she said softly, placing it back on the leather. "I don't know how you did it, but it's an exact match. All my expertise, and I can't tell it's a fake. Your work is exquisite."

He shrugged and waved a dismissive hand. A few quiet seconds ticked by before he said softly, "He's in love with you, you know."

Fresh grief made her sore, tear-weary eyes well up again. "People in love don't lie to each other."

"You're wrong. They lie the most."

She couldn't stop her gaze from flicking to Stella. He noticed. Whether or not he guessed that Lowe had told her about their past, she didn't know. But the sadness behind his eyes was too much for her to endure.

"If the museum finds out what Lowe's been up to, and that I've been seeing him, my career is ruined. And he knows how important that is to me. It's everything. My life's blood is wrapped up in the antiquities wing, and . . ." No use in explaining further. It didn't change the reality of the matter. "I guess I underestimated his carelessness."

"I don't think Lowe's problem is a lack of feelings," Adam said carefully. "Just the opposite, in fact. When he makes mistakes, he's so focused on righting the wrong, and so overconfident about his ability to fix it all, that he loses sight of the big picture and ends up making things worse."

She looked away to gain some control over her wayward emotions and dug an envelope out of her pocket. "Here," she said, handing it to Adam. "For his bail. He's being held at the Richmond precinct station. I wrote down the captain's direct telephone line inside."

He tried to give back the envelope. "You do it. Go talk to him."

"Did he tell you why my father wants the amulet?" she asked in a rough voice. "Did he tell you . . . about me?"

Adam seemed genuinely confused. "I know the amulet pieces are hidden around the city, and I know how much your father is willing to pay Lowe to find them."

"My father is very ill, and that amulet might save his life."

Adam blew out a long breath. "You know how Lowe's parents died?"

She nodded. "Car accident. That is, I only know from the newspapers. Lowe never talks about it."

"Not surprising. It was a bad time. But you do know that his brother, Winter, was the one driving the car?"

She nodded once.

"Winter took it hard. Blamed himself. Lowe, on the other hand, spent a couple weeks grieving before taking off to

Egypt. Thought he could outrun it, you know. And maybe he did, for a while." He shrugged. 'But I guess my point is that Lowe would not under any circumstances choose money over your father's life. He may be a lot of things, but he's not a monster."

She ducked her head and twisted her jaw to stop from crying.

After a few moments, Adam slid the third crossbar toward her along with the real amulet, affixed with the first two crossbars. "Take it. If you sort out things with Lowe and still want to copy the rest of it, you know where to find me. And if not?" He gave her a wry smile. "Well, let's just say he owes me."

"Are you sure?"

He made a shooing gesture with his hand. "Take it," he insisted, placing the amulet's copy inside the box.

"Then you keep the crocodile. After all, you made it." She pocketed the amulet. "That is, if you want to risk holding on to the thing. I made sure I wasn't followed here, but Monk Morales might have ears to the ground."

He slipped the crocodile inside the box before closing it and rapping his knuckles on the lid. "This old gal will keep it hidden. Velma said the iron alone would probably do the trick—people have hidden things in iron for centuries. But her magic makes it doubly safe."

Hadley smiled tightly as she pulled on her gloves. A thought stilled her hands.

Iron.

She knew something made of iron. Something right in her own family's backyard. She mentally summoned the pictograms on the last urn—the one they couldn't crack or match up to any names on the list. It was the right number of letters, but she'd been through every possible interpretation a thousand times.

Every interpretation but one.

Funny how one wrong letter could change a word so completely.

"Are you all right?" Adam asked.

"No, I'm really not," she mumbled as a buzzing brightness filled her mind with a singular, enormous idea—one that was so distracting, she failed to notice the dark car parked across the street, or the man who stepped out of the driver's seat, as she sped away inside her taxi.

THIRTY

———◆———

LOWE COLLECTED HIS THINGS FROM THE HOLDING WINDOW AND nodded at the captain before heading upstairs to the police station lobby with Bo.

"Thanks again," he told Winter's assistant.

"You should've called last night," he chastised, his slender, sinewy body outpacing Lowe's as they ascended into dreary midday light filtering in from gray windows. "If Chief Ryan knew they had a Magnusson locked up on trumped-up charges, he would've gotten out of his bed to come here and personally haul their asses over the coals."

Lowe straightened his necktie and attempted to brush out the wrinkles in his suit jacket. His back was killing him. He'd dozed off in the jail cell once or twice, only getting enough sleep to make him grouchy. He was also vaguely aware that he hadn't had anything to eat since yesterday's lunch. And yet, none of those discomforts matched the unyielding heavy ache in the pit of his stomach.

Monk wanted him dead.

Levin was eager to expose him for a forger and rip away any credibility he had as an archaeologist.

The hunt for the crossbars was now hopeless, so he'd certainly voided his payout from Bacall. And in the process, he'd likely resigned the man to his death, thereby leaving his daughter exposed to his dangerous ex-partner's dark magic and unhealthy obsessions.

And—the worst of it all—he'd not only lost Hadley; he might very well have ruined her reputation and career.

"Christ, Bo. I've fucked up."

Bo tugged the brim of his newsboy cap and agreed heartily, confirming his fears with an enthusiastic expression in Cantonese that Lowe could only guess meant "thoroughly."

"I'd appreciate if you wouldn't tell Winter about this," Lowe said.

"I'm sure you would," Bo agreed. "You're a decent man, despite your faults, and I like you. But my loyalty is to Winter, and you know that."

"Just take me home. But I need to stop by Adam's first and find out why he never showed."

The captain had said Adam had called at ten, promising he'd be there in a half hour. It was now past one. Anything could've held him up, but with Lowe's recent luck, chances were it wasn't good. And though he desperately wanted to head straight to Hadley's, he had to check on Adam first.

Bo pointed to the curb. "I drove Lulu here. Jonte's waiting out front in the Pierce-Arrow. I'll ride with him to the theater and pick up the Packard. You'd better hope to God it's still in one piece or Winter might have to kill you twice."

"Once is more than enough," Lowe said.

"Hey," Bo said in a kinder voice. "Chin up. You'll find your way out of this. Always do."

There was a first time for everything.

Lowe buttoned up his coat and watched Bo jog down the station's front steps and slide into Winter's limousine. But as Lowe started out the door, the police operator said something to one of the detectives that caught his attention.

He backtracked to the front desk. "Did you just say Fillmore?"

The operator glanced up at him, eyes wary, and darted a questioning look at the detective.

"Yeah, Fillmore District," the detective confirmed. "Earlier this morning."

"A homicide?"

"We don't know that yet. What's it to you?"

Lowe felt the blood drain from his face. His fingertips began tingling. He nearly tripped as he rushed out of the building, unable to say another word.

His mind was numb as he sped away on Lulu, flying through the city. Stop signs blurred. He ignored honking horns and gave no thought to recklessly cutting corners as he wove in and out of traffic on wet pavement.

He brought Lulu to a screeching halt, her back end fishtailing as he skidded behind two police cars. A crowd of people looked to be disbanding behind a sawhorse blocking their view of the shop. A couple of uniformed cops guarded the door.

Lowe's heart dropped to his stomach when he spotted the black City Morgue truck rumbling away down the street. He jumped off of Lulu and rushed toward the shop's entrance, shouting in Swedish.

"Whoa." The police grabbed his arm. "You can't go in there. You speak English?"

Lowe switched languages. "Adam Goldberg is the owner of this shop, and I'm his friend. Where is he? What's happened?"

"Calm down, sir. What's your name?"

"Lowe Magnusson." He glanced at the men's faces, forcing himself to look closer and see if he recognized either as one of the many cops Winter paid off; he didn't. "I'm Winter Magnusson's brother."

Recognition clicked behind the first cop's eyes. He whispered something to the other man. And when Lowe tried to move around them, he said, "Whoa, whoa, whoa. You don't want to go in there."

"Yes, I goddamn do." Lowe shoved the man's hand away. "What's happened to Adam?"

"I'm sorry, buddy," the cop said, holding up both hands

to block him. "Your friend was found dead a couple of hours ago."

"We're real sorry for your loss," the other said solemnly, removing his hat to cant his head.

Lowe glanced back and forth between them as the words sank in.

Dead.

Gone.

Impossible.

A mistake.

Lowe blinked and tried to speak, but his throat wouldn't work. He licked dry lips and tried again. "How? Why? Oh, God—where's Stella? Is she . . ."

Please God, no.

This couldn't be happening. Not again. He'd grieved for too many people. He couldn't lose Adam and Stella. He just couldn't. This wasn't happening.

"Maybe he should talk to the detective," someone said. "Mr. Magnusson? You okay?"

He nodded.

They let him inside, but stopped him from going past the counter. The shop was wrecked. Broken glass, tools scattered. And all these cops inside here made it feel wrong—a place that he knew as well as his own home suddenly felt foreign.

"Detective Cohen," the first cop said. "This is Lowe Magnusson. Friend of Goldberg."

A dark-headed man in a long navy raincoat glanced up from his notepad. "Mr. Magnusson, you say?"

"*That* Magnusson," the cop clarified.

The detective gave Lowe a sympathetic nod. "I knew your father. I'm sorry for your loss. You were close to Mr. Goldberg?"

Lowe nodded, trying to look around the man's shoulders to see. "Where's Stella?"

"The little girl?"

"*Ja, ja.* Where is she?"

The detective put a hand on Lowe's shoulder. "She's all

right. In safe hands. Maybe a little traumatized—shop owner next door found her hiding beneath the table over in the corner."

"Oh . . . Jesus." Lowe began to unravel. His hands were shaking so badly, he clenched them into fists to make them stop. "I d-don't understand what's happening."

"When was the last time you saw your friend?"

Think. When? "I think it was two days ago. Three." When he'd come to tell Adam about the new plan. The plan to switch the amulet paperwork. Give Monk the real documents and the forged amulet. Give Dr. Bacall the real thing. "I brought sandwiches," he said, as if that mattered. They'd played hide-and-seek with Stella.

The detective scribbled down Lowe's answer in a small notepad. "And how did you know him?"

"We're childhood friends. I grew up in this neighborhood."

"How old was he?"

"What?"

"His age?"

"Same age as me," Lowe said, confused. "Twenty-five. What difference does that make?"

The detective squinted at Lowe, and then nodded toward the back of the shop. "It appears someone was looking for something here. You got any idea what that might've been? Did Mr. Goldberg have any enemies? Anyone harassing him?"

Christ. Was this his fault? Was it Monk or Levin? Couldn't be. How would they have known? One of Monk's men? He'd been so careful. And Monk acted like he didn't know who the forger was when he'd questioned Lowe in Levin's office at the theater last night.

"I don't think so," Lowe said.

"The couple next door—"

"The Ackermans," Lowe said. "The hardware store."

"Yeah. The wife said she saw a dame go inside around nine thirty."

Lowe stilled. "Who?"

"Didn't know her." The detective checked his penciled notes. "Black hair. Tall. Dark fur coat."

Hadley.

"Said she was in there for a quarter hour or so. Left by taxi. As soon as she was gone, a man got out of a blue Cadillac and entered the shop."

Lowe didn't know anyone with a blue Caddy. But God almighty, what the hell was Hadley doing over here? She'd tracked down Adam and someone followed her. Who?

"Mrs. Ackerman heard shouting," the detective continued. "Said she heard Mr. Goldberg telling the visitor to get out. Tried to get into the shop to see what was going on, but the door was locked. Had her husband knock on the door, but no one came. So they called us. We had a patrol car in the neighborhood, but by the time the officer got here, the man had raced out the door and taken off in the Cadillac."

"Did Mrs. Ackerman get a good look at him?"

The detective nodded. "Dark hair. Tall. Thin. Handsome guy, she said. Her husband got the tag number." The detective narrowed his eyes. "You know anyone named Oliver Ginn?"

It felt as though the floor suddenly washed out from under his feet. He put a hand on the counter to steady himself and tried to keep his voice light. "His name sounds familiar, but I can't place where I've heard it."

"Well, we can't seem to place him at all. Dispatch gave us the address listed for the registration, and it doesn't exist anymore. Destroyed in the Great Fire. Belonged to a man who died. Name of"—he checked his notes—"Noel Irving."

Oliver Ginn.

Noel Irving.

Inside his shock-fueled brain, the letters rearranged themselves without effort.

An anagram.

A goddamn anagram.

"Anyway, whoever the guy is, we figure he killed your friend and trashed the place looking for something. Probably got scared off when Ackerman banged on the door."

"How?"

"Pardon?"

"How did he die?" Lowe asked in a voice that sounded far away.

"We aren't really sure, yet. You say he was twenty-five. The Ackermans and a couple of other neighbors said the same thing, and his identification confirms it." The detective lifted his hat to scratch his head. "But when we found him, I know this might sound crazy, but he looked . . ."

"What?" Lowe demanded, trying to read the man's face.

"He looked like an old man."

Jesus Christ.

Lowe stared at the detective for a suspended moment, a thousand thoughts jumbling inside his head, and none of them jibing . . . until his gaze landed on broken crayons scattered across the floor.

Fall apart later, he told himself, fighting the onslaught of emotion threatening to bring him to his knees. *Just keep it together for a little longer.*

"Where have you taken Stella?" he asked.

"Pacific Hebrew Orphan Asylum, on Silver and Mission. Everyone said the next living relative would be Goldberg's father—"

"He's a drunk," Lowe said angrily. "Adam wouldn't let Stella anywhere near him. Not that the old man even gave a damn. Last Adam heard, he was somewhere in Philadelphia."

"Court will still try to contact him. Anyone else you know? An aunt, maybe? Deceased wife's family?"

"The girl knows me," Lowe insisted. "I've seen her every week since she was born. I'm her family."

"Legally?"

Oh, Christ. "She's deaf. She needs special care," Lowe argued.

The detective set his hat down on the counter, nodding. "The orphanage director is aware."

Lowe started to say something else, but another cop signaled for the detective outside. "Listen," the detective said, "you can petition the court for guardianship. And you can go talk to the ladies at the orphanage—maybe even set up visitation. But we can't just release her into anyone's care. I'm really sorry, and I know you're distraught. Believe me, I'll do whatever it takes to make sure we find out what happened here today. Give me a number where we can contact you. Hold on, I'll be right back."

Blindly, Lowe pulled out a business card and left it on the counter next to the detective's hat. And when the man stepped outside to talk with one of the cops, Lowe strode to Adam's curtained-off storage room at the back of the shop. Without hesitation, he pushed aside an empty crate and popped open a secret panel in the wall. The iron box was still there, thank God.

The key was hidden separately. Lowe rummaged through a tray of old tools. Found it at the bottom. Quickly unlocked the iron box.

The crocodile statue stared back at him. It took Lowe several moments to get over the surprise of seeing it there. Another moment to realize that he couldn't feel any strange energy. But when he moved the statue and found only one amulet—not two—he had a damn good idea where the other had gone.

Hadley certainly hadn't come here to make small talk about the weather.

And if Noel Irving had just killed Adam to get his hands on the amulet, what the hell would he do to Hadley?

THIRTY-ONE

◆

HADLEY SPENT HOURS SEARCHING HER FATHER'S HOUSE FOR THE key to the family mausoleum. The staff thought her mad. She didn't give a damn. Father would be back any minute from his checkup at the hospital, and she was prepared to outright tell him what was going on—that she knew everything about her mother and Noel Irving. That she'd been helping Lowe search for the crossbars the entire time.

That he'd betrayed both of them.

And that she'd fallen for someone who'd broken her heart.

It was all bound to come out sooner or later. Levin might've already called Father, for all she knew. Regardless, she had to get inside the mausoleum. If she had to bloody her fists to knock the door down with her own hands, she would.

"Miss," the oldest housekeeper said, blowing a stray hair out of her reddened face. "I really don't know where else to look. It's probably in your father's safe. When he gets home, we'll ask him for it. But if he comes back and finds you've torn through the house, he'll be very upset. And we're not to be upsetting him in his condition."

"If we don't find that key, his condition will get a hell of a lot worse on its own. And what safe are you talking about? The one in his study?"

The housekeeper's plump face flushed a deeper shade of red. "I meant the other one."

"What 'other' one?"

"Can't we just—"

Hadley narrowed her eyes. "Show me the safe, Charlotte. *Now.*"

She followed the woman up the grand staircase to her father's bedroom. The nightstand next to his bed had a drawer that didn't open. The housekeeper lifted off the lamp and pulled the piece of furniture away from the wall. The back opened up to expose a black safe, the size of the front drawer.

"I don't know the combination," Charlotte insisted.

But Hadley did. Her father used the same predictable numbers he always used: Hadley's date of birth. And after a few quick turns of the knob, the lock clicked open. She tried not to look too hard at the few things that lay inside: photographs of her mother, some legal documents, a stack of cash. Several keys were stuffed inside a small envelope, but she had no trouble finding the one she needed: one large key and one small, both on a hammered ring.

The mausoleum was built by her mother's grandfather in 1856, a year after the house was built with the Murray family's newly acquired gold rush fortune. The story was that Great-Grandfather Murray wanted to build it in Laurel Hill Cemetery—back when it was called Lone Mountain—but got into a fistfight with someone from the records office when he attempted to purchase a plot of land. Angry at the city, he was resolved to build it in his own backyard.

It wasn't large. The roof of the neoclassical structure was barely two feet above Hadley's head. And though it was much deeper than tall, half the back end had been swallowed by huckleberry bushes, and the entire building was dwarfed by the cover of her grandmother's prized Blackwood Acacia tree. One of the two columns sported a large crack—earthquake damage—but both it and the house had been spared during the Great Fire, as they were on the northwestern side of Russian Hill.

With afternoon drizzle misting her hair, Hadley fitted the heavy key into the mausoleum's ironclad door. The rusty lock gave way, but the door was a little more work, requiring all her weight and strength to budge. Its squeal of protest made Hadley wince as she finally heaved it open.

She switched on a flashlight. Six crypts, three on each side, all covered in a pale sheet of dust. Great-grandmother and -father, grandmother and -father. Hadley looked past those and focused on the top two crypts near the ceiling.

VERA MURRAY BACALL
WIFE AND MOTHER
BORN 1875–DIED 1906

Her coffin lay on the other side of the carved granite door. No crossbar inside, of course. Her father would've found it when he defied the law that forbid burial within the city and sneaked her remains into the mausoleum during the chaotic aftermath of the Great Fire.

But the last crypt, her father's future resting spot, remained empty. If her mother was going to hide something, that would be the place.

"Here goes nothing," Hadley murmured to herself, and inserted the smaller key into the iron crypt door.

Dread hit her like a slap against the cheek.

Bad energy she'd recognize anywhere. Adam had been right about iron keeping things contained.

She directed the flashlight's beam into the dark space. The final canopic jar. The human-headed lid representing Imsety, protector of the liver.

What a fine joke her mother played, hiding the crossbar in a place that no one would have reason to open until after her father's death. When it was too late for him to use the amulet.

She'd never hated her mother more.

After flicking off the flashlight, Hadley hauled the canopic jar out of the crypt and took one last look at the pictograms before dashing it against the granite floor. A flash of gold danced over the ceramic shards and skipped out of the mausoleum chamber, into the muddy ground outside.

Hadley stepped into the gray light and saw the thing more clearly. It wasn't a plain crossbar like the others. This one had a loop on top, onto which a long gold chain was attached. The top of the amulet. Once it was attached to the other pieces, it became a necklace.

Hadley stepped over a gnarled root of the Acacia tree and stooped to pick it up. Her fingers met someone else's. She looked up and found herself face-to-face with Oliver Ginn.

"Hello, Miss Bacall," he said, snatching the crossbar out of the mud.

She jerked away and stumbled to her feet.

"Doing a little afternoon grave robbing?" He wiped mud from the crossbar with the cuff of his dark coat sleeve as drizzle beaded on the brim of his hat.

"That doesn't belong to you," she said, grabbing.

Long fingers closed around the chain as he yanked it out of her reach. "If we're being accurate, it doesn't belong to anyone but the ancient priestesses back in the desert. Your father was a fool to track down the pieces. A bigger fool to send children out to reclaim it after your mother spent all that effort to keep it out of his hands."

"She apparently meant to keep it out of *your* hands as well, Oliver. Or Noel. Whatever the hell you want to call yourself."

"Ah," he said, lifting his head to squint at her. The face she'd once thought handsome and young hadn't changed, but the knowledge that he was unnatural made the hollows of his cheeks seem gaunter; the light behind his eyes, dimmer. "I've been Oliver for many years now," he said softly. "But I won't lie—I enjoy hearing 'Noel' on your lips. Reminds me so much of Vera."

"Don't mistake me for my mother."

"No, you are so much colder than she ever was. But I see now that the aloofness is a defense. You grew up alone, without the warmth that a mother provides."

"Indeed, I did. Because even when she was alive, she was no mother. She handed me over to the staff and went about her merry way. She was too busy cuckolding my father to bother raising a child."

"She loved you. You and your father, unfortunately. Archie certainly didn't deserve the emotion she wasted on him. He was more concerned about advancing his career than giving her what she needed."

"Yes, he certainly didn't give her what you did—namely, an arcane magical spell that took her life."

Oliver's brows snapped together. "It *saved* her life. And yours, as well."

"It also cursed me!"

"Cursed? How? You didn't die after eight years like your mother. You're standing here now, aren't you?" he said, his gaze sliding over her in a way that made the hairs on her arms stand on end. "You know, when I heard the amulet base had been found, I expected to see your father scrambling to get his hands on it. I did not expect to find you—looking more like your mother than I could have ever dreamed."

"Why? Did you expect the Mori specters to have taken my soul eight years after my mother died and passed along her curse to me?"

His eyes flicked to hers. "I had no idea that would happen. Or that it had. Not until the night of the museum party. When I saw the reapers climbing the walls, I thought they were finally coming for me. Then I thought they were coming for you, that it was happening all over again. I'd just found you, and they were taking you away from me again—"

Hadley opened her mouth to protest, but he was in another world, eyes glazed over and haunted. After a moment, he floated back down to terra firma. "But when I realized the reapers were responding to your command, it was the most extraordinary revelation. Hadley, don't you understand? You wield the power of a goddess. The hounds of Set respond to your command. You took down my griffin—"

"You sent those magical creatures to kill us."

"I sent them to fetch these," he said, holding up the chain. The crossbar swung in the air, dangling in the mist. "Neither would have harmed you."

"Your fire-breathing golem burned Lowe."

His eyes darkened. "I said they wouldn't harm *you*, not that Nordic cretin. And you should be blaming him for putting you in harm's way, right from the beginning. Both him and your greedy father—you can't imagine how furious I was to discover that he'd sent you to meet Magnusson at the train station in Salt Lake City."

Hadley recoiled. "You sent those two goons after Lowe?"

"I paid them to retrieve the amulet base using whatever means necessary. Magnusson should've been dead in Chicago, and if it weren't for their incompetence he would have been. I only learned after the fact that the woman with whom he escaped on the train was you. And when your loud-mouthed lover, George Houston—"

"George?" Dear God! His name alone was enough to flip her panic into a true anger that stirred up the Mori. She felt them sniffing from the hedgerow, beyond the great Acacia tree.

"Oh, yes. A lout who can be bought with a single drink is no one you should be sharing a bed with," he scolded in a manner that exposed the old man hiding behind his youthful facade. "Houston told me he'd overheard your father instructing you to meet up with Magnusson at the Flood Mansion party. I couldn't believe he'd use his own daughter to do his dirty work."

He was mistaken about that, but she didn't say this. Her gaze shot beyond Noel's shoulder to see her father in his wheelchair, blindly cutting two muddy ruts through the dead grass.

"Hello, Archie."

"Hello, Noel, you filthy piece of shit."

Noel barked a cruel laugh. And in that moment, Hadley lunged and snatched the crossbar dangling from his fist. The chain snapped—one of the links broke open. But she got it!

"Now, now, my dear." Noel glanced at her father, but his focus was fixed on her. "That wasn't nice. Is your allegiance really so firmly entwined with your father? I challenge you to remember that the man betrayed you in front of his peers, selling away your career to the first clod treasure hunter who happened to stumble upon the amulet base."

"For the love of God, I didn't do it to *spite* her." Her father came to a stop a few yards away. "It was merely a carrot to lure Magnusson. And I'd do it again a million times over if it meant I'd get even half a chance to put your rotten corpse in the ground. Hadley," he called out. "Stay away from that man. He's dangerous."

"I know who he is," she said. "I know everything. I know about the Deathless magic and his affair with Mother and that she passed on the specters to me when she died."

"Hadley," her father said in a broken voice.

Tears stung her eyes as the Mori crept closer. "Why didn't you tell me? I had a right to know. I'm not a child."

"I just wanted to keep you safe. And I didn't want you to think badly of your mother."

"Why should she?" Noel said. "Vera was brilliant and filled with endless potential. Her mistake was trusting you'd recognize that."

"Of course I did—she was *my wife*!"

Anger tightened Noel's face. "She may have been your wife on paper but she died in *my* arms," he said, thumping his chest.

"A sight I'll never forget," her father snapped. "The entire city was in chaos, and I raced home to find you in my bed. My bed. My house. My wife." His arms began shaking. "And you killed her. You infected her with that disease in Egypt. You made her sick while she was pregnant with my child. And you're the one who insisted I call that unholy witch—Hadley's curse is your fault!"

"My God, Archie," Noel shouted. "It's not a curse. She

commands those reapers—that's a gift from the gods. Then again, I suppose this is not something you'd appreciate if you've misled her all these years."

"That spell has rotted your brain."

Noel shook his head and turned to Hadley, speaking in a softer voice. "Come with me. I can take you to Cairo and show you incredible things. Things your mother loved."

Smoky shadows circled the base of the Acacia tree and climbed the wet bark as Noel's voice grew more persuasive. "Think about it, Hadley. I understand if you have doubts about us. I even accept that you've taken this Magnusson fellow as a lover. But you can't deny that there's something bigger drawing us together. It's fate, Hadley. We're two halves that can make a whole—you with the power to wield death, and me, the man death cannot touch."

Her father made a choking noise. "Are you mad? First my wife and now my daughter? Death isn't good enough for you! I should've dug a hole and cemented you inside."

"And I should've done the same to you, but I made a promise to Vera that I wouldn't kill you."

"You're killing me with this goddamn aging spell."

"I'm just giving you a shove in the right direction. But if you want an even bigger push, I'm happy to oblige."

The Mori were making Hadley dizzy. So many of them. Some were pulling on her anger and panic; others were focused on something else. And when she realized what that thing was, she pulled herself together long enough to retrieve the amulet base from her coat pocket.

"Hadley," Noel warned when he saw the gold gleam.

"Father may have made a lot of mistakes, but my mother obviously cared enough to stay with him. And I guess there are some similarities between my mother and me after all, because I stand by him, too."

"Hadley," her father called out in warning.

"Don't worry, Father," she said, backing away from Noel into the mausoleum doorway. "I've got all the pieces now. You should've asked me to find them in the first place."

"Hadley—"

Bracing for the unknown, she slipped the last crossbar into the top of the amulet. It greedily attached itself, as if it were magnetized. As if it were alive. With shaking, rain-slick fingers, she twisted it together, and the metal snicked into place.

THIRTY-TWO

———⋁———

THE AMULET WAS WHOLE, ALL THE PIECES ASSEMBLED. HADLEY expected something big and dramatic and frightening to happen. But . . .

Nothing.

No door to the underworld. No flash of light. No swirl of magical smoke. She wiggled it while glancing around, looking for something that wasn't there. She shook it, grunting. Still nothing.

Noel's slow chuckle grew into a laugh. "Oh, Archie. If you could only see the look on her face. Your precious Backbone of Osiris doesn't seem to work. I'm afraid someone's been deceived because I don't see any sort of magical doorway to a dark netherworld."

Dear God. Had Adam given her the wrong one? Had she just attached the last crossbar to a forgery? She cried out in frustration. Her Mori wailed along with her, teeth gnashing. Wanting to be loosed. A rumbling noise gathering somewhere in the distance grew closer and closer.

"Hadley!" her father bellowed. "Put it around his neck. It must be around his neck!"

She stared at the broken chain. Glanced up at Noel. His slow grin sent a shiver of fear across her skin. Stupid, arrogant bastard. She might not kill him, but she could damn sure hurt him enough to make him wish he were dead.

That distant rumble grew louder, until her bones shook with it. And with a furious wail, she unleashed the Mori and willed them upon Noel with all her might.

Shadows coalesced above the mausoleum as her specters swirled around a tree limb that was fatter than a man's chest and easily twenty feet long. The grand old Blackwood Acacia shook. Wood groaned. Bark splintered. And with a terrible *crack!* the hulking limb came crashing down through the misting rain.

Noel lunged to the side as the limb exploded near Hadley's feet, hitting the ground with such force, it made her teeth clack together. Hadley's gaze met his over the fallen branches. His mouth screwed into a snarl. His eyes squeezed shut momentarily. "Forgive me, Vera," he mumbled before whipping around to face her father. A string of familiar words floated from his lips. What was that? Egyptian Arabic?

Wind rustled through her hair as Noel shouted something at the sky.

Her father screamed. His legs twisted around each other. Bone cracked.

"Father!" Hadley stumbled over the mausoleum steps and slipped in the mud as the Acacia tree shook again. She saw her specters rocking another bough a moment before a streak of red flew across the grass.

The rumble wasn't coming from the Mori.

It was *Lulu*.

A dark figure leapt from the bike—one she barely recognized as Lowe. His soaked clothes clung to lean muscles. A wild crown of burnished gold curls dripped over narrowed eyes as his long legs carried him across the lawn with dangerous grace. He looked as if he were the devil himself, risen from hell, bent on ripping someone's heart from their chest.

That someone turned out to be Noel.

As Hadley pushed herself out of the mud, she spied Lowe reaching under the flap of his suit jacket. Silver winked in the mist as he fisted his curved dagger.

"Lowe!" she shouted.

His eyes briefly flicked to hers, but they barely registered recognition. He looked possessed. How in the world had he known to come here? Had Adam told him? She couldn't remember what she'd muttered to the watchmaker when she left his shop.

"The amulet!" her father bit out between pained breaths. "Get it . . . around his n-neck."

Lowe charged at Noel and tackled him. Knocked the man clear off his feet like he was nothing more than a leather-bound punching bag, sending his hat flying off. And Hadley nearly slipped again as their combined weight hit the felled tree limb and pushed it backward several inches toward her.

Growling, Lowe grabbed the man's hair with his disfigured hand and slammed the back of his head against the branches—once, twice. Noel flailed. Struggled. Then regained some strength and struck Lowe across the face so violently that Hadley cried out.

But Lowe just shook it off and changed tactics, spitting out Swedish curses. His bad hand came down on Noel's wrist. The dagger rose up in the rain as Lowe lifted his arm, grunted savagely, and swung down with brutal force. The blade sliced through the middle of Noel's palm and jammed into the tree limb.

Noel screamed. He tried to lift his arm and failed as blood pooled in his palm.

Lowe had pinned the man's hand to the wood.

And the wound was already mending itself, trying to close up around the blade.

"Hadley!" Lowe shouted. "Give it to me, now."

She hesitated, gripping the muddy amulet in her fist. The chain was broken. She needed to tell him that. And so much more. She wanted all of this madness to disappear, for the landscape to be wiped clean. For one minute alone with him, so they could assess the situation together and find a solution, like they had done so many times before everything went so terribly wrong.

Before he smashed her heart into a thousand pieces.

God, how she wanted him to be the man she'd trusted.

More than anything.

Some part of her must have had faith, because her arm jerked forward on its own accord, offering up the amulet to Lowe.

In a flash, he seized it from her hand. Wild eyes met hers. Just for a moment. But when she failed to get a single word out of her mouth, he dropped his furious gaze onto Noel and wrapped the loose ends of the chain around the man's neck like he was trying to choke him with the amulet.

The Mori let out a collective wail. A warning. Something was happening.

The ground shook. The bough cracked. And the amulet's nasty energy suddenly intensified as a dark void opened up beneath Noel's back.

It was working!

The void spread like a black halo over Noel's shoulders, down his legs. The Mori flew down from the tree and circled the men like dark angels.

Noel screamed in horror. But he wasn't the only one. Lowe struggled to push himself off of Noel. They were sinking together into the void, as if the darkness was made of quicksand—a hungry, pitch-black mouth eager to swallow them alive.

Hadley rushed forward, and with both hands, grabbed Lowe's arm and pulled.

"Hang on," she shouted, digging one heel into the muddy ground and pushing one against the fallen tree limb for leverage. It was impossible. She could feel the dark suctioning energy of the void sapping at her strength. And Lowe was too big. Too heavy. His wet clothes slipped under her hands and she nearly lost him.

Nearly.

Heart galloping, she quickly adjusted her grip, gritted her teeth, and tugged harder.

Noel screamed again. Near her foot, his flesh tore away from the dagger. His body sank into the void all at once and . . . disappeared.

And as if she were on the winning side of a tug-of-war game, Lowe's torso suddenly gave way and flew over the tree limb. They both toppled into the mud, a tangle of arms. She gasped for breath as he flipped around and drew his legs over the bough. Then they both scrambled to their knees.

One by one, the Mori dove into the shrinking void like a flock of black birds arrowing into a pool of water. What was seconds ago big enough to swallow Noel's body was now the size of a dinner plate as the last specter flew in.

Out of the corner of her eye, Hadley saw gold glint. The amulet. It lay strewn across the tree limb, one side of its broken chain caught on the dagger jutting out of the wood.

Lowe saw it, too. His hand shot out. He snatched the amulet off the chain and tossed it into the closing void. As if it finally had everything it wanted, the black mouth snapped shut and disappeared completely.

A weary grunt pulled her attention across the lawn.

She raced around the branches and stopped short in front of her father's wheelchair, where he was prying his twisted legs apart. He was still in pain, his eyes still pale. But he was alive. "Father," she said, unable to hold back the tears that streaked down her cheeks.

Her father's staff came running from the back porch, terror and fear in their eyes. "Call an ambulance," she shouted out to them.

"It worked," her father said between labored breaths. "I can feel the magic leaving."

But it wasn't the only thing.

Lulu's rumbling engine sputtered to life again. Hadley tried to call for Lowe, but whether he heard her or not, she didn't know. He just leaned forward into the motorcycle's handlebars and sped away without a single look behind.

And he was gone.

THIRTY-THREE

ONE MONTH LATER . . .

HADLEY SET A FULL GLASS OF CHAMPAGNE DOWN ON THE EDGE of the desk as distant laughter from the office party floated through the doorway. She'd never shaken so many hands in all her life. All that bare skin was hard to get used to, and now that it was over, she had to fight the urge to wash her hands, exchanging one phobia for another. But she did fight it—a small victory.

She just needed to take a breather. If she stuck around any longer, Miss Tilly might've damn well tried to hug her. She gritted her teeth and shuddered at the thought.

Small steps.

"That's the last one," her father said as he hobbled into the room on crutches. He nodded to a box of odds and ends that sat at her feet.

"You sure you want to give up this desk?" She leaned back against the edge of it. "Last chance to withdraw your retirement. The staff's already half-cut. I'm sure they'll be more than happy to toast to you changing your mind."

A smile lifted his lips. "Can you imagine the paperwork? Besides, they've already printed your business cards. How does it feel to be department head?"

Strangely, not as satisfying as she once imagined, but she merely said, "Daunting."

"Pish. You'll be fine. Oh, and while I'm thinking of it, I had Miss Tilly place notices in the trade publications that we're seeking a replacement for George's position. And if you need help interviewing—"

"I think I can manage."

He blinked at her, studying her face while motes of dust fluttered within a slice of afternoon sun spilling from the nearby window. Though his sight had returned days after the final confrontation with his old partner, he still spent a lot of time looking at her more closely than he ever had before the blindness. "Don't be too proud to ask for help."

"I won't," she assured him, as her father's assistant, Stan, walked into the room.

Stan picked up the box of her father's things. "We should get going, sir. Driver is waiting outside."

"Take that out to the trunk," he said. "I'll be there in a minute or two."

"When's your appointment with the doctor?" she asked her father as Stan left the office.

"Half an hour, but he can wait. There's something I wanted to talk to you about."

"Father, I appreciate all your concern, but I really can handle things here."

He leaned on one crutch and shook his head. "It's not that. I wanted to talk to you about Mr. Magnusson."

Just the sound of his name sent a pang through her chest. Had it been a month since she'd last seen him, riding away out of her father's backyard? Because it felt like an entire year's worth of sleepless nights.

"What about him?" she said, trying to make her voice sound normal.

"Are you in love with him?"

She balked at the accusation, crossing her arms below

her breasts. Yes, her father had seen her fall apart a few times in the first days after Lowe had disappeared out of her life, when she was intermittently racked with anger and hurt. But she'd pulled herself together. Mostly. "I don't know why you're asking about this. Nothing's changed. He's made no attempt to contact me."

"That wasn't what I asked."

"What you asked doesn't matter. I wouldn't be surprised to never see the man again." Admittedly, she'd once or twice taken a taxi past the Magnusson house to see if she could spy his red motorcycle in the driveway. She never did, and subsequently gave up trying. "For all I know, he's run off to Egypt again. And considering the way we parted, I feel quite sure he won't be trying to sell the museum anything else he finds in the desert."

Her father squinted. "He's not in Egypt. In fact, he stopped by the house this morning before I came over here."

Her stomach pitched and a tingling sensation raced through her limbs. A dozen questions popped into her head at once, but the only one she could get out was: "Why?"

"He was showing me a few things he found in Philae."

Oh. Not to ask about her, then. Just business. And the thought of her father doing business with him made her chest spark with quick anger. "You've got to be joking. Are you mad? You met with him, knowing that he hawks forgeries?"

"These were authentic. Mostly ceramics, a few tools."

"Father"

"Don't look at me like I'm an imbecile," he said grumpily. "I can see just fine now, you know. And I asked him to bring them to me—not the other way around."

Impossible. How in the world . . . ? Her pulse spiked. "Are you saying you've had contact with him before this?"

"I didn't want to upset you."

"You're doing a fine job of it now."

"Now, now. Calm down and send those things away."

She glanced in the direction he was looking. A couple of

Mori were crawling out from the shadowed space behind a row of books.

Noel's descent into the underworld might've removed the aging magic that the man had embedded inside her father, but it hadn't severed her connection to the Mori. When she'd first realized this, she'd nearly destroyed her father's kitchen in a tear-filled rage. But she'd come to terms with it and was now resigned to the fact that they were there to stay. Curse or blessing, it was hers to keep.

And her responsibility to control. Shutting her eyes, she quickly willed them away and took a deep, cleansing breath. "I'm fine," she mumbled. "Go on."

"The last time I saw him, Magnusson mentioned he was thinking of donating some of his finds to Berkeley, and I asked if I could see the ceramics."

"How many times have you seen him?"

"We had unfinished business. Naturally I asked him to call on me."

"What sort of unfinished business?"

"Payment, of course. Think of it this way—your mother got us into this mess when she took up with Noel. Therefore, using her family's fortune to get us out of it was the least she could do for us." Hadley was taken aback by her father's frankness. He never spoke of her mother this way. Perhaps he was moving on, in his own crotchety way. "And a deal is a deal," he finished. "The sum we originally agreed on wasn't really for the amulet itself."

"You paid Lowe?"

"Two weeks ago."

"He was planning to cheat you."

"Regardless, the amulet was found—"

"Mostly by me!"

"—and Noel is gone. Magnusson fulfilled his part of the bargain, so I fulfilled mine. I would've felt guilty not doing so. And the fact that he didn't demand it made me feel better about him." He nodded his chin toward her and spoke in a softer voice. "If I can look beyond his mistakes, perhaps you might consider doing the same. He's gone to great lengths to ensure Levin didn't taint your professional career with gossip."

How, she didn't know, but she'd be damned before she begged her father to tell her. "He has shown no interest in contacting me, so I don't see what difference any of this makes."

"Perhaps you should give him the benefit of the doubt," he said, tucking his crutches beneath his arms. "And that's all I'll say on the matter. Your life is your own. But do keep in mind that no matter what fulfillment you'll find inside these walls, it's a poor excuse for failing to search for other fulfillments outside them. Don't let your drive for success be your only happiness."

Funny words coming from a man who'd done exactly that, but she watched him leave the office without comment—mostly because she was too upset to speak. All the hurt and grief she'd so carefully managed to keep locked up inside her head came rushing to the surface.

"Miss Bacall?"

She shook away her chaotic feelings and glanced up at the doorway to see the accounting secretary who was watching the front desk while Miss Tilly drank herself silly at the office party. The woman held out a bright orange tiger lily in her hand. "This came for you."

Hadley silently cursed Miss Tilly for not informing the woman. "That goes in the trash."

"The trash? But why?"

Because no matter how many times she told the delivery boy to stop bringing them, he insisted that he'd get in trouble at work, and didn't she know who the Magnussons were? As if the family would come after him with machine guns if he failed to deliver a stupid flower. Ridiculous. Hadley sometimes wondered if Miss Tilly told the delivery boy to keep coming because she was sweet on him.

"Never mind," she told the secretary, suddenly feeling more defeated than angry. Her father's speech had confused her. Fifteen minutes ago, she'd been perfectly fine. Well, that was a lie. Not fine, but coping. Enduring. And yes, maybe occasionally grieving what she'd lost with Lowe, especially after she stopped hoping he might show up and at least try to explain why he'd lied to her.

But he didn't.

Truth be told, she was probably more upset with him for giving up on her and what they'd had together than she was about the lying. After all, her father had lied to her, too, and they'd made amends. Did Lowe not think she was worth the effort?

A heavy sigh inflated her chest. She just didn't think she could survive grieving for him all over again.

"What was the name of the florist?" she asked the secretary.

"Lunde Flowers."

Maybe it was time to admit that it was truly over between them. And time to cut the last tie to him, once and for all.

She called a taxi and left the office early, giving the driver the florist's name. The cab carried her south of the park, into the Fillmore District. Not more than a block or so from Adam's shop. She should've known.

After asking the taxi driver to wait, she strode into the florist's, a calm resignation propelling her steps, and rang a bell at the front counter.

A blond middle-aged woman with pink cheeks appeared from a door. "Good afternoon," she said with a heavy Scandinavian accent. "How may I be helping you?"

"A couple of months ago, someone ordered flowers to be delivered to me at my office. A daily delivery of lilies—"

"Oh! Mr. Magnusson, *ja*." She smiled. "You are at the museum."

"Yes, that's me."

The woman's brow creased. "You have been getting your deliveries?"

"Yes, no problem there. I came because I want them stopped."

"Why? Is the quality not good?"

"The quality is fine." Hadley inhaled a calming breath.

"Mr. Magnusson and I are not seeing each other anymore, and I suppose he forgot to come in here and halt the deliveries himself."

"Oh, that is terrible. Poor man."

For the love of God, not her, too. Was everyone cheering for Lowe today?

"He has lost so much," the florist said solemnly. "First Mr. Goldberg, and now his sweetheart."

Hadley tilted her head. "Did you say Mr. Goldberg? The watchmaker?"

"*Ja*. What a terrible tragedy. We are so sad for his passing."

She stilled. Surely the woman's message was lost in translation. "You do not mean he's died, do you?"

The florist nodded. "He was killed in his shop. The police still do not find killer. You did not hear? It was in the newspaper."

Hadley stood stiffly for several moments, desperately trying to steady her nerves and think rationally. "When did this happen?"

"A month ago."

A month. That was . . . when she last saw Lowe. When he'd torn into her father's backyard in a rage, and attacked Noel and—*Oh, God!* "What about the little girl? Did she? That is, I mean, was she killed?"

"No." The florist intently shook her head, frowning at Hadley like she was a horrible person for even thinking such a thing.

Hadley blinked rapidly and backed away from the counter. "I have to go. Thank you."

"Wait! What about the deliveries?"

"Never mind," she mumbled, racing out of the shop.

Between labored breaths, she gave the taxi driver an address and clutched her handbag in her lap the entire way, her mind empty and bright with shock. When the cab rolled up in front of the Magnussons' Queen Anne on Broadway, she nearly leapt out before he came to a full stop.

As she was racing to the front door, a familiar blond head peered from the driveway.

"Miss Bacall?"

"Astrid!" She changed directions and strode to the big gate at the side of the home. "Is Lowe home?"

Lowe's sister scratched her ear and twisted her mouth. "Uh, well, not exactly . . ."

Winter's assistant, Bo, walked up behind Astrid. "Afternoon," he said, canting his head.

"I'm looking for Lowe," she repeated.

An unspoken conversation passed between Astrid and Bo. She nodded, giving him some sort of permission.

Bo nudged the brim of his cap up with a knuckle. "Actually, the two of us were headed over to see him. If you'd like, you can ride along."

She couldn't even answer properly. She just nodded and ran to pay the cabbie. A couple of minutes later, she was in the backseat of a Pierce-Arrow limousine with Astrid, and Bo was driving them out of Pacific Heights.

Astrid tried to make small talk, but Hadley was too wound up to be anything more than the worst of conversationalists. An awkward, uncomfortable silence stretched out over long city blocks. It wasn't until they passed through Russian Hill that Hadley realized she hadn't asked where they were going.

When they started the long ascent up Filbert, snatches of memories resurfaced from the day she climbed Telegraph Hill with Lowe. Riding in the taxi with him from the Columbarium. The green and red parrots. Pretending to be a couple looking to purchase a house from that poor, bedraggled real estate agent selling the old Rosewood house. Gloom Manor, Lowe had called it.

And there it was, sitting near the top of the hill.

Trucks were parked at the curb. Workers were loading up debris and clinging to ladders, painting the trim. The twin windows on the third floor had been replaced.

Hadley stared at the window as the car slowed to park. "What's happening here?"

"Believe me, I asked the exact same thing when I first saw this tumbledown shack of a house," Astrid said, waving her hand dismissively at the Italianate Victorian home. "Lowe said I had no vision, and maybe he was right. Come on, we'll take you inside."

In a daze, she followed them down the sidewalk where she and Lowe had fought off the griffin, past workers who tipped their caps, and up the front stairs into the open door. It was so much brighter and warmer than she remembered. Electricity and heat, she realized dazedly. And she smelled fresh paint; the lewd graffiti was gone. So was the old furniture. A new Craftsman hall tree sat at the end of the foyer. And here, above a carved bench, a cap and two coats hung— one achingly familiar, and one small.

A deep voice several yards away made her throat tighten.

"No, you can't go up the stairs. They're working up there, *sötnos.*"

Lowe stood at the bottom of the staircase, tugging the hand of a small child in a red and white polka dot dress.

Hadley stood, rooted to the floorboards, as Astrid and Bo walked into the room. Spying them, a smile lit up the girl's curl-framed face, and she forgot all about the stairs. Astrid bent low and rushed toward her.

"Stella-umbrella," Astrid said in a silly voice, scooping the child up in her arms. "What have you been doing? Your hands are positively filthy."

Stella held out her palms and wiggled her fingers, clearly delighted with herself.

"She tried to catch a wild parrot in the yard," Lowe said. "I'm going to have to get someone to build a fence around . . ."

Lowe's gaze connected with Hadley's.

A strange heat washed over her skin. She wasn't sure if she wanted to cry or run.

"We brought someone to see you," Bo said to Lowe. "Astrid, why don't we take Stella outside and see if we can find another parrot."

Hadley concentrated on breathing as they led the girl outside. Lowe stood where he was, several feet away. His umber suit was the same shade as the new wood stain on the staircase, and he wore his brown leather riding boots. A memory of her crouching to untie those crisscrossing laces added more kindling to the emotional chaos threatening to burn down her heart.

"Hello, Hadley."

"Hello, Lowe."

Her mouth went dry. There were too many things she wanted to say at once, but she couldn't remember what any of them were. A month without him, and it was as if her dumb heart didn't care about all the pain he'd caused. She had to fight the urge to run to him and press herself against his solid chest so that she could feel his arms around her, his steady heartbeat under her cheek. She finally pretended to look around the room in order to gather her wits about her. "You bought Gloom Manor," she finally managed, trying to sound normal.

"I did," he answered. "My brother helped to rush the sale through the bank. They were eager to get rid of it. Haunted houses aren't desirable properties, apparently."

She tried to force a casual smile, but her mouth was having trouble remembering how. "You don't say."

"It's not actually haunted, in case you were wondering." He shoved his hands in his pants pockets and took a few lazy steps in her direction. "Aida has given it her all-clear approval. So I suppose all that ghost graffiti was wishful thinking."

A part of her wanted to smile, but she quickly sobered up and remembered the panic that had brought her to him today. "Why didn't you tell me?" she said in a near whisper.

His head dropped, and he looked down at her with bright blue eyes. Two deep lines crossed his forehead. "Hadley . . ."

"You should've told me. I didn't know." The words tumbled out so fast. She blinked away tears. "I went to the florist in Fillmore and she told me Adam was dead and I couldn't believe it. I went straight to your house—"

"Hey, hey," he said softly. "It's okay."

"It's not okay. It's terrible. Don't you see? I went to Adam's shop. I went to talk with him because I was angry at you for lying to me, and I wanted to know the truth. I thought I was being careful—"

"Noel Irving followed you," he said in a cracking voice. He blinked several times and cleared his throat. "He was looking for the amulet, and I guess when he didn't find it, he went to your father's house and found you outside."

A terrible hollowness stretched inside Hadley's chest. "You should've told me."

"I thought you knew."

"My God, Lowe. If I had known, I would've . . ."

"What?" he challenged. "What could you have done? He's gone, and unlike your father, I didn't know any dark magic to bring him back."

"That's not fair," she whispered, tears stinging her eyes.

"None of it's fair. Do you know how many people I've grieved for over the last few years? First Miriam, then my parents—both at the same time, Hadley. And now Adam."

"And I'm so sorry for that. It wrecks me to imagine how much you've been hurting, but you didn't have to go through it alone. All you had to do was talk to me."

"Why would I have any reason to believe you wanted me to? I lied and you walked away."

"You better believe I did," she said, blinking away angry tears. "I've been betrayed by a lot of people in my life, but I never saw it coming from you. You might as well have stuck that dagger of yours in my belly, because I think that would've hurt less."

Lowe's eyes brimmed with emotion. "I truly never meant to hurt you."

"But you did, and you should've at least tried to talk to me—if not about us, then about Adam. After what we'd been through together, I would think you owed me that much. Or did you . . ." She waited for her throat to stop clenching, but when she spoke, her voice still sounded rough and torn. "Do you blame me for what happened to him?"

His gaze dropped to the floorboards. "I wanted to blame you, believe me. But I'm the one who found the damned amulet and brought it here. I'm the one who asked Adam to duplicate it. So in the end, it was easier to blame myself."

"Lowe—"

"When I botch things up, I do it spectacularly. I lost you and Adam the same day, all because I wasn't man enough to own up to my lies. It's impressive, really, how far I had to fall to realize that."

She didn't know what to say. All the fight drained away from her.

"So, yes. I blamed myself," he finished in a softer voice. "But after a few days passed, I started thinking about your father."

"My father," she repeated in bewilderment.

He jiggled the change in his pocket and exhaled heavily. "When your mother got eight extra years from that spell, instead of your father spending that time trying to fix what was broken between them, he spent a fortune traveling the globe, trying to find a three-thousand-year-old object to kill his best friend. Granted, his friend was a monster, and the complete opposite of Adam in every way."

"Oh, Lowe."

He shook his head, as if it was over and done, and he wasn't interested in rehashing it. Then he returned to his explanation. "But see, it didn't even stop there. After your mother was gone, your father spent decades more clinging to this idea of revenge. Decades. That's a damn long time to be angry. Maybe all of this could've been avoided if he'd just accepted that he was partly to blame. Perhaps he should've asked himself if your mother turned to Noel because your father forgot that a relationship needs tending."

A long pause hung between them.

"The same thing happened to you and Adam," she murmured, suddenly realizing. "When you and Miriam . . ."

"Everyone makes mistakes. Forgiving yourself for

making them is much easier when the people you surround yourself with are willing to give you the same consideration."

She quickly swiped away tears with gloved fingers. "You got Stella?"

"Yes and no." He looked toward the back hallway, where Astrid and Bo had taken her outside. "The court doesn't like to give guardianship to single men who aren't family. Especially ones who don't own property and spend half their year in other countries. They also frown on having a police record. Apparently you need high morals to raise a child these days."

"Hard to believe," she said with a wry smile.

"Lucky for me, it turns out the judge owns stock in one of the hotels that the Magnussons supply with booze."

"Ah." She nodded. "Very convenient."

"Indeed. So he granted temporary guardianship to Winter and Aida. We got her released from the orphanage about ten days ago. She was a little shell-shocked at first, but she warmed up to the household pretty fast. Turns out a girl's fancy *can* be swayed with large amounts of sponge cake and shiny toys."

Hadley murmured her agreement, low and softly. "I seem to remember you swaying me with lemon pie."

"And I'd do it again in a heartbeat."

Warmth bloomed across her chest. She looked away. "So you bought Gloom Manor to get guardianship of Stella?"

"Partly. The family house is crowded, what with Winter and Aida having a baby. Stella's a little intimidated by Aida's mastiff. And I've wanted my own place for a while. Your father's money made that possible."

"He told me about that this afternoon. He also mentioned you'd squared things up with Levin?"

"Your father helped me with that. He gave Levin the forged amulet base with the real paperwork. If it had come from me, Levin would've sensed something was up. But your father was able to convince him that he was trading

Levin's silence about the crocodile forgery for a real artifact."

"Dear God," she mumbled. "He tricked Levin?"

"Dr. Bacall is quite the actor."

"I didn't know he had it in him."

"Now everyone's happy—Levin thinks he owns a rare piece of history, your reputation remains intact, and Monk is satisfied. And I think Adam would be pleased to know that his last masterpiece went to righting a wrong. He would definitely approve."

They looked at each other for a moment, and a terrible shyness crept over her. She looked away and fidgeted with the cuff of her coat. "I don't know what to say. I feel like I've been living in another world while all of this was going on."

"You've been busy. Congratulations on the department head position. Well deserved."

She thanked him as loud hammering on the floor above them drew their attention. Lowe gestured further into the house. She nodded and walked with him, leaving the noise behind. "And what will you do?" she asked, matching her steps to his. "Now that you have Stella, will you go back to digging for treasure?"

"Actually, I somehow snagged a job at UC Berkeley. I'll be teaching fieldwork in the anthropology department and overseeing small digs in the area for graduate students."

"A teacher?" Another surprise.

"Figured I'd give it a try. I've been known to tell an entertaining tale or two. Might come in handy in a classroom."

"Yes, I think it might."

"Winter's letting me keep a runabout boat at the Magnusson pier. Saves me from having to take the ferry to Berkeley. And it'll make it easier to get back home to Stella. I'll have to hire a staff and a nanny, of course. Find her a tutor, so she can learn to sign properly. But I don't start teaching at Berkeley until August, so I've got plenty of time to get things settled."

They stopped in the doorway of the kitchen, which had been freshly painted and tiled. A new icebox and washing machine were waiting to be installed, and a long table sat in the middle of the space.

"Sounds like you've thought of everything," she said. "And the house looks like it might be ready for you to move in soon."

"In a couple of weeks. Still a lot of work to be done, but Winter's pulled in some favors to get extra workers."

Hadley's gaze dropped to the table legs. She leaned forward and looked again, not believing her eyes.

"Talented crew of men," he continued. "They figured out how to bolt the table to the subfloor before they laid tile. But they're having the damnedest time figuring out a way to bolt the icebox down. Perhaps the men who did yours can let them know how they managed it?"

"Lowe?"

"Yes?

"I don't—Why . . . ?" She tried again. "What are you doing?"

He turned to face her and spoke in a soft voice. "I hadn't worked out all the details yet. I know it's a hell of a thing to hope you'd forgive me, but it was more that I was confident in your capacity to do so than whether I deserved it. And I know it's a lot to ask that you'd have to accept not just me, but Stella, too. It's an enormous request. But I'm not expecting you to waltz in here and play her mother. I'm sticking with Uncle, myself. Keeps things simple."

"Lowe." She shook her head several times in disbelief, stuttered a nonsensical response, and then realized she didn't even know what she thinking, much less saying. Her heart was beating so fast, she feared he might hear it. "I thought you'd given up on us. I thought . . ."

"Like I said, I botched things up spectacularly, and I worried if I showed up on your doorstep with nothing but an apology, you might tell me to go to hell. So I'd planned on getting this all fixed up first, you see. Then I thought I'd try to win you back through sympathy. Pretend to have a

crippling disease that gave me six weeks to live, perhaps."
His words were lighthearted, but his voice was rough with
restrained emotion. He hesitantly lifted a hand and traced
a lock of her hair, a barely-there touch that sent goose bumps
over her arms. "And if that didn't work, I was prepared to
disguise myself as someone different. Dye my hair, affect
a limp. Maybe introduce myself as someone impressive—a
duke, perhaps, or a wealthy heir who hunts wild game in
Africa. Sweep you off your feet with my charming conversation and a big, fancy ring, then wait until we were married
to reveal my identity and pray you didn't divorce me."

She choked out a gravelly laugh. "And if that didn't
work?"

"If you want me on my knees, I'm prepared to grovel.
I've spent most of my life making mistakes, but if it takes
me the rest of it to prove to you that I can be a better man,
I'll gladly die trying."

He was very close now. So close, she could smell his
hair and clothes, and the achingly familiar scent of his skin.
She kept her eyes on his shirt collar and tried to keep her
heart from racing ahead of her scattered thoughts. "It's a
long drive to the museum from here."

"Plenty of room in the staff quarters for a full-time
driver."

"I don't have much luck with staff."

"That's where my family name comes in handy."

A funny sort of euphoria made her legs feel weak. "And
I don't know how Number Four will feel about country
living."

Slowly, he reached for her hand and began removing one
of her gloves as he spoke in a low murmur. "This isn't
the country, *min kära,* but Stella loves cats, so at least he'll
have a partner in crime if he finds himself longing to chase
parrots."

"Lowe," she said, grasping his fingers to still them.

"Yes, Hadley?"

"I can forgive mistakes. And I don't care about all the
cons and rackets. If you want to tell the president that you're

the Pope, it makes no difference. All I ask is that you refrain from lying to two people."

"And those people would be . . . ?"

"You and me."

With a final tug, he removed her glove and enfolded her bare hand in both of his. "Miss Bacall," he said, kissing her knuckles. "You've got yourself a deal."

EPILOGUE

HADLEY SQUINTED INTO THE MORNING SUN AS SHE APPROACHED the porter loading their luggage onto the waiting train. The Twin Peaks station was bustling with travelers going to and from San Francisco, and she was both ecstatic and nervous to be one of them. She'd dreamed of this trip since she was a small child. Her stomach was a riot of butterflies and she couldn't stop smiling.

"It's just that I also noticed two last names, sir," the porter was saying to the unusually tall man with wheat-blond hair. Hadley stopped behind him, out of sight, and listened for his answer.

"You're a perceptive fellow," Lowe told the porter conspiratorially. "Yes, it's true. We're bound for an Atlantic-crossing steamer ship, see. And Miss Bacall is a famous newspaper journalist who's been sent along with me as a traveling companion to write my memoirs. Distant lands, exciting adventures. That sort of thing."

"Oh," the porter said, eyes wide. "Well, forgive me for

being blunt, sir, but her luggage is tagged with your compartment number. Should I put it in the neighboring compartment with the child and her caretaker—Mrs. Geller?"

Arms crossed, Lowe rocked on the heels of his riding boots before leaning closer to the attendant. "No, the luggage is marked correctly. Miss Bacall's should go to my compartment. She'll be taking a *lot* of notes, if you catch my drift."

The porter slowly raised his brows. "I do, indeed. And is there—Mrs. Geller and the child, and Miss Bacall and you . . . Is there a Mrs. Magnusson making the trip as well?"

"Just the four of us."

"I see," the porter said, looking positively shocked. "Not to worry. I'm discreet."

Hadley stepped to Lowe's side and gave him a sidelong frown.

"Ah, here she is now," Lowe said, placing a firm hand on her back.

"Yes, it's me. Your traveling companion," she said dryly. "I'm afraid I've forgotten to pack a typewriter, Mr. Magnusson."

"I hope your longhand's good," he said as his warm palm slid down to cup her rear.

"Did I hear you mention an extra sleeping bunk in Mrs. Geller's compartment?" she asked the porter, struggling to pry away his hand without drawing attention.

"He said it would be far too crowded in there," Lowe said quickly and let go of her to fish out a ridiculously large bill for the porter. "Keep the assignments as they are. And if you could personally ensure our service is top-notch all the way to New York, there's more where that came from."

"Yes, sir. Anything you need, I'm your man," he said before carting the luggage away.

"So it's 'Miss' Bacall, and we aren't married now?" Hadley said when the man was out of earshot.

"He noticed you weren't wearing a ring—"

She couldn't travel with it. The thing was so big and

showy, they'd be robbed before they made it out of the state. It was currently hidden in a panel inside their bedroom closet.

"—and our last names."

For professional reasons. She'd kept Bacall for her career, nothing more. Explaining this to strangers was almost more trouble than it was worth. For her, at least. For Lowe, it was an opportunity to invent a new madcap story at every dinner party they attended. God only knew what he'd told his fellow professors at Berkeley. Their staff at home had believed Hadley to be some sort of royal princess when she'd first moved in after the wedding.

"You know that's going to spread through the train like wildfire," she said.

He waggled his brows. "Nothing more exciting than salacious gossip."

Before she could decide if she wanted to wallop him on the arm with her handbag or lean into the kiss he was pressing to her temple, the rest of their party appeared: the entire Magnusson clan, her father, Mrs. Geller, and Stella—who dropped Mrs. Geller's hand and bounded for them, slinging her arms around Hadley and Lowe's legs like they were a jungle gym. She gave a little squeal of excitement into Hadley's skirt before grinning up at both of them.

"Enjoy it now, *sötnos*," Lowe said. "Once you get your first bout of motion sickness on that train, you'll wish Uncle Lowe and Auntie Hadley had done the responsible thing and left you at home."

Stella pushed dark curls out of her face and made the humplike sign for "camel" with her hand.

"Yes, we're going to ride a camel," Hadley said, smiling down at her. "I'm excited, too."

"Satanic beasts that stink and spit," Lowe mumbled, but his eyes twinkled with merriment. He ran a hand over Stella's head. "I swear, that is Adam's smile exactly."

And it was. The girl looked more and more like Adam with every passing week. Hadley worried Lowe might be disappointed with this realization, but it only seemed to strengthen their bond. The adoption went through three months ago, making their small family of three official.

It had taken a while for Hadley and Stella to warm up to each other. Mostly Hadley's fault. She'd never been so nervous about her specters. Number Four was one thing, but a small child without nine lives was quite another. Thankfully, the girl couldn't see them, and over the last year, Hadley had rarely been upset enough at home to draw the Mori's attention.

Funny how someone she'd once considered the most irritating man she'd ever met could now be the source of so much serenity.

Even when he was spinning tales to train porters.

"You sure you have everything?" her father asked. "You packed the revolver?"

"We're staying in luxury hotels and going to major tourist sites, not digging up treasure in the desert," Lowe reminded him. "If I thought anyone might be shooting at us, I wouldn't be escorting a five-year-old and my wife there. And you, Mrs. Geller," he added.

The gray-haired woman looked more titillated than wary. "Don't worry, Dr. Bacall. I've packed a small wooden club in my steamer trunk, just in case we face bandits."

Lowe had lured Mrs. Geller away from the Pacific Hebrew Orphan Asylum to serve as Stella's live-in tutor and nanny. She'd been teaching the child sign language at an astonishing rate. And as someone who'd never crossed the California state line, she was positively exuberant about accompanying them on the trip to Egypt—which was a miracle, considering all the garish stories Lowe had shared with the woman about his last trip there.

"No one will be raiding our hotel rooms except the maids taking away dirty linens," he assured everyone.

"Better safe than sorry," Winter said, slinging his arm around his spirit medium wife's shoulders. Their small infant was wrapped up in a stroller and being cooed over by Astrid. Bo stood next to her, watching both of them.

"It will take you two weeks just to get to Europe?" Astrid asked.

"A little less. Four days by train to New York," Lowe said, counting the time off on his fingers. "Six days on the S.S. *Olympic* to England. A ferry to France, then a train ride to the coast the next morning to catch another three-day steamer to Alexandria."

Hadley stopped herself from mouthing the schedule along with Lowe; she'd memorized every leg of their journey weeks ago. "Which means that exactly two weeks from now, we'll be stepping foot on Egyptian soil." Just thinking about it made her stomach flutter.

"Be sure to take lots of photographs at the pyramids," Bo said.

"And at the museum," her father added. "You have my letter to Director Amir inviting him to San Francisco?"

"You've asked me twice already, Father." A stronger relationship between their museum and the Egyptian Museum in Cairo could help bring touring exhibits to San Francisco. Hadley was eager to meet the director and discuss opportunities.

Eager for that, and eager to see the country that birthed the civilization she'd spent her life studying, and that changed her family's lives so profoundly. Without it, her world would be so different. She wouldn't have lost her mother nor been cursed with the Mori. But she also wouldn't be running the antiquities department, and she wouldn't have met the man at her side.

And those gifts alone made her curse feel almost like a blessing.

The first whistle sounded to announce the train's impending departure.

"Adventure awaits, Mrs. Bacall," Lowe said, smiling down at her. "You ready for this?"

She threaded her arm through his and linked elbows. "Darling, I was born ready."

TURN THE PAGE FOR A PREVIEW OF THE FIRST
ROARING TWENTIES NOVEL FROM JENN BENNETT

BITTER SPIRITS

AVAILABLE NOW FROM BERKLEY SENSATION!

ONE

AIDA PALMER'S TENSE FINGERS GRIPPED THE GOLD LOCKET AROUND her neck as the streetcar came to a stop near Gris-Gris. It was almost midnight, and Velma had summoned her to the North Beach speakeasy on her night off—no explanation, just told her to come immediately. A thousand reasons why swirled inside Aida's head. None of them were positive.

"Well, Sam," she muttered to the locket, "I think I might've made a mistake. If you were here, you'd probably tell me to face up to it, so here goes nothing." She gave the locket a quick kiss and stepped out onto the sidewalk.

The alley entrance was blocked by a fancy dark limousine and several Model Ts surrounded by men, so Aida headed to the side.

Gossip and cigarette smoke wafted under streetlights shrouded with cool summer fog. She endured curious stares of nighttime revelers and hiked the nightclub's sloping sidewalk past a long line of people waiting to get inside. Hidden from the street, three signs lined the brick wall corridor leading to the entrance, each one lit by a border of round bulbs. The first two signs announced a hot jazz quartet and a troupe of Chinese acrobats. The third featured a painting of a brunette surrounded by ghostly specters:

WITNESS CHILLING SPIRIT MYSTERIES LIVE IN PERSON!
FAMED TRANCE MEDIUM MADAME AIDA PALMER
CALLS FORTH SPIRITS FROM BEYOND,
REUNITING AUDIENCE MEMBERS WITH
DEPARTED LOVED ONES,
—PATRONS WISHING TO PARTICIPATE SHOULD
BRING MEMENTO MORI—

One of the men standing next to the sign looked up at her when she passed by, a fuzzy recognition clouding his eyes. Maybe he'd seen her show . . . Maybe he'd been too drunk to remember. She gave him a tight smile and approached the club's gated entrance.

"Pardon me," she said to the couple at the head of the line, then stood on tiptoes and peeked through a small window.

One of the club's doormen stared back at her. "Evening, Miss Palmer."

"Evening. Velma called me in."

Warm, brassy light and a chorus of greetings beckoned her inside.

"The alley's blocked," she noted when the door closed behind her. "Any idea what's going on?"

"Don't know. Could be trouble," said the first doorman.

A second doorman started to elaborate until he noticed the club manager, Daniels, shooting them a warning look as he spoke to a couple of rough-looking men. His gaze connected with Aida's; he motioned with his head: *upstairs.*

Wonderful. Trouble indeed.

Aida left the doormen and marched through the crowded lobby. At the far end, a yawning arched entry led into the main floor of the club. The house orchestra warmed up behind buzzing conversations and clinking glasses as Aida headed toward a second guarded door that bypassed the crowds.

Gris-Gris was one of the largest black-and-tan speakeasies in the city. Social rules concerning race and class went unheeded here. Anyone who bought a membership card was welcome, and patrons dined and danced with whomever they pleased. Like many of the other acts appearing onstage, Aida was only booked through early July. She'd been working here a month now and couldn't complain. It was much nicer than most of the dives she'd worked out East, and to say the owner was sympathetic to her skills was an understatement.

Velma Toussaint certainly stirred up chatter among her employees. People said she was a witch or a sorceress—she was—and that she practiced hoodoo, which she did. But the driving force of the gossip was a simpler truth: polite society just didn't know how to handle a woman who single-handedly ran a prosperous, if not illicit, business. Still, she played the role to the hilt, and Aida admired any woman who wasn't afraid to defy convention.

Though it was a relief to work for someone who actually believed in her own talents, all that really mattered was Aida was working. She needed this job. And right now she was crossing her fingers that the "trouble" was not big enough to get her fired. A particular unhappy patron from last night's show was her biggest worry. It wasn't her fault that he didn't like the message his dead sister brought over from the beyond, and how was she supposed to have known the man was a state senator? If someone had told her he preferred a charlatan's act to the truth, she would've happily complied.

Grumbling under her breath, Aida climbed the side stairs and sailed through a narrow hallway to the club's administrative offices. The front room, where a young girl who handled Velma's paperwork usually sat, was dark and empty. As she passed through the room, her breath rushed out in a wintery white puff.

Ghost.

She cautiously approached the main office. The door was cracked. She hesitated and listened to a low jumble of foreign words streaming from the room, spoken in a deep, male voice. Beyond the cloud of cold breath, she saw a woman with traditional Chinese combs in her hair, on which strings of red beads dangled. Bare feet peeked beneath her sheer sleeping gown. She stood behind a very large, dark-headed man wearing a long coat, who stared out a long window that looked down over the main floor of the club.

Aida's cold breath indicated that one of them was a ghost. This realization alone was remarkable, as Aida had only encountered one ghost in the club since she'd arrived—a carpenter who'd suffered a heart attack while building the stage and died several years before Velma came into possession of Gris-Gris—and Aida had exorcised it immediately.

In her experience, ghosts did not move around—they remained tethered to the scene of their death. So unless someone died in Velma's office tonight, a ghost shouldn't be here.

Shouldn't be, but was.

Strong ghosts looked as real as anyone walking around with a heartbeat. But even if the woman with the red combs hadn't been dressed for bed, Aida would've known the man was alive. He was speaking to himself in a low rumble, a repeating string of inaudible words that sounded much like a prayer.

Ghosts don't talk.

"Is she your dance partner?" Aida said.

The man jerked around. *My.* He was enormous—several inches over six feet and with shoulders broad enough to topple small buildings as he passed. Brown hair, so dark it was almost black, was brilliantined back with a perfect part. Expensive clothes. A long, serious face, one side of which bore a large, curving scar. He blinked at Aida for a moment, gaze zipping up and down the length of her in hurried assessment, then spoke in a low voice. "You can see her?"

"Oh yes." The ghost turned to focus on the man, giving Aida a new, gorier view of the side of her head. "Ah, there's the death wound. Did you kill her?"

"What? No, of course not. Are you the spirit medium?"

"My name's on the sign outside."

"Velma said you can make her . . . go away."

"Ah." Aida was barely able to concentrate on what the man was saying. His words were wrapped inside a deep, grand voice—the voice of a stage actor, dramatic and big and velvety. It was a voice that could probably talk you into doing anything. A siren's call, rich as the low notes of a perfectly tuned cello.

And maybe there really was some magic in it, because all she could think about, as he stood there in his fine gray suit with his fancy silk necktie and a long black jacket that probably cost more than her entire wardrobe, was pressing her face into his crisply pressed shirt.

What a perverse thought. And one that was making her neck warm.

"Can you?"

"Pardon?"

"Get rid of her. She followed me across town." He swept a hand through the woman's body. "She's not corporeal."

"They usually aren't." The ghost had followed him? Highly unusual. And yet, the giant man acted as if the ghost was merely a nuisance. Most men didn't have the good sense to be afraid when they should.

"Your breath is . . ." he started.

Yes, she knew: shocking to witness up close rather than from the safe distance of the audience when she was performing onstage. "Do you know what an aura is?"

"No clue."

"It's an emanation around humans—an effusion of energy. Everyone has one. Mine turns cold when a spirit or ghost is nearby. When my warm breath crosses my aura, it becomes visible—same as going outside on a cold day."

"That's fascinating, but can you get rid of her first and talk later?"

"No need to get snippy."

He looked at her like she was a blasphemer who'd just disrupted church service, fire and brimstone blazing behind his eyes. "Please," he said in a tone that was anything but polite.

Aida stared at him for a long moment, a petty but sweet revenge. Then she inhaled and shook out her hands . . . closed her eyes, pretending to concentrate. Let him think she was doing him some big favor. Well, she *was*, frankly. If he searched the entire city, he'd be lucky to find another person with the gift to do what she did. But it wasn't difficult. The only effort it required was the same concentration it took to solve a quick math problem and the touch of her hand.

Pushing them over the veil was simple; calling them back took considerably more effort.

After she'd tortured the man enough, she reached out for the Chinese woman, feeling the marked change in temperature inside the phantom's body. Aida concentrated and willed her to leave. Static crackled around her fingertips. When the chill left the air, Aida knew the ghost was gone.

She considered pretending to faint, but that seemed excessive. She did, however, let her shoulders sag dramatically, as if it would take her days to recover. A little labored breathing was icing on the cake.

"Your breath is gone."

She cracked open one eye to find the giant's vest in front of her. When she straightened to full height, she saw more vest, miles of it, before her gaze settled on the knot of his necktie. It was a little annoying to be forced to tilt her face up to view his. But up close, she spotted an anomaly she hadn't noticed from a distance: something different about the eye with the scar. Best to find out who the hell this man was before she asked him about it.

"Aida Palmer," she said, extending a hand.

He stared down at it for a moment, gaze shifting up her arm and over her face, as if he were trying to decide whether he'd catch the plague if they touched. Then his big, gloved hand swallowed hers, warm and firm. Through the fine black leather, she felt a pleasant tingle prickle her skin—an unexpected sensation far more foreign than any ghostly static.

TWO

———◆———

WINTER MAGNUSSON WASN'T SUPERSTITIOUS. IF ANYONE would've asked if he believed in ghosts a week ago, he might've laughed. He wasn't laughing now. And after a lousy week marred by one bizarre event after another, he frankly wasn't sure what he believed anymore.

First, a crazy old woman had accosted him on the street and shouted some hocus-pocus curse at him. After that, a specter began appearing in his study every afternoon—something no one in his household could see but him. Then, during a business meeting tonight at a bar in Chinatown, someone spiked his drink with a foul-tasting green concoction. And before he could spit it out, a prostitute with a gaping hole in her head walked right through a wall from the brothel next door.

Like the specter in his study, no one but Winter saw the dead prostitute, but she'd damn sure followed him from Chinatown to North Beach. All she did was stare at him, but until the spirit medium walked in the room, he'd been questioning his sanity.

Now he was too unsettled to question much of anything.

After the medium's breath returned to normal, the first thing Winter noticed about her was her breasts, which were respectable. Much like looking into the sun during an eclipse, staring at her breasts would only lead to harm, so he quickly shifted his gaze upward. Slender fingers combed through blunt caramel brown bangs covering her forehead. Straight as a ruler, her sleek hair was styled into a short French bob that fell to her chin in the front and tapered to the nape of her neck. When she introduced herself and extended her hand to shake, it drew his attention to her skin, which was pale as milk and densely covered in bronze freckles. Not the kind you'd see smattered on the sun-kissed face of a child.

Freckles *everywhere*.

They began in a sliver of pale forehead above arched brows, gathered tightly across her nose and cheeks, lightened around her neck, then disappeared into the dipping neckline of her dress.

Winter's gaze raked over her breasts again—still respectable—down her dress to the jagged handkerchief hem below her knees. He followed the path of the spotted skin around her calves, half hidden by pale stockings, to the T-bar heels on her feet. Freckles on her *legs*—how about that? For some reason, he found this wildly exciting. Increasingly lurid thoughts ballooned inside his head after he wondered *exactly* what percentage of her skin was speckled. Did freckles cover her arms? The curving creases where her backside ended and her legs began? Her nipples?

He pushed away the enticing reverie, shook her hand, and successfully remembered his own name. "Winter Magnusson."

Her enormous brown eyes were ringed in kohl like some exotic Nile princess. A strange heat washed over him as their gazes connected.

"Good grief, you're a big one, aren't you?"

He stilled, rooted to the floor, unable to think of a response to that.

If he was big—and at four inches over six feet, he definitely was—then Miss Palmer was *very* small. Average height for a woman, legs on the long side, but there was something petite and slender about her frame. Graceful. She was also unusually pretty—far more attractive than the sketch of her on the poster outside Gris-Gris's entrance.

"I suppose everyone jumps when you snap your fingers." The way she said this, in a calm manner, almost smiling, made him think it wasn't a criticism as much as an honest assessment. Maybe even a compliment.

"They jump when I snap my fingers because without me, they have no income."

"*Aha!* I knew I'd heard your name around here. You're Velma's bootlegger."

She had such a disarming, casual way about her. Very straightforward, which was off-putting and exciting at the same time. Women didn't speak to him this way—hell, most *men* didn't speak to him this way.

"Not Velma's alone," he said. "And on the record, I'm in the fish business."

And he was: fish during the day, liquor at night. Both were considered some of the best in the city. Quality is an unusual thing to specialize in when your enterprise is illegal, but that was his niche. Winter's father owned boats before Volstead and fished up and down the coast, from San Francisco to Vancouver. His old routes and the contacts he'd collected made it easy to set up bootlegging from Canada. And like his father, Winter sold no bathtub gin—nothing cut, nothing fake—which allowed him to cater to the best restaurants, clubs, and hotels.

It also earned him the status of being one of the Big Three bootleggers in San Francisco.

Aida nodded as if it were of no consequence, then said, "They're different colors."

"What's that?"

"Your eyes."

Strangers never had the nerve to comment on his maimed eye or the hooked scar that extended from brow to cheekbone. Either they'd already heard the story behind it, or they were too intimidated to inquire. He wasn't used to explaining, and even considered ignoring the medium's questioning tone altogether, but her curious face swayed him.

Or maybe it was the freckled ankles . . . and what he'd like to do with those ankles, which started with licking and ended with them propped on his shoulders.

He cleared his throat. "One pupil is permanently dilated."

"Oh?" She stepped closer and craned her neck to inspect his eyes. The sweet scent of violet wafted from her hair, disorienting him far more than the foul drink and the damned ghost already had. "I see," she murmured. "They're both blue. The big pupil makes the left eye look darker. Is that genetic?"

"An injury," he said. "I was in an auto accident a couple of years ago."

God, how he detested the disfigurement. Every time he looked in the mirror, there they were, wounded eye and scar, reminding him of the one night he wanted more than anything to forget: when his family was brutally snatched away from him, crushed by the oncoming streetcar. Dumb luck that he survived, but some days he truly believed his continued existence was really a curse in disguise.

The medium made no comment about the scar; though, to her credit, she didn't appear to be revolted or frightened by its presence, nor did she politely pretend it wasn't there. "Can you see out of the wounded eye, or does the dilation affect your vision?"

He smelled violets again. Christ alive. She was intoxicating, standing so close. A pleasurable heat gathered in his groin. Any more pleasurable and he'd be forced to hide a rampant erection. He pulled his coat closed, just in case.

"My vision is perfect," he answered gruffly. "Right now, for instance, I see a tiny freckled woman in front of me, asking a lot of questions."

She laughed, and the sound did something funny to

Winter's chest. Maybe he was getting ill. Having a heart attack at the age of thirty. He hoped to hell not. He'd rather be burned alive than tolerate another wretched doctor's so-called assistance. Between the parade of psychiatrists who treated his father's illness before the accident and the over-priced surgeons who sewed up his own eye after it, he'd seen enough doctors to last a lifetime, no matter how short.

When the medium finally turned away, he let out a long breath and watched the spellbinding sway of her ass with great interest as she strolled toward Velma's desk to set down her handbag and the cloche she'd been gripping in her hand. The view only got better when she shucked off her coat: freckles covered every inch of her slender arms.

He might pass out from excitement. His legs were definitely feeling unsteady. Wobbly, even. He felt high as a kite. Feverish. But when the room started to spin, he had the sinking feeling Miss Palmer's freckles weren't the cause.

After Aida set her things down, the bootlegger silently stared at her for several beats, an unnerving intimidation that chilled the sweat prickling the back of her neck. And because she was clearly depraved, a thrill shot through her.

God above, he was well built. Like an enormous bull. Just how tall was he, exactly? Her gaze stuttered over the solid bulk of his upper arms, which stretched the wool of his expensive coat, then ran down the rather distracting length of his meaty legs.

This was a body built for conquering. For smiting enemies. Ransacking villages.

Ravaging innocent women.

Maybe even some not-so-innocent women.

He wasn't pretty or conventionally good-looking. More savagely handsome, she decided. Rough-hewn and dark and intense. A barbarian stuffed inside a rich man's suit. Not her usual taste in men, but for some reason, she found his big body rousing.

"So tell me," Aida said, attempting to get her mind refocused on the reason she was called here. "How long was that ghost following you, Mr. Magnusson?" His name sounded Scandinavian. He looked it. Something about the combination of those ridiculously high, flat cheekbones and the long face . . . his reserved, intense nature. No accent, so she assumed he wasn't fresh off the boat.

"A couple of hours."

"Any idea why?"

He made an affirmative noise. His mouth didn't seem to know how to smile—it just stretched into a taut line as he stared at her with those strange, otherworldly eyes. Eyes that fluttered shut momentarily. When they reopened, he looked dazed.

"Are you all right?" she asked.

"I . . ."

He never finished. One second he appeared cognizant; the next, he was swaying on his feet. Before she had time to react, he was leaning toward her like a felled giant sequoia. Instinct opened her arms—as if she could catch someone his size. But she did . . . rather, he crashed into her, a dead weight that overtook hers.

"H-help!" she cried out as his big body took hers down in a series of awkward, slow motions that had her bending backward, dropping to one knee—"Oh, God . . . dammit, Mr. Magnusson . . ."—then finally crumbling beneath him.

Her mind made great, panicked leaps between the mundane—*He smells pleasantly of soap and witch hazel*— and the practical: *How could another human being weigh so much? Is he filled with rocks?*

A thunder of footfalls shook the floorboards, and before she could fully wonder if it was possible to experience death by crushing, the impossibly titanic weight of Giant was lifted from her. Sweet relief! While two club workers lifted Mr. Magnusson, Aida's boss helped her to her feet.

"You hurt?" Velma Toussaint's briar rose dress had a softly sweeping neck that revealed sharp collarbones and pale nutmeg skin of indeterminable ancestry. Her shiny brown hair was sculpted into a short Eton crop, with slicked-back finger waves molded close to the head.

"Fine . . . fine," Aida replied between breaths.

Velma was a former dancer in her mid-thirties who moved to San Francisco from Louisiana a few years back and began running the club after her wayward cheat of a husband—the original owner of Gris-Gris—died of an aneurism. Rumor had it that his untimely death came after Velma used a pair of scissors to cut his photo in half during some midnight ritual. Aida didn't know if this was true, but if it *was*, no doubt the man deserved what he got.

"The poison's settling in," Velma said.

"You poisoned him?"

Velma made an impatient face. "He *came here* poisoned. Hexed. Someone sneaked poison in his drink and left a written spell on the table. Appears to be some sort of Chinese magic that acts like a supernatural magnet. Draws ghosts."

"Like the one that was in here."

"So you got rid of it? Thank you," Velma said. "I've got a friend in Louisiana who might know an antidote. Called the operator to set up a long-distance call a quarter hour ago. Should be coming through the line any minute now, but he's getting worse."

Everyone gathered around the downed bootlegger. With disheveled hair falling across his forehead, Mr. Magnusson lay on the floor with his eyes shut, groaning. Looking down at him, Aida thought he really did look like a giant, and that she wouldn't be surprised to see an army of tiny men scurry over him to tie him down with ropes.

Hurried footfalls drew Aida's attention to the doorway as a slender Chinese boy burst into the room. Dressed in a well-tailored cedar green suit and a newsboy cap, he couldn't have been a day over twenty, twenty-one. His face was pleasant, his body sinewy and strung tighter than a guitar, bouncing with energy.

"Aida, meet Bo Yeung," Velma said. "Bo, this is Miss Palmer."

Bo turned a friendly face her way and touched the brim of his cap in greeting, then tilted his head as if he'd just worked out a crossword puzzle answer. "Oh, the spirit medium," he said, looking her up and down with a quirky smile. "I'm Mr. Magnusson's assistant."

"A pleasure."

"Bo," Winter mumbled from the floor, attempting to prop himself up on one elbow and failing. "Did you get a chance to have the symbols on the paper deciphered?"

"Yes, boss," Bo said coolly. "Unfortunately, it seems you've been poisoned with *Gu*."

FROM *NEW YORK TIMES* BESTSELLING AUTHOR

M E L J E A N   B R O O K

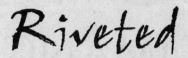

A NOVEL OF THE IRON SEAS

Annika is searching for her sister while serving on an airship.
David is intent on exposing her secrets—until disaster strikes,
leaving them stranded on a glacier where survival depends on
the heat rising between them.

PRAISE FOR THE NOVELS OF THE IRON SEAS

"*Riveted* is the standard against which I am
currently measuring all steampunk."

—*Smart Bitches, Trashy Books*

"A stunning blend of steampunk setting
and poignant romance."

—Ilona Andrews, #1 *New York Times* bestselling author

meljeanbrook.com
facebook.com/AuthorMeljeanBrook
facebook.com/ProjectParanormalBooks
penguin.com

M1402T1113

LOVE
ROMANCE
NOVELS?

For news on all your favorite romance authors,
sneak peeks into the newest releases, book
giveaways, and much more—

"Like" Love Always on Facebook!
 LoveAlwaysBooks

M1063G0212

Enter the tantalizing world
of
paranormal romance

Christine Feehan

Lora Leigh

Nalini Singh

Angela Knight

Yasmine Galenorn

MaryJanice Davidson

Berkley authors
take you to a whole new realm

penguin.com

M4G0610

Penguin Group (USA) Online

What will you be reading tomorrow?

Patricia Cornwell, Nora Roberts, Catherine Coulter,
Ken Follett, John Sandford, Clive Cussler,
Tom Clancy, Laurell K. Hamilton, Charlaine Harris,
J. R. Ward, W.E.B. Griffin, William Gibson,
Robin Cook, Brian Jacques, Stephen King,
Dean Koontz, Eric Jerome Dickey, Terry McMillan,
Sue Monk Kidd, Amy Tan, Jayne Ann Krentz,
Daniel Silva, Kate Jacobs...

You'll find them all at
pengu

*Read excerpts
find tour schedules an
and ente*

Subscribe to Penguin
and get an excl
at exciting new titles a
long before eve

PENGUIN GROUP (USA)
pcnguin.com

M224G0909